JANGO

William Nicholson

JANGO

THE SECOND BOOK
OF THE
NOBLE WARRIORS

HARCOURT, INC.

Orlando   Austin   New York   San Diego   Toronto   London

www.HarcourtBooks.com

First published in Great Britain 2006 by Egmont Books Ltd.
First U.S. edition 2007

Library of Congress Cataloging-in-Publication Data
Nicholson, William.
Jango/William Nicholson.—1st ed.
p.   cm.—(The noble warriors; bk. 2)
Summary: Seeker, the Wildman, and Morning Star discover
that the mysterious warrior sect they had been so desperate
to join is not quite what it appears from the outside.
[1. Self-realization—Fiction.   2. Conduct of life—Fiction.
3. Faith—Fiction.   4. Fantasy.]   I. Title.
PZ7.N5548See   2007
[Fic]—dc22   2006019971
ISBN 978-0-15-206011-4

Text set in Bembo
U.S. edition designed by Cathy Riggs

First U.S. edition

A   C   E   G   H   F   D   B

Printed in the United States of America

❊ CONTENTS ❧

JANGO

The Nomana Catechism

Who is the All and Only?
The All and Only is the power that existed before the world came into being.

Did the All and Only make the world?
The All and Only shared itself into many parts. This sharing brought the world into being, and all its creatures, and you and me.

Why did the All and Only bring us into being?
To become gods.

Can I become a god?
Of course. Every one of us has within us the power of the All and Only.

Why do I not feel this power?
It's locked within you.

Why has the All and Only locked the power within me?
Because power can destroy.

Does the All and Only not trust me?
The All and Only has made you free. You must show
yourself to be worthy of trust.

How do I show myself to be worthy of trust?
By taking the true way.

What is the true way?
That you must find for yourself.

*Why does the All and Only not come before me in power and
glory and show me the true way?*
Such greatness would make you little.

So will the All and Only never come?
The All and Only is with you now.

Will I ever see the All and Only face-to-face?
You will.

When?
When you are a god.

THE FIRST STAGE
IN THE TRAINING OF
THE NOMANA

LEARNING

*In which the novice receives the skills,
wisdom, and memory of the Community.*

❉ 1 ❉

The Secret Skill

SEEKER ADOPTED THE COMBAT STANCE KNOWN AS THE Tranquil Alert: feet a pace apart and flat on the ground, arms loose at his sides, head erect, balanced and steady. He softened the focus of his gaze so that his eyes became sensitive to the smallest movement. He calmed his breathing until his breaths were slow and even. For a single brief moment he attended to the feelings in his bare feet: the prick of grit on the worn pavers, the slickness of water on stone.

A chill winter rain was falling steadily from the gray sky. It soaked into his hair and his tunic and formed puddles among the loose stones of the courtyard.

He heard his teacher's intake of breath and knew he was about to be given the first command. He exhaled a single long slow breath and slid into the attack stance called the Hammer and Nail. Two fingers of his right hand were the nail, tingling and still by his side. The entire combined force of his being, which his teachers called "the lir," was the hammer. He had chosen his weapon and his initiating strike.

"Pay respect!"

The scratchy voice came from his combat teacher, a short middle-aged Noma with a sleepy face. All his features—his eyebrows, his cheeks, the corners of his mouth— seemed to droop downwards, and his heavily lidded eyes were half closed. However, as Seeker well knew, he was far from sleepy.

Obediently Seeker bowed, first his upper body from the waist, then his head: paying respect. Only as he straightened up did he allow himself to see his opponent, standing a pace away from him in the rainy courtyard, beneath the shadow of the high dome of the Nom.

It was the Wildman: his friend and fellow novice, and the only one of their group of eight he had never yet defeated. In the course of nine months of training, during which Seeker had felt his body grow strong and the lir flow to his command, he and the Wildman had met in combat fourteen times, and he had lost every bout. He had never yet, facing the Wildman, achieved that sudden overwhelming strike which breaks the opponent's guard and shatters his concentration. With Jobal he could do it, and with Felice, but never with the Wildman.

His friend was now also straightening up from the respect. Their eyes met, unseeing as strangers. Seeker tracked for clues over the Wildman's beautiful rain-streaked face.

The throat. He'll strike for my throat.

It was the Wildman's usual move. But he was so fast and so strong that knowing it was coming was not enough. Seeker's mind moved smoothly and rapidly, using the few seconds now left to him. When the teacher gave the second command, the combat would begin. It would last for one, or two, or possibly three strikes—no more. Trained Nomana did not require lengthy bouts. Each fighter had at his disposal a single devastating blow, the blow into which his lir was concentrated, like the force of a great river funneled into a narrow jet. If this win-all or lose-all blow was struck too soon, or fell wide, the fight was lost. Timing was all.

Seeker's web of feelings, instincts, and thoughts fused into a single bright blade of decision. Roll the attack, play the riposte, follow with the kill. His plan formed, he let his entire body hang loose, dangle in the rain, swing in the wind.

Don't think. Never think.

React into action.

Meet your plan like a stranger.

Surprise yourself.

So much teaching. So much training. "Know everything and then forget everything," their teacher told them.

To one side stood the line of silent novices, watching the combat that was about to begin. Morning Star, third in line, watched like the rest, hands clasped before her, silent in the rain. A thought flickered in Seeker's brain.

Who does she want to win? Me, or the Wildman?

On the other side rose the stone pillars of the cloister,

and beyond, the great outer wall of the Nom. Slots pierced this wall at intervals, and through the slots could be glimpsed the sea, stretching away, horizonless, into the iron gray sky.

The voice of the combat teacher sounded as if from far off.

"Engage."

The Wildman struck first, for the throat, as Seeker had guessed. Seeker swayed back, outreaching the strike hand, and stabbed at the crook of the attacking arm, but only playing the riposte. If the Wildman went for the kill now, Seeker knew he would break him.

No time to hesitate. On he flowed, pouring his lir into the about-to-be-launched strike, begging the Wildman to make his throw now, at the bait moment, when he seemed so vulnerable, on the second strike, which had always been the Wildman's strike of choice.

But not today. With dismay Seeker realized he had committed, and the Wildman had not. His timing was off. In his frustration Seeker lost perfect concentration and felt the lir spreading from the two speeding fingers over his right hand and up his arm, dissipating his force. His blow powered through, hammer on nail, and caught the Wildman's left shoulder, rocking him back, but it was not enough to break him.

At once Seeker sucked back what lir was left and locked himself to the ground, but even as he did so the Wildman struck, the heel of his hand to Seeker's brow: the kill blow. Not all his power was in the strike, of course. Seeker was not killed. But he was broken.

He fell as he must, crippled by pure force and by shame. The Wildman had pulled his blow and had still broken him. The impact of the wave of power rippled from his stunned brow all the way down to his stomach, making him want to retch.

"Withdraw."

The teacher called the moves as if nothing of any significance had taken place. Seeker rose and bowed, a little shakily, and resumed his place in the line of silent novices, as did the Wildman. They stood still, hands clasped before them, maintaining the rigid discipline that had been drilled into them.

Their sleepy-eyed teacher now proceeded with the analysis, dabbing at his wet head with one end of his badan. His name was Chance.

"What did he do wrong? You."

He pointed at Morning Star.

"He committed too soon," said Morning Star.

"Could he have done otherwise?"

"Yes," said Morning Star softly, glancing towards Seeker. "He could have waited. But he knew his opponent had the longer reach. His decision to attempt a first-strike win was sound."

"Therefore predictable."

"Yes, Teacher."

The teacher nodded, then raising his hands above his head, he clapped twice. This was the signal for a break. The novices retreated into the shelter of the cloister—all but the Wildman, who stood apart from the rest, by one of the slots in the wall that looked out over the sea.

Morning Star came to Seeker's side. The last nine months had changed her greatly, as it had changed them all. In appearance she was the same, with her round face and her little button of a nose and her gentle blue eyes; but she seemed to Seeker to have grown older and more serious. Seeker found himself admiring her more each day.

"Almost won that time," she said.

"What do you call someone who almost won?"

"Loser."

He grinned. This was what made him feel so close to Morning Star. Their minds worked the same way.

But her attention was directed to the Wildman.

"Look at him," she said. "He doesn't smile any more. Why is he so unhappy?"

"Is he unhappy?"

Morning Star turned reproachful eyes on him.

"You hadn't noticed?"

"I don't see people's colors like you."

"Yes, he's unhappy."

Seeker had noticed how silent his friend had grown and how he liked to stand apart from the rest, but he had put that down to the training. Before all else, the Nomana were taught the art of stillness. Now that Morning Star voiced her concern, he saw that she was right, and was angry with himself for not having seen it before.

"I'll talk to him."

Seeker crossed the courtyard in the rain and touched his friend lightly on the arm.

"You win again," he said. "But I'll have you one day."

He wanted him to feel some pleasure in his victory.

The Wildman turned and looked at Seeker. It was clear from his face that he hadn't heard him. He gave an indifferent shrug.

"Yes," he said. "Why not?"

"They're saying you could be the best warrior ever."

"Are they?"

He shook his long golden hair, now dark with rain, and looked up at the high dome of the Nom. On the far side of the dome, invisible from this courtyard, lay the silver-walled enclosure called the Garden. In the Garden, at the heart of the great castle-monastery, lived the god of many names: the All and Only, the Always and Everywhere, the Reason and the Goal.

Seeker followed his friend's gaze, and he thought he understood. He knew how fervently the Wildman longed to enter the Garden. There, he had been told, he would find peace.

"You're tired of waiting, aren't you?"

"One day soon," said the Wildman.

"When we're ready."

"I'm ready now."

He spoke so quietly, so unlike his old bold voice with which he had cried out his heedless demands.

"There's so much we don't know," said Seeker. "We have to be patient."

"Like Noman was patient?"

He flashed Seeker a sudden grin, a glimpse of the old Wildman. Noman was the warlord who had come to

Anacrea long ago, made curious by the reports of a child god who lived there. Noman had not waited for permission to enter the Garden.

"You think I can't climb that silver screen?" said the Wildman. "I'd be over it before they saw me move."

Seeker was appalled.

"What are you talking about? The Garden's defended in ways we don't even understand."

"Only one way to find out."

"Are you crazy? You'd be caught! You'd be—you know what they'd do to you."

"I'd be gone."

"Gone where? The doors are locked. There's no way out."

"There's one way."

"This is all wrong. This isn't how you're supposed to be feeling. Why haven't you said this before? You should talk to a teacher. Or talk to the Elder. He'd understand. He'd tell you what to do."

The Wildman turned his dark eyes back to the gray infinity of sea and sky beyond the wall.

"Why do you think I don't know?" he said.

"Don't know what?"

"They don't want me here. They never have."

"That's not true."

"Look out there," said the Wildman, as if Seeker hadn't spoken. "Down there, the open sea. One perfect dive, and I'd be gone forever."

Seeker looked down. Three hundred feet below, the waves smashed against the rock on which the great walls were built. Anyone who jumped would be dashed to pieces in that roaring surf.

"Impossible," he said.

"One perfect dive," said the Wildman again, softly, to himself.

The teacher returned, and clapped his hands, and the novices took their places in line in the open courtyard. The rain was still falling, and the air was filled with the sound of water gurgling down gutters.

Chance looked at his class from beneath his heavy drooping lids and was silent for longer than usual. They waited patiently, accustomed by now to their teacher's methods. The longer the silence before a class began, the more significant the teaching.

At last they heard the slow exhalation of breath that preceded speech.

"It has been my task," he said, his voice sounding weary, as if he grudged the effort, "my task and my duty, over these last few months, to teach you to fight. I have taught you to command the life power that we call lir. I have taught you to deliver that power in combat."

He then shook his head and let out a sigh.

"But you are not yet Noble Warriors. You do not yet possess the secret skill."

A tremor ran through the line of novices. Seeker stole a look at Morning Star. The secret skill! Every one of them knew it. For all their recently acquired strength and stamina, they had not yet learned to fight as the Nomana fought. The Noble Warriors in action rarely struck with their fists, and never with weapons. They felled their opponents without touching them.

"Remember," said Chance, "the Noble Warriors do not seek dominion."

He looked from face to face, to satisfy himself that each one had heard and understood.

"However strong you become, you will never seek to exercise power over others."

They all knew this: it was the fundamental teaching. Their vow called them to bring justice to the oppressed and freedom to the enslaved, and no more. The Rule of the Nomana was absolute on this point. The Noble Warriors were not, and never would be, a ruling class.

"You're cold," said Chance. "You're wet. You're hungry. You're weary of these long slow weeks of training. All this is as it should be. Now I am going to show you what you still have to learn."

He scanned their faces.

"You."

He pointed at the Wildman.

"Come before me. Pay respect."

The Wildman stepped forward and bowed to his teacher, first from the waist, then the head.

"Prepare."

The two stood a pace apart, as earlier Seeker and the Wildman had done.

"Engage."

The teacher made no move of any kind. For a few trembling moments, the Wildman stood his ground. Then, abruptly, as if he had been hit with a club, he buckled and fell. He lay on the rain-soaked stones, curled onto his right side, breathing deeply as he had been taught, rebuilding his strength.

The teacher turned to the class.

"What did I do?"

None of them could answer. The teacher gestured to the Wildman to rise.

"Did I use force?"

The Wildman pushed the wet hair from his face and shook his head.

"No," he said. Then, "Yes. I suppose so."

Morning Star watched and listened intently. She could not explain what she had just seen any more than the rest of them, but she had an additional cause to be perplexed. She could always predict an act of aggression long before it took place. She could see the change in the attacker's colors. The faint aura that hovered round him would turn an angry red. But the teacher's colors had given no warning. It was as if he had made no assault at all.

"Something I did caused you to fall," said the teacher to the Wildman. "Did you feel the effects of force?"

"Yes. I think so."

"What did this force feel like?"

The Wildman shook his head. The questions confused him, and they made him feel stupid in front of the class.

"I don't know."

"Did it strike you like a fist?"

"No."

"Like a gust of wind?"

"No."

The teacher turned to the rest of the class.

"Any suggestions?"

Sweet-faced Felice spoke out, in her soft voice.

"Your spirit struck him?"

"No. That's not the answer."

Jobal, the slowest-witted member of the class and the most good-natured, reached up his hand to speak.

"You whacked him," he said. He swiped the air with one fist to demonstrate. "You whacked him so fast that none of us could see."

Chance shook his head, smiling. Everyone smiled at Jobal.

"No," he said. "I'm fast, but I'm not that fast."

"Maybe," said Winter, raising one eyebrow, "he just got tired and wanted to sit down."

Winter was the oldest of the novices and liked to tease his younger companions with wry and cynical comments. But this time, to his surprise, the combat teacher clapped his hands.

"There!" he said. "Now we're getting there."

Seeker picked up the clue and followed it.

"You took away his strength?"

"Go on. More. How did I do that?"

"With your mind?"

"Simpler, simpler. What did I do?"

Seeker frowned and concentrated.

"You looked at him."

"Aha! Yes, I looked at him."

He beckoned to the Wildman.

"Come closer." To the others, "Watch closely. See if

you can work out what I'm doing." And to the Wildman, "Hit me. Strike me with your open palm."

The Wildman raised his right hand and struck.

He missed.

"Try again."

He struck again and missed again. His blows either landed short or skidded off to one side. To the watchers it was as if the teacher was protected by an invisible shield.

"Wildman," called Seeker, following his earlier hunch, "close your eyes and then hit him."

The Wildman closed his eyes and struck. This time his palm caught the teacher square across his cheek.

"Bravo!" cried Chance, rubbing his stinging cheek. "Enough."

The Wildman stepped back and allowed himself a quick grin. It was the first blow any of them had ever landed on their teacher. Morning Star caught that mischievous smile. His long hair was swept back off his face, and for a moment he looked quite different. He looked older, with his high cheekbones gleaming in the rain-bright light.

"I know!" cried Jobal, one step behind everyone else as usual. "You do it with your eyes!"

"What do I do with my eyes?"

The teacher looked up and down the line of soaked novices. He raised one hand and passed it through the air, from left to right. All down the line they jerked their heads to the right, one after the other, as if he had slapped them.

"There," he said. "You all felt it. But what did you feel?"

None of them were able to answer.

"You."

The teacher beckoned to Morning Star. She stepped forward.

"Pay respect."

Morning Star bowed. She braced herself for combat.

"Stand," said the teacher.

Morning Star adopted the Tranquil Alert stance. She studied her teacher's colors closely but could see only the soft blues of a quiet spirit.

"Why don't you fall down?"

"You haven't struck me, Teacher."

"If I were to strike you"—he reached out a hand and pushed at her, but only gently—"you would harden your muscles against me. You would resist me. I would have to overpower your resistance with my force."

"Yes, Teacher."

"I am not doing that."

"No, Teacher."

"And yet you don't fall down. Why is that?"

"Because I don't want to fall down, Teacher."

"Ah, I see. So if you were to want to fall down, you would release the muscular tension that keeps you upright, and you would fall. I need do nothing. Is that so?"

"Yes, Teacher."

"Like this."

She caught a flash of red and felt her legs give way beneath her. Unable to stop herself, she fell to the ground.

"She falls," said Chance to the class, "because she wants to fall. Her body obeys her will."

"And her will," said Seeker, "obeys your will."

The teacher nodded, pleased.

"That," he said, "is the secret skill of the Noble War-riors. The stronger will controls the weaker will."

He gestured to Morning Star to rise and return to her place. Morning Star did so in thoughtful silence. In that moment of power, when her teacher had overwhelmed her, she had seen something curious. His colors had flowed out and embraced her. She had felt it as well as seen it. Never before had she known that the colors of one person could unfold like a cloak and embrace other people.

She listened closely as the teacher explained.

"When my friend here"—Chance indicated the Wild-man—"tried to hit me and missed, he was not failing in his aim. He was choosing not to hit me. I had control of his will. I made him not want to hurt me."

Of course, thought Morning Star. The colors are more than just a picture of feelings—they're the force of those feelings. So maybe other people's colors can be changed.

If it was true, it meant you could make other people do whatever you wanted. And then what? What sort of world would it be where everyone and everything surrendered to your desires? Morning Star shook her head, wanting to banish such wild fancies. It couldn't be so, she told herself. I don't want it to be so.

Meanwhile Winter, thinking himself ahead of his teacher, stepped forward out of the line, a pretend-innocent smile on his face.

"Make me fall down," he said.

He shut his eyes.

The combat teacher nodded approval.

"Without eye contact," he said, "I can't control an-other's will. However—"

He swept one hand through the air, boxing the side of Winter's head so hard that he staggered and fell to the ground.

"People with their eyes shut can't see you coming."

The class laughed. Winter sat on the ground and rue-fully rubbed at his ear.

"In the normal course of events," said Chance, "those who fear you will watch you. If they watch you, you can control them. But only if you have the stronger will."

Winter rose to his feet and rejoined the line. The com-bat teacher surveyed the class with his heavy-lidded eyes in silence for a long moment.

"For that, you need true strength."

He made the class a formal double bow: the bow of farewell.

"And for that, you need a new teacher."

The novices entered the study hall, grateful to escape the persistent rain, and took their accustomed places on the semicircular bench before the fireplace. A novitiate meek came scurrying in to light the fire that was already laid. The dry kindling caught with a crackle. Soon the split logs were ablaze and a welcome heat was reaching out to the novices' chilled wet bodies.

The combat teacher had not followed the class into the study hall, so they sat quietly on the bench and let their cold hands grow warm and waited for the promised new teacher.

A resinous log caught fire and exploded in a series of small pops, sending out sparks. Morning Star, inattentively watching the fire, still absorbed in her own thoughts, caught a flicker of color in the air beyond. Looking up, she saw with surprise that there was a person sitting by the window. It was a young woman, in full view of them all, her tall figure outlined by the light from the window, on the far side of the room from the only door. She must have been there when they came in. Somehow they had not noticed her.

She had short-cropped fair hair and wide-spaced dark eyes and soft smooth skin that was golden brown as honey. She met Morning Star's surprised stare with silent amusement. From her dress it was evident she was a Noma, about thirty years old, and perfectly, effortlessly lovely.

Morning Star was about to speak, but the new teacher raised one finger to her lips. At that, all the class saw her, and all were as surprised as Morning Star. The teacher kept her finger to her lips, so no one spoke, but they all rose to their feet and bowed. The teacher bowed in return, from the head only, and made a sign for them to sit once more.

The novices waited for the teacher to speak. They sat on the bench in silence and kept their eyes on her, and she sat with her hands folded on her lap and said not a word, half smiling, seeming to show interest, but revealing nothing. The firewood hissed in the grate, and the rain tapped at the windows, and nobody moved. They heard the cries of the gulls circling the dome of the Nom, and the rush and suck of the waves on the shore far below. They heard the humming of the wind and the changing rhythms of

the rain, now sweeping over the tiles above like a soft
broom, now drumming with a marching beat.

So time passed.

When at last the great Nom bell sounded noon, the
new teacher spoke.

"My name is Miriander," she said. Her voice was low,
but they heard every word. "It is my task and my duty to
teach you true strength."

She met their eyes one by one, giving no more time
to one than to another, but causing each of them to feel
he or she was the object of her special interest.

"Please prepare yourselves. In order to find your true
strength, you will be stripped of everything that protects
you."

The bell's last deep boom sounded, and the vibrations
slowly faded into the hiss of the rain. Through the high
windows, the ocean mist was closing in.

"This," she said, "will hurt."

⊰ 2 ⊱

In the Glimmen

THERE WAS A STRANGE NEW SOUND IN THE FOREST, A distant rustling and throbbing, coming from the west.

"Wagon train," said Sander Kittle, swinging idly from his branch. "Wagons on the road."

"It's not just the road," said his sister Echo. "Listen. It's all over. It's like a wind."

"So, why aren't the treetops blowing?"

"Maybe it's a ground wind."

"Ground wind?" snorted Sander. "Whoever heard of a ground wind?"

"Orvin has," said Echo. "Haven't you, Orvin?"

This was unkind of Echo, but she was annoyed that Orvin had joined them there, high in the branches of the old beech tree. This was Echo's own special place, and Orvin should have allowed her some privacy. Also he had such a long face and such a gloomy way of gaping at her that sometimes it made her want to scream.

"Yes," said Orvin. "I've heard of a ground wind."

"Orvin doesn't count," said Sander. "He'd say up's down if you told him to."

Orvin was known to be sweet on Echo. In this he was not unusual. Echo Kittle, seventeen years old, pale, slender, and beautiful, filled the dreams of most young men in the great forest called the Glimmen. But it was Orvin Chipe her parents encouraged, with the result that Orvin Chipe was the one admirer of them all that Echo found the most tiresome.

"You wouldn't say up is down, would you, Orvin?"

"No," said Orvin.

"But it is, you know. Up is down." She swung round on her branch so that she hung by her legs with her head dangling, long blond hair flying. "See. Up is down. Say up is down, Orvin."

"All right. Up is down. I don't mind."

Hanging there, feeling that she wanted to pull Orvin's nose till he squealed, Echo heard the strange sound again. It was coming nearer.

She swung herself back onto the branch.

"Let's go and see," she said. "Race you to the road."

Sander grinned. A recent light rain still clung to the leaves and branches, creating just the perfect slickness for sliding down. Echo was older than him by two years, but they were evenly matched when it came to tree racing. Orvin, however, was slow and clumsy. This was Echo's way of getting away from him.

"Ready when you are."

"Go!"

Off they went, swinging from branch to branch, and Orvin made no attempt to follow. They sprang from tree to tree, sliding down poles placed there for the purpose, scampering up notched stairways, running along bouncing rope walks. The dark network of high branches that stretched for miles in every direction was their familiar home, and their slight and slender forms slipped as effortlessly through the trees as fish swim in the sea. They raced past the homes of other Glimmeners, clusters of timber huts perched high in the branches, where friends and neighbors were to be glimpsed as they flashed by. They raced on into the uninhabited regions of the forest, some way apart now, seeking any and every advantage to overtake each other. Echo found a springer and, using the branch's bounce, sprang up high into the next tree, catching at fronds of leaves to guide her landing. Now she was sure she was above Sander—in tree racing, height gave critical advantage—but she didn't stop to look. The race was too close.

On they hurtled from tree to tree at breakneck speed, leaving behind a trail of flying spray and tumbling pinecones, racing each other through the permanent twilight of the Glimmen towards the wide cut of the road. They had both forgotten their original purpose and were entirely caught up in their contest.

Echo lost sight of Sander in a pine grove, but as she came out on the far side, she reckoned she was a whole tree's reach in front of him. Ahead she saw the brighter light, where the high road wound through the forest and

the trees were cut back to let the pale winter light fall on
its stony ruts. She slowed herself down and swung panting
into a high fork in an old yew, directly above the road.
Here she braced herself and looked back, face glowing
with triumph. But there was no sign of Sander. She looked
all round and finally caught a slight movement ahead. It
was Sander, dropping into the hide position, a good two
trees in front of her. Somehow he had overtaken her. But
there was no time to find out how. In the same moment
she saw him, she heard once more the strange sound that
now filled the whole forest.

Not wagons. Not a wind. It was a low thundering roar,
like the rolling of the sea.

Echo hugged close to the yew trunk, also adopting the
hide position. Then, barely moving, she shifted her head
and shoulders until she could see round the trunk and into
the road. She saw only trees, and the pools of light between the trees. But that sound! Ever closer, ever louder—
she focused her attention and was sure she could hear the
beating of many hooves. Could it be a bullock team? Only
a thousand bullock teams could make such a roar. Whatever it was must be very close now, but the spreading foliage below prevented her from seeing clearly.

She glanced ahead at Sander, guessing that his nearer
perch would give him a better view. Sander had his eyes
fixed on the road. On his face was a look that Echo had
never seen before. His eyes were wide, his mouth open.
It was a look of wonder.

Echo turned her own gaze back to the road. Now it
was her eyes that opened wide.

A strange and beautiful creature came prancing into view down the track. On its back rode a thickset man with long dark hair, wearing a silver fur jacket and glinting armor. But the girl's eyes were not on the rider: they were on his mount. This was no bullock. It was a pale ginger color, its long neck fringed with strands of sandy hair, its prominent eyes set wide on a long narrow head. Its slender and muscular legs rose and fell in a prancing dancing rhythm that was beautiful to watch. From time to time the creature lifted up its elegant head and flared its wide fragile nostrils and made a sound like the wind in long grass. This, Echo thought, was how the wind would sound if it could talk. And as if to prove her right, there came from farther back down the road an answering sound, and another, and another. And all the while the great beating roar drew nearer.

The rider did not look up. He was an outlander, that much the watching girl knew, and one who was clearly unaware that there might be people living in the trees above. Echo risked a quick silent swing from her tree to the tree where Sander was hiding.

"What is it?" whispered Sander, his voice trembling.

"I don't know. But I've never seen anything so beautiful in my life."

The roar of sound was taking on a recognizable shape now, the sound of many hooves drumming on the worn stone of the road and on the softer ground between the trees, mingled with the strange breathy cries of the beautiful beasts. They caught sight of a second making its way between the trees, some way from the road. It was followed by a third, and then two more, and then many more. In a short time they had lost count. There were hundreds of riders advancing through the forest. Soon they had filled the road, in a stream of bobbing forms; and on either side, as far as the hidden watchers could see, there were riders swarming through the trees.

They carried weapons in their belts: swords and coiled whips. They rode in orderly files, one behind the other. These were not travellers. They were warriors.

As the riders advanced eastward along the road, Echo and Sander followed them, keeping pace in the trees above, fascinated by the immense array of beautiful animals on which the warriors rode.

Then a new sound drew their attention. It was the tramp of a column of marching people, coming from the east. The marchers sang as they came. Echo recognized the sound.

"It's the axers," she whispered. "They're going to get a surprise."

Every week for many months now a band of axers had come marching through the forest, escorting a column of pilgrims dressed in white robes. They marched through the Glimmen and on out the other side, and there vanished into the region of mist known as the land cloud. What they did there no one knew; but they had never been seen coming back.

It was the pilgrims who were singing now. The words of their song became audible, though they were not yet in sight.

"Take me up into the harvest!
Take me up into the harvest!
Take me up into the harvest!
To live for evermore!"

The riders also heard the sound of the singing. Those in the lead slowed their mounts to a stop. Their hands went to their sides and untied the whips that were coiled there.

The approaching column of singers now rounded the bend of the road and came into view. There were about thirty of them, both men and women, their hands reached up above their heads, waving from side to side as they sang.

"Take me up into the harvest!
To live for evermore!"

On every face was the same look of ecstatic hope. Before them, and on either side, marched their escort of axers, tall men in heavy armor, the enforcers of the rich and cruel empire of Radiance. These giant guardians carried spiked chains, looped in their right hands, ready at a moment's notice to snake out and swing with devastating force. Echo and Sander kept very still in the high branches. Like all Glimmeners, they feared the axers, and Radiance, and its priests, and its worship of the sun.

Now both the white-robed pilgrims and the axers saw the mounted warriors massing before them, and they came to a shambling surprised stop. The axers stood with their legs apart and their chains at the ready, staring through the visors of their helmets. The pilgrims fell silent. All were speechless at the sight of the unfamiliar beasts.

Then the chief axer, recalling that his heavy armor and his immense strength made him invulnerable, boomed out through the slit in his helmet.

"Give way, in the name of our Radiant Leader!"

The mounted warriors made no answer. Their mounts frisked and capered, wanting to be moving forward.

"Clear the road!" boomed the axer. "Get your skinny cattle out of our way!"

Still the mounted warriors said nothing. The chief axer then loosed his chain with a jerk of his arm, which sent it hissing through the air into the space between them, at knee height. Echo gasped, in the tree above, terrified that the heavy iron links would snap the fine-boned legs of the fragile beasts. Instead, in a swift smooth movement, one of the mounted warriors slipped over the side of his mount and sent his whip curling at ground level to wind round the axer's ankles. A single tug, and the axer and his chain came crashing to the ground. The whip curled, snaking back to its owner, even as he was righting himself on his mount.

The other axers, seeing their chief felled, gave out a roar of rage and loosed their own chains. The mounted warriors responded with a flurry of movement and a snapping of whips. Shortly every one of the escorting axers was sprawled on the ground.

The white-robed men and women looked on in dismay.

"Who are you?"

"We are Orlans!" The lead warrior spoke in a harsh voice, in an accent they had never heard before. "We are the masters now."

The boldest pilgrim spoke up.

"We must go on down the road," he said. "We are the chosen ones."

The felled axers were now climbing back to their feet and grimly drawing their long-handled axes. The invaders were not big people, nor were the beasts they rode much larger than calves, and the axers towered over them. But Echo, watching from above, knew now that the beautiful beasts were in no danger. They were too fast and too skillful.

The leading axer plowed into the middle of the mounted army, swinging his weapon, but wherever he struck, all he hit was air. The Orlans danced round him like children taunting an aged bear. Their whips caught him round the helmet and the wrists and the ankles, and without quite knowing how it had happened he found himself on his knees, by the side of the road, his axe tossed far out of reach.

"Now you kneel!" cried the Orlan. "All men kneel before the Great Jahan!"

Mounted Orlans on every side loosed their whips and snapped them in the air.

"Kneel!" they cried.

The other axers and the white-robed pilgrims, awed by this display of power, dropped fearfully to their knees.

All the time that this confrontation had been taking

place, more and more Orlans had been riding up, massing
in a dense array of mounted warriors that stretched back
through the trees as far as the eye could see. Now the ranks
were parting, and a new sound was heard: the blare of
trumpets, the beat of drums, the shrilling of pipes, and the
clash of steel on steel. There came a flashing of lights from
among the mass of the men, and the sound of cheering,
and a ripple of movement as riders dismounted.

Echo, peering down through the foliage, saw the ador-
ing faces of the riders as they fell to their knees; but she
could not yet see the object of their adoration. She heard
the beat of the music and saw the kneeling riders take up
their swords and beat in time on their breastplates, and she
heard them cry out.

"Jahan! Jahan! Jahan!"

The Orlans who had overpowered the axers now
themselves dismounted and knelt, and joined in the chant.
The white-robed singers, already on their knees, looked
on in awe and terror.

"Jahan! Jahan! Jahan!"

The music was loud now, a pealing, clashing fanfare of
praise, augmented by every man in earshot striking his
sword against his breastplate. The flashing lights dappled
the tall trees on either side. The warriors closest to their
leader cheered wildly as he passed.

"Jahan! Jahan! Jahan!"

Echo and Sander, motionless as lizards in the trees
above, watched in amazement. A striking figure was advancing slowly through the lines of kneeling men, seeming to glide over the ground, and bright lights illuminated

his tawny face as he came. The light was reflected from some twenty mirrors, held in the skilled hands of riders who accompanied his progress on either side, angling their discs of polished steel to catch the pale daylight above and send it bouncing onto their leader. Beside the mirror bearers rode the musicians, the pipers and drummers and trumpeters, filling the air with their pounding fanfare. Behind the leader rode three young men with haughty faces. On either side the swarthy Orlans clashed their swords and cheered.

"Jahan! Jahan! Jahan!"

As the leader drew close, the axers and the white-robed singers alike could see that he was standing in a high open carriage, drawn by a team of four of the beautiful beasts. The carriage was so finely made, its two high wheels so slender, that he seemed to be floating through the air. He looked about him as he advanced, with a gaze of indifference that was almost contempt.

Echo stared at him in fascination. He was mesmerizingly ugly. Every feature on his broad nut-brown face was oversized, from his lowering eyebrows to his powerful chin. Hard black eyes stared ahead at nothing. A great jutting nose, a wide fleshy mouth. Thick springy black hair dragged back and bunched at the nape of his neck. Silver fur jacket and steel breastplate, like all his men. Hips and shoulders swaying to the beat of the drums, with the arrogant swagger of a monster who believes he is beautiful.

"Jahan! Jahan! Jahan!"

He raised one hand, in which he clasped a silver-handled whip, and the carriage came to a stop. The music and the cheering ceased. The Great Jahan cast his eyes over the axers and the white-robed pilgrims who knelt in the forest road before him. He made a sign to one of the three young men who rode behind him.

"Alva!"

The young man rode forward, to the axers. The other two, his brothers, looked on, glowering with envy.

"Explain yourselves," said Alva. "Speak clearly, and be brief."

"We are soldiers of the imperial army of Radiance," said the chief axer, trying his best to sound defiant while still kneeling.

"Who is your lord?"

"Radiant Leader, the beloved son of the Great Power above."

"Go back to your lord. Tell him that my father, Amroth Jahan, demands his submission. Tell him that when the Great Jahan enters his territory, he expects to be welcomed by him on his knees, as you are now. If he fails in this, he and all who follow him will be destroyed. Now go!"

The axers rose to their feet and looked at one another uncertainly. Then, all reaching the same decision at once, they turned and strode back down the road home.

Amroth Jahan had no more interest in the kneeling pilgrims. He motioned to his men that they should continue. But the boldest of the pilgrims rose to his feet and cried, "We are the chosen ones! What have we to fear?"

The Great Jahan's oldest son, Sasha, still angry that his father had picked one of his brothers, drew his whip and snapped it in the air.

"Clear the way for the Great Jahan!"

"But we must go forward! We go to eternal life! It's been promised to us. We've been chosen!"

"Let them pass."

This was the deep voice of Amroth Jahan himself. He showed his uneven yellow teeth in a wide smile.

"They've been chosen. Let them pass."

The white-robed men and women formed up once more into their marching column. The ranks of Orlans parted to make way for them.

"Eternal life, eh?" said the Great Jahan; and he laughed a rich booming laugh.

The column of pilgrims set off. As they began to move, they waved their hands from side to side above their heads and raised their voices once more in song.

"Take me up into the harvest!
Take me up into the harvest!
Take me up into the harvest!
To live for evermore!"

The Orlans too now resumed their forward progress. Echo and Sander kept up with them, slipping from tree to tree above, dropping lower and closer all the time. Echo was entranced by the four riderless beasts that drew the Jahan's carriage, and she longed to touch them.

"Oh, they're so beautiful!"

They were beneath her now, so close. She reached down a hand—

"Careful!" cried Sander.

Too late. For the first time in her life, Echo Kittle fell out of a tree.

She dropped directly onto the back of one of the four beasts. She was so light and her reactions were so fast that she was able to throw her arms round the animal's slender neck and so break her fall before tumbling to the ground.

Whips hissed out from either side and spun round her, binding her tight. She was then dragged to her feet, and there before her, gazing down at her, was the craggy pockmarked face of Amroth Jahan.

"A tree sprite!" he said. "Fallen from the sky!"

Echo knew she was in trouble and could do nothing to save herself, so she did what she always did: she pushed the distressing thoughts out of her mind. Her arms were bound at her sides by the whips, but she could move her head. She was close to the animal who had broken her fall. Its nose was reaching towards her, its nostrils flaring gently. Its coat was a soft fawn color, with a white mark in the shape of a diamond between its eyes. She laid her cheek on the animal's nose. She felt it snuffle at her, then nuzzle her with the softest of lips.

"You're perfect," she whispered.

Amroth Jahan watched, and a smile formed on his broad craggy face. The girl was extraordinarily beautiful, with her pale flawless skin and her symmetrical face and her delicate features. Also, she was showing no fear. The Jahan respected that.

"You like my Caspians?"

"Caspians?" She turned her gray eyes to his. "Is that what they are?"

"Horses. Caspian horses." He signed for the whips to be released. "Have you never seen a horse before?"

"No. Never."

"There are no horses in the world as fine as my Caspians."

"There are no horses in my world at all."

The Jahan made a sign to his men. He had made a decision about the girl: she would travel in his carriage. Echo found herself lifted up and deposited by the Jahan's side. She caught a flurry in the branches above and guessed that it was Sander racing away to get help. But they were far from their home village.

The carriage began to move forward once more. The entire great army advanced through the trees.

"Would you like to have a Caspian for yourself?" said the Jahan.

"Yes," she replied faintly, feeling as if she had fallen into a dream.

"Pick one."

Echo pointed to the one with the white mark on its nose.

"That one."

"An excellent choice. His name is Kell. What's your name?"

"Echo," she replied. "Echo Kittle."

"Then I give him to you, Echo Kittle. Kell is yours. Do you ride?"

"No."

"I will teach you. You have the frame of a good rider."

"Thank you."

But even in the midst of her confusion, Echo knew that she couldn't accept the gift.

"Please don't think I'm ungrateful. But I have to go home."

She looked around. Already they had covered far more distance than she had realized. These horses moved much faster than bullocks. She looked up into the branches above: no sign of her people.

"No, Echo Kittle. I've decided to take you with me."

The Jahan smiled as he spoke, but the tone of his voice told her that he meant what he said.

"Take me with you? Why?"

"Because it pleases me. It will give me pleasure to teach you to ride."

He turned and gestured to the young men riding behind his carriage. At his sign, they came forward.

"These are my sons. It pleases me to give you to one of them as his wife. You may choose."

At this Echo forgot her fear. Her mother was always proposing husbands for her. There was no surer way to provoke her anger.

"I don't want to marry one of your sons."

"Yes, they're not very attractive, are they? Still, it is my will."

"You can't make me."

"Young lady," said the Jahan, frowning, "I can do as I please."

"I'll run away. You'll never catch me. No one can race through the trees as fast as me."

"If you run away," said the Jahan, now greatly displeased, "I will burn every tree in the forest, and kill every man, woman, and child who lives there."

Echo gasped.

"You wouldn't! No man could be so cruel!"

"I do whatever is necessary to get what I want."

"Then you're no better than a monster!"

"I don't understand. How am I a monster?"

"You don't care how much you hurt other people, so long as you get what you want."

"And are you different? Do you care more for others than for yourself?"

"I don't go about burning and killing."

"Very well. We shall see."

He raised his whip hand high, and the advancing army clattered to a halt.

He turned to his oldest son.

"Sasha. Those singing fools. Ride back and fetch me one."

The young Orlan saluted his father, wheeled round on his horse, and cantered away down the road.

The Great Jahan stood silent in his carriage and tapped on the harness bar with the handle of his whip. Echo's father tapped like that when he was cross with her. Sometimes, after a period of silence, her father would explode for no reason at all and go into a long shouting tirade about all the things that were wrong with her, how she was selfish and stubborn and never said sorry and would end by driving everyone to distraction. At such times, she would stand quietly before him and not listen. This was her great discovery: when something unpleasant was happening, all you had to do was not think about it. If you didn't think about it, it might as well not have happened.

So they waited in a gathering drizzle that misted the Orlans' armor and glistened on the horses' coats. Once or twice Echo looked up into the trees, but without any real hope of being rescued. Even if her people caught up with her, what could they do against these whip-wielding warriors who had overcome the giant axers?

In a little while Sasha Jahan returned with one of the white-robed pilgrims on his horse's back, slung sideways like a sack of grain. He rode up in front of the carriage and tipped the pilgrim down onto the ground. The poor man was white-faced with fear. He lay curled up on the ground, clearly expecting to die.

The Jahan smiled grimly and addressed Echo.

"Now, young lady," he said. "You see this man before you. I give you the power of life and death over him. Give the order for his death, and his throat will be cut. Here, on the ground, as you watch."

"Never!"

"Give the order for him to be set free, and he'll go free. But you must pay a small price for his freedom. The little finger of your left hand will be cut off."

"You wouldn't!"

"I'll do it myself."

Before she could stop him, he had gripped her left wrist in his massive hand and drawn a short sharp knife from his belt. Echo let out a stifled cry of fear.

The Jahan held the gleaming blade before him. The lightly falling drizzle began to bead on its bright surface.

"If you want this stranger to live, say: live. Then pay the price. If you want him to die, say: die. If you remain silent for as long as it takes for the rain to run off my knife, he dies."

Echo was paralyzed with horror. Her left hand felt numb, he gripped it so tightly. She looked once at the pilgrim crouching on the ground, then quickly looked away. She fixed her gaze on the knife. She saw the mist of moisture forming into droplets of water, and the droplets growing and merging. The sight hypnotized her. She shut her thoughts to everything else. She saw the droplets shiver and start to roll along the blade, gathering other droplets as they went, growing into a trickle. She followed the runnel of rainwater to the tip of the blade, and saw how it hung there, swelling into a fat shining pearl. She saw it shudder and drop, and heard the soft pat of sound as it struck the carriage floor.

She had not spoken.

There came a sharp cry. A cold chill seized her heart. It was as if the blade had plunged deep into her, even as it killed the stranger she could have saved.

Then came a groan, followed by the scuffle of running feet. She looked around and saw the pilgrim running for his life down the road. She shut her eyes tight and blushed a deep hot red.

She heard the rattle of the wheels and the tapping of countless hooves on the stony track as the carriage began to move once more. She felt her left wrist released and the tingle of blood returning to her fingers. She felt the tears rolling down her cheeks.

Then came the mocking voice of the Jahan.

"So now you know."

"You didn't cut his throat," said Echo. "I knew you wouldn't."

"You knew only one thing. That you cared more for your little finger than for another man's life. If I'm a monster, so too are you."

Echo said no more. She couldn't begin to find words for the storm of fear and shock and shame within herself. She had never known men could be so cruel. She had never known she could be so afraid. She had never known she could let a man die.

"Now you will kiss my hand."

He held out his huge hand before her. She took it, then bowed her head and kissed it.

"No more talk of running away."

She hated him then, more than she had ever hated anyone in her life: this great ugly man who made her hate herself. She wanted more than anything to hurt him, and to see him cry as she had cried. She knew she had no choice for the moment but to stay with him. But secretly she vowed that she would die before she married one of his sons. And one day, she would make him in his turn kiss her hand.

✢ 3 ✣

The Shadow of Noman

MIRIANDER LED THE EIGHT NOVICES INTO THE SHADOW Court. Morning Star, walking in line immediately behind the Wildman, was surprised to see that his colors had changed. The amber brown tones that told her he was un-involved and unhappy had turned to a pale yellow glow. It was as if he had awoken from sleep. There was something he wanted very much, and his colors told her that he now expected to get it soon.

Once they were in the Shadow Court, Miriander spoke to them.

"We will enter the Night Court," she said, "and sit there for a little while, and I will show you something of the past of our Community. To see this, you will need to share my memories."

She smiled at them as she spoke, and every one of them, not realizing they were doing it, smiled back. This new teacher was so strong and so beautiful that they all wanted to please her.

"These memories will become visible to you as pictures in the air. They are memories that were shown to me by my teacher, and to him by his. In this way the Noble Warriors have forged an unbroken chain of memory from the early days of our Community to today. You will now join this chain."

She led them on into the darkness of the Night Court, and they sat down cross-legged on the ground. The high-domed windowless space was lit only by hundreds of pencil-thin shafts of light, which entered through small holes in the curving roof high above. The stripes and speckles of brightness fell on their faces and clothing, on walls and floor, dissolving their forms into the shadows.

"Look upwards," said Miriander. "Look at nothing. Expect nothing."

Seeker did as he was told. He let his attention fall on the motes of dust that hung in the fine beams of light, and then on the shadowy emptiness beyond. From somewhere outside he thought he heard cries and the pattering of many feet. He felt a rumble in his stomach and realized he was hungry. He wondered what they would be given for lunch. He particularly liked the custard that the meeks sometimes made, when the hens were laying well and there was a surplus of eggs. He even liked the skin that formed on the custard, which most of the others hated. And if they were allowed butter biscuits with the custard, his happiness would be complete.

He smiled at the thought. Then he caught a shifting

of the light in the air, and there appeared above him a line of ghostly men and women, all kneeling, with their heads bowed.

"You are seeing a memory of a memory," said Miriander. "You are seeing the first brothers and sisters of our Community."

The images were faint, and the thin shafts of light passed through them, further distancing them. But the kneeling people were visibly dressed as the Nomana were dressed to this day.

"They kneel," said Miriander, "because they expect to die. A warlord has come to Anacrea, and they know his power is too great for them to resist."

"Noman," murmured the Wildman.

They all knew the story of the warlord who had become the founder of the Noble Warriors.

"Yes," said Miriander. "This is the coming of Noman."

Now in the memory-scene above, the novices saw a man stride towards the kneeling figures. In his right hand he held a long straight slender sword. Little more than a shadow among shadows, he came to a stop before the kneeling group, and they looked up at him and spoke to him, though no sound could be heard. Then he raised his right arm, and holding his sword horizontal over his head, as if to guard himself against attack from above, he strode onwards, between the kneeling figures, across the domed space of the Night Court, and so out of sight.

The Wildman's eyes tracked the figure all the way. He half raised one hand, as if he too might hold a sword above his head, but then he lowered it again.

Seeker made no move, but he shivered as he watched. It seemed to him that somehow he had seen this before.

Miriander's quiet voice told the familiar story.

"Noman was the first and last man to go into the Garden. He remained in the Garden for a day and a night. He never spoke of what he found in the Garden. But when he came out, he disbanded his army and joined our Community."

"How long ago did Noman die?" This was Morning Star, gazing up at the ghostly figures above.

"Noman lived on Anacrea over two hundred years ago," said Miriander. "But I never said he died."

The class heard but did not understand. Above them now in the speckled shadows, the kneeling figures were rising to their feet and reaching their arms high in the Nomana salute. And now others were joining them and standing close behind them, saluting also; and more came and stood behind them, and more, until the entire vault of the Night Court was thronging with a great crowd of Nomana, all reaching upwards.

"Memories of memories," said Miriander. "You are seeing every Noble Warrior that has ever lived. They salute you. This is your Community, past and present."

The novices looked up and marvelled at the vast gathering, and in all of them, there swelled the same sensation of pride and fellowship, that these were now their brothers and sisters for all time.

"Go to them," said Miriander.

The novices then rose up from the ground on which they sat and passed among the ghostly figures above, who embraced them and gathered round them with smiling faces. No one of these faces was clearly recognizable, but from them all flowed a current of love and power that warmed them and made them feel as if they had come at last to their true home.

"We are always with you." The murmur of deep voices seemed to come from the mouths of all that great gathering of ghosts. "Our strength is always with you."

Seeker felt it then; so did Morning Star and the Wildman and the others: a new force sprang to life within them, which they knew was not theirs alone, but was the force of the Community.

Then the insubstantial figures in the air began to melt away, and the novices were seated once more upon the ground.

"You are not alone," said Miriander. "This is the beginning of true strength."

She rose to her feet. The novices too rose. From outside came the sounds of some distant commotion to which Miriander paid no heed. She led them through the open doors of the Night Court into the Cloister Court. Here, in the tranquil light diffused through the pearlstone ceiling, they gazed through the forest of white pillars towards the distant silver screen and prayed the entrance prayer.

"Wise Father, you are the Clear Light. You are the Reason and the Goal. Guide me in the true way."

Then Miriander resumed her instruction.

"Noman understood that the Lost Child was weak and that his defenders must be strong. He feared that the evil in the world would overwhelm this precious seed of truth.

He devoted the rest of his life to building defenses that would stand against all that the future years might bring."

"Was he so fearful?" said Seeker.

"Fearful, and fearless," said Miriander. "His last words were 'My life is an experiment in search of the truth.'"

Seeker shivered again as he heard this. It was so like his own name, the name he had always hated: Seeker after Truth.

"His last words?" said the Wildman. "So he did die."

"His last words before he left us, to submit himself to his last test. He was never seen again."

She led them forward to the space before the silver screen so that they could each offer themselves to the All and Only in their own way. Morning Star approached the Garden with rising nervousness. She kept her eyes on the ground, fearful of the power of the light that streamed through the piercings in the screen. She longed to be close to the Loving Mother, who was also the Lost Child, but the colors were too intense for her, and she dared not look.

This was Morning Star's most secret shame. Because she was unable to look into the Garden, she believed she must be unworthy. How if she was unworthy could she ever become a true Noble Warrior?

The Wildman, meanwhile, was standing very still, staring into the green depths of the Garden. Without realizing he was doing so, he was clenching and unclenching his fists.

He had felt the surge of power as he had entered the Community memory. He had listened to every word spoken by Miriander. The warlord Noman, the greatest of the

Noble Warriors, had gained his power by fearlessness. He had forced his way into the secret guarded place. The Wildman saw no reason why he should not do likewise: no reason but fear of the unknown, and the Wildman had no fear of the unknown. The greater the risk, the more he embraced it.

Morning Star guessed what he planned to do just a moment too late. She caught the surge of glowing red that burst from him, and cried out—

"No, Wildman!"

But he had already thrown himself at the silver screen, and finding fingerholds in the piercings, he was pulling himself up, moving so fast that he was almost at the top before Miriander responded. He had his back to her: there was no question of controlling his will.

She jumped.

It was a single spring, but it carried her up and over the Wildman's head. It seemed to the amazed novices that her heel did no more than brush his temple, but he dropped like a stone. Miriander landed and was standing still once more, as if she had never moved. The Wildman lay unconscious on the ground.

"Carry him out."

Morning Star knelt by his side, tears stinging her eyes. "Is he dead?"

"No," said Miriander. "But his time with us has come to an end."

Morning Star gave a low cry and covered her face with her hands. Seeker felt a shudder of horror at the teacher's words. At an end? That could only mean one thing. The

Wildman would be cast out. Therefore, according to the promise he had made to the Elder, Seeker must be cast out, too.

But as they carried the Wildman out into the Shadow Court, their private fears were overtaken by a greater commotion. The Pilgrim Gate had been opened, and a line of Nomana were standing between the gate and a shouting crowd out in the Nom square. The crowd was made up of villagers: farmers, herdsmen, fishermen. They were shouting, but not in anger. They were afraid.

"Help us! Only the Noble Warriors can save us! Come to our help before we lose everything!"

The Nom bell began to ring: not the slow booms of the hour, but a rapid bing-bing-bing of alarm.

Miriander hurried the novices through the side door into the novitiate and told them to take the unconscious Wildman to his bed in the novitiate dormitory.

"He won't wake for many hours," she said. "I must leave you for a short time. Use that time to prepare for your training. Once the training begins, you will each be alone."

As she spoke, members of the Community were hurrying past, heading for the Chapter House. The villagers' cries could still be heard, coming over the high wall. Miriander now followed in her turn.

Seeker's brother appeared, walking fast.

"Blaze!" cried Seeker. "What's happened?"

"Trouble on the mainland," said Blaze. "A new warlord on the rampage. The Elder has called a council."

———

The novices laid the Wildman on his bed in the dormitory and covered him with a blanket. He looked peaceful in his sleep. Morning Star brushed the golden curls away from his face, then lightly stroked his cheeks. The others left, all but Seeker.

Morning Star spoke to him in her distress.

"He will wake, won't he?"

"He'll wake," said Seeker. "But he shouldn't have done that."

"What will they do to him?"

"He'll be cleansed. He'll be emptied of everything he's ever learned. He'll be like a child again."

He said nothing of the risk to himself. Morning Star's concern was all for the Wildman.

"Like a child!" she exclaimed.

Morning Star looked down on him. He was so fragile in his sleep, so helpless and so beautiful.

"We mustn't let that happen, Seeker. He's our friend."

"Yes, of course. But I'm afraid it may be too late."

"We have to help him." And she said again, "He's our friend."

As she spoke she was swept by a sudden overpowering memory. She was remembering the beautiful golden youth who had stood on the prow of his riverboat and cried out to the noonday sun, "Do you love me?" With the memory, with the image of his bold laughing face, came a piercing sensation that made her gasp with its intensity. For a moment she was unable to breathe. Then, as she breathed again and felt the chill air fill her lungs, it seemed to her that everything had changed. This beautiful broken boy sleeping before her had become infinitely precious to her.

She had never loved him before, in his crazy arrogance. But she loved him now. She didn't want to love him. She was angry with herself for loving him. But as she stroked his sleeping brow and watched his blond eyelashes tremble in his dreams, she longed for him to cry his echoing cry once more, so that she could answer him, "Yes, Wildman. I love you."

It was impossible to say any of this to Seeker. She was ashamed of her feelings and did not understand where they had sprung from. Better to say nothing and hope that the storm of emotion would pass.

Seeker had noticed nothing. He had troubles of his own. He was gazing out through the narrow windows of the dormitory over the terraced streets of Anacrea, all the way down to the little harbor. He was remembering the days he had passed in the school yard, staring up at this very window, waving to his brother, wondering if he ever saw him.

Morning Star looked round at him and saw the blue-gray color of sadness. She felt a pang of guilt.

"Now you're unhappy, too."

"Yes." There was no point in denying it. She could read his every mood. But that didn't mean she understood its source. "Just one of those passing feelings."

"Like a cloud shadow."

"Not shadow, exactly. More like emptiness. As if I'm going to lose everything."

His searching gaze located the street where he had lived all his life. He could just make out the corner of his house. He realized he was looking for the house as if he would never see it again.

"Why should you lose everything?"

He couldn't tell her. She was so grieved over the Wildman: how could he tell her that the Wildman's rash act might drive him too from the Nom? Moreover there was a shyness in Seeker that made it impossible for him to ask for Morning Star's pity—a shyness that was edged with pride. She could read his colors. His feelings were open to her, if she chose to look.

"I don't know," he said. "It's only a feeling."

"You'd tell me, wouldn't you?"

"Yes. I'd tell you."

They often spoke in this kind of shorthand, without naming the fears or sadnesses that were their true subject.

"Wildman never told me," she said. He caught the slight tremor in her voice.

"But you saw his colors. You knew."

"I wish I didn't know."

"You have a great gift, Star."

"Do you think so? Most times I'd rather not know."

"I like your knowing," said Seeker. "I like not having to explain."

She looked at him closely then, and it seemed to him that she guessed.

"But knowing isn't enough, is it? I can't make the emptiness go away."

"No. But at least there's someone who knows what I'm feeling."

"You're lucky. I wish—"

He understood what she couldn't bring herself to say.

"You wish there were someone like that for you."

She nodded.

"There're so many things inside me I can't say."

"Yes, you can. You can say them to me."

But she shook her head.

"I can't. It's not that I don't trust you. You're my best friend in all the world. It's just that I'm ashamed."

"You? What have you got to be ashamed about?"

He looked so surprised, it made her laugh.

"There!" she said. "I knew it. You think I'm all pink and good and uncomplicated. But I'm not."

"What are you?"

"I'm dark and wicked and mysterious."

Then Seeker laughed too, because it was so absurd to think of her that way; and so they left the dormitory to join the others.

The meeting in the Chapter House lasted longer than expected, and twilight shadows were gathering when at last the members of the Community emerged. Miriander came to the waiting novices and told them there had been a division of opinion within the council.

"Some say we should help the villagers against this new warlord and his army. Others say our Rule forbids us to fight battles and win wars. We were not given our powers to rule the land."

"But the Noble Warriors can't refuse to help," said Morning Star.

"We do what we can," said Miriander. "We can't do everything. That we owe to the wisdom of Noman. Our powers have limits."

"All except for Noman," said Seeker. He didn't know why he said it, or how he knew it. It just came out.

Miriander stared at him.

"Yes," she said. "Noman alone came to possess power without limits. That is why he left us. He knew that un-limited power is a terrible thing."

Blaze now entered the courtyard of the novitiate, ac-companied by a second Noma, called Arden.

"I've come to say good-bye," he said to Seeker. He embraced him. "We're off to meet this mighty warlord who calls himself the Great Jahan."

"What! Just the two of you?"

"Two's enough to do what's needed."

"Why not all the Noble Warriors? Why not drive the invaders back where they came from?"

Blaze laughed.

"That would be war," he said. "The Noble Warriors don't fight wars."

"Are we afraid of losing?"

"No," said Miriander. "We're afraid of winning."

Blaze and Arden left the Nom by the Pilgrim Gate. The crowd waiting outside raised a cheer. The novices heard that cheer with pride. The frightened villagers had perfect faith in the Noble Warriors. They believed that as few as two had the power to save them from destruction.

Miriander now addressed the novices.

"You have shared our memories. You have been admitted to our Community, past and present. You have felt our strength. Now you must be taught to accept that strength and make it your own. For that, all your present supports and comforts must be stripped away."

Seeker listened with the others, expecting with each passing moment that the teacher's eye would fall on him and that he would be asked to stand apart from the rest. But this did not happen.

"You will go now to the cell assigned to you and remain there entirely alone until the training is complete."

"How long is the training?" asked Felice.

"It's different for everyone. A day and a night, at the very least."

"A day and a night!" said Jobal. "Are we to be fed?"

"Yes," said Miriander with a smile. "There'll be food."

Morning Star said, "What will happen to the Wildman?"

"That is for the Elder to decide. He has not yet been told of the incident. There have been more pressing matters to consider."

Seeker felt a mixture of relief and dread. So he was to go on with the training—but for how long?

"The meeks will lead you to your assigned cells."

The room was just wide enough for a plank bed, an upright chair, and a small table. The bed was made up with a blanket. Beneath it stood a bucket. There were no windows. The sloping roof above contained a single pane of glass, through which fell such light as remained in the darkening sky. On the table there was a candle, unlit, and beside it a basin, a jug, and a half-full glass of water.

There was nothing else.

Seeker lay on the hard bed and watched night come through the glass above. He saw some of the brighter stars appear, and then disappear again as clouds spread across the sky. After that he could see nothing.

Pictures, sounds, memories floated through his mind. He thought of the faint trembling image in the stippled air of the Night Court, the one glimpse he had had of Noman, his sword raised over his head, and the strange feeling that had come with it of familiarity. But Noman had lived and died generations ago.

He realized then that this memory, if it was a memory, came not from outside himself, but from deep within. He was not simply learning about the great founder of the Noble Warriors. He was following in his footsteps. He was embarked on the same journey.

My life is an experiment in search of the truth.

The warlord had gone into the Garden to seek the Lost Child and had come out changed utterly. Of course he was changed utterly: he had come face-to-face with the All and Only. He had seen the Clear Light. He had known the Reason and the Goal.

One day, Seeker told himself, whatever decision the Elder reached, he too would come to the end of his own journey, and he too would go into the Garden.

———

Morning Star lay on her narrow plank bed in the darkness, and she too was filled with thoughts of the day now ending. But where Seeker had found his way to a defiant conclusion, she was caught in unending turmoil. All she could see in her mind's eye was the sleeping face of the Wildman, and all she could feel was the longing within her to lie down with him and fold him in her arms, and kiss him, and keep him by her forever.

Why this passion had come upon her, she did not know. It had caught her entirely by surprise. Always until now she had thought of the Wildman as amusing but stupid, like a cock pheasant. Now none of that mattered. His beauty alone was enough. His beauty made him fine and good, even though she knew him to be vain and selfish. She could only conclude that this groundless passion was yet another proof of her base nature. She was unable to look into the Garden for fear of drowning in her own confusions. And she had fallen in love with an unsuitable boy, solely because he was beautiful.

Morning Star despaired of herself. This next phase of her training would surely find her out as an unworthy candidate. Then she would be expelled, as the rebellious Wildman would be expelled. First they would both be cleansed. Then, their minds as empty as babies, they would go out into the world and start their lives all over again, together.

To her shame, Morning Star found that she was smiling to herself at the thought.

⊁ 4 ⊱

Blood and Ashes

ALL THAT DAY, THE LONG LINES OF RIDERS CAME STREAM-
ing out of the trees. They pitched their low dome-shaped
tents in open farmland by the banks of a river, seized and
killed all the cows, pigs, and chickens they could find, and
lit fires. Their horses, set free to roam as they willed, formed
into herds several hundred strong and grazed up and down
the water meadows. By nightfall the tents and the campfires covered the land as far as the eye could see.

For Echo Kittle, everything in this new life was strange
and frightening: the swarthy male faces that stared at her
from all sides, the taste of the mare's milk she was given
to drink, the stinging smoke of the campfires. Only the
Caspian horse called Kell seemed to her to be a gentler
creature, and a friend.

She hugged Kell's neck and pressed her cheek to his
soft breathy nose and talked to him.

"You're not cruel, are you? You're beautiful and kind."

Kell nodded his head at this and looked at her in what she took to be a friendly way. This made Echo a little less lonely and afraid.

The Jahan set her a place before his own fire, to eat beside his sons, and for the night, he assigned her a tent of her own. He treated her with respect, which meant that his sons and his officers respected her, but he did not attempt to converse with her. Having forced her to accompany him, he seemed to want little more to do with her.

His three sons had evidently been told their father's plan that she was to be married to one of them, and when they got the opportunity, they stared at her with their dull shifty eyes. However, for the most part, they kept away from her, and she was glad of this. All three were as ugly as their father, but lacking his dynamic power and his outrageous swagger, they held no distinction for Echo. She could barely tell them apart. Sasha, the eldest, was the most self-important of the three. Alva, the second son, was the tallest. Sabin, the third son, was the only one she ever saw smile. On the whole, they were a miserable trio, always to be seen together but always bickering. It never occurred to Echo for one second that she would truly have to marry one of them, so she didn't trouble to ask herself which one she preferred.

That evening, in the flicker of the great campfire, she listened to their talk and tried to comprehend what sort of people they were. In some ways they were like her father and his friends, whom she had heard drinking and laughing and showing off to one another often enough. But

Glimmeners had no desire to leave their treetop homes and make war on strangers. Did these Orlans not have homes of their own?

From time to time they would leap to their feet and hold their drinking mugs high and shout out a toast. These toasts were all about war.

"To the battle charge!"

"Blood and ashes!"

"To the conquest of the world!"

Why did they want to conquer the world? The army of the Orlans was so huge that it seemed to Echo nothing could stand against them. No doubt they would conquer the world. Then what would they do with it when they'd got it?

As for herself, she thought only of when and how she could run away. She didn't believe the Jahan would carry out his threat to burn the Glimmen. The great forest was behind him now, and his eyes were set on the imperial city of Radiance ahead. He wouldn't turn his whole army back on itself just to spite her.

She was not tethered, and as far as she could tell, she was not watched. The decision was not so hard: she would run away in the night. It would be a long walk to the forest, but she reckoned she would be back in the familiar world of trees by sunrise. Once high up in the slender branches, she knew they would never catch her.

She lay in her bedroll that night and waited until all round her the camp was silent. Then she rose and crept noiselessly out of the tent. Before her stretched the giant camp, its tents reaching into the distance, its fires burning low. Here and there bands of Orlans were still up, laughing softly and telling tales into the night.

She made her way slowly, not wanting to seem to be in flight, passing from campfire to campfire. The encampment was larger than she had realized. By the time she reached the last of the tents, the night was so dark she could not see her way beyond the pools of firelight. Then in the darkness ahead, she heard the low snuffling noise of a group of Caspians. She walked on in darkness until her outstretched hand touched the horses, and they gathered round her and pushed at her gently with their soft noses.

She stroked their hot smooth coats and ran her fingers through their straggly manes. She pressed her face against their necks and blew softly at them as they blew at her. She sensed in them just the same nervous energy that she felt in herself, and just the same untamed spirit. The Orlans rode them, but they did not rule them.

Echo longed to learn to ride herself. The Jahan had promised he would teach her. But he was cruel, and she hated him.

She looked ahead into the darkness and hesitated. She turned and looked back at the thousand twinkling lights of the great camp. The horses began to make their way towards the river, brushing past her as they went. Now she could make out their shapes outlined in the firelight, merging and separating as they went, picking their way with delicate hooves over the thistled ground.

Would he burn the Glimmen?

Suddenly she felt unsure. The Jahan was proud. What

if he saw it as a matter of honor? It would not take so many men to set the fires. He need not turn his entire army back.

It came to her then with a terrible clarity that she could not run away. She longed to go back to her own familiar world, but she could not draw down on everyone she loved the threatened destruction. She saw them now in her mind's eye—her brother forever competing with her, maddening her with his taunts; her mother, with her clumsy efforts at matchmaking; her father forever planning new and unnecessary extensions to their house in the treetops; even Orvin Chipe's doglike gawping—and sharp tears pricked into her eyes. She had not known how much she loved them until she was taken from them. But this she knew: she would not let them come to harm on her account. She was not worth it.

A picture sprang into her mind, a memory of her father teaching her how to recognize the unsafe branches.

"Look," he said, snapping the branch, showing her the dry pulp within. "Nothing good left in it."

It was the same with her. There was nothing good left in her. This morning she hadn't known this. But between this morning and now had fallen a bright blade glistening with droplets of rain. That knife had cut her life in two.

With the fingers of her right hand she felt her left little finger, as she did all the time now.

I was willing to let a man die to save myself pain.

This was the most hateful thought of all.

She tried to push the thought away, but the feeling remained: the hard grip of a hand on her wrist and the hot flush of her own shame. All her life she had been happy, because she had been able to push away the bad thoughts. Now she had become a bad thought herself. How do you push yourself away?

"You do something," she said aloud.

She had no idea what she meant by this, but oddly, she found it helped. It made the future possible.

"I won't run away," she said to herself. "I won't let them hurt the Glimmen. I'll do something."

So she made her way back across the night camp and into the tent, and she wrapped herself up once more in her bedroll. No one stirred. She believed she had not been seen.

She was wrong.

At sunrise next day, as the camp came alive and breakfast was being served, the Jahan stopped before her and said in a low voice, for her alone, "So you decided to stay with us after all."

Echo flushed.

"I don't know what you mean."

"You went for a walk last night."

"Did I?"

"I followed you. I thought you were running away."

"What would you have done if I had?"

"Sent a man after you."

"So I'm a prisoner?"

"But I didn't send a man after you."

"Because I came back of my own free will."

"So you're not a prisoner."

It was a curious exchange. To Echo's surprise, she found her spirits improved afterwards. The fact that she had shown independence by leaving, and had made her own choice in returning, gave her back some self-respect. Also she was much struck by the image of the Great Jahan following her across the camp. He must have moved quietly, and without an entourage, because she never spotted him. It made her feel odd to know he'd been there all along. It made her feel both trapped and protected. It also made her feel that she was special to him. She liked that.

"Would you have burned the forest if I'd got away?"

"Of course."

"Why do you care whether I stay or go?"

"What I have said I will do," he replied, "I will do."

"Then say I'm to go."

"You will marry one of my sons."

"I won't."

"I've not yet decided which one." He spoke as if her objection was of no importance at all. "I may make them compete for you."

"You can't force me to do it."

"But first you must be made fit for an Orlan prince."

"You'll have to kill me first."

"For that, you must learn to ride."

"Oh."

"Or do I have to kill you first?"

"No," said Echo. "I'll learn to ride."

The Jahan gave an order, and Kell was led up with a halter round his neck. It was the first time Echo had seen any kind of harness on any of the Caspians.

"He's strong," said the Jahan, taking the halter himself, "and he's fast, and he's not the easiest to control. If you prefer, we can start with a quieter animal."

"No," said Echo. "I like this one."

"Then you must let him get to know you and trust you."

"How do I do that?"

"Just as you would with anyone. Spend time with him. Show him respect. Don't be in a rush."

"So I'm not to ride him yet?"

"That will be the very last stage. By the time you mount him, you'll know all you need to know. The rest is easy."

Echo was disappointed, but she was also impressed. Much as she wanted to spring on the Caspian's back and fly across the land, as she saw the Orlans doing round her, she felt the rightness of this slow approach. So, as the tents were rolled up and the field kitchens stowed, she and Kell walked soberly up and down the riverbank, side by side, going nowhere and doing nothing.

Yesterday's rain had passed, but pale gray clouds still filled the sky, and the grass was heavy with moisture. The breath of men and horses misted in the early morning air. The wide river, swollen by the recent rain, rushed high and fast between its banks, churning into froth round fallen trees.

The river was too deep to ford. Scouts reported a bridge some twenty miles to the north, so it was northward that the army now turned. The horses that had grazed in herds as freely as if they were still wild had rejoined their riders, and every Orlan, from the lowliest kitchen-hand to the Great Jahan himself, was now mounted.

Only Echo walked, with Kell by her side. She held the halter in one hand, but the rope hung loose between them. Kell seemed to accept that he was to accompany her. They followed the river path, and the faster-moving mounted army streamed by them, until they found themselves falling behind. Echo hardly even noticed. All her attention was on the horse.

Improbable though it surely was, it seemed to her that she and Kell were conducting a conversation. There were no words involved. It was a conversation of nods and shakes and twitches. When the horse shook his head, making his mane flick away from his eyes, she shook her head in return. When she turned to glance at him, he flicked his ears. Sometimes Kell looked down and then up again, in one quick movement. When he did this, Echo gave a little jump as she strode along. Kell always kept pace with her. Once she stopped, wanting a short rest, and Kell stopped long before the rope of the halter tightened. He swung his long lovely head round to gaze at her, and she bowed her head in a small show of thanks, and he bowed back.

After that she removed the halter. They walked on, side by side, like two companions. Echo felt as if Kell had chosen her, and this made her feel glad and proud.

The army was now out of sight. The Jahan trusted her to follow alone. Only she wasn't alone. She had Kell.

The pale cloud-dimmed sun was high above when Echo saw a barge approaching on the river, riding low in the water, carried swiftly downstream by the current. It was crowded with people—men, women, and children. Seeing the girl with the horse plodding northward, they called out to her, waving their arms.

"Turn back! Killers ahead!"

"No, look! She's one of them! That's one of their beasts!"

"Then, curse you! May you rot and die in pain!"

They spat and made hateful gestures at her as they were swept on down the river.

Echo was shocked by their anger and wanted them to know she was not one of the invading army; but they were beyond the reach of her voice. Looking ahead, now fearful of what she would find, she saw thin trails of smoke climbing up into the winter sky. Then she saw a column of slow-moving people approaching down the river path. As they came nearer, she saw they were women and children. Some of the women were carrying babies.

The women avoided her eyes when they met. She knew it was because of Kell.

"So you'll be dancing now," hissed one woman, holding her baby close. "Now your killers have murdered our menfolk and burned our homes."

"No," said Echo, a sick feeling forming in her stomach. "I'm not one of them. I'm a—"

She was going to say "prisoner" but stopped herself in time. She was no prisoner.

"She's only young," said another of the women.

"And wasn't my boy young?" cried the one with the baby. "And did they show him mercy?" She spat furiously on the ground before Echo. "Murderers! Go and dance on the ashes of our lives!"

The sad little procession continued on its way. Echo stood still, her head bowed. Kell came up to her and nudged her chin with his nose. She put her arms round his neck and rested her cheek against his prickly-smooth hide and was grateful for his quietness.

"I want to go home, Kell," she whispered. "Shall we run away home to the forest?"

Kell turned his head round and butted her gently again.

"No. You're right. We can't."

They continued on their way.

In a little while they came up with the rear guard of the Orlan army, which had stopped to rest men and horses. The lines of warriors were now in the process of forming up again for the onward march. The men and riders circling round her were agile and graceful, the men smiling, their teeth bright in their tawny faces, the horses lithe and strong. Echo, passing through their midst, found it hard to believe that these handsome laughing beings were responsible for killing and destruction.

Then she reached the village.

There was very little of it left. Smoke was still rising from the burned houses, now reduced to fallen timbers and piles of ash. Bodies lay here and there, some still clutching the scythes and hoes with which they had tried to defend themselves. The immense army was riding in formation through the scene of devastation without a downward glance, the horses picking their way over the limbs of dead men as if they were tree roots.

Echo saw it all and felt a stinging in her eyes and thought: am I too a part of this?

"So, there you are!"

It was the Jahan, coming up behind her on horseback. She turned to him, and he saw the tears running down her cheeks.

"Why, what's the matter?"

She pointed silently at the burning houses and the dead men. The Jahan shrugged his broad shoulders and looked round with contemptuous indifference.

"They shouldn't have fought back," he said. "Those that stand in my way, I destroy."

"Did you have to burn the houses?"

"Houses? What houses? There were only shacks and hovels here. We'll sweep this garbage away and build a real town. You'll see."

His three sons came galloping up to their father, pretending not to race, but each one eager to be the first to come to a stop before him. The Jahan watched them, his face expressionless. His second son, Alva, was the winner, by a head. Sasha Jahan, his older brother, rode on past, as if to show he had been racing for a different goal, and so had not lost. He rode up to Echo.

"Why do you walk?" he said to her. His face was still contorted with anger at his brother.

"Because I haven't yet learned to ride," she replied.

"I could ride when I was three years old. What's wrong with you?"

He wheeled away and rejoined his father.

The army was now moving through the burning village in three long columns, heading up the west bank of the river towards the bridge, which Echo could see ahead.

It was a broad timber roadway, carried on heavy piles and braces, strong enough to bear the weight of a convoy of loaded bullock wagons. The vanguard of the Orlan riders would shortly be clop-clopping onto its stout boards.

Echo felt sick and miserable. She would have turned away at once, and begun the long trudge home, but for this hateful itchy sensation that somehow she too was responsible for the killings and that she could not leave this monstrous army until—until what? There was nothing she could do. But still it persisted, this stubborn conviction.

"I shall do something," she said to herself. "I will. You'll see."

Voices called out from the far side of the river. She saw figures there, people from the village on the eastern bank. They were gathering at the end of the bridge, on the far bank, and shouting—though to what end it was impossible to see. If they tried to stop the Orlan army crossing the bridge, they would be slaughtered and their village burned.

It was one thing to weep for those already dead. But these people were still living, and in immediate danger. Echo thought no more. She set off at a run, and Kell trotted by her side. She ran between the columns of mounted Orlans, trying to overtake the Jahan before he reached the bridge.

The Jahan had now mounted his carriage, with its escort of drummers and trumpeters. The columns of riders in the vanguard had come to a standstill. Panting from her run, walking now, Echo passed through the ranks towards the Jahan. Round him she saw the mirror bearers taking up their positions, turning their gleaming discs this way and that to find the angle of the pale winter light. The drummers began to patter softly on their drums, creating the first rhythms of expectation that would soon burst forth as a driving martial beat. The Jahan swung a bright scarlet cape over his shoulders and, grasping the rail of the carriage, looked round with a proud gaze at the immense gathering mass of his men.

From the far side of the bridge there went up a sudden cheer. The crowd of villagers had grown to a hundred or so. They carried farm implements and kitchen knives, and a few swords, which they now raised defiantly above their heads as they cheered. Then from their midst stepped two men, who walked out onto the bridge and came to a stop halfway across.

They appeared not to be armed. They wore pale gray tunics and loose breeches, tied at the ankles, and they were barefoot. Over their heads they wore hoods of the same gray material. They stood quietly, side by side, their hands clasped before them, their gaze on the lead riders of the Orlan army. From the way in which they had positioned themselves, it seemed they meant to block the passage of the Orlans across the bridge—except that such a thing was clearly impossible. One mounted Orlan with his whip could lay them low without coming near them.

Amroth Jahan did not consider them worth even this much effort. He sent one of his junior officers to order the two men to give way. Echo watched as the officer trotted onto the bridge and then returned. She was near the Jahan's carriage now and heard the officer's report.

"They ask us not to cross the bridge unless we come in peace, Excellency."

The Jahan frowned.

"I will cross the bridge when and how I please. Tell them to give way immediately."

The officer rode back to the two hooded men. He spoke a little more with them, then returned.

"They say the same as before, Excellency."

The Jahan became angry.

"Then seize them!" he ordered. "Drag them before me on their knees!"

The officer beckoned to two of his men, and all three rode onto the bridge, unhitching their whips as they did so. Echo watched, dreading what would now follow. She saw the whips curl out, snapping in the air. But the two hooded men were just beyond the reach of the whips and were not touched. The three Orlans rode closer, and the whips cracked all round them but failed to connect with their targets. A murmur rose up from the ranks of mounted men, and some good-natured jibes were called out to the three on the bridge.

"Open your eyes, soldiers!"

But still the whips snapped harmlessly in midair.

Now the riders could be seen to be close to the two hooded men and to be exchanging words with them. Then they turned and rode back. The Jahan glowered at them.

"Why have you not done as I ordered?"

"Why, Excellency?" The men seemed confused. "We thought—we thought—it seemed best to leave them alone."

"Arrest these three!" said the Jahan, with an abrupt wave of one hand. The unfortunate men were led away.

"Which company is in the van?"

"The Sixteenth, Excellency."

"Tell the captain of the Sixteenth to charge the bridge."

"You wish them brought back alive, Excellency?"

"No. Make an example of them."

Echo watched as the company of twenty men and horses formed four lines, packed close, jostling and rubbing against one another. At the first command, the men drew their short curved swords. At the second command, falling into pace, the company set off at a canter towards the bridge.

The horses rose and fell together as they moved, in a beautiful display. As they quickened their pace and hit full gallop, the twenty melted into a single thunderclap roaring over the land, their raised swords flashing like lightning as they went.

The two barefoot hooded men on the bridge stood still and watched the charge sweep towards them and did not flinch. The villagers behind them fell silent with apprehension. As the horses' hooves struck the booming boards of the bridge, the riders let out wild howling cries and braced themselves for the impact and the kill.

The two hooded men made a slight movement—the bridge shuddered—and the compact squad of Orlan warriors burst apart. They exploded outwards, horses rearing, twisting, leaping. Men were tossed from their mounts, some falling, some skidding sideways and toppling over the low parapet into the river, some turning about, spinning in confusion, until they were facing back the way they had come.

When the cries of men and horses had faded, and the last of the bewildered Orlans had pulled themselves from the tangle of crashed riders and limped back off the bridge, there stood the two hooded men for all to see, as still as before, untouched. Each had one hand raised before him, with two fingers extended. But they had made no move. They had stood on the bridge like rocks in the river, and the charge of the Orlans had broken against them.

Echo Kittle saw, and she felt the same awe that she saw on every face round her. She turned to look at the Great Jahan. He stood raised on his carriage, staring impassively at the bridge, his face giving away no emotion. His sons, riding just behind him, were exchanging glances. Then Sasha Jahan spoke.

"Send me, Father!"

Then Alva Jahan called out, more loudly.

"Send me, Father!"

Amroth Jahan shook his head. Moving slowly, he stepped down from the carriage and strode towards the bridge. He had given no orders to his sons or to the rest of his army, so no one moved. But Echo, who was not a warrior under his command, slipped forward through the frozen ranks and followed him to the start of the bridge.

There she halted and watched as the Jahan strode over the boards to the two hooded men. The immense army behind her was silent, as were the villagers before her. She could hear every word that was spoken in that encounter.

"I am the Jahan of Jahans. Who are you?"

"We are Nomana."

The hooded man replied in a low voice. He sounded weary.

"What are Nomana? Are you devils? Are you spirits from the land of the dead?"

"We're men like you."

"Then let us pass."

"If you come in peace."

"Peace!" roared the Jahan, his caged fury breaking out. "I am peace! There is no peace without order, and I am the bringer of order! In all the lands I rule there is peace, because I enforce peace!"

The taller of the two hooded men sighed, and he raised one hand.

"You carry a heavy burden," he said. "Peace for all, but no peace for you."

The Jahan was silent with surprise.

"Ask forgiveness. Seek your own peace."

He extended two fingers and touched the air before him. Amroth Jahan sank slowly to his knees. There, kneeling on the bridge, he bent his head, groaned, and wept. Echo saw it and heard the low sobs. The men of the army lined up behind her saw and heard also. The unthinkable was happening before their eyes. No one had ever seen the Great Jahan cry.

The two hooded men then turned and padded away over the bridge. They linked arms as they went and leaned a little towards each other, as if overcome with exhaustion. Then they were lost to sight among the crowd of villagers.

After a few moments the Jahan rose slowly to his feet, and without brushing the tears from his eyes, he returned to his army. All watched him, in fearful uncertainty. He gazed at the massed ranks of his warriors, his cheeks still glistening, and raising his silver-handled whip, he gave the sign for the army to advance over the bridge.

The companies of mounted warriors began to file slowly across the river. The villagers on the far side parted to let them go by.

Echo was watching the Jahan as he climbed with weary movements into his high-wheeled chariot. One impatient wave of his hand dismissed the mirror bearers and the music makers. He turned to his three sons, who were staring at him in utter confusion. Sasha spurred his horse to the chariot's side.

"Father, command me!" he said. "Let me avenge you!"

The Great Jahan fixed dull angry eyes on his son.

"For what?"

Sasha Jahan saw that he had said the wrong thing, and not wanting to anger his father further, he bowed his head and was silent.

"We will cross the bridge," said the Jahan. "No one bars our way. There is nothing to avenge."

"Yes, Father."

The Jahan and his sons then crossed the bridge in the midst of the vast Orlan army. There was no sign of the hooded strangers on the far bank. The villagers offered no resistance. The army passed on down the road in silence.

After a little while the Jahan sent for Echo and asked that she ride with him in his carriage.

"You saw what happened," he said to her, not meeting her eyes.

"Yes."

"They call themselves Nomana. Do you know them?"

"I've heard of them."

"What have you heard?"

"That they are the only good people who are also strong."

"Good, and strong."

He said no more for a while. She watched the muscles twitching on his swarthy face.

"I'll not forget," he said at last, speaking more to himself than to her. "They did what no one has ever done before. They made me cry."

"They wanted you to find peace."

"Peace? Yes, I'll find peace."

With this the Great Jahan's face distorted in a smile of passionate cruelty: the smile of one who inflicts great pain and finds great pleasure in it.

"My peace will be in their destruction."

Echo said no more. But she too knew she would not forget those silent figures in gray. She had no interest in the peace they spoke of; she was interested in their power. Here was her means of escape from the Jahan, without harm to the Glimmen; and here was her means of revenge. She would find her champion among the Nomana.

⊰ 5 ⊱

Nothing Lasts

ALONE AND WITHOUT OCCUPATION IN HIS CELL, SEEKER found the hours passed slowly and unmarked until they merged into a single unending moment. Food was brought to him by a silent meek, and his bucket was emptied. Day came with the brightening of the panel of glass in the roof above, then departed again with the fading of the panel into the night. For hours at a time he lay on the hard bed and watched the distant clouds above, finding in their many forms, and in the way they were forever changing, his only reminder of the world's variety and ceaseless activity. The silence and the emptiness were hard to bear, but he sensed that here, alone in his cell, he was being given a last chance. If he failed this test—whatever it was—he would follow the Wildman into exile from the Nom.

So he looked for ways to occupy his mind.

He studied his room, becoming familiar with the cracks and stains on its old plaster walls, imagining that they were rivers and roads and forests on a map of an unknown land. He chose not to eat his breakfast all at once, but to hold back the apple for later—breakfast was a slab of dark bread, an apple, and water—and to eat every part of the apple but for the pips. He kept the pips on his table in a row and played games with them, making them into warriors who went on adventures. He discovered that there was a very small spider living in a corner by the door and that close to the spider's web was a hole in the wall, no more than a pinprick, through which tiny crawling insects came and went. From time to time one of the little creatures became caught in the web.

He did his physical exercises, as he had been taught on first entering the Nom, and afterwards the more important mental exercises. Standing upright, he focused his attention first on his outer extremities—fingers, toes, scalp—and so worked slowly in towards the pit of his stomach. At each stage he felt for and found the lir that tingled through his nervous system and drew it inwards, until he could feel the concentrated heat of its power throbbing in his belly. From here he shot it like a bouncing ball into his hand, or his eyes, or his foot, like an acrobat who can balance his entire weight on any part of his body.

When he had done everything he could think of to do, he lay on his bed and tried to guess the purpose of this strange isolation; and from that he fell to thinking about Morning Star, also alone, somewhere very near. He thought about the way she had wept over the Wildman.

Morning Star was not afraid of solitude. She had spent
many a night alone on the hills, watching over her father's
sheep, and was used to her own company. What she found
hard to bear was the closeness of the walls and the narrow-
ness of the horizon. After the first few hours, the confines
of her cell became unbearable to her, and she took to closing her eyes and keeping them closed. She found her way
about the room by feel, letting her fingers patter over table
and walls, until she could move as freely as if her eyes were
open. For a time this trick made the spaces round her seem
bigger. But then the unseen walls began to loom as large
to her fingertips as they ever had to her gaze, so she stopped
her circling of the cell and stayed for long hours, with her
eyes closed, on the bed.

Alone in the darkness she thought of the Wildman and
wondered what was happening to him.

"Are you still there, Wildman?"

She realized she had spoken aloud. There was no one
but herself to hear, but the sound of her own voice com-
forted her. Also she liked saying the Wildman's name.

"Are you still asleep, Wildman? I want to be there
when you wake. I want to be with you, Wildman."

This talking aloud made her ashamed and made her
happy; but since shame requires the presence of others,
and there were no others, she was left with the happiness.

"I've always been alone," she told the Wildman, as if
the beautiful youth were standing by her side in the darkness. "I'm a good companion because I ask for very little.
When you wake up from your sleep, maybe they'll send

us both away, and we won't mind. You're bold and strong, and I'm really quite clever, so we'll find a way to survive."

Once launched into this daydream, she saw no reason to deny herself; and so, by small stages, she talked herself into an entire future life with the Wildman by her side. This life was vague as to what occupied her days, and how they obtained their nourishment, but was very detailed about the time they spent sitting close together and the sweet moment when they curled up in each other's arms to sleep.

"There, Wildman, lay your head on my arm, just here. And I'll rest my head on your chest, like so. We'll keep each other warm, shan't we? We'll say nothing, for there's nothing needs to be said. So shall we sleep now, my friend? Shall we sleep in each other's arms? And when morning comes, shall we wake and find ourselves still warm in each other's arms?"

Such thoughts were so strong and clear to her that she almost believed her friend was there with her, and she felt a deep calm contentment. But he was not there. It was only a trick she played on herself. Then, seeing the reality in a sudden flash, the daydream vanished and she was alone again in the darkness, more afraid than ever.

"Wildman! Help me!"

But the Wildman did not come. So, not thinking or caring what she did, she called for Seeker.

"Seeker! Don't let me fall into the darkness! Reach out your hand. Let me catch it. Let me hold your hand!"

She stretched her hand up into the darkness, there in

her solitary cell, and imagined that Seeker took it and held her, and so the panic subsided once more.

"I'm going mad," she said to herself. "I can't do this any more. I'll tell them they have to let me go. I'm not strong enough to be a Noble Warrior."

The Wildman, meanwhile, had woken from his long sleep, to find himself alone in the novitiate dormitory. He rose from the bed and saw a meal waiting on a table. He was very hungry and ate all of it. His head throbbed, but he was not in pain, and his sleep had refreshed him. However, he was very confused. He tried to recall how he came to be there, but found he had no memory after the time he and the other novices had entered the Cloister Court.

He left the dormitory, passing down the bare wooden stairs and out into the courtyard. He hadn't been there long when he saw Miriander approaching him through the low archway.

"Are you well?" she said. "Are you better?"

"Yes," he replied. "Have I been ill?"

"Not ill, no. You've eaten?"

"Yes."

"Do you understand what has happened?"

"No."

"You're going to have to leave the Nom."

She looked at him with such gentleness as she spoke these words that the Wildman still didn't grasp her meaning.

"Does that distress you?"

"What?"

"Leaving the Community."

"Leaving? No, I want to leave."

He looked around.

"Where are all the others?"

"They're in training."

"When am I to go?"

"You'll be made ready for your departure soon, and then you'll go."

"Made ready." The Wildman felt his mind clearing. He knew what that meant, and he knew he didn't want it. "I don't want to be made ready."

"I'm sorry," said Miriander. "You can't leave the Nom until the Community permits it."

"I'm a prisoner?"

"Only until you're ready. You'll be free soon."

The door to Seeker's cell opened, and his teacher Miriander entered. She looked at him carefully.

"How is it?" she asked. "Is it hard to be alone?"

"Yes," he replied.

"The door isn't locked," she said. "Whenever you want to go, you can go."

"I'll go when you tell me to go," he said.

She looked round the room. Her eyes took in the apple pips, in a row on the table.

"What do you do to pass the time?"

"Watch the clouds," he said.

"Nothing is dependable," she told him softly. "Nothing lasts."

She left him alone.

After that there were changes. There came a scrabbling on the roof above, and unseen hands pinned a drape of white cloth over the pane of glass. Daylight still entered his room below, but more faintly now, and his view of the clouds was gone.

When the next meal came, there was no apple. The meek who brought it swept the apple pips off the table and took them away.

"Very well," said Seeker to himself. "My powers of endurance are to be tested to the limit. I won't fail."

It was hard without the clouds to watch. He spent more time on the floor, by the door, watching the movements of the spider and the tiny ants.

Later a meek came with a brush and swept away the cobweb, and the spider with it, and stopped up the little hole by which the ants came into the room.

"No matter," said Seeker to himself. "I can tell myself stories."

He lay on his bed and gazed at the cracks on the wall and turned the dusty plaster into a land of empires at war.

Then there came more scrabbling on the roof, and a drape of black cloth was drawn over his one source of light. From then on he was in darkness.

This was hard indeed.

"No matter," he said to himself. "This testing time will end. All I have to do is endure."

He still did his exercises. For recreation he now moved round the room, feeling the walls as he went, learning to be familiar with each bump and crack. When his fingers reached the door, and passed by the latch, there were times when he felt a rush of longing to lift the latch and open the door and step out into light and noise and company. But he controlled the impulse. He was determined to complete the training.

Miriander returned.

"Is it still hard?" she asked.

"Yes," he replied.

"Whenever you want to go, you can go."

"I'll go when you tell me to go."

"What do you do to pass the time now?"

"I do nothing, Teacher."

"And yet you don't go."

"I know that this is my training."

Miriander heard this and was silent for a moment. Then she said, "You are no longer under instruction. You must do as you think best."

She left.

Seeker was bewildered. Was the training over? How could it be? He had learned nothing. All the hours of loneliness and darkness must surely be for a purpose. Perhaps, he thought, he was meant to leave his cell and seek that purpose outside. His heart leaped with hope. He went to the door, in the darkness, and felt for the latch.

But she had not told him to leave. She had told him only to do as he thought best. All his instincts cried out that to leave now would be failure. The very intensity of his longing to leave was a clear warning.

"No," he said to himself. "This too is a test. I won't fail."

But now he found the passing of the dark hours was much harder. He had to struggle against the doubt that squatted like a seagull on his shoulder and nudged him with its beak.

What's the point? said the seagull. *You're achieving nothing here.*

"But I am," Seeker replied. "I'm showing that I can pass this test."

What test? You do nothing. Anyone can do nothing.

"This is a test of strength," said Seeker to his doubt. "I'm showing that I'm strong."

Even as he told himself he was strong, he felt himself weakening. He began to suffer from a confusion in his thoughts. Once or twice, when talking to the gull on his shoulder, he found he was speaking aloud.

"I'm talking to myself. I'm not so strong after all."

If this testing time was not making him strong, if it was doing the very opposite and he was becoming weaker all the time, then what was the point of going on?

Again he went to the door and put his hand to the latch. Again his heart soared at the hope of release.

"So will I fail after all?"

His hand jerked back from the latch as if it had burned him.

"There," he told himself. "That's why I'm to go on. Because I refuse to fail. Nothing else matters. I won't fail."

Morning Star too received a visit from her teacher and was told that she was free to leave her cell when she was ready to go. Like Seeker, she wondered if this was some further test; but even if it was, she knew she could not stay alone in that darkness.

"If I'm to fail, let me fail," she said to herself.

So she found the door latch and opened the door and went out into the passage beyond. A pale evening light flowed down the passage from the courtyard, softly illuminating the stone walls. Morning Star touched the archway as she passed through, grateful for the simple gift of light. Then she heard voices and found other novices gathered in the courtyard, all recently emerged from their cells, all wearing the same dazed expression. They were sharing their experiences and puzzling over the purpose of them. Two nights and two days had gone by. What were they meant to have learned? What had the training been for?

Winter greeted Morning Star.

"Almost the last," he said. "How was it for you?"

"Hard. I'm glad to be out."

Their voices sounded unusually clear.

"It was horrible," said Jobal. "I wanted to scream."

But they were all smiling. They kept touching each other and laughing.

"Has anyone seen the Wildman?"

"He's gone. He's not in the dormitory any more."

"Gone?"

A sudden dread filled Morning Star's heart. How could he be gone already? She looked round for Seeker.

"Where's Seeker?"

"Still in his cell. He's the only one who hasn't come out."

That night was the worst of all for Seeker. A whole flock of gulls now descended on him, and his doubts tore at him without ceasing. A hundred times he reached for the latch, and every time, he let his hand fall back to his side.

"If I go now, what's it all been for? Nothing."

His doubts screeched at him, saying, "Of course it's all for nothing. So why go on?"

"I will not fail."

"Fail what?" said his doubts. "There's no test here."

Then, deeper into the night, came a doubt that was even harder to dismiss.

"Look at you," said this doubt. "Unable to sleep. Tormented by uncertainty. As miserable as you've ever been in your life. Is that strength? Is that endurance? Of course not. You've failed. Why not admit it?"

He felt his way to the bed and lay down to sleep, worn out by the turmoil in his mind.

"Tomorrow. I'll decide what to do tomorrow."

He closed his eyes. The darkness in the room was so complete that it made no difference.

I could sleep with my eyes open, he thought.

So he opened his eyes and slept.

He was woken by a light. The light came from the passage. His door was opening, and someone was coming into his room, carrying a candle.

It was Morning Star. She was wearing bright-colored clothes and had glittering bracelets all up her arms, like a bandit.

Seeker sat up, overjoyed to be able to see and to talk and to have company.

"Oh, Star! You don't know how good it is to see you!"

She put the candle down on the table, beside the half-full glass of water.

"You're the only one who's failed," she said.

"What?" Her voice was different. She sounded glad that he had failed. "Have I failed?"

"You weren't strong enough."

"But I tried so hard. It isn't over, is it?"

"Of course it's over. You're the only one still in here."

She turned to the door, which still stood half open. Reaching out one hand, she called to someone waiting outside.

"Come in."

The Wildman came in. He too wore the gaudy clothes of a bandit. He clasped the hand that Morning Star held out to him, looking strong and handsome and happy, as in the early days.

"He doesn't know it's over," Morning Star said to him. "He doesn't know he's failed."

The Wildman shrugged.

"Just not strong enough," he said.

He smiled at Morning Star, and she smiled back. Seeker saw those smiles and could hardly think at all, so many conflicting emotions were rising up and churning within him. He felt sick, and hurt, and angry, and he wanted to burst into tears.

"Please," he said at last. "Help me."

"Too late," said Morning Star. "We have to go now."

Still holding hands, their bracelets jingling, she and the Wildman left the room, and the door closed behind them.

Left alone, Seeker groaned.

"When did it happen?" he cried. "When did I fail?"

His teacher's voice answered him.

"When you called for a candle."

She was sitting on the chair by the table, the candlelight rimming her lovely face. Seeker had not seen her come in.

"But I didn't call for a candle."

"Then why is there a candle here?"

"She brought the candle with her. My friend, Morning Star."

"Your friend took her candle away with her. Don't you remember?"

He remembered now: Morning Star leaving the room, holding the Wildman's hand with one hand, the other hand carrying the candle. There had been darkness after they had left. Now there was light.

"Did I call for a candle?"

"You weren't strong enough."

"So it's true. I've failed the test."

"Yes," said Miriander without pity. "You have failed."

Seeker let his stinging eyes close and was thankful to feel the soothing flow of tears. There was nothing more to strive for. He could release himself and slide into the warm waters of exhaustion. He could give up.

He slept.

He woke to darkness. The candle was gone. His head ached and his body was stiff. He sat up on the bed and rubbed at his temples, and the terrors of the night slowly returned to him. He felt his face burn with shame, even as a cold sweat of misery broke out over his body.

"What now?" he asked himself. "What's to become of me?"

No need to remain in the utter darkness of this hateful room. This room that had witnessed his failure.

He stood and staggered, then found his balance with difficulty.

"Even my own body fails me."

He walked unsteadily to the door and felt for the latch. There was no latch. He felt all round where it should have been. There was no door.

Slowly, feeling his way with his fingers, he worked round the walls and so came to the door at last. Somehow it had moved to the opposite wall. He lifted the latch, and the door opened.

The passage outside was in darkness. That meant it was still night. He could feel cool air on his face but could see nothing at all.

When he had been brought to this room the door had been on his left. So now he turned to the right and felt his way along the wall. Before, there had been other doors in the passage, but now, as his hands passed over the smooth plaster, he could feel no doors. His only guide was the cool air that blew towards him. He shuffled blindly towards the source of the open air.

It must have been the darkest and most moonless of nights, because in a little while he sensed he was in the open courtyard but still could see nothing at all. Following his memory only, he set out across unmarked space, hands before him.

Now he sensed he had entered another hallway. He must have gone through an open door without knowing it. On he went, telling himself that soon he must come upon a light. Somebody somewhere in the Nom would be awake and on watch. This now was all he craved: the comfort of another human voice. The loneliness had lasted too long.

As if in response to the intensity of his need, he saw the glimmer of soft light ahead. He was crossing some great empty space, on the far side of which loomed the rectangular shape of a doorway. The glow of light lay beyond.

As soon as he reached the doorway, he recognized where he was. The great space he had just crossed was the Night Court. He was now entering the pillared hall of the Cloister Court. Some way ahead, beyond the silent forest of pillars, rose the silver screen that protected the Garden, the screen pierced by many thousands of patterned holes. The light glowed through these holes. It was shining from within the Garden itself.

A wash of relief and gratitude flowed through Seeker's entire being. The All and Only would never leave him. He was not alone after all. The Wise Father would take him in his arms. The Loving Mother would kiss his aching eyes. The Quiet Watcher would protect him. Here at last he could rest.

He made his way forward through the pillars to the screen, his eyes fixed on the source of light within. He heard a faint sound, the familiar scrape-scrape of a broom sweeping the stone floor. Somewhere, even now in the middle of the night, a meek was at work. He looked around, but could make out no one in the darkness. Then, turning back to the silver screen, he saw that the light had grown brighter.

There had never been such a light in the Garden before. The Garden was open to the sky above, and by day he had seen it bathed in sunlight. But at night no lamps were lit there. For who was there to light them?

Who but the Lost Child himself? For was he not also called the Clear Light?

Suddenly, overwhelmingly, it came to Seeker that he was about to see with his own eyes the being who had created the world.

Hurrying now, he blundered past pillars, his feet skidding on the marble floor smoothed by the prostrations of pilgrims. The light that shone from within grew brighter the nearer he came, until it was dazzling him. He blinked and scrunched up his eyes, wanting to see through the pattern of star-shaped and diamond-shaped holes the source of the light, but all he could see was brightness.

Now he had reached the screen. Now his flushed face was pressed to its cool surface. Now his eyes found a single star hole and gazed through the silver metal, which his breath misted all round. Now he saw the light clearly. It was immense, like the disc of the rising sun, and it would have blinded him with its power, except that sitting before it, cross-legged on the ground, was the figure of a man. All the light was behind him, so he was entirely in silhouette. The edges of his silhouette shimmered and melted into the brightness—it was impossible to tell who or what he was. But he was inside the Garden, and he was irradiated by this nighttime sun. There could be no question as to his identity.

Seeker was in the presence of the Here and Now.

He slipped to his knees, face still pressed to the screen, and abandoned himself to a helpless torrent of prayer.

"Wise Father, forgive me for failing you. I need light to see my way. Don't leave me in the darkness. All I ask is to serve you. All I ask is to know that my days have a purpose. Don't let it all be for nothing."

Exhausted, he slipped farther down, to the cold marble floor. Involuntarily his eyes closed. He heard a voice speak to him.

"Nothing is dependable. Nothing lasts."

"No!" he cried. "Don't fail me!"

Rising to his feet, he spread his arms wide and pressed all his body to the silver screen. The dazzling light filled his eyes and the burning heat scorched his skin.

"Show me my way! Tell me what I'm to do!"

But no answer came. Instead, the light and the heat from within the Garden flowed on through the silver screen, melting his body into helplessness. The one terrible word echoed in his brain, mocking his hopes.

Nothing! Nothing! Nothing!

So there was nothing after all. Nothing to strive for, nothing to believe in. Only this annihilating light. Its pure stream pierced him and flooded him, washing away his fears and his desires until there were no shadows left in him and he was formed of light.

After this came Seeker's surrender. He surrendered all

ambition and all hope of meaning. He surrendered his pride and his dreams. In their place came an immense emptiness; and in the emptiness lay limitless power.

Seeker had found his true strength.

The candle burned on the table beside the half-full glass of water. He moved his head, which was lying on the bed, and saw the walls and the sloping ceiling of his room. Then he looked back at the candle. It burned with a steady flame. Its light was reflected in the water glass, refracted and re-peated many times. The glass was transparent, and the water was transparent, and yet he could look and say: there's water, there's glass. How?

He laughed to himself.

"Why am I laughing? Am I happy?"

He stood up, then stretched and yawned, reaching his arms as high as he could go, feeling his fingers tingle. Then he went to the table and sat himself down on the chair be-side it and looked closely at the water glass.

Really, now that he noticed it, water in a glass was something quite extraordinary. It was, in a sense, nothing surrounded by nothing.

"I'm a nothing, too," he told himself, smiling for no very good reason. "I'm a nobody going nowhere for no reason."

He laughed at that more than ever.

"Hey ho!" He chuckled. "I must be jango."

Jango?

"What am I saying? There's no such word."

But now there was such a word, because he had said

it. Jango. What was more, he knew just what it meant. It meant playfully mad. Crazy, but in a harmless and delightful way.

"Yes. No doubt about it. I'm jango."

At that he rocked back and forth on his chair and laughed until the tears streamed down his cheeks.

"I suppose I've lost my mind," he said to himself. "But I don't see that it much matters. I didn't need it."

He reached out for the glass of water, meaning to have a drink. But it wobbled about in the glass in so very interesting a manner that, instead of drinking it, he looked at it, then looked through it at the candle flame, which it made smaller and farther away.

"Well, well, well," he said aloud. "The glass of water is jango, too."

Then it struck him that quite possibly the whole world was jango. He liked that idea so much that he explored it further.

This was how his teacher found him: sitting on the chair, holding the glass of water before him, contemplating the oddity of all things.

"How is it?" she asked him.

"Terrible," he said, putting down the glass. "Couldn't be worse."

"Whenever you want to go," she said, "you can go."

"Certainly I can," he replied. "And certainly I shall. Just as soon as I can make up my mind that there's more point in going than in staying. And since there's no point in either, that may take me some time."

He laughed merrily.

"Hey ho, jango!" he added, feeling that this made the situation much clearer.

Miriander looked at him intently.

"What did you say?"

"Jango!" cried Seeker. "It's my new word."

"Can it really be so?" she said.

"Yes," said Seeker. "Everything is so. So very so."

"What have you learned in the night?"

"Nothing," said Seeker. "Nothing is dependable. Nothing lasts."

Miriander kept her gaze on him, searching his face.

"I'm jango," he said happily.

She reached out one hand and stroked his face, from his eyes to his mouth. He became calm at last.

"Perhaps you really are," said Miriander softly.

"It doesn't matter," said Seeker. "I've failed. I'm the only one who's failed."

"Why do you say that?"

"Morning Star told me. When she came in the night."

"No one came to you in the night."

"Yes. She did. And the Wildman came. And you came."

"No one came to you in the night."

"And I went to the Cloister Court, and there was a light in the Garden, and the Wise Father was there."

Miriander heard this in silence.

"It was he who told me. Nothing lasts."

"Seeker," said his teacher at last. "This is very important. Look me in the eyes."

He did so.

"Was this a dream?"

"It might have been a dream," he replied, "but I don't think so."

"You saw a light in the Garden? You saw the Wise Father?"

"Yes."

"Did you see his face?"

"No. The light was behind him."

"The light was very bright?"

"Brighter than bright! So bright there was nothing else."

"If this is true, you've seen more than I've ever seen."

She took the glass of water from the table, and with a sudden twist of her wrist, she threw the water at Seeker. It splashed cold on his face, shocking him.

"Stand!" she said, and he stood.

She herself stood before him.

"Look into my eyes."

He looked into her eyes.

"If you are my master now—make me fall."

Seeker was puzzled and was about to ask how he was to do this. But then, looking into his teacher's eyes, it struck him that it was simple. He had only to want it enough, and he could will her to fall.

He willed it.

Miriander fell.

⊰ 6 ⊱

The Flying Onion

A SHARP WIND WAS BLOWING OFF THE LAKE AS THE crowd waited, shivering, in the temple square. A bank of gray cloud to the east threatened rain. Some of the patient people had been in the square since dawn and had brought thick blankets to keep themselves warm. Some had come every week for months, in the hope of being chosen. One of them, a small balding man in a fur coat, was at the Choosing for the first time. At his feet, attached to a short cord, stood a peculiar wheeled carriage, a little like a child's toy wagon, only narrower and taller. Its owner had come early to secure a position near the front of the throng. He wanted to make sure that the priest-king of Radiance saw him.

Now at last there were signs that the ceremony was about to begin. A detachment of axers filed out and placed themselves between the crowd and the temple steps, facing the people and rattling chains in their hands. A buzz of anticipation ran through the crowd. A surge from the back drove the front rows forward until they were stumbling against the axers.

"Back!" roared the axers. "Make room!"

Then the great temple doors began to part, pushed from within by scarlet-clad servants of the priest-king. When the doors were fully open, a line of gong bearers filed out and stood on either side of the doorway. They struck their gongs, making soft shivery sounds, and a column of lower priests came marching out of the temple, bearing fire basins. The smoke streamed in the wind, and the smell of burning cedarwood filled the square. After the lower priests came the higher priests, in their gold capes and holding long thin canes that reached high above their heads. And after the higher priests came the priest-king himself, a full head taller than the others, his golden corona gleaming in the orange light of the fires.

"Choose me, Radiant Leader! Choose me!"

The people sighed and crowded forward, and the axers pushed them back. From all across the temple square, like dry leaves in the wind, came the rustling whisper of sound.

"Choose me! Choose me!"

But none looked up at the priest-king. The priests on either side lowered their gaze in his presence. No one looked directly on the glory of the son of the Great Power, for so it was ordered. Nor did the people shout loudly to draw attention to themselves, much as they longed to be chosen. They knew that only the humble deserved the reward, and they believed that Radiant Leader had the power to see into their hearts.

The soft jangling of the gongs now ceased, and Radiant Leader spoke to his people.

"Who seeks eternal life?"

"We do!" murmured the crowd. "We do!"

"Who is worthy of eternal life?"

"We are! We are!"

They called back in low voices, without raising their eyes.

"Who will wear the white of the pilgrim, and live forever?"

"I will! I will!"

"Prepare for the Choosing."

The people stood now in utter silence with their heads bowed. The higher priests reached out their long slender canes and watched the priest-king's right hand. With one jewelled forefinger extended, Radiant Leader pointed into the crowd. A cane dipped, then tapped the head of a young woman.

"Saved!"

She raised her hands high above her head and cried out ecstatically, "Take me up into the harvest!"

The priest-king pointed again, then another cane dipped, and another supplicant was chosen. And another, and another. As they were chosen, they were led away by lower priests standing at the edge of the crowd.

Radiant Leader's gaze, passing back and forth over the bowed heads before him, came to a sudden stop on one balding head that was not bowed. Alone among the hundreds in the square, this man looked up boldly, even impertinently, evidently determined to catch the priest-king's attention.

Radiant Leader recognized him at once.

The audience room in the temple was long and high, with a magnificent vaulted ceiling supported by golden pillars. Radiant Leader's receiving throne stood at the far end on a raised dais. The little man entered, pulling his wheeled contraption behind him, and marched boldly down the hall. He seemed to be singing as he came. Radiant Leader, seated on his throne in solitary splendor, watched him approach with conflicting emotions. This absurd man might prove to be a serious problem for him, or he might prove to be the answer to all his problems.

Now that he was closer, the song became audible.

"High, high, watch it fly!
Like an onion in the sky!"

So he had gone mad. That wasn't necessarily a bad thing.

The little man came to a stop before him at last. He did not avert his gaze. He didn't bow. He stood there grinning like a fool.

"Professor Evor Ortus," said Radiant Leader. "Why aren't you dead?"

"Why should I be dead?" said the little man. "I'm not sick, nor am I old enough to die of natural causes."

"I searched for you. My men searched for you. You were nowhere to be found."

"That may be so. But lost is not dead."

He tipped his head to one side and studied the priest-king like a bird.

"Have you grown taller?" he said. "I remember you as quite a shorty. Ah yes, I see the trick of it. The furniture round you is made small. And your attendants out there— picked for their small stature, I suppose."

Radiant Leader's face turned a dull red. It was many months since anyone had dared to speak to him with such irreverence.

"I am Radiant Leader!" he said sharply. "I can have you thrown from the temple rock."

"You won't do that," said the professor, quite unafraid. "And you're not Radiant Leader. You're the old king's secretary in a shiny frock."

Radiant Leader stared at the insolent man, in grim silence, for a few long moments. His first instinct was to summon his axers and order them to dash out the professor's brains. But he controlled himself. There was a matter of vital importance to be settled first. Once, not so long ago, Professor Ortus had held the key to the most powerful weapon ever made.

Could he do it again?

"They won't stop me this time," said the little man, with a chuckle.

"Who are you talking about?"

"The hoodies." He nudged his wooden toy with one foot. "This time I've got a flying onion. This time we destroy Anacrea."

Before Radiant Leader could ask for an explanation, the far doors burst open and in hurried an attendant priest, his eyes on the ground.

"Radiance!" he cried. "Danger! War!"

Behind the priest came three travel-stained axers. They threw themselves to their knees and bowed their heads and cried out their news in a wild jumble of words.

"A terrible enemy—thousands upon thousands—strange beasts of war—a great warlord—invasion—"

Radiant Leader rose from his receiving throne and walked to the kneeling axers. He commanded them to be calm and to speak more clearly; and so he learned the grave news. An immense army had come out of the forest. Its leader called himself the master of the world. He demanded the submission of the priest-king of Radiance.

"He says," whispered one of the axers, fearful even to frame the words, "he says you're to greet him on your knees."

"On my knees?"

"Or the city will be destroyed."

"Destroyed?"

Radiant Leader laughed a short contemptuous laugh.

"And these strange war-beasts? What are they?"

"Like cattle, Radiance, but light and fast-moving. The warriors cling to their backs, and they attack so fast—they have whips—Radiance, strong as we are, we could do nothing. They could have killed every one of us."

"Then why didn't they kill you?"

"Because we knelt to their leader, Radiance."

"You knelt!" The priest-king heard this with proud anger. "You should have died. Better to die than to submit."

"We live only to warn you, Radiance."

"Very well. I am warned. But I'll not kneel."

He raised his arms high on either side, his palms facing outwards.

"I am Radiant Leader, beloved son of the Great Power on high! I do not kneel to any man!"

The axers were suitably awed and reassured.

"How long before these invaders enter our territory?"

"Within days, Radiance. Perhaps even as soon as tomorrow."

"Very well. You may go. I shall do all that is necessary."

The axers rose and bowed and departed, followed by the priest. Radiant Leader then turned his attention back to the little scientist. Ortus seemed to have taken in none of the axers' news. He was crouched over his wheeled contraption, crooning to it quietly.

Radiant Leader spoke to him in a slow clear voice, as if he were addressing a child.

"Professor Ortus. The laboratory where you made your great weapon. The laboratory that was burned down. You remember it?"

"Of course," said Ortus.

"Can you build it again?"

"Of course." Ortus smiled a crafty smile and tapped his head. "This is my laboratory. It's all in here. And I'm the only one who can do it."

"So you could make a second great weapon?"

"Why else have I come to you now?" Once more the

scientist pointed proudly to his wheeled toy. "My flying onion will destroy Anacrea."

"I don't want to talk about flying onions."

"Allow me to demonstrate."

"Professor, we face a real and imminent danger."

But it was no good. The little scientist would only do what he had come to do. Now he was kneeling beside his device, winding a small handle. Radiant Leader decided to humor him.

The contraption was a high ramp on wheels. The back end of the structure rose vertically for about three feet, and up its struts ran a little elevator platform. This platform was now rising as Ortus wound the handle below. On the platform was a toy truck the size of a pack of cards. In the truck was an onion.

When the truck reached the top, it rolled off the elevator and onto the highest part of the steep railed ramp. This ramp curved all the way down, and then rose up again to a lower height.

"The onion," said Ortus, "will now fly. Watch."

The little truck was already gathering speed as it rolled down the slope. Reaching the steepest part, it hurtled downwards and was swept up the other side to the ramp's end. Here a trip tipped the truck up, and the onion went sailing on through the air in a high parabola, to land on the floor some twenty feet away.

"A flying onion!" said Ortus, beaming with pride.

"Very good, Professor. A flying onion. Excellent. Now, to return to the matter of rebuilding your laboratory—"

"This is only a model, of course, constructed on a scale

of one to a hundred. The onion, you see, is the container of charged water. We send it down the ramp, and it flies across the channel that divides the mainland from the island of Anacrea, and—boom-bang! No more Nomana."

At this he danced a little dance of delight. Radiant Leader gazed at the wooden structure thoughtfully. He understood the flying onion scheme now; it was not entirely half-witted; but the Nomana would never stand idly by while a tower three hundred feet high was built facing their island. The charged water, however, was a very different matter. If the little scientist really could rebuild his laboratory, and pack the explosive power of the sun into some portable form, then Radiant Leader was happy for him to prattle on about onions as much as he liked.

"Remarkable, Professor," he said. "Simple, but effective. Now tell me. How long will it take you to establish a laboratory and produce the necessary charged water?"

Ortus pursed his lips and made mental calculations.

"If the materials were to hand, and if I had the manpower, a matter of days."

"Shall we say three?"

"Three days! That is very little time."

"I shall give orders that you are to be supplied with all that you need."

"Excellent!" The scientist clapped his hands and did another little jig. "I knew that once you had seen the onion fly, you would be convinced."

"I'm happy you're happy, Professor."

"Happy indeed! All any scientist asks for is the chance

to carry his projects through to their conclusion. Now I know I shall complete both."

On retreating to his private quarters and shedding the burdensome paraphernalia of his office, Radiant Leader turned his ingenious mind to this new development. If the mad professor could truly fulfill his promise, it would make Radiance once again the greatest power in the land. If he could destroy Anacrea, and with it the hated Nomana—

We are waiting.

Radiant Leader heard the soft voice, and his excitement evaporated. I'll never be free, he thought bitterly to himself. The voice will always return.

"Here I am, Mistress."

He had tired of it long ago, the insatiable demands of the mysterious old people he had never seen, their dry hunger for the moisture of young lives. He hated it all now, it disgusted him, but how could he escape? The voice lived inside his own head.

We need more.

"I'm tired."

Tired?

The voice in his head sounded mocking. And to think he had loved her once, this never-seen mistress.

What right have you to be tired? You rule only to serve us.

"I have served you!" In his frustration he shouted his reply, which was absurd, since she could hear even his most silent thoughts. "When will you be satisfied?"

When the harvest is complete.

"It never ends! How many have I sent you? Thousands! Thousands upon thousands! And still you want more."

It will end soon now. Be patient.

He bowed his head and was silent. His unseen mistress, feeling the passing of his brief resistance, became gentle.

You have done well. We are pleased with you.

He accepted his reward in silence; but the brief jolt of bliss no longer pleased him as it once had. He would gladly have done without it, to be released from the demands. But the old people would not let him go. He was too successful. To feed the hunger of his mistress, he had told his subjects he could give them eternal life; and by making this reward available only to the chosen few, he had caused them to clamor for it. All he had to do was point, and off they marched. He had no idea what happened to them after that, nor did he care. They never came back. Maybe they did get eternal life. If not, they were contributing to it. Wasn't that what the old people wanted them for?

He sighed as he rubbed the heaviness from his face. Then, lowering his hands, his eyes fell on a goatskin drum that had been used by his predecessor. He picked it up and began to beat a rhythm, to release the tension in him.

Bam! Bam! Ba-ba-bam!

It was the rhythm of the hate training he had invented for the old king, back when he was his lowly secretary Soren Similin. How did it go?

"Uh! Uh! Gouge out their eyes!"

Simple, but in its way satisfying.

He beat the drum harder.

Bam! Bam! Ba-ba-bam!

"Uh! Uh! Rip out their hearts!"

The old king had hated the Nomana. Now that he beat the same drum and chanted the same chant, Similin realized he hated the Nomana, too. He hated them because they were more powerful than Radiance, and he hated them because they were free. Everyone had to submit to someone—even he, Radiant Leader, son of the Great Power above, must obey the commands of his mistress. But the Nomana obeyed no one.

Ba-ba-ba-bam! Ba-ba-ba-bam!

"Nomana die! Nomana die!"

Maybe now they would. Maybe the professor's mad scheme would work.

That reminded him of the day's news. Radiance was in danger from a new threat: this so-called master of the world, who demanded that he, Radiant Leader, greet him on his knees. He needed to buy time—three days, if possible. Somehow he must stall this new warlord until he was armed and protected by Ortus's explosive power.

But on one matter he was in no doubt. He would kneel to no one.

Power without Limits

SEEKER STOOD BY HIS TEACHER'S SIDE, IN THE CENTER of the Chapter House, and all round him, on the three tiers of benches that lined the walls, were the members of the Community. Directly in front of him sat the Elder, his head sunk and his eyes closed. Beside the Elder sat the sallow-faced Narrow Path. It was Narrow Path who had found him when he first strayed into the Nom, and who had urged that he be cleansed.

Now they'll tell me I'm to leave the Nom, thought Seeker. The Wildman and I will be cast out together.

Only a few hours earlier this prospect would have devastated him. But now he felt no dismay, and no fear. He could still feel within himself the glow of that intense light and, with it, the sense that somehow his life had changed and all that had concerned him before was now of no importance.

High above, the dull light of the new day fell through the central lantern in the roof to illuminate the windowless octagonal room. He saw Blaze looking at him. He smiled to show his brother that he wasn't afraid, but Blaze didn't smile back. Narrow Path murmured to the Elder, and the Elder nodded without opening his eyes. Narrow Path then signed to Miriander that she could begin.

"Brothers and sisters," said Miriander, "this young novice is called Seeker after Truth. I tell you nothing about him. I ask you only to watch."

Watch what? thought Seeker. What am I to do?

He had no idea. But this did not seem to him to be a difficulty. Clearly this was some kind of test. Well, he had faced tests before and had survived. He recalled the leap from the temple rock in Radiance, into the night, into nothing, and how afraid he had been. Now he knew he would never be so afraid again. This wasn't bravery, it was something else. He had stopped minding.

It's all because I'm jango, he thought, and he smiled.

Miriander now bowed to Chance, the novices' combat teacher. Chance rose from the bench on which he'd sat and padded forward to stand before Seeker. He gave him a brief glance, then let his heavy lids droop low over his eyes, and adopted the Tranquil Alert.

So I'm to try my strength against my teacher, thought Seeker. That will be interesting.

"Pay respect," said Miriander.

He made his bow as he had been taught.

"Engage."

Seeker met his teacher's eyes. The older man made his first move, a simple pulse of power, but Seeker was able to deflect it. Chance struck again. Seeker rocked under the impact but did not fall. Neither of them had so far lifted so much as a finger.

Seeker focused his attention on the lir within him and drew it into a long thin rod, an imaginary blade that extended from his right forefinger. While he was doing this, Chance took two light steps forward and caught him with an actual blow to his left flank. The blow was so powerful that Seeker was sent tumbling to the floor, scrabbling and sliding all the way to the feet of the watching Nomana.

A murmur went up from the crowded benches. Seeker, struggling to his feet, caught sight of Miriander and saw on her face a look of perplexity mingled with shame. She expects me to win, thought Seeker. Very well. I shall win.

He returned to the combat. He took his position facing Chance, and once again let all the lir in him flow down his right arm into his forefinger, then out from his forefinger into the invisible blade that streamed from him into space. He raised his arm and reached forward—not fast, not hard, more a push than a strike.

Chance saw it coming, of course. He was ready to block it. But there was nothing he could do. The blow lifted him off his feet and tossed him through the air, to land, winded and gasping, on the top benches of the watching Nomana.

A sigh of surprise went round the spectators. Miriander allowed herself a brief smile. Narrow Path wrinkled
his high shiny brow.

Seeker was as surprised as the rest of them. It had cost
him so little effort. He believed he could do better. He
wanted to find out.

Chance was assisted down the tiers to the floor. Shaking himself, he resumed his position in the combat. This
time he did not look as if he was half asleep. Every fiber
of his being was alert and ready to strike.

He held Seeker's gaze. For a long moment he wrestled
with him, attempting to control his will. But he could not.
Seeker, by contrast, did not wrestle. He looked back with
a limpid gaze, untouched. Then the combat teacher
launched a triple attack: changing his tactics so fast that his
moves could not be anticipated, he struck high, then low,
then sprang through the air in the horizontal full-body
strike called the Mortal Arrow.

Seeker stopped him dead in mid-flight without making a single move. Then he rotated his right wrist and gave
a flick of his hand. Chance jerked as if hit by a beam across
his midriff. He seemed to snap and fold. He dropped to
the floor and did not move.

Silence in the Chapter House.

Seeker felt a surge of exaltation burn through his body.
What he had just done, he knew, was one-tenth—one-
hundredth—of what he could do. Intoxicated by the discovery of his immense power, he lifted his hand and swept
it over the lines of watching Nomana, as a child rattles a

stick along a picket fence. One after another, in rapid succession, the Nomana jerked their faces to one side, as if they had been smacked.

Then he turned and bowed to his teacher, Miriander.

Narrow Path leaned forward and fixed Seeker with a sharp look.

"Now, boy," he said, "are you weary?"

Weary? Not at all. He was surging with energy.

He shook his head.

"Do you feel stronger than before?"

"Yes, Brother."

Now that he said it, he knew that it was true. He did feel stronger. But how could that be?

He looked towards the slumped body of his combat teacher. Chance hadn't moved. Only then did it occur to Seeker that his teacher might have been badly hurt. Forgetting the staring faces of the Community, he went and knelt by his side.

"Forgive me, Teacher," he said.

Chance stirred, then raised his head to look on his pupil. He tried to speak but could not.

"I didn't know my own strength," said Seeker.

Chance nodded and smiled faintly.

"Your own," he whispered, "and mine."

Then Seeker understood. The blow that had crippled Chance had sucked the strength from him. That force, that lir, had flowed into Seeker himself.

Every blow I strike makes me stronger.

He reached out one hand and helped his combat

teacher rise to his feet. He felt the weight on his arm. Chance had aged ten years.

When Seeker turned round once more he saw that the Elder had woken, if he had ever been asleep. His eyes were open, and he was watching Seeker. On his face was a look of unbearable sadness. Seeker looked beyond him at the rows of watching faces. The Nomana were staring back at him in utter silence, as if he was something terrible and monstrous. A great ache grew in his heart as he looked from face to face and found there no answering kindness.

What have I done? Why do they fear me? My strength is their strength. Such power as I have comes from the All and Only. Am I not sworn to protect the Lost Child? Am I not a brother among brothers?

He turned to Miriander. Her beautiful face looked on him with compassion.

"We've been waiting for you for a long time," she said. "Now that you've come at last, we're afraid."

"Why?" said Seeker. "What is there to fear?"

"Power without limits," she said softly.

Seeker felt an icy coldness pass through him, and all round him it seemed that the world stood still. The row upon row of gray-clad figures retreated into the distance, became paintings on a shadowed wall. The lantern above climbed through space to become the white sun, a distant blur in the clouds. The floor beneath his feet fell away, and he was standing on the tops of trees, on the windblown leaves themselves.

He was beyond the reach of humankind. Alone, forever.

Overwhelmed by desolation, he dropped to his knees and put his hands to his face and wept.

The Wildman looked out from the storeroom where he had been hiding and saw that the courtyard was empty. No one had come looking for him. It seemed that the Nomana had more urgent concerns. The doors and gates that led out of the novitiate were all locked. They had no reason to fear he would escape.

The Wildman knew exactly what he would do. He had imagined it so many times, it was almost as if he had done it already. But this time, in place of his imaginings, would be the act.

One perfect dive.

He swung himself up onto the lower part of the wall, and from here, using the uneven blocks of stone to offer hand- and footholds, he heaved himself up to the parapet itself. Here, crouching, fingers spread on the wall's top, he found his balance and slowly rose to his feet. He was standing now with his back to the courtyard and with the wide ocean horizon before him. He felt the wind lift his long golden hair and ruffle the badan that lay loose over his shoulders. Then he looked down.

Far, far below the waves were rolling in, to crash and burst against the island's rocky base. The tide was high and the wind was off the sea, and the entire lower part of the Nom's great soaring wall was hazed with spray. No way of knowing how deep the water was and how far out the rocks lay.

"Soon find out," he said to himself. It was the kind of crazy risk he had taken time and again in the old days. "If you win, you win. If you lose, it's all over, and what do you care?"

He was physically fitter than he had ever been. The Nom's training had transformed a powerful young man into one who knew how to use every muscle in his body to maximum effect. He had never understood the notion of lir, but he had learned how to control it and knew that he was now ten times the fighter he had been before. He admired the Nomana with all his heart and knew he would regret to the end of his days that he couldn't be one of them. But he wasn't staying to be cleansed.

He heard a cry from the courtyard below and, turning, saw one of the meeks pointing up at him, calling to him.

"Come down! Come down!"

He turned away again and focused his attention on what he was about to do. Using his training, he gathered his lir, drawing it into the pit of his stomach—not to deliver a strike, as in combat, but to preserve his own life for as long as possible when he slammed into the water. As he felt the lir flow at his command, his lean body became still and alert.

Now there were more shouts from the courtyard. He thought he recognized Morning Star's voice, and Seeker's, too. He raised one hand above his head and waved in a gesture of farewell. He heard the scrabble of hands and feet climbing the wall towards him. Too late, he thought. Where I'm going, you won't want to follow.

He stretched up onto the tips of his toes and leaned into the wind. As he felt himself begin to fall, he kicked with all his might, to propel himself clear of the wall. And so, curving in the morning air, he turned over in a graceful arc and fell arrow-straight down towards the foaming waves.

He heard the torn edge of screams. He felt the slap of air. He smelled the onrushing ocean. And for a few moments, dropping without effort, he was perfectly, blissfully at peace.

Through the slots in the high wall, they saw him vanish into the turbulent water far below. They watched the heaving, rolling surface of the sea and looked for a head breaking through to air, or strong arms striking for the shore; but they saw nothing. They watched until they knew that the Wildman could not still be alive. Then they turned away.

Miriander had charge of Seeker.

"Come now," she said.

Instead, Seeker went to Morning Star, who was kneeling on the stone floor of the yard with her face in her hands. He knelt with her and put his arms round her, and she began to sob.

"He's gone," she said. And then, in time with her sobs, as if she was trying to cry him out of her, she said again and again, "Gone. Gone. Gone."

Seeker felt her shudder in his arms, and he looked up to his waiting teacher.

"Give me a little time with her."

Miriander nodded.

He drew Morning Star gently to her feet, thinking he knew a way to bring her comfort.

"We could have stopped him," she said. "We were his friends."

"No," he said. "We can't live his life for him."

Now that she had begun to talk, the words came tumbling out of her, and Seeker let her talk, hoping it would ease her pain.

"He was so unhappy and I did nothing. What could I do? He told me he felt crushed and trapped and tied. Why did he feel that? He wanted peace. He wanted it so much. And now he'll never find it."

Seeker led her down the passage that opened into the Shadow Court, his arm round her the whole way.

"Don't tell me he's gone," she said, holding tight to his hand. "Tell me he'll come back one day, the way he used to be, laughing and golden and beautiful. He didn't have to dive. Don't let him dive. It's too high, and there are rocks beneath the waves. And even if he dives . . ."

They were in the deep gloom of the Shadow Court.

She stopped and pulled Seeker round so that she could see his face.

"Even if he dives," she said, her eyes burning, "it doesn't mean the sun will rise again. Will you tell him that? Tell him the sun won't rise. If he dives, the dawn will never come. Tell him. Please tell him."

He put both arms round her now and held her close, to soothe her bewildered spirit.

"I'll tell him."

"But he's gone. How could I forget? It's too late."

She wept in his arms.

"Come," said Seeker. "Let's lay our grief before the Loving Mother and ask for comfort."

She went with him through the speckled light of the Night Court, not noticing her surroundings.

"Don't tell him I love him," she said. "He doesn't want me to love him, so I'll not love him. Tell him so, and maybe he'll come back. Tell him I love him so much I'll not love him."

"I'll tell him," said Seeker sadly.

They entered the cool white space of the Cloister Court. Ahead glinted the silver screen that bounded the Garden. The closer they came to the Garden, the tighter Morning Star gripped Seeker's arm.

"No," she said. "No nearer. I'll be punished."

"Punished? For what?"

"For the madness in me."

"There's no madness in you," he said. "Only sadness. Let the Loving Mother comfort you."

But she would go no farther. She shook with fear.

"The colors," she said. "Don't let me dive into the colors. If I dive, I'll drown."

He held her tight, pressing her head to his chest so that her eyes would close.

"No dive," he murmured to her. "No dive. No colors. Only me, holding you tight."

As he held her, he felt an ache in his heart. But this was no time to be thinking of himself.

"The Wildman dived," she whispered. "Did I see him dive? I think I did. But you must tell me the truth."

"Yes," said Seeker. "He dived."

"And will the sun now rise again?"

"Yes. The sun will rise again."

"Will you tell him I'm stronger now? Tell him I'll not love him any more."

"I'll tell him."

"We can be friends again, the way we used to be. You and me and the Wildman. We were good friends, weren't we?"

"Good friends."

Then she was silent. Her breathing grew even against his chest. He stroked some stray hair back from her flushed cheek. He heard a soft sound behind him, and there was Miriander, waiting for him.

"We have to go back now," he said.

Morning Star walked back with him, and with every step she took she became calmer and her mind became clearer.

"I'm sorry," she said. "I've been confused."

"It's the shock," said Seeker. "We're all shocked."

"I don't know what I've been saying. Forget it all. It's all nonsense."

"I'll take you back to your room. Let you rest."

They returned to the novitiate. At the entrance to the long passage where the novices had their cells, he came to a stop.

"I'm all right now," she said. "Thank you."

She held out one hand. Absurdly, after he had held her close to him and stroked the tears from her cheeks and felt her cling to him so tight, he now shook her hand.

"You'll always be my friend, won't you?" she said.
"Always."

Miriander led Seeker down a flight of steps into a lower
level of the Nom, which he had not known existed. The
passages and rooms through which they passed had been
cut out of the rock itself and were windowless, dimly lit
by small lamps placed on the floor.

After a while he could see bright light ahead. A shaft
had been cut through the rock to the open air, and down
this shaft streamed the cold clear daylight, so much more
powerful, even on a cloudy winter's day, than the little
amber glow of the lamps.

In this last room, in the pool of daylight, sat the Elder,
in his wheelchair. His weak old eyes were on Seeker with
the expression he had worn before, of an overwhelming
sadness. He made a sign to Miriander. She bowed and left
them.

"So you are the one," the Elder said. "As I have suspected since you first came to us."

He spoke with difficulty. He had grown much weaker
since Seeker had last been alone with him. Seeker waited,
feeling the beating of his own heart, for the soft creaky voice
to begin again. Now at last he would be told the meaning
of the changes that were taking possession of him.

"Your coming, at this time, warns us that we are in
great danger. This has been long expected."

The Elder fell silent, exhausted.

"If I have more power than others, Elder, it's at the service of the Nom. Only tell me what I'm to do."

"More power, yes." The Elder sighed. "Our strength is as the strength of a wounded warrior, and victory makes us weak. You remember?"

"Yes, Elder."

"But not for you."

Seeker bowed his head in acknowledgment and in obedience. If extra powers had been given him, it was the will of the All and Only. He waited to be told what to do.

"What was it the voice said to you, Seeker, all those months ago?"

Seeker spoke the well-remembered words.

"'Surely you know that it's you who will save me.'"

"So, so," murmured the Elder. "You can save, or you can destroy."

"Why would I want to destroy, Elder?"

"Power is a terrible thing, my boy."

Then he crinkled his worn face into a small smile.

"But you're a boy no longer."

"I haven't asked for this, Elder. None of this is my doing."

"Do you fear the power?"

"Yes, Elder."

"Good. That's good." He thought for a while. "You know you can be released."

Seeker knew of only one way: he could be cleansed. That would drain him of his power, but also of his past and everything that made him who he was. He would be returned to early childhood.

"There are those in the Community," said the Elder,

"who say that it should be done. They say it is our duty not to loose such unlimited power into the world."

"And what do you say, Elder?"

The Elder gave another long sigh.

"I don't know, boy. My mind is not as clear as it was."

He held out one hand before him.

"See. My hand trembles. I can no longer stop it."

Seeker took the trembling hand and drew it to his lips and kissed it. The trembling ceased.

The old man saw this and tears came to his eyes. He bowed his head to Seeker.

"Thank you."

He raised one hand, and out of the shadows stepped his attendant meek. This came as a shock to Seeker. He had thought they were alone.

"Now I will go back to the meeting," said the Elder. "We meet to decide what is to be done with you. You will wait here."

"Yes, Elder."

The meek then wheeled him out of the room. Somewhere in the darkness of the passage Seeker heard a door close and a key turn in a lock. It seemed he was a prisoner.

He went to the shaft of daylight and looked up into the white sky above. The shaft was no more than twelve inches wide at its widest. On either side, the walls were solid rock. He explored the passage and found the door and felt it. It was heavy, but he knew his own strength now and reckoned he could break it down if he chose. But this imprisonment was the will of the Community. So he returned to the light and sat himself down on the floor and waited.

He recalled the tears in the Elder's eyes, and there came back into his mind the words the Elder had spoken to him long ago.

"We weep for pity of those we must hurt, and our hearts break for those we love."

❅ 8 ❅

Learning to Ride

THE IMMENSE ARMY OF AMROTH JAHAN MOVED SLOWLY across the fertile plains of the Great Basin, devouring all the winter-stored grain and slaughtering all the cattle as they went. Word of the Orlans' ruthlessness went before them, and they met no resistance. The people of the regions through which they passed gathered in silent clusters to watch them go by, and stared in awe at the warriors' elegant Caspians. They were the first horses ever seen in these parts.

Echo Kittle, carried along as part of the Great Jahan's entourage, had still not mounted the horse that had been given her to ride. Each day she asked the Jahan if she was ready, and each day he shook his head and said, "Not yet."

It must be soon now. The more time she spent by Kell's side, the better he seemed to understand her. Often she would look round and see him gazing at her, his wide-spaced eyes thoughtful and steady, and she would say, "What, Kell? What is it?" Then he would toss his beautiful head and come to her and stand close, and she would feel he wanted her to know he would look after her.

To add to the hardship of her life on the road, the Jahan's sons had become bolder in her presence and were turning into a constant irritant. Everywhere she went, there was Sasha moodily brushing his fingers through his long bushy hair, which he believed to be his most attractive feature; or Alva, as often as not stripped to the waist, showing off his well-muscled torso; or Sabin, who never spoke, but who watched her like a hungry puppy.

Small gifts began to appear in her tent: a plate of honey cakes, a beaded bracelet. There was never a written note to say who they came from, so Echo didn't know who to thank. This suited her well enough, as she didn't feel at all grateful. She felt harassed. She put the gifts outside her tent, where the Jahan saw them.

"What's this?" he said.

"They're not mine," she replied. "Someone left them in my tent by mistake."

"These are love gifts."

"Then why are there no messages?"

"Messages?"

"To say who they're from."

The Jahan laughed.

"My sons can't write. These are gifts from them, to win your favor."

"Then please tell them not to waste their time."

"I will not tell them so. At my command, they are competing for you. The winner will receive you as his bride at a celebration in the city of Radiance. Do you know the city of Radiance?"

"I've never been there," said Echo.

"I'm told it's very rich and very beautiful. It will please me to have the king of Radiance offer his homage. Afterwards, at the victory feast, you will be married."

"Am I to be given away as a prize?"

"You will give yourself away. To the one you favor."

"I don't favor any of them. They're all as dull and ugly as each other."

The Jahan sighed at this.

"I don't deny it. I'm hoping that the competition for your favor will bring out qualities that have not yet been revealed."

"I won't do it," said Echo. "You can't make me."

"Of course I can make you. You will do what is necessary to please me. What displeases me, I crush beneath my feet."

After this the love gifts ceased. In their place came words. Echo found this even more aggravating.

"Your eyes are like ripe plums," said Alva Jahan to her one morning. He spoke without preliminaries, coming up behind her as she was stroking Kell. She made no reply. After a few moments, he wandered away.

Sasha Jahan was more persistent.

"Your mouth is soft as a foal's," he told her, "sucking the udder of love."

Echo pretended she hadn't heard him. He went on.

"My beloved's head is a cake. Her skin is pale as marzipan."

This was too much. She rounded on him.

"Where do you get this nonsense?"

"From the matchmaker," he said, blinking a little.

"Then you need a better matchmaker."

"It's true," said Sasha gloomily. "All the best match-makers are women. But we're on campaign, and we have only men."

Later that day Echo heard scuffles and cries, and came out of her tent to find a man bent over a barrel, being whipped. He was one of the camp cooks.

"What's he done?" she asked, flinching at his piteous cries.

"Been making out he's a matchmaker," came the reply. "He should stick to making pies."

That evening Echo sought out the cook. He was lying on a cot with a cold mud poultice on his raw back.

"I'm sorry you were whipped," she said. "It wasn't your fault."

"My love words failed," said the cook sadly. "I don't know what went wrong. They've always worked well before."

"They came out a little suddenly," said Echo.

"Ah, well. There you are. They do need leading up to. You do have to prepare the ground."

"Yes, I expect that would have made all the difference."

"Your buttocks," the cook recited tenderly to himself, "are the pillows of my dreams."

"They didn't use that one."

"I think that's my favorite."

"Tell me," said Echo. "These love words. Is your method to work through the parts of the body, and then find something to compare them with?"

"That's exactly what I do!" exclaimed the cook, very surprised. "But don't tell anyone. They might set up a rival business once they understand the method."

"I won't tell."

Echo would have laughed at the cook-matchmaker but for the whip wounds on his back. And as for herself, it was all very well to sneer at the Jahan's sons, but their father had let it be known throughout the camp that one of them was to have her for his wife. His immense pride would never allow her to refuse all of them for much longer.

The most persistent of her suitors was Alva, the Great Jahan's second son. The most athletic and warlike of the three, he announced one day that he would challenge all comers in the traditional Orlan mode of courtship: a contest of skill and strength called the jagga.

"I fight for you," he declared to Echo. "If I win, you must give me a kiss. That is our custom."

"It may be your custom," said Echo, "but it's not mine."

The great army had made camp at the end of the day. Word spread rapidly that Alva Jahan had called a jagga, and a number of young men lined up to try their skills. Echo had no notion what a jagga was, and at first was curious enough to linger and watch.

Mounted, naked to the waist, armed only with his whip,

Alva faced his first opponent across a cleared space. He raised his whip in salute to Echo and then gave a great shout.

"Ya, jagga!"

He rode at his opponent, whip cracking, and the two tangled in a blur of combat. Both were agile and adept at evading the flying whips; and so they parted unharmed.

The Jahan himself came to watch, and he applauded loudly.

"Ha, Alva! Bring him down, boy!"

Echo understood that the object of the sport was to unseat your opponent. As she watched she saw Alva's whip curl and catch and tug, but the other rider made his horse spin round on the spot, and so he escaped. This dexterity amazed Echo. At such times horse and rider seemed to fuse into a single being.

"Don't let him go, boy!" yelled the Jahan. "Follow! Follow!"

Alva was dominating the contest. There was little doubt of the outcome. Even now he was dancing round his opponent, taunting him, readying a winning strike. Then he would come prancing over to Echo, glowing with glory and sweat, and demand his winner's kiss.

Echo waited for his attack, when the attention of the onlookers was all on the combat, and she slipped away.

"Come, Kell," she whispered; and Kell picked his way with delicate hooves over the tussocky grass to her side.

But she had left it just a little too late. A shout went up from the spectators, and turning, she saw that Alva Jahan had just unseated his opponent.

"Sorry, Kell," she said. "No more time to get to know each other. I need you now."

She swung herself up onto the horse as she had seen the Orlans do, and lying low over his back, she wrapped her arms round his neck and gripped tight with her thighs. Kell set off at once at an easy canter across the camp. Echo was quite unable to look behind her, so she had no idea whether Alva had seen her go and was chasing after her.

Kell cantered faster and faster, past the last of the tents and into open farmland. Echo felt herself being thrown from side to side, but she clung on grimly for as long as she could. When her grip began to slacken out of sheer exhaustion, she decided to risk sitting upright. She rose up and at once felt herself tip to the left. She threw her weight to the right and fell off.

Kell came to a stop just ahead, then turned round to gaze at her with big reproachful eyes.

"What do you expect?" she said. "I've never done it before."

She climbed to her feet, and Kell trotted back to her side. She looked around. No sign of any pursuers.

It struck her then that she had now ridden for the first time—badly, it was true, but she had begun.

"Let's try again," she said. "And, this time, slowly."

She climbed onto Kell's back once more and gripped tight to his mane. Kell set off at a slow walk. She felt the rolling rhythm beneath her and wondered very much how she could possibly stay on at a faster pace without clinging to his neck. She tried to anticipate each roll with a shift in her own body weight, and got it wrong. Once again she tipped too far to one side, and once again she fell off.

Falling off hurt. She felt annoyed. It looked so easy when the Orlans did it.

She mounted once again.

"Please, Kell," she whispered, "don't make this any harder than it needs to be."

Kell started off walking sedately once more, and Echo rolled from side to side on his back, staying on only by means of the viselike grip of her thighs. Then Kell broke into a trot, and everything changed. Up and down she bounced, like a pea on a drum, and every moving part of her body from her teeth to her toes jiggered and jaggered, so that she supposed very soon now she would fall to pieces. Then, with a sudden lurch, Kell broke into a canter. After the bone-rattling jog of the trot, this was a far easier matter, but they were now moving fast, and with each swoop of motion, Echo so very nearly fell off that she threw herself forward and wrapped her arms round the horse's neck as she had done before. But then Kell changed rhythm again, and now he was thundering over the hard earth at a true gallop.

Now Echo knew she would fall—and would fall hard.

"Kell! Please, Kell!" she gasped.

But on they swept, down the cart track and along the edge of a leafless wood. The trees flashed by in flickers of light and dark. Echo lurched this way and that, expecting each lurch to land her in the ditch. Then it seemed to her that Kell was slowing down. She felt the kinder rhythms of the canter and sighed with relief. Then came the trot.

Shaken and aching as she was, the trot was more than she could manage. She released her tensed legs and let herself be jiggled to one side; and from there she slithered gracelessly to the ground.

So that was riding. Not the elegant birdlike flying she had imagined. Not sweeping and effortless, like racing through the trees. It was bumpy and scary and made her ache all over.

"Not your fault, Kell. I'm just not doing it right."

Kell pressed his nose against her shoulder, as if to say, Come on, get up.

"Let's just walk for a while."

She had no idea of the way back to the camp. She had been too busy holding on to take account of where they had come. So she let Kell lead as they walked, trusting that he knew where he was going.

Soon they were on a roadway that ran alongside an old tumbledown wall. Sitting by the wall, on nothing at all that Echo could see, was an elderly man. He had long tangled gray hair, and his face was the wrinkliest face she had ever seen. The wrinkles went up and down, and running across the up-and-down wrinkles were sideways wrinkles, and all round his eyes were arrow wrinkles. Even his nose seemed to have been scrunched up and left out in the rain. The effect of so many wrinkles was to give him a permanent expression of humorous kindliness.

His brown eyes peered shortsightedly at Echo and Kell as they approached. He was wearing clothes of a style that was unfamiliar to her. The outer coat was dark blue and long, with buttons up the front, and split at the back like a bean pod. The inner coat was gray and belted at the waist. He was barefoot.

"Good afternoon," he said, rising to his feet. He drew from behind the split in his coat a stout walking stick with a hinged handle that doubled up as a small seat. He made Echo a small bow.

"Is your horse injured? Perhaps I can be of assistance."

"No," said Echo. "My horse isn't injured."

"But you don't ride."

"I haven't yet learned to ride."

"Not learned to ride?" He chuckled as if she had said something comical. "No need to learn to ride. Your body knows how to ride a horse."

"Not my body, I'm afraid," said Echo. "I fall off."

"That is because you want to fall off."

"Want to fall off? Why would I want to fall off?"

"Oh, fear, of course. Fear lies behind most foolish behavior. Riding the horse frightens you, so you arrange to fall off."

Echo was about to say that falling off frightened her more. But she decided not to. She was interested in the old man's notions.

"So how do I stop myself?"

He squinted at her.

"You don't think I'm talking nonsense?"

"No. That is, I'm not sure."

"Very well. If you truly understand what I'm telling you, there's nothing more to be done. Your desire will already have changed. Remember, dear girl, everyone always gets what they want."

Echo didn't agree with that at all. But she didn't want to argue. She wanted to learn to ride.

"So what do I do?"

"Ride. If that's what you want."

So Echo scrambled up onto Kell's back once more and told herself she wanted to ride and not fall off. Nothing felt any different. It still seemed to her that she would crash to the ground at any moment.

Then Kell gave a funny little shiver. As he did so, she felt her thigh muscles relax. She hadn't realized how tightly she'd been gripping with her legs. As her muscles let go, Kell's back and flanks changed shape beneath her. Or perhaps her legs changed shape. Whatever it was, she slipped into a new posture that was much more comfortable. All at once it seemed her body fitted on the horse's body. Sensing this, a ripple ran up her spine to her shoulders and down her arms, and the stiffness of her back softened into a shallow curve.

Was I so stiff? she thought, amazed.

With each adjustment of her position, Kell shifted, too. It was exactly like the business of getting into her bedroll at night: a kind of wriggling and snuggling to achieve just the right warmth and safety for the surrender to sleep.

Kell began to move. Now Echo certainly did feel different. She felt the thigh muscles on his right foreleg shift beneath her, and the same shift flowed upwards into her muscles. So it was with the left rear leg. As the position of balance changed, her weight rolled like water into the still center.

"Oh, you're so beautiful!" she cried to Kell.

The horse had done no more than take two paces, and Echo was entranced. The old man had been right. She had never learned this, and never could. This sweet true motion was something she could only accept, with gratitude and joy.

She leaned a little forward, not thinking to give any command, and at once Kell picked up speed.

"Oh, Kell!" she whispered. "Shall we ride? Shall we ride and ride forever?"

Kell twisted his long lovely neck before her and drew breath into his lungs and lengthened his stride. The old man looked on, nodding approval, unsurprised. The wind began to gust on Echo's cheeks, stinging her eyes, and the trees down the track came dancing towards her. There was no bumping, no juddering. She was like the mane on Kell's neck, she flew free but never far. She was part of him, and they were racing over the land.

Never anything like this before, not even swinging through the trees at home. The power of the horse had become her power, his heartbeat thundered in her blood. Together they could sail the world like a cloud blown on the wind. She looked up as this thought came to her and saw the clouds above, and she felt her body shift weight once more so that she remained responsive to the horse's rhythms. She no longer looked to see where they were going. The sensation was extraordinary. The great mass of winter sky, shifting its grand gray continents above, moved with her own body here below, wild as a bird and unafraid.

Why did I ever fall off? she wondered. To fall now would take such a deliberate effort, such a perverse determination to overbalance. It was as easy as walking. Walking demands a thousand tiny shifts of the muscles with every step, but staying upright is natural—the body can be trusted to do it without being asked. It's falling that's unnatural. So she felt now, riding Kell. She needed no skill but trust.

She closed her eyes and rode blind, feeling Kell sweep round in a long curving turn, leaning her body the way it must lean to flow with him on the turn. He was cantering more slowly now, and all of her skin was tingling with the wind and the speed. She heard the pull and blow of his breathing, and the catacat-catacat of his hooves pounding the earth. Then he was slowing to a trot, then to a walk, tossing his head, and whiffling with his nose.

She opened her eyes.

They were back before the old man.

"You turn out to be a fine rider," he said.

She smiled, her eyes still far away and dreamy from the intoxication of the ride.

"Thank you for showing me how to ride."

"Oh, my dear." He raised his arms in a delightful shrug. "Thank you for being so lovely."

"I think I must go back now."

"Yes, yes. Off you go."

Echo patted the side of Kell's neck, and Kell started to move. As they went, Echo twisted round for one last look at the old man.

"Who are you?" she called back.

"They call me Jango," he replied, and he waved his sitting-stick in the air to bid her farewell.

Now Kell was moving fast. Down the track they rode, back the way they had come, and the tumbledown wall and the old man who waited beside it passed out of sight.

As she rode, it struck Echo how easy it would be now to turn and head back west to the Glimmen. For a few moments the temptation was very strong. Never had her modest tree-bound world of home seemed so sweet to her. She thought of her father at work on his homemade furniture, beaming with pride at the way he contrived to make his couches both comfortable and light. She thought of her mother devising new color schemes for the living room and concluding, reluctantly but happily, that new curtains were needed yet again. Her parents had always seemed ridiculous to her; but now she saw and felt what she had not understood before, that in the outward form of furnishings, they filled their treetop rooms with love.

"I'll be back," she said aloud.

But not yet. Not with an Orlan army at her heels, under orders to burn the Glimmen. First she must find the Nomana, who alone had the power to humble the Great Jahan.

THE SECOND STAGE
IN THE TRAINING OF
THE NOMANA

SEEKING

*In which the novice goes on a journey
to encounter the unknown.*

⇥ 9 ⇤

Back from the Dead

THE SPIKER CHILDREN FOUND THE FUNNY ASLEEP ON A mound of fallen leaves by the side of a stream. They could tell he was a Funny because his clothes were all torn and his face was scratched and streaked with mud. They gathered round to stare at him and nudged each other and giggled.

"Let's wake him up. Let's make him dance."

"No, don't. He'll curse us."

"I want to see him do his funny dance."

The boldest of them found a stick and poked the Funny until he emerged from his sleep, while the others stood well back. The Funny swatted the air with sleepy fists, and then he grumbled and said, "Leave off, old lady. Leave off."

The spiker children shrieked with laughter.

"Old lady! He said old lady!"

Their laughter woke the Funny, and he jumped to his feet and roared at them. He was tall, taller than they'd expected, and he had goggly eyes, and his roar was like an animal's. They scattered into the trees, still laughing. The Funny thrashed the air with his fists and then fell silent, peering crossly round him.

"Yah, Funny!" shouted the children. "Loony old Funny!"

They picked up stones and threw them at him.

"Make him growl some more!"

"Make him dance!"

The stones maddened the Funny. He set off at a loping gallop through the trees, and the children ran from him, squealing. They thought he was chasing them, but when he caught up with them, he went crashing past, heading for the beach. They realized then that he was running away from them. This made them bolder.

"Come on! Let's get him! He's trapped now!"

They followed the Funny out of the trees and onto the wide pebbly beach. It was high tide on a windy day, and the waves were rolling in and breaking in cascades of creamy foam. The Funny ran right into an oncoming wave and got drenched, then staggered back, bewildered. The children picked up pebbles, and when he turned to come back up the beach, they threw the pebbles at him, some of which struck him.

The Funny came to a stop and waved his hands in the air and made a low groaning sound.

"Yah, Funny!" yelled the children. "Dance!"

They threw more pebbles at him. He turned aside to

protect his face from being hit. Another wave came rolling in and broke over him. He uttered a great roar. Then, to the children's delight, he began to dance.

Filka, who had once been a goatboy, who had once heard voices in his head, began to dance. It was all he could do when the world became too unkind. His dance never brought back the sweetness that for a time had been given to him, but it made it possible to stop feeling the hurt of his life. The dance began with spinning. Round and round he went, arms outstretched, feeling the splash of the salt water and hearing the mocking laughter of the children. Then, as the spinning became faster and faster, he started to wail and then to jump, working himself up into a frenzy. Round and round, eyes open but seeing only a blur of sky, wailing turning to howling, long body convulsing, Filka drove himself faster and faster, seeking the trance.

As a wave cascaded over him, another wave broke in his head, washing through his mouth and nose and eyes and ears, and the trance came. He went on spinning, no longer consciously exerting himself, and he uttered no more cries. His mouth hung open, and his eyeballs rolled upwards in his head, and he smiled as he went round and round.

"He's dancing! He's dancing!"

The children laughed and shouted and spun round and round themselves, in imitation of the Funny. Then the laughter stopped.

Sweeping towards them on an incoming wave was a

black bobbing shape. Up it rose on the wave, and they saw arms reaching out, a white face. Screaming, they ran back.

"Dead man! Dead man!"

The sea threw the dead man straight at the Funny, knocking him down as he danced. And then the great wave sucked and growled and drew away. There on the hissing beach lay the dead man, his arms wrapped round the Funny, who lay beneath him.

"He's come for him!" squealed the children. "The dead man's come to take the Funny away!"

The Funny was struggling now, pushing himself out from under the sodden weight. He pulled himself free and stood up, but giddy from his spinning, he fell again, and his hands reached down to break his fall. His fists sank into the soft gut of the drowned man, and out of the drowned man's throat shot a squirt of seawater.

"Yeck!" screamed the watching children. "Oh, yeck!"

Then a new wave rolled over both the Funny and the dead man, hiding them from view. When it sucked back again, the children saw an astonishing sight. The Funny had hold of the dead man by one hand, and the dead man was rising up. He was moving. He was alive.

"He's made him alive! The Funny touched the dead man, and he's made him alive!"

They all saw it, with their own eyes. There on the wave-battered shore, a miracle had taken place. Awed, eager to tell the news, the children turned and ran back towards the camp where their families were waiting.

———

The Wildman woke from a dream of trying to run and not being able to make his legs move. He knew he must run, but it was so hard; they were holding him with their great hands, they wouldn't let him go.

"Let me go! Let me go!" he cried.

Then he woke. His arm was being jerked. There was thunder behind him. He was choking and couldn't breathe. He convulsed, bringing his knees up to his chest, and he vomited, again and again, pumping bitter juice from every cavity in his body.

Water crashed over him. Fear gave strength to his shattered limbs. He heaved his head out of the shallow sea and staggered to his feet and drove himself, step by heavy step, up the beach to dry land.

Here he collapsed and lay pulling in long bubbly breaths. A face loomed over him, the face of a puzzled youth of his own age.

"You was dead," said the youth, eyes solemn wide. "You was dead. Now you're alive."

In the spiker camp, no one paid much attention to the children at first. They were overexcited and ran about shouting something about a dead man, but their mothers were busy skinning an ox, and their fathers were building a fire to work iron to mend the wagon wheels, so no one was listening. It was only later, over the noon meal, that the story began to come out. Of course the grown-ups didn't believe a word of it. But the children all told the same story, and seemed so sure of what they'd seen, that a group of grown-ups agreed to go with them to the beach, to see for themselves.

The beach was empty.

The children said, "He's taken him into the trees." They ran into the trees, calling as they went. "Heya, Funny! Where are you?"

They found him back where he had been sleeping before, on the mound of leaves by the stream. The dead man was with him, his back propped up against a tree. The Funny was giving him water from the stream, in a tin cup.

The children pointed. The grown-ups gathered round. They questioned the Funny.

"This man you have here. Where did you find him?"

"Came out of the sea," said the Funny, avoiding their eyes.

"He was a dead man," piped up a child.

"That so? Was he a dead man?"

"Dead and drowned," said the Funny.

"Not dead now, is he?"

"Not dead now."

"He touched him!" cried the child. "He touched him, and he made him alive!"

"Is that so? Did you make him alive?"

The Funny frowned and pondered. Then after a few moments he nodded.

"That's it," he said. "I made him alive."

The spikers now fell silent in awe. They looked on as the dead man sipped water, and they saw his eyelids flicker, and his chest move slowly with his breaths. Everyone had heard of the strange powers that went with being a Funny.

Mostly it was telling fortunes, or putting on small curses. This was the first time they had heard of a Funny bringing a dead man back to life.

They became respectful.

"We have meat back at the camp," they said. "Will you eat with us?"

The Funny felt it at once, the change of tone, and understood that it was connected with the dead man.

"And him, too?" he said, nodding at the limp figure.

"We'll carry him."

They made a simple stretcher out of branches and carried him back to the camp. The Funny followed behind.

The Wildman slipped in and out of a half sleep, too weak to speak. He saw trees going by, and clouds beyond the bare branches, and he felt a lurching motion and heard voices. Then he knew he was being lowered to the ground. He felt the blessed heat of a fire. Turning his head, he located the flicker of flames. His soaked, chilled body shivered as sensation began to return to his skin. He smelled roasting meat.

Hands pulled at him, hoisting him to a sitting position. A piece of cooked meat was pushed into his mouth, but his tongue was thick and heavy, and his jaw couldn't move. The meat fell from his numb lips.

"Soup," a voice said. "Give him soup."

Now a ladle was at his mouth, and a warm rich broth was trickling down his throat. He choked, but he swallowed. The soup pooled in his belly and warmed him. He opened his eyes, tried to smile his thanks.

A spiker woman was stooping before him, looking intently into his face.

"I know you," she said. "You're the Wildman."

The Wildman could only blink in reply, but what he blinked was yes. The spiker woman stood up and called out in a loud voice.

"It's the Wildman! We've got the Wildman!"

"Not so wild any more," shrugged the old woman by the pot.

"And guess who wants the Wildman, eh?"

This produced laughter. Everyone, it seemed, knew the answer.

When the Wildman next woke, unaware that he had fallen asleep, he found himself in motion, on the bed of a wagon jolting down a stony road. He lay still and looked up at the sky. The dull winter day was drawing to a close. He tried to lift himself up but found he was still too weak. But at least his mind was now clear.

Where am I?

He remembered standing on the high wall of the Nom. He remembered his dive. He remembered that moment of perfect stillness as he fell.

If I could live like that forever, he thought. If I could dive forever.

He twisted his head and saw the dangling legs of the man driving the wagon, and the rolling flank of the cart-ox beyond. He could hear other footsteps too, treading the path alongside the wagon. Judging by the openness of the view, they were east of the Great River, most likely in the hill country. That was Morning Star's country. She was one of the hill people. He recalled her friendly face, with its puzzled gaze. Then he remembered Seeker, his one true friend.

But that's all over now, he thought. Our ways have parted forever.

Then they were leaving the road and rumbling over a streambed. He could hear the splashing of the wagon wheels in the water. The wagon entered a tunnel. The rock roof of the tunnel was not far above his head. He could see the water dripping down its sloping sides, and the sleek green weeds growing there. Then there was daylight again, and a crisscross of shadow breaking the light, and the wagon lurched to a stop.

Voices all round him called out, harsh threatening voices. The ones who had accompanied him answered, laughing, confident.

"That's it, throw us out! But see what we've got first."

Now once more the Wildman felt himself lifted and carried a short distance. When he was set down, he was on the ground, but his back was against a timber wall, and for the first time, he could get a proper look at where he was.

He was in a hollow in a hillside, the walls formed of rock and grass, with a roof built over it of interlaced branches. Bramble and bracken were woven into the branches, to create a cover that was in no way wind- or rainproof, but was designed to conceal the space beneath. The Wildman recognized the style. He had been in many such hides in his younger days. This was a bandit camp.

Within the hollow, on either side of the stream, there

were several huts walled with wattles and thatched with straw. Between the huts a fire was burning, with wet wood baffles above to break up the smoke. The camp was well made and well hidden, and judging by the number of men and youths standing staring at him, it was the home of a large band.

One of the youths came close, to peer at him. The Wildman realized with astonishment that he recognized him.

"Shab!" he said, his tongue thick in his mouth.

"Is it really you, Wildman?" said Shab, shocked.

The Wildman gave a feeble nod.

"Is it true you've come back from the dead?"

Again he nodded.

Shab backed away, as if he were face-to-face with an unnatural being.

"Shouldn't have done that, Wildman," he said. "Dead should stay dead."

"The Funny did it," put in one of the spikers who had come with the wagon.

"Never known anything like it," said another.

"Better tell the chief."

Shab gave a surly shrug.

"Dead should stay dead," he muttered.

"If the chief finds out, it'll be you who'll be dead."

"Finds out what?"

"That we had the Wildman here and we let him go."

"Who's letting him go? Look at him! Like a drowned cat. He's not going anywhere."

"So you'll tell the chief."

Shab shrugged again. The Wildman had followed this exchange without understanding why Shab was showing so much reluctance. Back in the old days of Spikertown, he and Shab had run together for weeks at a time. Why now wish him dead? If he had been stronger, he'd have smacked Shab round the head and it would all have been settled soon enough.

"Heya, Shab," he said weakly.

Shab turned his back on him. He gestured to his companions, saying, "Put him in the rest house. I'll tell the chief."

The Wildman was picked up by two of the band, one on each side, his arms round their shoulders, and heaved into one of the huts. Here there was a bunk piled with straw. They laid the Wildman down, then left him alone in the shadows. Outside the hollow, dusk was gathering. Here, beneath the double roof of canopy and thatch, there was almost no light at all.

He closed his eyes. Shab will tell the chief, he thought, and the chief will come, and he'll explain to me what's going on.

And after that? The Wildman had no plans after that. He had fled the Nom in fear of the cleansing and because they hadn't wanted him there. But he had no new destination. Maybe he would go far, far away.

He heard footsteps approaching, then the swish of the door curtain as someone entered the small dark space of the rest house. He turned to look, but all he could see was a black figure against the deep shadows.

"You the chief?" he said.

"That's right." It was a woman's voice: one he knew well. "Remember me?"

"Caressa?"

"Always knew you'd come back."

She turned in the doorway and called out, "Light!"

"You don't want to see me, Princess."

"What's this about you being dead?"

"I don't know. Maybe I was dead."

"And now you're back."

A burning stick was handed through the doorway. Caressa carried the flame to where the Wildman lay, and by its flickering light, she studied him. He too looked at her. In the months since he had last seen her, she had become even more handsome. The mass of dark hair framed big black eyes, broad cheeks, full lips: but there was an authority in her that had not been there before. Caressa had always been demanding. Now she had the look of one who expected to have her demands met.

"Those are hoodie clothes you're wearing," she said.

"Yes."

"You a hoodie, Wildman?"

"Not any more."

"Let's get you some dry clothes."

She gave orders to the unseen men outside the door. Then she knelt down by the Wildman's side and brushed his long wet hair with her fingers, as the flame crackled on the burning stick.

"They sucked you dry, Wildman. They turned you into dust."

"I'm back now, Princess."

"Back from the dead."

The clothes came.

"You need help?"

"No," said the Wildman, ashamed to be dressed by others.

Caressa left him alone in the hut, with the burning stick stuck in the earth floor. The Wildman heaved himself up into a sitting position and explored his limbs. He raised first one arm, then the other. His strength was returning.

Moving slowly, resting between each move, he peeled off his wet clothing and dressed himself in the borrowed garments. The flickering flame dwindled and went out. He finished dressing in darkness. Then he drew back the door cloth and sat watching the scene in the campsite outside.

It was dark now, and the members of the band were gathered round the fire holding pieces of meat on the points of their knives, roasting them in the glowing embers. The firelight played on their faces, and their quiet voices drifted across the hollow with the smoke. It was the kind of scene that the Wildman had been part of all his life, before he became a hoodie. Now, looking from outside at that ring of firelight and comradeship, he felt a sudden ache of longing for the old days.

Always was a no-good, he thought. Always was a bandit. This is where I belong.

He saw Caressa's high beauty as she moved among her men, and Shab's face as he looked up at her, seeking signs of favor that would never come. Easy to understand now why Shab didn't want him to return from the dead. But the Wildman knew Shab had no chance. There was too much longing in his face. That was the kind of look that made Caressa cruel.

So now she was the chief.

The Wildman laughed softly to himself. Good for her, he thought. Caressa the spiker queen, and no king any-where to be seen.

She turned then, as if drawn by his thoughts of her, and sensed that he was watching from the darkness of the hut. She left the fire and came to where he sat.

"Come to the light. Let's see you."

"Soon," he said.

So she sat with him, while her band roasted goat meat and drank brandy and bantered round the fire. Only Shab did not join in. He glanced round from time to time, his gaze reaching into the shadows where they sat, and kept a bottle of brandy to himself.

"So how's Shab doing?" said the Wildman.

"Shab's good," said Caressa.

"He's there for you, Princess. If you want it."

"So he is, if I want it. But I don't."

"You got other plans?"

"I said I'd wait for you, Wildman. And so I have."

She spoke softly, just a whisper in the night, but there was no tremble in her voice. The Wildman marvelled at her certainty.

"You don't want me no more, Princess."

"Why's that?"

"I've been away too long. There's not as much of me as there was."

"Maybe I don't mind about that."

"You're the chief now, Princess. You want more than I can give you."

"Maybe I do. And maybe I'll get it, too. But I always wanted you, Wildman. Since I was nine years old. And I always will."

Shab now rose from the fire and came over to them.

"You looking at me, Wildman?" he said.

"Some," said the Wildman.

"Back off, Shab," said Caressa.

"Nobody looks at me that way," said Shab. "Not unless he wants to do more than look."

"Go and lie down, Shab," said Caressa. "You're drunk."

"You want to do more than look, Wildman? Or are you getting too old and wise?"

"Don't do this, Shab," said the Wildman quietly.

"Seems like I'm doing it," said Shab.

"Look at him!" said Caressa, now angry. "He near died. How can he fight you? Shame on you, Shab. Wait till he's strong again."

"There's no place for him here," said Shab stubbornly. "He goes or he fights. That's my right."

"Best to get it over with," said the Wildman. "Give me a hand, Princess."

"I won't allow this."

"You must," said the Wildman. "You're the chief."

It was every man's right among the bandits for his quarrels to be settled man to man, under the eye of the chief. Caressa gave him her hand because she had no choice, but as she did so, she shook her dark mane with anger.

The Wildman rose and found his balance. He was so weak that one push would send him back to the ground. But maybe that would be no bad thing. Maybe if Shab forced him to his knees, Caressa would see him as he truly was, not as she had dreamed him when still a child.

He took one step forward and so came into the light. Caressa was gazing at him, and he caught a sudden smile on her face. It was his clothes. He looked down at himself and saw gaudy red and bright blue and flashes of gold thread. He was a bandit again.

Shab stood before him, flexing his arms and bouncing lightly from foot to foot. The others in the band, now aware there was going to be a fight, came and gathered round.

"This settles nothing, Shab," said Caressa, her voice sharp with anger.

"It's my right," replied Shab.

"Then get on with it. I'm tired of it all."

Shab took one step forward, to within striking distance. The Wildman stood still, arms loose by his sides. Without being aware of it, he had adopted the Tranquil Alert.

"You ready?" said Shab.

"I'm ready."

Shab stared at him, shaking with hatred. The Wildman looked back, amazed by the hatred, himself empty of all passion. He found he could read Shab's intentions long before he acted on them.

Shab lunged out with one fist.

The Wildman acted on instinct. Not moving a muscle, he flooded Shab's will with his own will. Shab's blow stopped short.

Shab struck again and again, and missed each time. The watching men began to laugh. Shab turned a deep red and threw himself into a hurricane of blows. Not one landed. The Wildman stood there, his eyes on Shab's, and never moved.

The laughter became loud and mocking. The Wildman realized he must end it now, for Shab's sake. He raised two fingers and, without touching him, forced Shab to his knees, then forced his head to bow down where he knelt.

The laughter died. None of them had ever seen such an absolute demonstration of power. Shab stayed kneeling, silent, defeated, humiliated. Caressa's eyes shone.

"Still the best, Wildman," she said. "And only the best is good enough for me."

The Wildman said nothing. It seemed he was still a Noma, whether he wanted it or not. He possessed the power, but he was not subject to the Rule. He could use his power for anything he chose.

The prospect did not excite him. He was weary and confused and couldn't say what it was he wanted.

Maybe he'd know tomorrow.

Moving with slow care, he went back into the rest house and felt for his discarded clothing. Now he was dressed in the bold flaunting colors of the bandits and had no need of the plain gray garments. He carried the bundle of wet clothing to the fire, and one by one he burned the fragments of his recent past.

But he kept his badan.

⊰ 10 ⊱

The Lords of Wisdom

SEEKER LAY IN THE DARKNESS OF THE UNDERGROUND room in the Nom and waited for the Community to reach its decision. Whatever that decision was, he knew that he would obey. What use were his new powers to him except in the service of the All and Only?

Then at last, late in the night, he heard a key turn in the lock of the heavy door and the creak of the door as it opened. A soft ray of light flowed into the room. Seeker jumped to his feet, expecting the return of the Elder.

It was Narrow Path, carrying a lantern.

He closed the door behind him but did not lock it. The light from the lantern threw deep shadows upwards over his bony face, giving it the look of a skull.

"Has the Community decided?" said Seeker.

"Yes."

Narrow Path held up his lantern and looked round the

room, to assure himself that they were alone. Satisfied, he turned his attention to Seeker.

"You are to be cleansed in the morning."

Seeker felt a shock go through him. He bowed his head in the sign of obedience; but as the shock passed, in its place came a secret stir of rebellion.

"The Community has decided my powers are too dangerous?"

"It has been so decided. After long debate."

"The Elder, too?"

"The Elder has been told that one of your friends has fled from the Nom. He was shocked to hear it. He took it as a sign."

"So it is," said Seeker. "The Wildman was my responsibility. The Elder told me so when we were both admitted to the Nom. He's gone, and so I must go."

With his words he seemed to accept the verdict, but in his heart he was not obedient. He did not want to be cleansed.

"Such is the decision of the Community," said Narrow Path. "But I believe that decision to be wrong."

"Wrong!"

"I am not here on the instructions of the Elder or the Community. I am here to save the Nom."

Seeker looked at the gaunt face of the Noma in astonishment. Narrow Path, so well known for his austere and unwavering observance of the Rule, was the last member of the Community he would expect to break the vow of obedience.

"How?"

"The first time you entered the Nom," said Narrow Path, "before you were a novice, I was the one who found you."

"I remember."

"I feared it even then," said Narrow Path. "I wanted it not to be so. I wanted to believe you were no more than a disobedient child, snooping where you had no business to go. But I was wrong. You are the one we've been waiting for. You have come to save us."

Seeker no longer knew what to think. Narrow Path spoke the very words that were always before him. But if Narrow Path knew this, why did the Elder not know it, too?

"We are in mortal danger," said Narrow Path. "Our enemy is preparing to strike."

Shock upon shock: Seeker could only stare.

"How do I know these things? Because you have come. You would not have been revealed to us unless the need was desperate."

"But what am I?" said Seeker, struggling to understand. "Who am I?"

"You? You are nobody. You have no significance. All that matters is that you have been given the power, and that you use it."

He came very close to Seeker and whispered with a terrible intensity. "You must kill our enemy."

"Who is our enemy?"

"The old enemy who has stalked us through the years and has sworn to destroy us."

"The Assassin?"

"The Assassin is a legend. The Assassin may be the name given to the one who strikes. But the orders come from the true enemy."

Again Seeker asked, "Who is this enemy?"

"I will show you."

Narrow Path then turned the covered lantern to the wall so that its light no longer fell on him, and he took Seeker's hands in his. Seeker understood that this was not a gesture of fellowship. The older man was passing on a part of himself through touch.

"Look up."

Seeker looked up.

"Memories of memories," said Narrow Path.

There above in the darkness a group of ghostly figures slowly appeared. There were seven of them, kneeling in a ring. Impossible to tell whether they were men or women, but from the stoop of their backs and the slowness of their movements, it was clear they were very old.

"This is not my memory. I share with you a memory of the Community."

"I see them."

"Now look more closely."

Seeker tried to make out the figures in the darkness, but they were insubstantial as smoke. Then, as he stared, they gained definition, and he saw that there were other indistinct figures forming a kneeling circle round them, resting their hands on the shoulders of the old people and bowing down their heads on their outstretched arms. Round this kneeling circle knelt a wider circle, their hands on the shoulders of those before them, their heads too resting on their arms; and yet more who knelt beyond; and so the ever-widening circles, linked by touch, disappeared into the shadows.

Seeker stared at the faces of those in the outer circles and saw that they were not old like the seven at the center. They were gaunt and pale, with unblinking eyes and white bloodless lips.

His gaze travelled back through the rings to the seven old people kneeling at the center. As he reached them it seemed to him that they turned their faces towards him and studied him with their ancient indifferent eyes.

"Who are they?" he asked.

"They call themselves savanters. The lords of wisdom."

"And who are those gathered round them?"

"The ones who give them life. The savanters are old—too old to live—and yet they live."

"And do they still live today?"

"Still today. Each life is sustained by many other lives. It's a kind of immortality."

"And they are our enemy?"

"They have sworn to destroy us."

He passed one hand through the air and the ghostly images faded away.

"Can they do that?"

"They are old, but they use the strength of others. They can turn armies against us. We have great powers, but our powers have limits."

"But I," said Seeker slowly, "am different."

"Yes."

"Am I stronger than them?"

"That is what you will find out."

"But I'm to be cleansed." The folly of this decision at such a time of danger bewildered him. "Why? Why doesn't the Community use my powers to protect the Nom?"

"Maybe there are those who don't want to protect the Nom."

"What! In the Community?"

"There's a traitor in the Nom. I've suspected it for some time. I believe this traitor, following the orders of the savanters, has caused the Community to make the wrong decision."

"Even the Elder!"

"The savanters have great power."

Seeker looked at the burning eyes of his informant and felt how intensely Narrow Path was willing him to believe in his words. For this very reason, he felt sudden doubt. Why should Narrow Path alone see how his powers must be used?

"You're thinking," said Narrow Path, "that I might be the traitor."

"How can I be sure of anything?"

"If I'm the traitor, if I'm lying to you, if the Elder and the Community are right and wise—then tomorrow you will be cleansed. The door you now see opening before you will be slammed shut."

No! cried Seeker in his heart. My whole life, my struggle to be accepted as a Noble Warrior, my training and my power, it must all be for a purpose. The voices that have spoken to me, the words of the Elder, my own deepest instincts—all tell me I have a task to do that's not yet done. I can't let the door close on my life.

Surely you know that where your way lies, the door is always open.

Narrow Path was watching and waiting.

"Where is this enemy?" said Seeker.

A glint of triumph flashed in Narrow Path's sharp eyes. "You believe me."

"I believe there's more I must do."

"You must leave tonight, while the Community sleeps. You must travel fast. There are armies on the march. We have very little time. As to where you're to go—you've heard of the great forest called the Glimmen?"

Seeker nodded.

"Follow the high road through the Glimmen. Where the trees end you'll see a band of mist lying low over the ground. They call it the land cloud. Go into the cloud."

"I'll find them there?"

"Find them. And kill them. Don't hesitate. Kill them all."

"And if I fail?"

Narrow Path shrugged. "The day of the Noble Warriors will be over."

He took up his lantern.

"Wait for two hours at least. I'll leave this door unlocked. As for the other gates, each one has a gatekeeper. Your will is stronger than the will of a gatekeeper."

He turned to go.

"Wait," said Seeker.

Narrow Path stopped, his eyes cast down.

"Who else has the key to this door?"

"No one else," said Narrow Path.

"So the Community will know it's you who sets me free."

"They will know."

"And what will become of you?"

Narrow Path looked up then, and on his gaunt face there appeared a wry smile.

"Each of us serves in our own way," he said. "I give what I have to give."

With that he left, and the cell was plunged once more into darkness.

Morning Star lay on her hard bed, unable to sleep. In her mind, over and over again, she saw the Wildman dive. In her mind, she called out to him, "Don't go! Wait for me!" as she had wanted to do at the time. But she had not dared to speak. She saw that long lean body flashing down into the mist, so pure and beautiful, so alive. How could he be dead? Though her reason told her no man could survive such a fall, her heart cried out that he was still living. And she—was she living? This no longer felt like life. Shut off from the one source of comfort, the Loving Mother in the Garden, driven away by her own terrors, her own worth-lessness, what was left to her in the Nom? Even Seeker, dear good Seeker, had been taken away for some unknown purpose.

I must go, too.

Not in search of some new goal, but to escape the burden of failure that weighed her down here on Anacrea.

I'm like my mother after all, she thought. I don't deserve to be a Noble Warrior. I live too close to the edge of madness.

Better to leave and go back to the mainland and build a new life for herself. And if the Wildman were still alive—

She left her bed and felt in the darkness for the little bundle of lamb's wool her father had given her when she left home. She had no other possession in the world. Even her clothes belonged to the Nom.

Moving with soft steps, she left the room and padded down the passage to the open air of the courtyard. On the far side was the door that led out to the Nom square. The door was locked. A gatekeeper dozed beside it.

For the first time, it struck Morning Star that she could not leave the Nom even if she wanted to. The Community would have to authorize her departure. And for that, she would have to be cleansed.

Her courage left her. Despairing, she sat down on the ground and put her head in her hands and wished she was home again with her father and mother and the dogs, gentle Amik and eager Lamb. She wished she was on the hillside with the flock. She wished she was little again.

Seeker waited until silence filled the great castle-monastery. Then he felt his way in the darkness to the unlocked door and followed the rock passage to the flight of steps. At the top of the steps was a door that was also unlocked, no doubt left that way by Narrow Path. Beyond the door, he found himself at last in the cold night air. It was a moonless night, but after the dark of the underground room, his eyes found light enough to know that he was in the lesser courtyard of the Community quarters. Facing him was the washhouse where they planned to cleanse him in the morning.

He crossed the raked pebbles, treading lightly, and passed down the Chapter Passage to the novitiate. The iron-barred gate in the stone arch ahead was closed. Beside it dozed a sleepy meek.

Seeker touched the meek on the arm to wake him.

"Open the gate," he whispered.

The meek blinked and stared at him.

"I've no orders to open the gate in the night," he said.

"Look at me."

The meek stared at Seeker. His blinking slowed and stopped.

"Yes, I do have orders," he said. "Somehow I had forgotten them."

He unlocked the gate and Seeker passed through into the novitiate. Moving rapidly, he made his way into the cloistered courtyard, heading for the exit door. There, curled up by the wall, was Morning Star.

"Star!" he whispered. "What are you doing?"

She looked up, and the unhappiness in her face shocked him.

"Where are you going?" she said.

"Away. I can't explain."

"The door's locked."

"The door will be opened for me."

She jumped up and seized his hand.

"Take me with you."

"I can't."

"No, Seeker, no!" She sounded as if she was going to burst into tears at any moment. "Don't make me stay here. Not if you're both gone."

The gatekeeper woke, then rubbed his eyes.

"What's this?" he grumbled. "What's going on?"

"Open the door," said Seeker. "As you've been ordered."

The gatekeeper frowned.

"Ordered?" he said. Then, "Yes. Ordered."

He took out a key and unlocked the door and opened it. Seeker passed through into the square outside, and Morning Star followed. The door closed behind them. It was the door through which they had first entered, the door with no handle.

Seeker turned to Morning Star.

"I shouldn't have let you leave, too. You've not had permission to leave."

"Have you had permission to leave?"

He shook his head. She was right. He too was breaking his vow.

"But you can't go where I'm going."

"I know that." She gave him that look of hers that he knew so well, that told him she understood him. "I've always known that."

"What will you do?"

"Look for him."

There was no need to say who she meant.

"He's dead. No one could make a dive like that and live."

"Maybe." But on her face there was a stubborn look that said she was going to go her own way nonetheless. "Come on."

Ahead rose the avenue of ancient pines that Seeker had known all his life. To the left were the steps that ran down the terraced streets all the way to the harbor. Morning Star was already beginning the long descent. Seeker followed.

When they reached the street where his home stood, he came to a stop.

"Wait for me. I won't be long."

Morning Star understood. He hadn't seen his parents for nine months. Who knew what dangers lay ahead, or whether he would ever see them again?

They padded along the dark terraced street, past the low wall where she had crouched and wept so long ago, where she had first touched hands with Seeker and had seen the sparkle of gold that shimmered round him.

When they reached his house, she waited in the street. Seeker found the front-door key in the crevice in the wall where it always lay, and he let himself into the silent house.

His eyes were now fully adjusted to the darkness, and though there was almost no light, he could make out enough to find his way through the familiar rooms. The house was not big, and it was simply furnished. There was the long narrow table, piled with books. There the outdoor coats hanging on hooks on the wall. There the worn wooden armchair in which his father always sat. There the basket for fetching the morning bread.

He climbed the short flight of stairs, knowing every twist of the handrail, avoiding the fifth tread because it squeaked, touching the projecting nail at the top. Ahead, his own tiny bedroom, its door closed. To the right, his parents' room.

For the first time since he had left home, it struck him that the house must be quieter, perhaps sadder, with both Blaze and himself gone. The child grows up and moves on to the challenge of a new life. But for the parents, there is no new life, only the old life, but emptier.

Their bedroom door was open. No need to close it at night when they were the only ones in the house. He stepped into the room, and there they were, lying side by side in the wooden bed, the covers drawn up tight round them. They were both deeply asleep, his mother on her side, facing his father; his father on his back. Seeker stood still and heard their breathing, listening carefully until he could distinguish his mother's more rapid breaths from his father's long slow exhalations. He looked at their faces.

His mother seemed peaceful, and younger than he remembered, her cheek smooth, her lips very slightly parted. His father, by contrast, looked older, the skin pulled more tightly over the bones of his face. All his childhood these two had been the lords of his life, his guides and protectors, the ones whose existence alone gave him the promise that all would be well. And now here they were, asleep and growing old, the same as ever and yet vulnerable, dear to him but already slipping into his past.

"I love you," he whispered. "I'll always love you."

His mother stirred in her sleep, perhaps hearing the murmur in the night, but she didn't wake. He dared not touch them, though he longed to do so. If they woke they wouldn't understand. They would try to stop him going away. So he kissed his own hand instead and then held it over them, giving them his kiss in their sleep.

"Good-bye."

So, he left them and returned to the night street.

Morning Star saw the soft violet shimmer round him and touched his arm. He was trembling. She put her arms round him, and he did the same, hugging her close. They remained like this for a few moments; then they parted and made their way to the steps, and so down to the port.

Neither of them had considered the matter of getting off the island in the middle of the night, a time when no boatmen sailed. But here was a small fishing boat moored by the quay, with a boatman asleep on his own bundle of fishing nets, beneath a tarpaulin.

Seeker nudged him awake.

"You're to take us to the mainland," he said. "As you said you would."

The boatman pushed his hands through his hair and shook his head. He was clearly about to protest that he had said no such thing, when it seemed to him that he had.

"Said I would, did I?"

"You did."

"Then, that's what I'll do."

They climbed into his boat, and the boatman cast off. The wind had dropped and the waters were calm. He

unshipped the oars and rowed across the narrow channel
to the mainland.

"There you are," he said, still puzzled. "If I say I'll do
a thing, then I do it."

"Thank you," said Seeker. "But you've already forgotten all about it."

He and Morning Star set off up the steeply rising shore
to the level land beyond. Here they paused for a moment
and looked back at the looming hulk of the island. Anacrea
rose out of the glimmering sea, its rocky sides, its walls and
houses, the roofs and domes of the Nom at the top, all
outlined against the night sky. Seeker lingered. Morning
Star, chilled by the cold night air, wanted to be walking.

"Come on."

Seeker nearly told her why he looked back for so long.
But it was only a feeling. There was no basis for it, and almost certainly it wasn't true. So he said nothing. After one
last look, he turned his back on the island and strode off
across the land.

He had been seized with the sudden premonition that
he would never see Anacrea again.

⊰ 11 ⊱

Kneeling and Standing

THE IMPERIAL AXERS MARCHED OUT OF RADIANCE IN full armor, eight abreast. Their looped chains clinked in their belt hooks as they strode slowly forward, swinging their huge armored legs, pausing with each third step in the slow ceremonial parade. Each one carried a shiny polished axe in a holster on his right thigh. They wore their parade breastplates, etched with intricate designs, and their parade helmets, topped with scarlet plumes. Rank upon rank wound its solemn way through the city gates, watched and cheered by the people of Radiance. This was not an army going into battle; this was a guard of honor. They cheered from the city walls because they were saved from destruction. Somehow, no one knew how, a solution had been found. Their king, Radiant Leader, was to greet the new warlord as a friend. There was to be no war.

"He's given in," said some. "He'll kneel to the warlord."

"Never," said others. "Radiant Leader is the favored son of the Great Power above. He submits to no man."

The long column of axers came to a halt on the high road west. The order sounded for the ranks to part by three paces, thus forming a human corridor from the city gates all the way down the western road.

Out of the archway came a golden palanquin, carried by sixteen scarlet-robed priests. In the palanquin, partially obscured by the golden curtains that flapped in the breeze, rode Radiant Leader, his head framed by a massive corona of artificial sunflowers fashioned from hammered gold.

Amroth Jahan had learned that morning that the priest-king of the city of Radiance was proposing to present himself in his full glory.

"He can come with the sun in a bucket for all I care," he said, "so long as he kneels to me."

Echo Kittle, riding now with the Jahan's entourage, saw the parade of the imperial axers and wondered very much how the king of such a magnificent army could bear to make a public submission. She herself, with no followers of any kind, still burned with shame each time she thought of how she had knelt and submitted. Then she remembered how the Jahan too had been made to kneel, when he faced the Nomana on the bridge, and how he had wept before her.

"If this priest-king refuses to kneel to you," she said to the Jahan, "will you really destroy his city and all the people in it?"

"I will."

"Out of pride?"

"What I have said I will do, I will do."

"Except with the Nomana."

His ugly face went still, his craggy features set in stone.

"The Nomana too will pay the price of defying me."

With this the Great Jahan dismounted from his horse and climbed into his waiting chariot. The music makers and the mirror bearers formed up on either side. His three sons took up their positions behind him. The companies of mounted Orlans formed orderly ranks that stretched back into the distance. Amroth Jahan meant to match glory with glory.

The golden palanquin advanced between the lines of axers. Rank by rank, the axers fell to the ground, abasing themselves in advance of their Radiant Leader. The leading priest of those bearing the palanquin then intoned, "Stand before our Radiant Leader!" The prostrate axers rose up, to stand tall and motionless as their priest-king went by.

This created a ripplelike effect, as the magnificent soldiers dipped and rose again. Amroth Jahan, advancing to meet the ruler of the city, noted the perfect formation of the axers, and the mounting potency of the ruler's approach on the waves of motion, and he nodded his head in professional appreciation.

"Prettily done," he murmured to himself. To have such a king kneel to him would be satisfying.

"Stand before our Radiant Leader!"

The Jahan could hear the cries of the priests clearly now. It didn't strike him as strange that the ranks of soldiers were required to stand to show respect. He himself was advancing, standing tall in his chariot, to the sound of drums and horns, and lit by the flashing of reflected light. The front rank of his immense mounted army was moving with him, spread out on either side like the rolling surf of a sea that must sweep all before it.

Now the palanquin had reached the front rank of the axers, and the leading line had fallen to the ground and risen again. The scarlet-robed priests came to a stop and stood like statues, bearing the full weight of the palanquin. Radiant Leader could be clearly seen within, magnificently draped in cloth of gold.

Amroth Jahan led his advancing line of Orlans to within ten paces of the unmoving axers and raised his hand. At once, with perfect discipline, the entire mounted army shuddered to a halt. The Jahan then spoke to his sons, without taking his gaze from the gold curtains that fluttered in the wind.

"Ride forward to this king. Tell him I wait for him to kneel before me, as a sign of his respect for me."

All three of his sons urged their Caspians forward and trotted across the space between the two armies. Echo, mounted on Kell beside the Great Jahan's chariot, saw Sasha Jahan lean forward from his mount and speak to the king behind the gold curtains and receive an answer. Then the three sons returned to their father.

"The king asks you to stand before him," said Sasha Jahan in some confusion, "as a sign of your respect for him."

"But I am standing," said the Jahan.

"Yes, Father. I told him so."

"Will he not kneel to me?"

"The king is already kneeling, Father."

"Already kneeling?"

The Jahan now felt confused. Who here was showing respect to whom?

He flicked the traces of the Caspians harnessed to his high chariot and drove forward across the empty space to the golden palanquin. There he saw that the king was indeed kneeling, in that he was comfortably positioned with his lower legs tucked beneath his upper legs and his bottom resting on his heels.

Radiant Leader inclined his head towards the Jahan.

"We are equals," he said. "The Great Jahan does not need to stand before me."

"But I'm not—that is, I don't—"

The Jahan was nonplussed. He wished to make it clear he intended no show of respect by remaining standing, but could not think what else to do.

"The empire and the people of Radiance welcome you," said Radiant Leader. "In your honor I have ordered three days of celebration."

"But first," said the Jahan, "you must kneel—that is, submit to me—for all to see."

"Three days of feasting and games," said Radiant Leader, seeming not to have heard him. "Let your finest warriors try their strength against ours. Let our loveliest ladies delight your eyes."

"Do you or do you not," said the Jahan doggedly, "submit to me?"

"Ah, yes. The oath of allegiance. You refer to the solemn oath of allegiance."

"Yes," said the Jahan, liking the sound of this. "Your solemn oath of allegiance to me."

"The solemn oath of allegiance," said Radiant Leader, "will be the conclusion of our celebrations. It will be the climax."

"The climax? You mean it will come at the end?"

"Of course. The climax can't come at the beginning."

"But three days!" said the Jahan. "Am I to be kept waiting three days?"

"Sir," said Radiant Leader, dropping his voice to a whisper, "you and I are not common men. We are exalted above the herd. We are the principal actors on the stage of this world. Let the scene be set and the expectations of our audience prepared. Let there be a prelude, a time of mounting expectation. Then let the climax strike like thunder and lightning. Let you and I appear before the awed spectators as gods. You seek a triumph. Let this be the triumph of triumphs."

The Jahan considered this with his habitual suspicion. He was enough of a showman to appreciate the plan; and his men, he knew, would be grateful for the pleasures of the promised feast. If possible, he preferred to enter a conquered city unopposed. It left more of the service systems intact: the food suppliers, the woodcutters, the water car-

riers. Burning and slaughtering, though invaluable for es-
tablishing authority, left an unpleasant mess. Also, he reflected, he could always destroy the city after the feast.

"Very well," he said. "The Great Jahan is merciful."

"Excellent," said Radiant Leader. "It remains only to
decide the order in which you and I will enter the city.
The choice is yours, of course."

"I shall lead," declared the Jahan proudly.

"But you wouldn't want it to look as if I and my axers
were driving you before us, like sheep before a dog."

"Certainly not! You shall go before me."

"And look as if I lead, and you follow?"

"Great horns of hell! What am I to do?"

"I would suggest that we enter the city side by side.
But the choice, noble sir, is yours."

So it was done. The palanquin of Radiant Leader turned
about, and the chariot of the Great Jahan rolled slowly by
its side, and the two leaders entered the city of Radiance
together.

Echo Kittle rode into the city behind the Jahan's entourage, her mind full of the coming celebration and her
own dilemma. She memorized the route as they went, in
case she needed to escape in a hurry. The city gates were
clearly never closed. The streets were broad and lined with
imposing houses. Ahead lay the still waters of the lake.
And towering above all was the dark mass of the temple
rock, with the temple climbing its sides.

Between the temple and the lake, in the wide square
bounded by arcades, a series of large linked pavilions had

been erected. Radiant Leader climbed out of his con-
veyance, and Amroth Jahan stepped out of his chariot, and
together they entered the great tent. The Jahan's sons and
Echo dismounted and followed behind.

The Jahan was impressed. Long tables laden with food
were interspersed with cascades of bright flowers, even
now in midwinter. Lamps glowed on every pole of the
forest of supporting masts. Everywhere shone the glitter of
gold. Gold was the signature color of Radiance, and here,
in this palace of pleasure, the chairs were gold and the
tablecloths were gold and the elegantly bunched drapes
that formed the scalloped ceiling were all cloth of gold.

The Jahan felt himself mellowing. Radiant Leader, he
noted with satisfaction, was even shorter than he was himself. But he was clever. On the whole, the Jahan was forming a favorable opinion of the fellow. He was amused by
the way all who approached him averted their eyes from
his face, and murmured some low prayer. It was absurd, of
course, but it did have the effect of surrounding the priest-
king with a certain mystery. He found himself wondering
how Radiant Leader retained his hold on his people. He
took the trouble to listen for the words of the prayer, the
soft mumble that issued from the lips of everyone who
came close.

"Choose me," they were saying. "Choose me."

"What is it they want?" he asked curiously. "They ask
you to choose them. For what?"

"Ah, that." Radiant Leader now sounded grave. "The
chosen ones go to eternal life."

Then the Jahan remembered the procession in the forest.

"They go dressed in white, and singing?"

"Just so."

"But it's all nonsense, of course."

"Is it?" said Radiant Leader. "Perhaps you know more of the matter than I do."

"I only know death comes for us all."

"Even for the Great Jahan? I can't believe that. You are the conqueror of all the peoples of the world. Surely you can conquer death?"

"Show me the way and I'll do it."

"Ah, noble sir. To conquer death you must submit to a power greater than yourself. I think submission is not in your nature."

"What power greater than myself? A god? I've never met a god yet. There may be gods around, but they take good care to keep out of my way."

He laughed a proud, booming laugh. Echo, who had heard this exchange, presumed to speak.

"You met the Nomana."

The Jahan stopped laughing abruptly and scowled at her.

"Next time you speak out of turn I'll have you tied to a barrel and lashed."

"And stain my bridal dress with blood?"

"What do I care if you bleed so long as you do as I say," growled the Jahan. Then not wanting to prolong his confrontation with this unmanageable girl, he said to his host, "I plan to hold a wedding ceremony here. One of my sons is to marry this impertinent tree sprite."

"A wedding!" said Radiant Leader. "When is it to be?"

"The sooner the better. Tonight. Do you have any objection?"

"None whatsoever. The city and people of Radiance will be honored to host the happy event. Which of your sons, may I ask, is the joyful bridegroom?"

The Jahan glowered at his three sons. They stood in a row, eyes cast down, shuffling their feet.

"That has yet to be decided," he said grimly.

Soren Similin had good reason to be pleased with his day's work; but as he knew all too well, this was only the beginning. As soon as he could get free from his alarming new friends, he hurried into the temple and climbed the stairs to his private quarters on the third floor. Here his servants removed his corona, which gave him neck ache, and his gold cape, which made him sweat even in winter, and left him alone. He hastened through his private bedchamber to the courtyard garden beyond, a favorite retreat of his from the burdens and pressures of his elevated position. Now, however, the bay tree and the vines were gone. The courtyard was walled with tall racks of glass tubes. The central space was a scene of feverish activity as metalworkers assembled pipes and rods, and glassworkers attached yet more glass tubes.

In the middle of it all, the little scientist Evor Ortus ran back and forth measuring, checking, and admonishing.

"The angle must be exact! Not a single degree out. We have so little direct sunlight here."

Similin had to tap the scientist on the shoulder to attract his attention.

"How's it coming along, Professor?"

"Well enough. Well enough."

"When will you be ready?"

"Soon, soon. Within the week."

"Within the week? You promised me three days."

"It was you who said three days, not me. But we'll do our best."

He turned his attention to a side table, on which stood a small wire cage.

Similin became agitated.

"Listen to me, Professor. You must deliver me some of your charged water by the end of the day after tomorrow."

He didn't tell Ortus that this was when he was due to swear an oath of allegiance to the Great Jahan. He understood all too well that the crazy scientist would have little sympathy for his dilemma.

"I don't need much. Just enough to give everyone a glimpse of the power at my disposal. At our disposal, that is."

Professor Ortus seemed not to have noticed his slip. He was studying a little creature that was confined in the cage.

"And the ramp?" he said. "You've given orders for it to be built?"

"Of course," said Similin, though he had done nothing

of the kind. He regarded Ortus's giant ramp as sheer folly. Much as he would like to destroy Anacrea, some more subtle means must be found in due course. For the present, his concern was the Jahan and his vast army.

The scientist was now feeding the creature in the cage.

"What have you got in there, Professor?"

"A mouse," said Ortus.

"What do you want a mouse for?"

"For tests. The details need not concern you."

He turned round and, for the first time, addressed Similin directly, in a manner that was not at all respectful.

"Work on the ramp must begin at once. As for the charged water, I have calculated that I need twenty liters."

"Twenty? Last time it was only four."

"Last time a carrier was to take the weapon to the heart of the Nom. This time we send our bomb flying through the air. We can't be sure where it will land. Twenty liters of charged water will certainly destroy the island, wherever it lands."

"But so much! How long will it take?"

"It will take as long as it takes."

"Then please, when production begins, set aside the first spoonful for me. Without that, I can't protect you."

Ortus frowned with displeasure.

"You mean to use the explosive power of my charged water against this invader?"

"For the purposes of persuasion only."

"What is he to be persuaded to do?"

The little scientist clearly felt suspicious of any scheme that was not part of his own design. Similin had had no more in mind than a demonstration of power. But at that moment an entirely new idea formed in his head, which neatly linked all the objectives currently before him. The idea, which he saw in its entirety in a single flash of brilliant insight, pleased him so much that he beamed at the prickly scientist and clasped him by the hand.

"We must persuade him to turn his army on Anacrea," he said. "That way we can distract the Nomana from the true assault. Which will, of course, come from your magnificent ramp."

On returning to his guests, Similin found that a curious ritual was under way. The pale and elegant girl they had brought with them was seated on a raised chair, while the Great Jahan and all his entourage were gathered round like spectators at a show. Seeing his host enter the pavilion, Amroth Jahan hailed him and invited him too to watch.

"My sons are about to make their love speeches," he said. "The girl then chooses the one she likes best."

"Do they all love her?" said Similin, drawing up a chair.

"They do as I tell them," said the Jahan.

"And what if the young lady chooses none of them?"

"She'll do as I tell her," said the Jahan.

"Then surely, noble sir," said Similin, "it would be simpler all round if you were to make the match yourself?"

"Make the match myself? You mean marry the girl myself?"

"No, no. I mean pick one of your sons to marry her, and it's done."

"Ah, that. I thought you were suggesting I marry her

myself. But I have two wives already. And she's too young for me. Don't you think so?"

"Far too young."

"So one of my boys'll have her. Not that they'll appreciate her. She's a rare one. Beauty combined with spirit. Dropped out of a tree. That was a surprise."

He pointed to his eldest son, Sasha.

"Get on with it, oaf."

Sasha Jahan took a few steps forward and stood before Echo's raised chair. He licked his lips and began to speak, clearly reciting from memory.

"I am my father's first son. When he dies, I will become the Great Jahan and will rule the empire he has won. Out of respect for my father, and to carry on his line as he has indicated he wishes, it is your duty to become my wife and give me sons who will grow strong and proud and bring honor to the Orlan tribes. This is not a matter in which either you or I should consider our own wishes. The family of Jahan knows its duty. I will do mine. I ask that you do yours."

His father listened to this speech, nodding with approval.

"Not so bad, my boy. I can see you've given the matter some thought. However"—he raised his silver-handled whip—"I will make the final choice of successor, when my time comes. I may choose you. I may choose Alva or Sabin. I may choose someone else altogether."

Sasha, dismayed, started to protest, but his father silenced him.

"Alva. Your turn to speak."

The Jahan's second son stepped forward.

"My father has asked you," he said to Echo, "to choose not from duty, but according to your own wishes. Name any quality that a woman seeks in a man, and all the world knows I am superior in that quality to my brothers. I am the tallest. I am the strongest. I am the most handsome. I say this not to boast, but to tell you honestly what you can see for yourself. Take my older brother out of duty if you must. But if you follow your own desires, as my father has ordered you to do, you will take me."

The Jahan smiled at this, amused by his son's strutting confidence.

"Ah, Alva," he said, patting him on the back. "I was just the same at your age."

Echo looked on, expressionless and silent, stroking the little finger of her left hand.

"Sabin!"

The Jahan's third son stepped forward.

"My lady," he said, bowing respectfully towards her. "I have no empire to give you. I am the least of my brothers. But I've watched you since you came among us, and I think I know you better than they do. I've seen how you're afraid, but brave in facing your fear. You anger quickly, but you're wise in controlling your anger. You love your horse, and your horse loves you, and that tells me that you're a true Orlan, in spirit if not in blood. I know you want none of this marrying. I know you'd run away if you could. But my father has spoken and must be obeyed. Since you must choose one of us, choose me, and I will do my best to make you happy."

The Jahan laughed out loud.

"What a boy!" he cried. "Where did that all come from? Did you get that from the cook?"

"No, Father," said Sabin quietly. "It's from me."

Echo was gazing at him in some confusion. She had prepared herself to endure arrogance and indignity; she had not been ready for kindness. She found herself touched almost to the point of tears. But she felt the Jahan's eyes on her, and she steadied herself and revealed nothing. Here, years of habit came to her aid. She pushed the troublesome thoughts out of her mind.

Just don't think it.

The Jahan himself now rose and stood before her.

"So, Princess. My sons have spoken. Now you must choose."

Echo was ready. She had made her plan in the long sleepless hours of the night gone by.

"Great Jahan," she said. "Your first son asks me to choose him out of duty. Your second son asks me to choose him out of desire. Your third son asks me to choose him for my own happiness. But I want to do my duty and to follow my desire and to be happy, all at once. I want all three."

"Maybe you do," said the Jahan, "but you must choose one."

"I can't."

"Then am I to choose one for you?"

"You? Yes!" The idea seemed to come fresh to Echo, as a way out of her dilemma; though in fact this was just the plan she was working towards. "You are their father. If you were a younger man, I would choose you."

The Jahan blushed with pleasure, as Echo had fully intended.

"But since I can't choose you, you must choose for me. I ask only that you choose the one who is most like you."

"If I must," said the Jahan, well pleased, "then I choose—"

"But not here. Not now."

"What else? What are you talking about?"

"I would like you to show me the son who most deserves to take your place."

"How am I to show you that?"

"In the Orlan way," said Echo. "In the jagga."

"The jagga!"

"Whichever of your sons throws you to the ground deserves to take me as his wife."

"The devil!" cried the Jahan in admiration. "What a girl! You hear that?" He turned to his sons, his eyes shining. "There's an Orlan answer if ever there was one!"

His sons showed rather less enthusiasm.

"But Father," said Sabin, "you know I can't beat you at the jagga."

"Why not? You're half my age, boy."

"So you mean to do this?" said Sasha.

"Certainly! The girl's got it right. Let's see who deserves to take my place, the Orlan way!"

He turned back to Echo with a beam all over his powerful ugly face, swelling with pride.

"It makes me feel like a young man again just think-ing about it!"

He lashed the air with his whip, making it crack, and turning to the priest-king of Radiance, he spoke.

"Three days of feasts and games, eh? You'll never have seen sport like the Orlan jagga!"

⇥ 12 ⇤

Knock Me Down!

SEEKER AND MORNING STAR FOLLOWED THE GREAT
River as far as the first crossing point and there joined a
cluster of other travellers waiting for the ferry to the west
bank. The travellers stared at their gray clothing and their
badans and whispered among themselves until at last one
woman plucked up the courage to speak to them.

"Please," she said, "are you Noble Warriors?"

Seeker nodded an affirmation. It seemed too compli-
cated to explain that they had not completed their training. The woman dropped to her knees and tugged at the
hem of his tunic.

"Help me!" she said. "The invaders have burned my
home. They've taken our cattle and our grain. How are
we to live?"

"Be patient," said Seeker. "These times will pass."

"I have five small children, sir. How am I to feed

them? The invaders have taken everything. And I'm left to hear my children crying in the night."

The ferry drew in to the landing stage, and the travellers boarded. Throughout the short river-crossing the unhappy woman continued to plead, turning now to Seeker and now to Morning Star. At last, to calm her, Morning Star answered.

"Trust in the All and Only. The invaders will be driven away soon, now."

Once they were on their road again, and alone, Morning Star spoke.

"Was I wrong?"

"We do what we can," said Seeker. "We can't do everything."

"This mission of yours—it's to do with the invaders?"

"No."

"Then may the Loving Mother comfort such poor abandoned people."

Seeker said nothing. They made their way down the road in silence. On either side stretched winter fields gray with corn stubble; above, the rolling clouds of the winter sky. For a little longer they would share this westward road, until they reached the fork. Then Seeker would go on to the great forest, and Morning Star would turn north towards Spikertown. If the Wildman had survived, it was surely there that he would go.

A flock of geese passed croaking overhead, beating the air in orderly lines, making for the unseen coast. A spatter of rain blew in on a gust of wind and then blew away again.

They were nearing the fork in the road when Morning Star broke their silence.

"I think you're ashamed of me," she said.

"Ashamed of you?" Seeker was surprised. "Why?"

"You go on a great mission. But I have no mission. I've left the Nom at a time of danger because—because I'm weak."

Seeker understood her.

"It's not weakness to go to the help of a friend."

"It is weakness," said Morning Star. "I don't go to help him. I go to help myself."

Seeker said nothing. If he could have chosen, he would have asked not to hear any more. But he could not choose.

"Seeker, I'm so unhappy. There's no one I can tell but you."

"Then tell me," he said quietly, and he fixed his eyes on the road ahead.

"I feel such a fool. I never thought much of him, you know that. With his boasting and his vanity and—oh, his selfishness. And all that stupid hair. But somehow, as we were spending so much time together, in the training, I started to look at him. Do you ever do that? Start to look at someone you know well, and realize you've not seen them properly before?"

"Yes," said Seeker, watching the puddles in the rutted track, counting the puddles. "I've done that."

"At first I just thought I was looking for no reason. But when you look, you start to notice—just little things. Then it changes. He started to be beautiful to me."

"He always was," said Seeker.

"Yes, I know. But to me. It's different from looking at someone and thinking, There's a beautiful person. When you see all the little things that no one else notices, then he's beautiful in a secret way. I can't explain. I never meant it to happen."

"It's what people call being in love," said Seeker.

"How can I be in love with him?" said Morning Star. "I don't even like him."

"But you want to go to him. You want to find him again."

"It's the only thing I want."

Seeker heard the tremor in her voice. He knew she wanted him to comfort her.

"I hope you do find him again."

"Do you, Seeker? That's kind of you."

She slipped her arm through his in a comradely fashion.

"You're the only one I can tell. I can't even tell him."

"Not even him?"

"He won't want me. Not a girl with a sharp tongue and a face like a bun. Beautiful people want beautiful people."

"You don't know till you ask."

"If he's even alive to ask."

"But you think he's alive, don't you?"

"Yes," she said. "I'm sure of it. I don't know why."

They continued on their way, arm in arm, walking more slowly, and so came at last to the fork in the road, where they would part.

"Take care," said Seeker. "These are dangerous times."

"Oh, I'll come to no harm. I'm not important enough. It's you who must take care."

Seeker smiled and nodded and didn't speak. Morning Star looked at his colors.

"You're hurting. What is it?"

Seeker shrugged.

"I suppose I'm just afraid," he said.

"Oh, Seeker! What a bad person I've become."

"Why?"

"All I've thought about is myself. I don't know what it is you're going to do, but I'm sure it's dangerous."

"There is danger. But I've been given power, Star."

"So have we all."

"More than you. More than all the others. More than you can imagine."

She stared at him.

"What power?" she said.

It was the look in her eyes that goaded him: not a look of disbelief, exactly, but not belief, either.

"Look down," he said.

He pointed both his forefingers at a puddle in the ground before him and concentrated his mind. The muddy brown water in the puddle began to hiss and seethe. Then the ground itself erupted in a small spout of mud and stones.

Morning Star saw and was amazed.

"You did that? With your mind?"

"With my lir."

"And it hasn't made you weaker?"

"No. I never run out."

"How is that possible?"

"I'm taking the power from the land itself. I can take strength from all living things. My power—"

He shrugged, suddenly embarrassed to hear himself.

"I don't really understand it. I've been given it for a purpose. That's what I go to do now."

"To use your power—to kill?"

He looked away. "Yes."

"Who are you to kill?"

"They're called savanters. They mean to destroy the Nom."

"How do you know this?"

"I've been told."

She watched his colors and caught the faint shimmer of gold that hovered round him; but with it there was a rim of palest yellow that she had not seen on him before.

"I should come with you," she said. "You'll need help."

"No. They can't hurt me."

"But you—you'll hurt them. And then what will you feel?"

He looked up at that and half smiled. So like Star, he thought, to sense the true danger.

"I have to live with that," he said.

She too smiled, but now there was a sadness in her eyes.

"Dear Seeker," she said. "You've gone on ahead of us all."

"I didn't mean to."

"Don't go too far. Don't change too much. I like you as you are."

Seeker kicked at the mound of stones with his toes, as if to put back what he had caused to bubble up.

"We'd better move on."

"Remember this?"

She raised her hand, palm forward. Seeker remembered. He did the same and their hands met, palm to palm. Then he turned quickly and strode away down the road to the west, without looking back. Morning Star turned north, towards Spikertown.

Seeker walked at great speed, thinking no thoughts of any kind, until he became aware of an ache in his stomach. He thought at first that it was hunger. But then he knew that it was the other kind of emptiness.

So I miss her already, he told himself.

Without intending it to, the image of Morning Star formed in his mind. Her eyes were looking at him intently, and her face was pretending to be blank, while in fact she was laughing. She had that sort of a face. People thought she was plain-looking, because they didn't see how she disguised her real thoughts. But he saw. He could tell from the crinkles in the corners of her eyes, and from the twitching of her mouth. Then out would come some pointy jabby little remark, which showed just how much she did understand what was going on—which was almost everything.

She's my friend. Nothing to be sad about there. She'll go on being my friend whatever happens.

But the ache got worse.

Nothing is dependable, he told himself. Nothing lasts.

So in a little while he was able to continue on his journey in a calmer frame of mind.

———

The line of ancient stones by the side of the road grew higher as he went, and in time took the form of a wall. The wall had evidently been substantial in some former age, for here and there its crumbling upper sections rose far above his head. Now brambles climbed over the granite blocks, and grasses grew from old mortar, and at the wall's feet lay strewn the rubble of stones that must once have been part of an even higher rampart.

Seeker paid little attention to the old wall, or to the door in the wall that now came into view ahead, because by the door, supported by some unseen means, sat an old man with long straggly gray hair, who was staring at him intently as he approached. The old man had a handful of small stones in his lap, and picking out one of the stones, he threw it at Seeker. Then he threw another, and another. His aim improved with each throw as Seeker came nearer, and the little stones now hit him on the legs.

"Stop that! Don't do that!"

The old man paid no attention at all. He went on throwing stones, not hard, but accurately.

"Why are you doing that? Stop it!"

"You'll have to make me," said the old man.

"Make you? How?"

Another stone came sailing through the air.

"Knock me down," said the old man.

"Knock you down? You're an old man."

"So it shouldn't be too hard, should it?"

He threw another stone.

Seeker stared at him. Everything about the old man

was odd, from the way he sat on nothing to the long dark blue coat he wore. And yet there was something familiar about him.

"Do you know me?" said Seeker.

"I should hope I do. I've known you all your life. You're Seeker after Truth."

"How do you know me? I don't know you."

"Then you've nothing to worry about. Come along. Knock me down."

"Please stop that. I can't knock you down."

"Maybe you can and maybe you can't. That's the question."

"I don't pick fights with old men."

The old man threw another stone at him.

"What if old men pick fights with you?" he said.

"What do you mean by saying you know me? You've never met me in your life. You don't know anything about me."

"Oh, no?" said the old man, suddenly producing a gap-toothed grin. "I don't know how you used to wet the bed in the night when you were seven years old. And I don't know how you cried when your brother left home. And I don't know how lonely you were at school. And I don't know how you love Morning Star."

Seeker stared at him, speechless.

"Such a lot I don't know about you, I'd say."

"Who told you that? Who have you been talking to? Who are you?"

"Just a nosy old man."

"Have you been spying on me?"

"You might say so."

"Why?"

The old man threw another stone at him.

"Maybe you should teach me a lesson," he said. "Maybe you should knock me down."

"I'm not going to knock you down!" The whole situation was absurd.

"Then I shall have to knock *you* down."

The old man stood up, revealing that he had been sitting on a stick with a seat for a handle. He dropped the remainder of the stones, brushed his hands free of grit, and looked into Seeker's eyes. Then he nodded his head.

Seeker fell over.

"Down he goes!" the old man chortled.

Seeker got to his feet in a more thoughtful frame of mind. There was only one sort of person who could knock him down like that.

"You must be a Noma."

"Of a kind," said the old man. "Will you oblige me now by knocking me down?"

Seeker stood before him with more attention than before. He allowed his body to become still, as he had been taught, and he let the lir flow through him freely. Then he met the old man's eyes with his own, reached out with the concentrated power of his will, and—

Fell over again.

He had collided with an immovable wall of power. This peculiar old man possessed more power than any of his teachers in the Nom.

"Who are you?"

"Do you mean, when am I?"

"I don't understand."

"Time changes everything, doesn't it? You say, Who am I? That may seem a simple question to you, but I'm one person when I get up in the morning—a disagreeable, bad-tempered sort of person, I'm sorry to say. Then I'm quite another person after breakfast. A little on the silent side, perhaps, but amiable enough. Then again, should you meet me after I've had a good dinner, and perhaps a brandy or two, you'll make a friend for life. And that's all in a single day. Now only consider myself when young, or middle-aged, or—"

"Please!" cried Seeker, waving one hand in front of his face.

"I only mean to make the point," said the old man mildly, "that I am different things at different times."

"All I mean is, what is your name?"

"My name now, you mean?"

"Yes."

"I believe now they call me Jango."

"Jango!"

Seeker was about to exclaim that this was a word he himself had made up. But apparently it wasn't. He must have heard it before somewhere, and kept it tucked away in his memory.

"Names, names!" said the old man, with a sigh. "What policemen they are! What judges and jailers! Some people are obliged to be fettered to the same name for the whole of their natural lives. Imagine it! Like having to wear the same suit of clothes from the day you're born. So undignified. I once knew a man called Poopy. Naturally he came to nothing. So how do you like being called Seeker after Truth?"

"I don't," said Seeker.

"So get yourself a new name."

"I can't just change my name. No one would know who I was."

"What's wrong with that?"

"I want people to know who I am."

"But they don't, do they? They know someone they call Seeker, but they don't know you. They've got a lot of wrong ideas about you, haven't they? So why not shed all those wrong ideas, along with the old name, and start again? You could call yourself, say, Hero."

"Hero? I'm not a hero."

"But if you were called Hero, you would be."

Seeker just shook his head and said no more. However hard he tried to get onto firm ground with the peculiar old man, it all slithered away beneath him.

"Now," said Jango, "why don't you try again to knock me down? Only this time, try harder."

"I don't think I can."

"Just not strong enough, eh?"

"I may not be."

"Funny thing, strength," said Jango. "Not like a rock at all. Much more like water. It can be here, and then—slosh, slosh—it can be there. You can drink it in, and you can leak it out."

Seeker was watching the old man's twinkly brown eyes as he spoke, and suddenly he understood.

"All right," he said. "One more time."

They faced each other in combat stance. This time Seeker didn't attempt to overpower his opponent. Instead, he held him with his eyes, and he drank him in.

Hey ho, jango!

He felt the old man struggle, but he did not release him. There was nothing his opponent could do. If he used his power to strike at Seeker, that would simply deliver more of him more quickly into Seeker's control. He was being devoured. With each moment that passed he grew visibly weaker, while Seeker grew stronger.

"Enough!" he gasped at last, tottering on his feet.

Seeker let him go.

Every blow I strike makes me stronger.

The old man propped up his sitting-stick and sat down on it, breathing rapidly.

"My oh my!" he said. "That was most unpleasant."

"I'm sorry."

"No need to be sorry. I had to make sure. And now I'm sure."

"Sure of what?"

"That you're ready. That you're up to the job. There are seven of them, after all, and only one of you."

"Seven what?"

"Savanters." Jango seemed surprised that Seeker needed to ask the question.

"So you know about the savanters, too?"

"Of course. The longer you live, the more you know.

But at the same time, as you see, the weaker you get. It's all very badly managed, really. Life, I mean. Take the savanters. They're even older than me. By rights they should be dead. But don't underestimate them, young man. They have very little strength of their own, but they've learned how to use the strength of others. They will try to use yours."

He dabbed at his wrinkled forehead with the sleeve of his blue coat and, turning towards the door in the wall, called out.

"Wife!"

Once again Seeker was taken by surprise. But no answer came from beyond the door. By now Seeker had come to realize he was unlikely to get a straight answer from Jango about who he was or how he came to know so much; but he was determined even so to learn what he could from him before they parted.

"How should I defend myself against the savanters?"

"You must not defend. You must attack. Wife!"

This time there came a shuffling sound beyond the door and the clicking of the latch, then the old door creaked open. However, no one appeared.

Jango peered crossly into the dark space beyond the door.

"Come on out, woman," he said. "You might at least set eyes on the boy. Where's the harm in that?"

There was no answer. As far as Seeker could see, there was no one there.

"Attack?" he prompted. "How?"

"How? How?" The old man furrowed his brow and

pondered his answer. "The savanters are very clever, you see. And the only way to beat very clever people is to refuse to play their game. You have to be stupid. You have to respond in ways they can't predict. Yes, that's it." He nodded, satisfied that he'd reached the proper end of his chain of thought. "Fight them with craziness."

"Fight them with craziness," said Seeker.

He understood the theory but had no idea how to carry it out in practice.

"They must all die," said Jango suddenly. "You understand that? It's most important. The experiment has failed. All seven must be killed. Leave even one alive, and it will all begin again."

"What experiment? What will begin again?"

"Ah! There you are!"

A figure was peeping out of the doorway: a little old lady.

"Come out, come out!" said Jango, beckoning her. "Take a good look. Here he is."

But she would not come out. Shyly, she peeped at Seeker from within the shadows of the doorway, but she did not speak. She was as old as Jango, and a little stooped, and wore a dark head-scarf that framed a deeply lined face. She seemed to be smiling.

Seeker bowed politely.

"My wife," said Jango. "My dearest friend, my life's companion, my comfort in old age, and my one and only love."

Seeker found himself unexpectedly touched. The strange old man spoke with such tenderness.

"Now shake my hand, my boy. And go on your way."

Seeker gave him his hand. Jango took it and drew him close and embraced him.

"You know I only threw stones at you because I love you."

"I don't know anything," said Seeker. "I wish I did."

"The stones come from the wall. Once this wall was as high as the trees and stretched from sea to sea. It was built by the great king Noman, to protect his empire."

"Noman? The first Noble Warrior?"

"The very same. And look at the wall now."

Then Jango kissed Seeker on his brow with his dry lips, and let him go. He got up from his sitting-stick and, taking it in one hand, shuffled to the doorway, where his wife was watching. He put his arm round her, and she put her arm round him, and they stood there side by side, smiling at him. Behind them Seeker could just make out a plain white room and a wooden table. On the table, in a glass of water, was a single blue cornflower.

The sight of the loving old couple in their simple home pleased Seeker. He bowed to them both in farewell, then set off down the road.

When he had gone some way, he turned to look back, and he could still make out the old couple standing in the doorway. The image of their happiness together after all these years moved him. Long after Jango's many other mysterious utterances had faded in his mind, Seeker recalled how the old man had looked towards the old lady in the doorway and said, "My one and only love."

⊰ 13 ⊱

The Jagga

CARESSA'S BAND TRAVELLED NORTH TO RADIANCE TO share in the three days of public feasting and games given in honor of the Orlans, and with them came the Wildman. His strength was returning, and he could feel his old wild spirit reawakening within him; but he saw no clear way ahead. So for now he followed and watched and waited.

The bandits mingled with the great crowds between the dome-shaped tents of the Orlan camp, drank toasts to the Great Jahan with grinning imperial axers, and raised cheers to Radiant Leader with weather-beaten Orlan veterans. As the day ended, they warmed themselves at the bright fires and ate their share of roast mutton and sweet potatoes and marveled at the Orlans' beautiful beasts.

The Wildman looked on in amusement as a wealthy merchant of Radiance tried to buy one of the Caspians for himself.

"I have gold," he kept saying. "I'll pay in gold."

"Would you sell your own child?" said the Orlan.

"But I offer you gold!" protested the merchant, as if this argument overcame all others.

"Maybe we'll have your gold, anyway," said the warrior with a wink. "Once the feasting's over."

Caressa too was paying close attention to the Caspians. She had little interest herself in the feast or the games. She had come upriver for the horses.

"What do you say, Wildman? The word is they're fast and strong."

The Wildman watched a mounted Orlan ride by.

"They're beautiful," he said.

"If we had mounts like these, you and I, we could have it all!"

The Wildman said nothing to this, nor did he turn to meet her shining eyes.

Shab joined them.

"I've been down by the lakeshore," he said. "There's hundreds of the beasts there, roaming free."

"Are they guarded?" said Caressa.

"Not that I could see."

"We wait till dark," said Caressa. "Then we rope some for ourselves."

"Right, Chief," said Shab.

"Right, Chief," said the others.

"Right, Wildman?" said Caressa.

The Wildman gave a shrug.

"Could be," he said.

He was gazing at a troop of mounted Orlans who were

cutting back and forth, clearing a space in front of the city gates. They moved in a disciplined formation, maintaining their lines, all turning at once when they turned. In this way, twenty riders imposed their will on a crowd of many hundreds.

"Wildman," whispered Caressa, "don't do this."

"Don't do what, Princess?"

"You know."

"Just the way I am, Princess."

"Seems like you're better," said Caressa, a little ruefully. "So now I suppose you want to be chief."

"Not me, Princess. This is your band. You're the chief."

"So you'll take my orders?"

He turned his handsome golden face to gaze at her at last, then shook back his long golden hair.

"You want me to take your orders?"

"I want to slit your guts and stuff you with pig dung and bury you alive," she said.

"Sounds like that's a no."

She struck him on the chest with one hand.

"What did you have to come back for?" she cried. "I was doing fine till you came back. Look at them!"

She gestured at the rest of her band, who were standing round pretending not to hear what was happening.

"They take my orders. They know I'm the chief. Shab knows I'm the chief."

"That's why you don't want Shab," said the Wildman.

"I know! I know! Don't tell me what I know! It's you I want! I want you because you'll never take my orders! I order you to want me, and you don't want me, and the more you don't obey, the more I want you!"

She struck him again and again.

"You drive me crazy! Throw yourself back into the sea, and this time, stay dead!"

"You want me to go away?"

"No! I don't want you to go away! I want you with me. I want us to be together. You and me, Wildman—we could be the best!"

There came a banging of drums and a braying of horns, and out through the city gates streamed a procession of red-robed priests. Servants followed, bringing gold-backed chairs, which they lined up in a row. Torches were lit, framing the now wide empty circle before the gold chairs. Onlookers crowded closer to see what was happening, and the Wildman and Caressa and the others moved with them.

After the priests came Radiant Leader, resplendent in his golden robes and his glittering corona. All the citizens of Radiance lowered their gaze. He stood for a moment to acknowledge the bowed heads, then took his place on one of the gold-backed chairs. He gave a sign that he was ready, and out of the city gates rode three young Orlans, all abreast. Word spread through the crowd: these were the sons of the Great Jahan, and there was to be some kind of contest.

Next came a pale and slender girl, on foot, escorted by Orlan captains on either side. She looked unseeingly before her as she came, and allowed herself to be led to one of the gold chairs without a word. The Wildman looked at her curiously, as did everyone else in the great crowd, and a murmur passed from mouth to mouth.

"She's the prize. They're fighting for her."

Then the drums beat faster and the horns sounded louder, and there came a dazzle of dancing light in the city gateway. Heralded by trumpets, flashing with brilliance, out rode the Great Jahan. At once a mighty shout went up from all the Orlans, and their leader raised both arms high above his head as he rode, then clasped his hands together.

The Wildman stared, transfixed. All round him he heard the cry, "The warlord! The warlord!"

The Jahan was smaller than he had expected, and uglier, but his every move was charged with the authority of absolute power. The Wildman watched him accept the cheers of his warriors and saw the fear and admiration on the faces of all others, and he felt a surge of excitement. This was what it was to be a warlord.

There had been another warlord, long ago, who had built a great kingdom and been feared and obeyed by all. But he had gone further. He had used his power to force his way into the heart of the Nom, into the Garden itself. What had he found there? Whatever it was, it had changed him forever.

The Wildman watched Amroth Jahan as he rode round the circle by torchlight, and he thought of Noman. Had he too been born to live wild? Had he breathed free air, and never sworn obedience to any man, and gone his own proud way? And had he learned to hunger for this thing called peace?

The Wildman now knew he could never be a true
Noble Warrior. But he could be a warlord. He could take
his peace by force.

He laughed to himself as he framed this thought. Caressa, hearing him laugh, thought he laughed at the Great
Jahan.

"You think he's funny?"

"No, not him."

"The girl, then?"

The Wildman looked at the girl sitting among the
leaders on the gold chairs. She alone of all that crowd was
paying no attention to the coming contest. There close
before her, the three sons of the Jahan were stripping the
clothes from their upper bodies and cracking their whips
in the air. But she stared into the distance, making no attempt to conceal her indifference to all around her.

"I think she's funny," said Caressa. "That girl has a face
like a fish."

She turned her gaze back to the Great Jahan. He too
was now stripping off his coat and shirt to reveal a powerful, well-muscled body. In the glow of the torches, he
presented an impressive sight. One of his servants bound
back his springy black hair, exposing his high cheekbones.
His prominent features now fell into place, and he looked
magnificent.

Caressa was mesmerized.

"That man," she murmured, "must be the ugliest man
in the world."

———

Amroth Jahan had not taken part in a jagga for ten years, but as he unfurled his old familiar whip, the thrill of the sport came back to him. He breathed the twilight air deep into his lungs and felt its cold touch on his bare skin and knew that soon he would be fiery hot. His best Caspian, Malook, waited restlessly for him to mount, shivering her ginger skin.

"You've missed it too, Malook? We'll show them something worth the seeing, won't we?"

Then he nodded to the handler, and with a single powerful spring, he was on Malook's back. He looked towards Echo Kittle and saw that she was gazing at nothing, her lovely face grave and unsmiling. There's a girl worth fighting for, he said to himself. Whichever of my boys brings me down will win himself a fine wife, and good luck to him.

His sons were stripped and mounted and waiting for him. He eased his position, leaned a little forward, and Malook moved off, smooth as cream. Picking his way with delicate hooves, Malook crossed the open space to the far side, where the boys were gathered.

"So who's it to be first?" the Jahan asked his sons.

"I'm to go first, Father," said Sabin, his youngest. "I don't claim any great skill at the jagga."

"You're an Orlan," said his father. "You're born to this."

He looked round the mass of watching faces, letting his gaze end once more on Echo.

"And we have a crowd to cheer us on!"

He raised his whip and rolled it through the air to end in a sharp crack. The nearest spectators jumped. The Jahan grinned. He was feeling strong.

"Come on then, boy! On my cry!"

He spun Malook round, trotted to the far side, and turned again. All this Malook did without being told. Sabin unfurled his own whip and angled his horse to face his father. The young man looked slight, almost fragile, in comparison with his father, and on his face there was a look of uncertainty.

"Ya, jagga!" cried the Jahan. His whip sliced the air, and Malook set off at a rapid trot. Sabin swung left and cantered round the perimeter, but Malook turned deftly to cut him off, and they were engaged. The Jahan's whip curled and caught, winding round Sabin's left arm. The boy held to his mount. With a turning countersweep, he flicked his whip round his father's shoulders. The pull from both sides dragged them together. Both releasing at the same time, they slackened the whips, and with a shake of their naked upper bodies, both were free.

"Good boy!" shouted the Jahan. "And again!"

He urged Malook round in a tight circle, his whip cracking in the air, and Sabin turned with him, watching the whip to avoid its clasp. Veteran Orlans shook their heads and smiled.

"The old man has him now."

The Jahan chose his moment at leisure. A murmur in Malook's ear, and the Caspian bolted past Sabin. In the same fraction of a second, the Jahan's whip curled out and wrapped itself round Sabin's waist. Before Sabin could turn out of its grip the whip had tightened, and with a lurch he was jerked off the horse's back, to fall sprawling on the ground.

Applause broke out from the onlookers. Amroth Jahan raised his left fist in victory and flashed a look towards Echo. To his gratification he found she was watching him now. She had seen him win. He smiled for her, his broad chest heaving.

Sabin clambered to his feet and rubbed at the raw weal where the whip had torn at his skin.

"I told you I was no match for you, Father."

"You lost the lead," the Jahan replied. "Never wait for your opponent to strike. Lose the lead and you've lost the jagga."

Alva, his second son, now rode forward.

"Would you like to rest before the next bout, Father?"

"Rest? I'm only just warming up!"

"Then I'm ready when you are, sir."

The Jahan gazed approvingly at Alva's powerful torso. This was the one he expected to lose to. Alva was a fine jagga rider, with an excellent horse.

"To our positions!"

The Jahan rode back to the side where the guests of honor sat. He leaned down to speak to his host, Radiant Leader, but his words were meant for Echo to hear.

"What do you say to our sport?"

"Good sport," said Radiant Leader, "but soon over."

"You'll see a more equal match this time. The boy's a champion. I'll hold him as long as I can."

He looked straight at Echo then, and there she was,

gazing back at him with those beautiful gray eyes. A thrill of pride went through the Jahan. There was no telling what she was thinking, but now every time he turned to her, she was watching him. Not his boys. Him.

He took up his position facing Alva across the trampled grass. Alva was ready and eager.

"Ya, jagga!" he cried, and charged.

Malook stood stock-still until the last moment, and then skipped to one side. The Jahan calculated Alva's whip strike perfectly, and swung out and low. Alva missed. But at once he was circling round, whip snapping again. His father circled too, once, twice, then broke out of the circle and rode away. Alva gave chase and caught up, and his whip snared his father's whip arm, but because he was in forward motion, he could get no tension on it. Malook stopped dead. Alva swept past, the Jahan let his arm move with him, and the whip unraveled.

Now with Alva before him and his whip arm free, the Jahan shot out his own whip and struck Alva across his naked back. But he was not close enough for a catch.

The onlookers applauded. The combat was fast and relentless, evenly matched.

They broke apart, raced to the farthest edges of the combat ground, and turned in as if both were obeying the same signal to charge. No evasion now: just sheer strength. The horses passed so close that the riders' legs brushed against each other. Both whips slashed the air, both found purchase. Twisting round on their mounts, right arms straining, both men felt the sudden tearing tug jerk them backwards. But their horses felt it too and leaned into the pull and turned back. So neither man was unseated.

Malook raced to circle the other horse, but Alva was not to be had as easily as his younger brother, and he spun round too and broke away. Suddenly he was behind his father, and his whip was curling round his father's neck, and every Orlan watching held his breath, knowing the older man must fall now or there would be a death. But the Jahan did not fall. He hurled his whip to the ground, reached behind him, and seized the cord that was throttling him. With one violent and powerful heave, he toppled Alva from his horse.

Up went a roar of admiration. The Jahan unwound the whip from his neck and punched the air. He turned fist high to Echo, and she was watching him still.

Alva rose to his feet, walked over to his father, and held up his hand.

"Still the best, Father," he said.

"You nearly had me, boy."

Sasha, his eldest son, now rode up to join them.

"Father," he said in a low voice, "there's only me left. I'm your eldest son. I must win this bout."

"You'll win if you're good enough, son."

"No, Father. Please think what you're doing. One of us three boys has to win, and there's only me left."

"Yes, son. Yes, you're right."

The Jahan drew a long sobering breath and saw reason. The prize for the winner was the girl. He could never have the girl. So Sasha must win.

With this thought clear in his mind, the Jahan took up his position for the third and final bout. His oldest son was not as strong as Alva, but he was smarter. That was as it should be.

He raised his whip hand.

"Ya, jagga!"

He cantered slowly towards his son. Since he had agreed he would lose, he was in no hurry. Sasha came out to meet him, then made a dash to pass him, at the same time sending out his first sweep. It fell short and lacked power. The Jahan didn't even try to deflect it. Instead, he let Sasha pass him, and then with the slightest lean of his body, urged Malook forward. The horse, superbly responsive, catapulted forward, leaving Sasha behind and out of reach. Then as Sasha followed to close the gap, the Jahan turned, whip snaking, and caught him in a perfect curl. Really it was too easy, he thought.

Sasha struggled to release himself, but could not.

"Father!" he muttered angrily.

The Jahan reversed the whip action and the cord fell away. The Orlans watching saw the older man give up his hold and they murmured among themselves.

"Come on, then, boy!" said the Jahan. "Here I am!"

Sasha moved away and then jabbed his horse into a flurry of motion. He swept round the perimeter of the ground, and then curled inwards on his opponent.

Malook never moved. The Jahan watched his son with contemptuous eyes. All this racing about was for show—it gave no advantage in the jagga. The boy doesn't deserve to win, he thought.

Sasha closed in, whooping a war cry, and his whip came hissing out towards his father's left flank. The Jahan did what any Orlan would do under the circumstances, faced with a well-signalled attack. He met whip stroke with whip stroke. His own whip, snapping before him, caught Sasha's whip in midair, and the two cords tangled. The Jahan then braced himself as Sasha cantered past, and when the pull came, he was rock solid in his seat. If anything, Sasha got the worst of it, dragged to one side and almost off, before his mount turned and gave him slack.

The whips spun free. Sasha glared at his father. The Jahan shrugged, as if to say, You'll have to do better than that. Sasha rode towards him at a trot. As he passed by he whispered, "You must fall!"

If I must, I must, thought the Jahan.

Sasha turned sharply once he was well past, then his father turned, and facing each other, they raised their whips. This was a well-known maneuver in the jagga, one that relied solely on strength. The two horses moved slowly towards each other until they were within striking reach. Then both men's right arms went up together, and both whips flew out. Each one wrapped itself tight round the body of the facing man. With a sharp simultaneous tug, both were pulled tight. Now it was a tug-of-war. Whichever man weakened first would be pulled to the ground.

Sasha kept his eyes fixed on his father as he strained. His father looked back with a half smile on his face. The watching crowd fell silent, captivated by the sudden stillness of the combatants. Both whip arms trembled with the strain. Soon now one would snap.

Father! Sasha didn't speak aloud, but his mouth formed the word.

The Jahan nodded very slightly, but he did not release his powerful right arm. He could feel it all down his arm and his back, right deep into Malook who was part of him, he could feel that he had the greater reserves of strength. He could win this. But he must not.

His eyes flicked away now and found Echo on the far side, still watching him. She was leaning a little forward, and her lips were parted. She too knows I can win, he thought.

So why am I about to lose?

I'm stronger than all of them. Why should I lose? I'm the Jahan! What has age to do with it? The best man wins. And she knows, she's known all along, that I'm the best man. Haven't her eyes been on me from the start? The jagga is to find the one who deserves to take my place. But no man deserves to take my place! Not while I'm still alive.

"Sorry, son!" he cried; and with a massive explosion of strength he pulled Sasha right off his mount, and sent him thudding to the ground.

The onlookers cheered. The Orlans grinned and clapped their hands above their heads. The Jahan threw down his whip and made a slow victory circuit of the ground, acknowledging the applause. Sasha clambered to his feet and joined his brothers. The three looked on in silence.

The Great Jahan's circuit brought him to a stop before the guest of honor.

"My congratulations," said Radiant Leader.

The Jahan ignored him. His eyes were on Echo Kittle. He dismounted and stood before her. She no longer looked at him. Her eyes were cast down. His bare chest glistened in the torchlight, and his ugly face shone with the glow of victory.

"We have done as you asked," he said. "Now you must choose."

Echo did not answer.

"I have two wives," he said. "But they are far away. I ask you to be the third, and the best."

She looked up then, and her gaze was unflinching.

"You're too old," she said.

There was no pity in her voice. Only then did he begin to guess at the depths of her anger.

"You think you can have whatever you want," she said. "But you can't have me."

She rose to her feet.

"I warn you—!"

"What?" Her eyes flashed at him. "You'll burn my home? Do it! Burn all the world, old man! Kill everyone! Then rule over a world of blood and ashes!"

She turned and stalked away.

The Jahan stood still as a statue, watching her go. No one else dared to move. Then, when she had disappeared into the darkness, he came back to life with a great laugh.

"Where's this feast of yours?" he said to Radiant Leader. "I could eat a bullock!"

Caressa had watched the entire jagga without saying a word. Now she turned to the Wildman, her eyes shining.

"I knew he'd win," she said. "I knew the ugly one would win. The rest of them are nothing."

The leaders and their entourage returned to the city, and one by one the torches were extinguished. The crowd dispersed, either to the feasting in the temple square or to their homes. Night had now fallen, and the great Orlan camp was bright with the glow of countless fires.

The bandits slipped away down the riverbank, to the meadowland where the herds of Caspians were grazing. As they went, Caressa talked on about the Great Jahan.

"Why do you think that great horde obeys him? He's not big. He's hideously ugly. Why don't they just laugh in his face?"

"Would you laugh in his face?" said Shab.

"I'd smack his face," said Caressa, "and then I'd laugh."

"Sure you would," said Shab.

Her hand shot out in a stinging slap. Shab squealed.

"You want to run with me, you show respect."

"Yes, Chief."

The grazing horses looked up as the bandits approached, but seemed unafraid. Caressa went to one of them, a mare, and stroked her neck and examined her in the faint light of the distant campfires.

"This shouldn't be too hard."

She uncoiled the rope she carried, then slipped it round the Caspian's neck. The others, following her lead, each picked out a Caspian in the darkness and did the same—all but the Wildman, who kept himself apart and watched.

Shab, still smarting from Caressa's rebuke, was the first to attempt to mount. He did exactly what he had seen the Orlans do. It had looked the simplest thing in the world.

He stood by the horse's side and sprang upwards, while swinging his leg wide and round.

The horse moved. Not far and not fast, but enough. Shab fell flat on his face on the wet grass.

The others laughed.

"Try holding on to your rope," said Caressa.

She herself then grasped her rope tight and swung herself up onto her Caspian's back.

"See!" she said. "Not too hard."

"Heya, Chief!"

The bandits were impressed. However, when Caressa urged her mount to move forward, nothing happened.

"Come on, come on." She tried rocking herself forward and kicking with her heels, but the mare just stood there. "Someone make it move."

Shab gave the mare a smart smack on the rump. This had a dramatic effect. The mare put down her head and kicked up her rear legs, and Caressa was thrown unceremoniously to the ground, taking the rope with her.

"Idiot!" she said to Shab as she got up.

"It's the rope," said the Wildman, who had been watching the Caspians carefully. "They don't like the rope."

"See if you can do better, then."

The Wildman went up to the mare, who was now watching the bandits with wary eyes, and stood before her. Hardly aware that he was doing so, he followed the training he had received in the Nom. He let himself go still, steadied his breathing, and felt the flow of lir within him. Then he brought the lir to a focused point and let it run down his right arm to his right hand. Then he raised his right hand and touched the Caspian lightly on the brow.

The mare looked at him in mild surprise but did not move away. The Wildman kept his hand in place and felt his own potent stillness streaming into the horse. Then he removed his hand, went to the mare's side, and vaulted onto her back.

"Now make her move," said Caressa.

Shab drew his spike.

"Let me help," he said.

He stabbed the sharp spike into the mare's leg. The mare kicked and bucked, the Wildman clung on tight, and in the same moment, with a hammer of flying hooves, a horse and rider hurtled out of the darkness. The Wildman's Caspian broke into a gallop, and the Wildman found himself being carried away down the river path, into the night.

"Wildman!" shouted Caressa after him. "Come back!"

But the mare was following the other horse and was entirely beyond his control. It was all he could do to stay on her back. He was lying forward, with his arms round the mare's neck, more like a sack of corn than a rider.

Ahead he could just make out the other horse and rider. Whoever it was seemed to have no intention of stopping soon. All down the river road they went, and with every hoofbeat, the Wildman was sure he would fall. But his arms were strong, and he gripped tight. Then at last, as the young moon rose in the night sky, the rider ahead slowed to a trot and so came to a stop. The Wildman's mare, still doing as she pleased without any reference to him, trotted up alongside, and the two Caspians touched noses.

The rider was the beautiful girl who had defied the Great Jahan. She was staring at the Wildman with fear-filled eyes.

"You're not an Orlan," she said. "Who are you?"

"Nobody," said the Wildman, panting, his heart hammering from the wild ride. "Just a spiker."

"Then how can you ride?"

"I can't."

"Why were you following me?"

"I wasn't. The horse was."

The girl now looked at his mare and saw how the two Caspians were nuzzling each other's faces.

"They were trace horses together," she said. Then her suspicious eyes returned to the Wildman. "You weren't sent to bring me back?"

"No."

"So where are you going?"

The Wildman nodded down the road.

"Spikertown."

"Is that on the road to the Glimmen?"

"Part of the way."

"I come from the Glimmen. The Great Jahan has sworn to burn the great forest to the ground."

"Why?"

"Because I won't be his wife."

The Wildman was shocked but also impressed.

"Can he do it?"

"He has enough men. No one can stand up to him. Except the Noble Warriors."

She gave the Wildman a searching look.

"Do you know anything about the Noble Warriors?"

The Wildman was silent for a moment, and then he looked away.

"No," he said. "Nothing."

They rode on side by side. The Wildman told his name and learned hers.

"Wouldn't it be better to be his wife than to have him burn the Glimmen?" said the Wildman.

Echo gave a shake of her body, as if to rid herself of a covering of dirt.

"I can bear almost anything," she said, "but not that."

"He's ugly," said the Wildman, "but he's magnificent."

He was thinking of the way Caressa's eyes had shone as she had watched him.

"I don't want to be anyone's wife," said Echo. "I want to be me."

In time they came to a roadside rest hut, built for the benefit of travellers, to offer protection from wind and rain.

"We should sleep a little," said the Wildman.

"The Orlans will follow me," said Echo.

"You sleep. I'll watch."

She dismounted.

"We'll take it in turns," she said.

The interior of the little low-roofed hut was window-less and blind dark. Echo lay down on the bare earth floor and was soon deeply asleep. The Wildman stayed outside and watched, and the Caspians grazed, and the moon travelled across the sky.

He thought about the Jahan and the Orlans who followed him. He pictured them in their camp outside Radiance. He saw again the crowds that gathered to watch the jagga. There were many Orlans, but there were many more spikers. The difference was that the Orlans were united in a disciplined army, while the spikers were a disorganized rabble. The spikers all belonged to different tribes, and within the tribes, they were divided into bands, and the bands were forever squabbling among themselves. In Spikertown alone, three chiefs disputed control of the streets, and their followers fought one another for territory, in frequent bloody brawls. But if one were to rise above them all and win the allegiance of every spiker in the land, he could build an army to rival the Orlans. Such a chief could truly call himself a warlord.

But how was it to be done?

When the light of dawn streamed in through the rest hut's doorway, Echo Kittle woke. Only then did she discover that she was not alone. A second figure lay huddled in sleep on the hut's floor. Echo stared in surprise. Then she crept quietly out into the open and whispered to the Wildman.

"There's someone in the hut."

"Who?"

"I don't know," said Echo. "But I think I recognize the clothing. I think it's a Noble Warrior."

The Wildman went into the hut to check for himself. As soon as he saw the sleeper, he let out an exclamation, and the sleeper awoke. Her eyes opened and looked up at him in confusion, still half in dreams. Then she smiled.

It was Morning Star.

⇥ 14 ⇤

The Whip and the Feather

A GRAND FEAST HAD BEEN PREPARED TO FOLLOW THE jagga, and since it was all there to be eaten, the Great Jahan and his sons and his entourage proceeded to eat it. No one spoke of the fact that the reason for the feast, the wedding of one of the Jahan's own sons to Echo Kittle, had now been abandoned. The Great Jahan sat in the place of honor at the top table and drank steadily, and ate almost as much as he drank, and repeatedly thanked his host, Radiant Leader, for the generosity of his welcome.

"This is the way to live!" he cried. "Why fight wars when friendship tastes this good?"

"Why indeed?" said Radiant Leader, raising his glass but not drinking.

"We only have the one life," said the Jahan. "Might as well enjoy it. Do you enjoy it?"

He leaned close to Radiant Leader, his face contorted by a bitter smile.

"Of course," said Radiant Leader.

"And how much longer do you expect to go on enjoying it? This enjoyable life of yours."

"I hope to enjoy this life," said Radiant Leader, "for many years to come." Noticing that many of his own people were listening with interest, though with lowered eyes, the priest-king added, "And I hope to enjoy the next life for all eternity."

"Eternal life, eh? And how about"—he leaned closer still—"eternal youth?"

"Ah. That's something very different."

"Very different. But very desirable."

Radiant Leader was all too aware that his guest was drunk and that not far beneath the smiling surface was a burning fury. He noticed that the Jahan's sons were watching their father with concealed agitation.

"I'm sure we all have many years ahead of us," he said.

"Are you? Are you sure?" The Jahan wouldn't let it go. "What makes you sure? How many years? How old are you? You're not pretty but you're not old. Are you thirty yet?"

Radiant Leader closed his eyes. This was not a good situation. The Jahan was treating him with a familiarity that bordered on disrespect. The priest-king's prestige depended crucially on the way those round him conducted themselves in his presence. As Soren Similin, he could pretend to be humble. As Radiant Leader, he must inspire awe.

He rose from the table. His priests at once rose with him.

"We are the sons of the Great Power above," he said. "We are all young in the light of eternity."

"Sit down!" roared the Jahan. "You know how old I am? Go on! Guess!"

He pointed a calloused finger at one of the priests.

"You! Red fellow! Make a guess!"

The priest looked at Radiant Leader, who shook his head very slightly.

"I'm forty!" bellowed the Jahan. "Forty years old! Is that old? Is my life over? Look at them!" His finger jerked towards his sons. "I'm a better man than every one of them! Who says I'm old?"

No one uttered a sound. The Jahan's face had turned a dark ugly red, and spittle flecked the corners of his mouth. The rage that had been gathering in him like a storm now burst into the open.

"What I want," he yelled, "I get! What I say I'll do, I do! I said I'd rule the world, and so I shall! Who's going to stop me? You? You?"

He glared round at them. No one moved.

"Insects!" he cried. "Worms! Maggots! I tread on you all!"

He became aware that Radiant Leader was still standing, and clearly preparing to leave.

"You!" he screamed. "I want you on your knees! I want your homage! Now!"

Radiant Leader was forced to play his trump card

before he had intended to show it. Anything to distract the drunken Jahan's attention from himself and his homage.

"You know who stands in your way," he said in a high, clear voice. "The Noble Warriors."

"Noble Warriors! I'll smash their skulls like eggs!"

He pounded the table before him.

"Noble Warriors! They'll kneel to me before they die!"

He lunged forward, as if to seize hold of his enemies there and then, and stumbled against the heavily laden table. As he thrashed about to right himself, he caught one of the legs, and the whole table came crashing down. Enraged by this, seeming to think it had been done by others to impede him, the Jahan turned and blundered in a new direction. Meeting another table, he picked it up and tipped it over.

"You can't hold me in!" he cried. "I don't want your feasts! You think you can stuff me like a cockerel? I'll show you how I crow!"

He crashed back and forth about the great pavilion, overturning the tables, shouting as he went. Radiant Leader, seeing that he had been safely forgotten, withdrew at a dignified pace, and his priests followed. The Jahan never even saw them go.

"On your knees! All of you! Who says I'm old? I tread on you all! On your knees!"

Orlans and citizens of Radiance sank to their knees amid the debris of the feast. The Jahan's sons watched in dismay but did nothing to stop their father's rampage. They had seen him like this before, and they knew how it would end.

The shouting stopped quite suddenly, for no obvious reason. The Jahan looked round at all the frightened eyes watching him. He grunted and passed one hand over his face. He frowned, as if trying to remember something that had slipped his mind. He pulled up a chair and sat down heavily. Then he fell asleep and began to snore.

Sasha Jahan signed to a group of servants. Together they lifted the deadweight of the snoring warlord and carried him out to his bed.

Radiant Leader passed through his private quarters in the temple, walking fast. Coming out again by a secret door, he crossed to the imperial arsenal. Here three tall buildings framed a yard in which carpenters and metal-beaters were hard at work. A giant timber structure was slowly taking shape within a latticework of scaffolding, lit by flares. As soon as he entered, the chief carpenter came hurrying towards him, clutching the plans of the structure and respectfully averting his eyes.

"I don't entirely understand, Radiance," he said, "what is to come here—where the rails meet the second tower."

He indicated the point on the plans.

"There seems to be a section missing."

"Nothing is missing. Build what is laid out in the plans."

"But Radiance, I don't entirely understand—"

"Understanding is not necessary. Build. It must be finished in two days' time."

"Two days!"

"Take as many men as you need. You'll be rewarded."

A second official was bearing down on him, also with his gaze carefully directed to one side. This was the imperial quartermaster.

"Radiance, I have received your orders. The barges will be ready. And the wagons."

"Good, good."

"But permit me to ask, Radiance—this immense structure—you mean to transport it and reerect it on the coast facing the island of Anacrea?"

"That is so. What of it?"

"It will be seen, Radiance."

"So? Your point?"

"Radiance!" The quartermaster spread his hands. "The Noble Warriors have great powers."

"The Noble Warriors will have other matters on their mind. They will be fighting for their very survival."

"Fighting who, Radiance?"

"That is not your concern. Look to your barges and your wagons. Greater minds than yours have conceived this plan."

He cast his eye round the arsenal one more time, to satisfy himself that the work was proceeding as fast as was humanly possible, and retraced his steps.

Back in his private quarters he found himself going over the plan once again, as he did many times a day. There were several points at which it could miscarry. The ramp might not be completed in time. The necessary amount of charged water might not be generated in time. The Jahan might prove harder to manipulate than had been the case so far. But on the whole, Soren Similin was confident of success—except for the one element that was beyond his control. It was precisely this that the quartermaster had spotted.

How could he be sure that the Nomana, even when under massive attack from the west, would not maintain their vigilance to the east?

Trust us.

Hearing his mistress's voice in his head, he dropped to his knees.

When you make your strike, the island will be deserted. Only their god will be left.

"Yes, mistress. But why would the Nomana leave their island?"

Do you doubt our power?

"No, mistress, but—"

That is a doubt. Extinguish it.

"Yes, mistress."

The god of the Nomana will die.

"Yes, mistress."

And you will be rewarded.

Similin bowed his head as if in submission, but in his secret heart he was rebellious. All those who believed themselves superior to the ugly little weaver's son were about to get a surprise.

He rose to his feet and hurried on once more, this time to the secret laboratory. Here he found to his gratification that the array of glass tubes was in place and the apparatus was humming. Clearly it was operational at last.

He looked round for Evor Ortus. The professor was asleep on a cot.

"Wore himself out," said one of the assistants. "Just collapsed. Couple of hours ago."

Similin wondered whether to wake him. He ran his eyes over the apparatus. Then he turned to the assistant and noticed the eager forward bend of his body and understood that this young man was excited by his king's attention. That could be used.

"When do you go into production?"

"We've started already, Radiance. Once the sun rises tomorrow, we'll see some results."

"Nothing so far?"

"Just a drop."

Similin followed the network of glass tubes with his intent gaze, tracking the process all the way to the final suspended needle point out of which dripped the charged water. The needle point itself was encased in a fine rubber membrane to keep the charged water from contact with the air. The membrane had swelled into a very small bubble, the size of a kernel of corn.

"Just a drop? But even so small an amount would make quite a bang."

"Oh, yes, Radiance. What you see there would blow up a house."

"A house, you say? But I suppose only Professor Ortus has the skills to handle such volatile material."

"Not at all, Radiance. I myself have handled the charged water many times."

"You're very young to be entrusted with so great a responsibility."

"Professor Ortus has full confidence in me, Radiance."

"Is that so? Would you be able, for example, to prepare me a small sample of the charged water? Enough to demonstrate the power we possess, without doing too much damage?"

"In what container, Radiance? It must be sealed."

"I have a container in mind." He looked round the laboratory. "There," he said, pointing. "Can you put the smallest drop into one of those and seal up the open end?"

The assistant looked very surprised.

"It could be done, Radiance."

"Then do it, please. At once."

Amroth Jahan did not sleep for long. When he woke, his head hurt and his throat was dry. His uncontrollable rage was gone. In its place was an implacable determination to revenge the humiliation and to reassert his power.

"Sasha!" he yelled. "Sasha! Where's that booby of a son of mine?"

He strode out of his quarters into the tented celebration hall. The mess had been cleared away. The great space was empty.

"Where is everybody?"

Sasha Jahan came running.

"Sasha! Take ten companies! Ride at full speed to the forest they call the Glimmen and set it on fire! Burn the whole forest, you hear? And when the people come running out, kill them! Burn the trees. Kill the people. Have you got that?"

"Yes, Father."

"Say it back to me."

"Burn the trees. Kill the people."

"Go and do it."

"Now, Father?"

"Now, now! Alva!"

The Jahan's second son came running.

"Alva! Find the little fellow in the gold dress and tell him I want him. Time for this homage of his. Where is everybody?"

"Asleep, Father. It's the middle of the night."

"Wake them all up! I want everyone to see this."

So in accordance with the will of the Great Jahan, the Orlan camp woke, as did many of the people of Radiance. The riders and horses of ten companies prepared to leave for the west with Sasha Jahan, and a makeshift throne was erected in the big tent for the Jahan to receive Radiant Leader's homage.

"Where is he?" cried the Jahan. "Why hasn't he come?"

"He's coming," said Alva.

Sleepy-eyed people came crowding into the tent, and the whisper went round that now at last Radiant Leader would be forced to kneel to the warlord. However, Radiant Leader himself still did not appear.

"I'll burn the city! I'll kill them all!"

The Great Jahan was pacing up and down with anger, on the point of making good his threat, when at last the procession of priests entered the tent. They carried with them a lectern, a scroll, and a quill pen standing in an inkpot. The Jahan took his place on his throne. Then he watched in surprise as the lectern was placed in the cleared space before him, the space where Radiant Leader was supposed to kneel to him. The scroll, pen, and inkpot were laid out upon it. In the tense atmosphere of the night, no one, let alone the Jahan, noticed that there was no ink in the pot.

"What's this nonsense?" he roared.

Radiant Leader himself now entered. He was in his most magnificent ceremonial dress, complete with the sunflower corona. His golden cape was held out behind him by six priests, all chosen for their small stature.

He came to a stop facing the Jahan, on the far side of the space in the center of which stood the lectern. He gave a sign. One of his priests scurried forward, took the scroll off the lectern, and carried it to the Jahan. With a deep bow of respect, he unrolled the scroll and held it up for the Jahan to read.

The Jahan's sons and the Orlan captains in his entourage all held their breath. The Jahan could not read.

"Out of my way!" With a roar of rage the Jahan swept the scroll from the priest's hands, sending it flying. "Take all this nonsense away! You!" He pointed his whip handle at Radiant Leader. "Kneel to me!"

"Sir," said Radiant Leader, clear and unafraid, "do not draw down upon yourself the anger of the Radiant Power."

"What? WHAT!"

"That scroll contains the oath that I will make before you—"

"Then make it!"

"—and you will make before me—"

"I swear no oath to you!"

"An oath of friendship and alliance. When you sign that declaration—"

"Sign? SIGN! The Jahan does not sign!"

He unleashed his whip and cracked it in the air before him.

"—we will unite our powers—"

"What power? What is your power?"

He cracked his whip again.

"You bring a whip," said Radiant Leader. "I bring a pen. A quill pen. A simple feather. And yet I say to you, there is more power in that feather than in ten thousand of your whips."

"A feather?" It was absurd. The Jahan broke into a roar of laughter. "A feather!" He pretended to be afraid of the feather, holding up his brawny arms to shield himself from its attack. "Don't hurt me! Save me from the feather!"

He rocked with laughter. The Orlans grinned. The people of Radiance looked puzzled.

The Jahan rose from his throne and readied his whip.

"I'll show you how much power you have in your feather," he said.

He took aim, then sent the whip curling out towards the lectern with deadly precision. The snapping end of the whip cut the feather clean in two—

A ripple in the air, a shudder, and a wave of force exploded outwards, extinguishing every lamp and every candle. Then came the blast. The Jahan and all his entourage were hurled backwards. Screams filled the dark-

ness. Tables and chairs crashed under the weight of sprawling bodies.

A single light came on. It was a lamp held by one of
the priests before Radiant Leader. His golden corona
glowed round his head. His face was a single spot of
brightness in the whole great space. His voice spoke, loud
and clear, and all heard him.

"Beware the anger of the Radiant Power! He who
gives life also gives death!"

"Uh! Uh! Who do we hate?"

Bam-bam! Ba-ba-ba-bam!

"Nomana! Nomana!"

Ba-ba-bam! Ba-ba-bam!

The Great Jahan took to the hate training with gusto.
Similin let him beat the drum himself.

"Uh! Uh! Rip out their hearts!"

Bam-bam! Ba-ba-ba-bam!

"Nomana die! Suffer and die!"

Ba-ba-ba-bam! Ba-ba-ba-bam!

By the end of the session, sweating and heaving, the
Jahan was in excellent spirits. He embraced Similin like a
brother.

"So you really think we can do it?"

"No question. You with your magnificent army—"

"And you with your big boom-bang!" His eyes wid-
ened at the memory.

"A drop, sir. That was no more than a drop. You wait
to see what I can do when I really mean business!"

"Kill all Nomana!"

"Wipe Anacrea off the face of the earth!"

"Smash them! Exterminate them!"

"And best of all—"

"What?" cried the Jahan. "What's the best of all?"

"Exterminate their helpless little god!"

THE THIRD STAGE
IN THE TRAINING OF
THE NOMANA

DOING

*In which the novice takes responsibility
for his own actions.*

⇥ 15 ⇤

The Land Cloud

MORNING STAR SMILED UP AT THE WILDMAN, THINK-
ing she was still dreaming. She reached up her arms to embrace him.

"Oh, Wildman! I knew you were alive!"

"Yes, I'm alive."

But instead of coming closer, he moved away. Morning Star let her arms fall back down. She was awake now.

The Wildman left the hut. Morning Star heard the
murmur of low voices outside. She rose to her feet and
brushed the dirt from her clothes. She felt the hot tingling
of a blush redden her face. She wished she hadn't reached
up her arms like that.

She came out into the bright daylight, blinking, and
forgot her shame in sheer amazement. There before her
were two strange and beautiful beasts. The beasts turned
their long narrow faces towards her and fixed her with

their large brown eyes. As she gazed at them she experienced a second shock: she could see their colors. The auras were faint but unmistakable, a whitish shimmer tinged with blue, like the winter sky. It was the first time she had ever seen the colors on an animal. It made her think they must be somehow human.

She moved forward, hand outstretched, and stroked their necks and cheeks. They permitted her to do so without turning away. She saw how her hand made a ripple in the aura but didn't change its color.

"They're called Caspians."

The voice spoke from behind her. Morning Star turned and saw a slender stranger. She too was beautiful.

Where am I? thought Morning Star. Everyone here is beautiful. Except me.

She looked then for the Wildman. He stood to one side, his eyes on the road. She took in his bright-colored clothes and the dull green of his aura, and understood immediately that he had cut himself off from his recent past.

"I'm glad you're alive, Wildman," she said.

"Didn't think to see you again," he said.

"You're one of the Nomana, aren't you?" This was the beautiful girl. She sounded excited and fearful. "Please. I need your help."

"I'm sorry," said Morning Star, struggling with a rising sadness. "I've left the Nom. I can't call myself a Noma any more."

"You, too?" said the Wildman.

The beautiful girl fell to her knees before Morning Star, and taking her hand, she kissed it.

"I kneel to you," she said. "I kiss your hand. I beg you to help us."

Morning Star blushed once more, with a new shame.

"I'm sorry. I can't help you."

"Then tell me where to find those who can. I have so little time. The Glimmen will be burned. Only the Noble Warriors can save my people."

Morning Star, hearing this, pushed aside her own troubles and did her best to make sense of what the beautiful girl was saying.

"Who is to burn the Glimmen? Why?"

So she learned about the Orlans and the passion of Amroth Jahan and the plight of Echo Kittle, and her sympathy was awakened.

"Anacrea is far away," she said. "I don't have the power to defend the Glimmen against an army. But there's a Noma walking this very road who has more power than any of us." Then, remembering Seeker's answer to the pleas of the women on the ferry, she added, "But I don't know that he'd agree to help you."

Echo Kittle sprang to her feet.

"How far is he from here?"

"I left him at noon yesterday, heading for the forest."

The Wildman stared at her.

"Who?"

"Seeker."

"Seeker!"

Echo then understood that the Wildman knew this great Noma, too.

"He's a friend of yours?"

"He was."

Morning Star watched his colors and saw a glimmer of shame. So the Wildman too felt that he had failed.

"Come with me," said Echo. "Beg him to help me."

The Wildman shook his head.

"I go another way."

"Seeker has a mission of his own," said Morning Star. "I don't think he'll stop for you."

Echo saw that she must rely on her own determination. She called to Kell, and the Caspian came to her side. Morning Star looked on in wonder as the beautiful girl mounted the beautiful beast. They were like magical beings from some other, finer world.

"I'll make him stop," said Echo. "Once he's in the Glimmen, he's in my world."

She urged Kell onto the track and into a canter. With a wave she was gone, down the high road to the west.

The Wildman and Morning Star were left alone together.

"Heya, Wildman," she said softly. "Looks like you're a bandit again."

He avoided her eyes. Her gaze made him uncomfortable.

"No telling what I am," he said.

"Any telling where you're going?"

He gave a shrug.

"Spikertown."

"Mind if I go with you? For now."

"I don't own the road."

This was permission enough. Morning Star turned her

attention to the second Caspian, grazing nearby. She approached her, and the mare lifted her beautiful head to gaze at her, curious but unafraid.

"She won't let you ride her," said the Wildman.

Morning Star put out one hand and touched the mare's shimmering colors. Then she stroked her neck. Then she laid one arm over the Caspian's back and rested her body against her flank. The mare did not move. Morning Star closed her eyes and pressed her brow to the mare's side and pictured her own aura merging with the aura of the mare. She had no idea what would result from this. She was responding instinctively to finding that the beautiful beast had an aura like hers.

The mare shuddered and tossed her mane. She turned her head round and pushed at Morning Star with her nose. Morning Star opened her eyes then and faced the mare, and slowly their heads bent towards each other until they were touching, brow to brow. As they touched, Morning Star knew, though she could not see, that they were sharing colors—that the same aura now enfolded them both.

This gave her a warm shivery sensation that she'd never experienced before. She and the mare were now linked, like sisters. She knew nothing about the Caspian beyond that, and of course the Caspian knew nothing about her. But from this moment on there was trust between them.

"She'll let me ride her now," she said to the Wildman. "Help me to mount."

The Wildman gave her his hand, and she jumped up onto the mare's back.

"Thank you."

The mare walked a little way, very slowly, to allow Morning Star to become familiar with the novel motion. She broke into a slow trot. Morning Star clutched at her mane and laughed at the jerky ride. Then the mare slipped into a smooth canter, sweeping up the road, turning in a wide curve, and so returned to where the Wildman stood watching.

He was smiling, clapping his hands in applause.

"Heya, Star!"

Morning Star waved to him, pink-faced, panting, happy.

"She's so beautiful. What's her name?"

"I don't know."

She leaned down and whispered into the mare's ear.

"What's your name, beauty?"

The mare flicked her ears, but of course could give no other response.

"I'll call you Sky," said Morning Star, "because you have the colors of the sky." And to the Wildman, "Jump up. She'll carry us both."

So the Wildman swung himself up onto the mare's back and put his arms round Morning Star's waist.

"How's that, Sky?"

The Caspian moved off at a gentle walk, her head nodding up and down as she went. Then, at Morning Star's urging, she increased her pace and broke into an easy canter. And so they rode east, towards the Great River.

Morning Star felt the cool of the wind on her face and the heat of the Wildman at her back, and for now she was happy. Her past was all failure. Her future was empty. This ride would come to an end. But she had found her

beautiful Wildman again, and she asked for nothing more
from life.

As dusk fell, Seeker was making his way down the road
that ran through the great forest. He was weary and hungry, and he had no way of knowing how far the forest extended, but he did not stop to rest. The shadows deepened
rapidly between the dark winter trees, and in a short while
he found he could barely see the road ahead. He began to
think it would be wise to stop and rest until dawn.

At this moment a light dropped out of the sky—or
rather, as he soon saw, out of the branches of the trees
above. It was a lantern with a flame burning inside a pierced
tin windshield, attached to a long cord. It dangled in the
roadway before him, illuminating his startled face and casting his shadow onto the surrounding tree trunks.

Next to drop from the branches was a basket, also suspended from a cord. In the basket was a long curving
sausage. He looked up, but he could see no one in the
darkness above. So deciding that questions could come
later, he took the sausage and started to eat.

The sausage was so tasty, and he was so absorbed in
eating it, that he never heard the Glimmeners descend
from their high perches and drop softly onto the forest
floor. He only became aware of their presence when they
began to appear between the trees, walking with soft tread
towards him, in the glow of the dangling lantern.

They came from every side, like ghosts, with slender
forms and pale lovely faces. There was no aggression in
their manner, and so he felt no fear.

In the lead was Echo Kittle.

"You are the Noble Warrior they call Seeker?"

"I am," said Seeker, now even more surprised. "How do you know my name?"

"I met some friends of yours on the road."

One of the older Glimmeners bowed and spoke.

"Darkness has fallen, sir. May we offer you the hospitality of our homes for the night?"

"Your homes?"

The Glimmener pointed up into the branches above.

"Our homes are very near," he said. "We can offer you food and drink and a comfortable bed. But you will have to climb."

Now that he had eaten a little, Seeker realized how hungry he was, and a bed for the night would refresh him more than a litter of damp leaves between the trees.

"Thank you," he said. "I accept your offer. But I must be on the road again at first light."

The lantern rose as he climbed, drawn by some invisible hand high above him. Echo's brother Sander went ahead, slipping upwards through the branches like a bird. Seeker followed, from foothold to foothold, feeling heavy and clumsy by comparison. And as he climbed, lights came on in the upper branches round him and sparkled like stars in the forest night.

"Have you got one of the new riding beasts?" Sander asked him.

"No," said Seeker, not knowing what he meant.

"Echo has. She's brought one back."

The nearer he climbed to the highest branches where

the Glimmeners lived, the more these lights revealed to him. There before his astonished eyes, seemingly suspended in shadows and air, were little homes made up of many rooms, all separate from each other but clustered close together, tumbled up and down and this way and that as if some storm had blown the houses into their various parts and tossed them into the high branches to perch wherever they fell. Each room had a roof, a door, windows; and through these windows, as he climbed, Seeker saw scenes of domestic tranquillity. A family seated round a table eating dinner; a mother tucking two children side by side into a quilt-covered bed; an old lady in a high-backed chair, at work on her embroidery by lamplight. He saw a line of jovial fellows on a bench, all with tankards in their hands, drinking and laughing. Altogether it was very like passing through a village at night, except that he was passing through it upwards.

"Why do you live in trees?" he asked Sander.

"We just do," said Sander. "Why do you live where you live?"

"If you don't like it, you don't have to come," said a voice from above. It was Orvin Chipe. He glowered at Seeker as he clambered up to the main living branch. "We don't get many groundlings up here. We keep ourselves to ourselves."

In this way Seeker was guided to the Kittle family home, and there he was greeted by Echo's mother.

"So you're the one who's to save us!" she exclaimed, bobbing a greeting and smiling even as she dabbed tears from her eyes. "My Echo says we're all to be destroyed, and what a wonder it is to have her returned to us! Do take the long couch, you'll find it very comfortable, like resting on air, though I say it myself."

Seeker sat on the couch and looked round him. Three glowing lamps illuminated a room papered in a pink and green floral pattern. At the center stood a polished table, with an arrangement of winter blossoms in a terra-cotta vase. All round were armchairs and couches, into which his hosts had settled themselves to gaze upon him. For all the urgency of his mission and his longing for sleep, it seemed impolite not to admire the domestic arrangements.

"What a pretty room."

"Oh, do you think so?" cried Mrs. Kittle. "It's just the way we like to do things in our family. It is true, I must say, that others have been kind enough to suggest that I have a knack. But in the end it's no more than what I call a home, and a home should be pretty, don't you think?"

Food and drink now appeared and were offered to Seeker. As he ate, the Glimmeners watched him with open curiosity and whispered among themselves.

"So you're the Noble Warrior, eh?" said Mr. Kittle.

"What's a Noble Warrior?" said Sander, impressed.

"It's just a name," said Orvin.

"Let him eat," said Echo.

"How do you find the couch?" said Mrs. Kittle.

"Very comfortable," Seeker replied.

"No doubt you're wondering who made it. He made it." She nodded proudly at her husband. "Tell him, my dear."

"No, no," said her husband. "He doesn't want to know about furniture."

"I don't see why not. If we're not to be burned to death, then we need somewhere comfortable to sit at our ease."

"Mother!"

"Oh, I'm not to talk." She looked round the room with bewildered eyes. "I don't know why it is, but apparently conversation is no longer appreciated. My daughter has come back from the dead—for we were all quite sure she had been murdered by those horrid hairy men—and as for the beasts they rode on, their color was most unusual, what I call biscuit, a color that I haven't thought to use before, but it would go very well with the reds I've used for the window curtains in this room, which I call earthy reds—"

She fell silent, quelled by her daughter's furious glare.

"Glimmeners keep to the Glimmen," said Orvin. "That's how to stay out of trouble."

"You can do as you please, Orvin," said Echo, "and I shall do as I please."

She had been watching Seeker with growing uncertainty. Though he was dressed as a Noble Warrior, he seemed to her to be too young and too soft to possess the kind of power she needed. His thoughtful face and wide brown eyes gave him the look of a student rather than a fighter. Nevertheless, he was her only hope.

"Sir," she said, when at last he put down his plate, "my mother has spoken of it already, and now I must tell you directly. We are in great danger. I have been told that the Noble Warriors are sworn to come to the aid of the oppressed. Sir, our homes, our people, the trees of this whole great forest round us—all are threatened with destruction. We ask for your help."

Seeker heard this with dismay and lowered his gaze. The Glimmeners fixed their eyes on him in silent entreaty.

"The Great Jahan," continued Echo, "has sworn that he will burn the Glimmen and kill all the people who live here. Only you can save us."

Still Seeker stared at the floor. Echo felt her hopes fade.

"You're a Noble Warrior. It's your duty."

Seeker looked up at last.

"I have a greater duty," he said.

"What can be more urgent than saving the lives of hundreds of innocent people?"

"Saving the All and Only who gives us life."

"The All and Only?" said Sander. "What's that?"

"Our god," said Seeker. "Everyone's god."

"There's a queer thing," said Mr. Kittle. "You're to save your own god? Are you stronger than your own god?"

"The All and Only is the weakest of us all," said Seeker. "We also call him the Lost Child."

"A weak god!" Echo felt anger rise up in her. "What use is a weak god?"

"We live our own lives," replied Seeker.

"If you don't have the power to help us," Echo said, "just say so. If you have the power and won't use it, then you don't deserve our kindness."

Seeker rose.

"I think I should go."

"No. I don't mean it." Echo found herself caught whichever way she turned. "Stay tomorrow, just for one day. If the Orlans come, they'll come tomorrow."

"I've no time to lose. Not even one day."

"Then go!" she cried out in her bitterness. "Go to your baby god and I'll do as the old monster wants and I wish I were dead!"

She turned away and bit her lip to stop the tears rising to her eyes. Her family and the other Glimmeners looked on in silence, awed by her anger and pain.

Seeker made them a bow in the Nomana fashion.

"Forgive me," he said. "You have your duty, and I have mine."

So Seeker slept that night on a bed of leaves after all, and slept fitfully and woke early. He set off at once down the road, unaware that he was being followed by a silent figure in the trees above. He reached the edge of the forest as dawn was breaking, then stopped by the last of the trees and gazed westward.

Ahead, across the plain, its upper surface silvered by the light of the rising sun, lay the land cloud.

It sat like an immense feather bed on the flat land. Its upper surface, hummocked and pillowed and creamy white, was in permanent movement, rising and falling, swelling and stirring, like some vast creature breathing in its sleep. It looked benign, even comfortable, from the safety of the forest. But this was surely not a natural creation.

Echo watched Seeker from her high perch in a tree

above. She understood now that he was going into the land cloud. She saw him leave the forest with confused feelings of anger and admiration. The Glimmeners had seen many singing pilgrims go into the cloud, but no one had ever come out. What was the point of doing something brave if you knew it would kill you?

Then she realized the fingers of her right hand were tugging at the little finger of her left hand. She blushed for shame, even though there was no one to see.

⚜ 16 ⚜

The Door in the Wall

THERE WAS A SHARP STING IN THE AIR THAT DAY, AND the clear white sky above gave warning of a frost. Ice had not yet formed in the wheel ruts of the road, but the stony earth was hard underfoot. The old man who had called himself Jango strode down the track at a swinging pace, stabbing the ground with his stick as he went. When the road reached the high stone wall that ran alongside it, he slowed down, first to a walking pace, then to a shuffle. By the time he reached the crowd in front of the roadhouse, he was moving like the old man he was, and no one paid him any attention.

The crowd had formed round a wagon, on which stood a short sly-looking fellow with one arm round the shoulders of a lanky youth. Jango knew them both. One was a rogue called Ease; the other was the former goatboy Filka.

"My friends!" Ease was crying. "We live in a time of suffering. Many of you have lost your homes to the invaders. Many of you have lost loved ones."

"And food!" cried a voice in the crowd.

"Your hearts ache," Ease went on, throwing an irritated glance at the one who had interrupted him. "You long to see them again. The loved ones you've lost."

"And the dinners we've lost," said the heckler. "They eat everything. They leave us nothing."

"But this is also a time of miracles!"

"It would be a miracle to get something to eat."

"Do you want to hear about miracles or not?" demanded the speaker.

"Miracles! Miracles!" cried the others in the crowd, shouting the heckler down.

"Very well," said Ease. "You see this lad here? You know what he is?"

The spectators looked up at the lanky youth, with his vacant, staring eyes.

"He's a Funny," they cried.

"And what's a Funny?"

"Simple in the head," said one.

"Came out feet first," said another.

Ease nodded.

"A Funny," he said, "is different from you and me. And different can be special. Different can be touched by the gods! Why would the gods choose to touch a poor Funny like this? Because he's simple! In his simplicity he's open to the favor of the gods. Are you open to the favor of the gods?"

His finger pointed accusingly down into the crowd.

"Are you? Or you?"

They seemed unsure.

"No! You are not! You're too clever. Too busy. Too important."

They nodded their heads at that.

"But this poor simple Funny isn't clever or busy or important. So the gods have touched him. And he—yes, this lad here—can do miracles! He's even brought a dead man back to life!"

A gasp from the crowd. One among them, more affected than the rest, cried out.

"Do a miracle for me!"

He forced his way forward to the wagon, panting and shouting, dragging one stiff crippled leg.

"Me! Me!" he cried. "Give me back the strength in my leg! Let me walk again on two good legs and I'll pay you all I have!"

"No money, good sir. All you need bring is an open heart."

"You're my last hope!" cried the cripple, and he wept aloud as he reached one hand upwards. "Let the gods touch me!"

"Stand back, good sir," said Ease. "The Funny will call down the favor of the gods. If the gods are merciful, he'll do what he can for you."

He murmured in Filka's ear, then moved back to give him space. Filka reached out his arms and began to spin. As he spun round and round on the wagon, he uttered a wailing cry.

The people in the crowd watched with interest.

"He's dancing! The Funny's dancing!"

"Hush!" called Ease. "Watch!"

At the height of his dance Filka suddenly stopped dead, rocking and staggering, and very nearly fell off the wagon. But he righted himself and began to wave his arms in a dreamy fashion. He smiled and babbled nonsense.

"Come closer," said Ease to the cripple. "He's ready now. Touch him."

The cripple dragged himself closer, evidently fearful, and reaching up his hand, touched the Funny's leg. No sooner had he made contact than he uttered a sharp cry and fell to the ground. Filka swayed and babbled as if nothing had happened. The crowd gaped.

"Rise, good sir," said the speaker.

The cripple hauled himself to his knees and an expression of astonishment formed on his face. He felt his bad leg. He stood up. He jumped on his bad leg. He sprang into the air. He cried out in joy.

"I'm cured! I can walk!"

The crowd cheered. The cured man pulled coins from his bag and held them up to Ease.

"No, no," said Ease. "No money."

"But you must eat—I'm so grateful—take it!"

So Ease at last accepted the gold coins.

"We shall treasure your gift," he said, "as an offering to the gods."

By now the crowd was in a state of ferment. Everyone was shouting at once, everyone seemed to have an ailment, everyone wanted to be touched by the Funny. They thronged round the wagon.

"My grippe! Cure my grippe!"

"Touch my eyes! Touch my eyes!"

"My hands! I can't use my hands!"

But before anyone else could be cured, Jango, who had been watching throughout, somehow got himself up onto the wagon. There, reaching out one bony hand, he touched Filka's cheek. Filka dropped his arms at once and came out of his trance. He looked at the old man, and his eyes were no longer blank.

"I'm so sorry, Filka," said Jango. "You've been badly used by this business."

"What do you think you're doing?" exclaimed Ease, pulling the old man away by one arm. "You take your turn."

Jango looked at him.

"I know you," he said. "We met long ago. Just as I know you." This was addressed to the cured cripple on the ground below. "You were partners then, as you are now."

"Lies!" cried Ease. "I never saw him before in my life!"

"Your name is Ease," said Jango. "And yours is Solace."

At this the two exchanged a rapid furtive glance. Ease came up close to Jango and whispered to him.

"Who the devil are you?"

"They call me Jango."

"Well, Mr. Jango, I've never seen you before in my life. But it seems we need to have a private talk."

He jumped down from the wagon and gave his hand to assist the old man down after him. Then he led Jango away from the crowd. The former cripple followed after them.

"You just walk on down the road, Mr. Jango," hissed Ease, pressing some coins into his hand, "and be glad nothing worse happens to you."

"I'm sorry," said Jango. "I can't let you abuse that poor boy."

"Abuse him? We're like family to him!"

"We look after his money for him," said Solace.

"He's no use for money, Sol," said Ease.

"But we look after it all the same."

"Out of kindness."

"Too much kindness. That's our weakness."

"Soft hearts, Sol. That's our weakness."

"So don't you concern yourself over us, Mr. Jango."

Ease wrapped one arm round the old man. At the same time, he drew a blade with the other hand, then touched the sharp tip to Jango's throat. "Or I shall have to concern myself with you."

Jango sighed.

"Stupidity," he murmured. "How little you see."

With that he gave a small shake of his head, and both men, who had been huddling round him, shot backwards as if punched by an axer, then fell sprawling to the ground.

Jango returned to Filka on the wagon, and while the crowd looked on in bewilderment, he knelt before him.

"Forgive me," he said. "You've suffered more than you deserved."

Filka wrinkled his brow in puzzlement. Then he too

went down on his knees—not to ask forgiveness, but so that he could clasp the old man's hands.

"I got special friends," he said. "Only they went away."

"I know," said Jango. "But I've come now."

"That's good," said Filka.

The crowd began to be angry.

"It's our turn now! We want to be cured, too!"

Jango rose and spoke to them.

"This boy can't cure you. What you saw was a trick to get your money."

"That was no trick," came a woman's shout. "Didn't I see him cure that cripple with my own eyes?"

"They never asked for money," cried another.

"Look," said Jango, pointing to where Ease and Solace now stood, rubbing their bruises and conferring in low voices. "They work as a team."

"You don't know that," said the woman in the crowd. "You just want to spoil it for the rest of us."

"He's just envious," said another. "He's an old man. He wants us all as crippled as he is."

"I saw that cripple. He was pulling his leg like a log of wood."

"And he never asked for money! He said we weren't to give him money. The old man's a liar if he says he did."

Jango gave up trying to convince them. He smiled at Filka and nodded at the road ahead.

"Shall we go?" he said.

The old man and the Funny climbed down from the wagon and set off together, leaving an angry and dissatisfied crowd.

"He just wants the Funny for himself," they grumbled.

Ease heard this. He beckoned to Solace to follow him back onto the wagon.

"My friends," he said to the murmuring people, "don't be dismayed because the Funny has left us. The favor of the gods falls on those who are deserving."

He put his arm round Solace's shoulders.

"The cripple has been cured. The gods are with him now."

Solace looked surprised. Ease whispered to him, "Dance."

"Dance?"

Ease reached out his arms in demonstration, copying the way the Funny had danced. Solace understood. He reached out his arms and began to dance.

Jango and Filka walked down the road together, through the bleak winter fields. After a mile or so, the road ran alongside a section of the old stone wall. Jango planted his stick before him with each stride.

"Never seen a stick like that before," said Filka.

"It's for sitting on," said Jango.

He opened out the handle into the small seat for Filka to see. Filka was entranced.

"Can I sit on it?"

"If you like."

So they stopped and Filka sat on the sitting-stick, as proud as a king on a throne.

"We must go on our way," said Jango.

"I don't have a way," said Filka.

"Then you can come on mine."

"All right. I'd like that."

On they went, following the long wall that ran ahead as far as the eye could see. The old man let Filka carry his stick. A flock of seagulls appeared, borne inland by the north wind, and circled in the air above them.

"You know how I'm a Funny," said Filka.

"Yes."

"Are you a Funny, too?"

"I suppose I am," said the old man.

"Do you like being a Funny? Because I don't."

"No, I don't like it so much, either. But, you see, the others need us."

"Do they? For what?"

"It's different for each of us. But we each of us have something important to do."

"Well," said Filka, "I don't know what mine is."

"No, mostly we never know. But we do it all the same."

"Once I had a herd of goats," said Filka. "I had to look after them. Then I had special friends. I had to do what they told me. But that's all gone now."

"Shall I tell you a story?" said the old man.

"All right."

"It's a story about a wall, much like this one. This wall went all the way across the land, from sea to sea. There was a door in the wall, and it was locked. Beside the door was a little house. In the house lived a little man, who kept the key to the door. He kept it in a bag that hung round his neck. His job was to open the door if anyone came by who wanted to go through to the other side of the wall. And people did come from time to time, and looked at the door, and rattled it to see how solid it was. But they never asked to go through."

"Why not?"

"Well, no one knew what there was on the other side. And I suppose you can't want something that you know nothing about."

"No. I suppose not."

"So the little man felt as if he wasn't much use to anybody. There he was, the keeper of the key to the door, and no one ever asked him for his key. He wished he was like the other people he saw, going about their busy lives with so many busy things to do."

"That's just like me," said Filka, greatly surprised. "That's how I feel."

"He thought of giving up being the key-keeper and going away. But what if someone came to the door after he'd left, and wanted to go through?"

"He could leave the key in the door," said Filka.

"He did even better than that. He unlocked the door, and he opened it."

"He opened it!"

"And then he went through."

"He went through!"

"And he was never seen again."

"So what happened to him?"

"No one knows."

"Oh." Filka was disappointed. "I thought the story was going to have a happy ending."

"It does," said Jango. "He left the door open."

At this point Filka realized that there was a door in the wall ahead.

"Look! There's a door here, too!"

"So there is."

Filka ran on, filled with excitement, and reached the door before the slower old man. He turned the handle. The door opened.

"It's open!"

"So it is."

"I could go through!"

"So you could."

"Shall I?"

He looked at Jango with apprehension.

"If you like," said Jango.

"I do."

So Filka went through the door. The old man did not follow him. Instead he unfolded his sitting-stick and settled himself down with a sigh to wait. The gulls that had been wheeling and calling in the air all round now flew down to land and settled on the top of the wall and on the ground by his feet. One of them came to rest on his shoulder.

"Back again," said Jango, closing his eyes.

⚡ 17 ⚡

Bedtime

SEEKER WALKED FAST. AS LONG AS HE WAS ON THE OPEN plain in the clear light of the chill winter day, he felt no fear. The land cloud lay ahead of him, heaving slowly in the wind. It formed a clearly defined mass, as wide as a valley but no higher at its highest point than the taller trees in the Glimmen. It was grayish white in color and seemed to be made of roll upon roll of vapor, not at all like the hazy mist that hangs over water meadows on an autumn morning. The land cloud was heavy and brooding and silent.

He thought as he went about the danger that faced him in the cloud and about how he would meet it. He was confident of his own strength, less so of his resolve. His mission was to kill. He had never killed before and was not sure he would be able to do it. These enemies, these savanters, these lords of wisdom, were old and weak; and yet somehow they were more powerful than the Nomana themselves and threatened the very survival of the Nom. So he must have no pity.

Leave one alive and it will all begin again.

As he came closer to the land cloud, it disappeared. The heaving gray-white mass was no longer before him. There behind was the open scrub leading back to the Glimmen. Above, the winter sun, white in a dappled sky. Ahead—nothing.

I must be in it, thought Seeker.

It was almost a disappointment. The feared shadow had not fallen over him. There were no waiting monsters. Just more of this stony weed-riven ground and a light haze.

He walked on. After a while he looked back, and behind him was the same haze that lay before him and to either side. Above he could still make out the white disc of the sun, and daylight illuminated the land round him. But farther away, in the far distance, the mist shut him in. As he walked, he carried a region of clear vision with him. After he had passed, the cloud closed in once more.

All this time he had been following a road—the continuation of the same road that passed through the forest. There were no wheel ruts to mark the way, but many boots had clearly tramped along it, and the beaten ground was easy to follow.

But where was the danger? Where were the enemies?

Seeker walked on into the nothingness, and the farther he went the less sure he became. What if nothing was as he had been told? Narrow Path might have been lying to him, for some secret reason of his own. And the strange old man called Jango was clearly half mad. Yet here he was, obedient to the instructions of a liar and a madman, losing all grip on normality.

Movement ahead. A blur of shadow. A figure in the mist.

It was a person standing by the road, waving. Indistinct as a ghost. Uttering a faint cry.

"Yoo-hoo! Yoo-hoo!"

Seeker approached cautiously. Shortly he made out the form of a woman: a strange-shaped head, a broad body, a raised waving arm.

"Over here! Yoo-hoo!"

Not a strange-shaped head, but a head-scarf. He was closer now and could make out more details. She wore an apron over an ankle-length wool work dress. She wore sheepskin boots. She was tubby. She was pink-cheeked and smiling.

She had no eyes.

"Yoo-hoo!" she sang out, still waving, although he was now quite near. "Over here!"

"I see you," said Seeker.

"There you are!" she exclaimed, evidently pleased. "You can never tell, in this nasty mist. People do get lost. But you must have kept to the road."

"Who are you?"

"Oh, I'm just here to show you the way. How many are there in your party? It seems to me it's very small."

"Just me."

"Only one? That's most unusual. But never mind. I mustn't keep you waiting—you'll catch cold. The beds are made up. Follow me, please."

She set off into the mist.

Seeker had no idea what she was talking about, but he followed. Whatever else she was, this pink-cheeked lady with no eyes did not seem to him to be a savanter. So he hastened after her, supposing that somewhere ahead a house would loom up out of the whiteness.

Instead he saw more hazy figures. His guide called ahead.

"Party of one!"

"One?" came the reply. "Only one?"

The figures ahead were more women wearing head-scarves and aprons. They too were eyeless.

Now, seeing several together, Seeker felt a chill of fear. Who were these people? Not normal people, born with eyes that had been lost. These women had no eye sockets and no eyebrows. From cheekbones to foreheads there was nothing but smooth skin.

"Come along, then," they said to him. "You'll be tired and sleepy."

"Who are you?" said Seeker.

"We're the nannies," said the stoutest of the ladies. "Just ask for Nanny, and one of us will come right away. Now hurry along."

"What do you want me to do?"

"Why, go to bed, of course. It's bedtime."

And there, just visible in the mist ahead, stood two lines of beds. The beds stretched away into the haze, so there was no way of telling how many there were. Each bed had a sturdy iron bedstead and a white pillow and was made up with clean white sheets and cream-colored blankets.

The nannies were already bustling on ahead. One of them turned down the bedclothes on the nearest bed. The others waited in a gaggle for Seeker to join them.

"I'm sorry," said Seeker. "I don't want to go to bed."

They pressed round him, patting and prodding him with their soft hands.

"They all say that," said the head nanny. "We're not tired, they say. We want to stay up longer. But Nanny knows best."

She urged Seeker towards the bed.

"I've come to meet the savanters," said Seeker.

"Mother will be along soon," said the head nanny as if she hadn't heard him. "She'll want to find you all tucked up in bed."

"Who's Mother?"

"Who's Mother? She's the one who loves you, of course. Now come along."

There were more of the nannies than he had realized. They were all soft and stout and seemed to use no force, but it proved difficult to withstand their urging. Seeker found himself pushed onto the waiting bed.

It was time to resist.

He discovered then for the first time that the secret skill was powerless against them. The nannies had no eyes. He must rely on brute force.

"Get back!" he shouted, and he hit out.

"Oh, the naughty boy!" said the nannies, surging ever closer round him. His blow landed, but it had no effect. The nannies were squishy but firm.

He felt himself being lifted up, and even as he struggled,

the bedclothes were being drawn tight over him and tucked in.

"There's a good boy," said the head nanny. "Bedtime now. You lie quiet."

He had very little choice. The bedclothes held him like bands of steel. He struggled but was helpless.

"Mother will be along soon to kiss you good night."

With that, the nannies all tiptoed away.

Seeker lay still, thinking what best to do. He was sure that if he followed his training and concentrated the lir in him he could break out of his bonds. But just as he began to still his mind, he heard the soft shuffle of approaching footsteps. Strapped down as he was, he had limited vision. He made out a stooping black-clad figure. He heard a voice that was sweet and low.

"There, there. Is my baby sleepy? All safe now. Mother's come to kiss you good night."

She was by his bedside now, gazing down at him. Seeker saw a beautiful smiling face—not the face of his real mother, but the face of a perfect mother, the mother who would never age and die, the mother in whose arms he would always find comfort and rest. He felt a warm softness flow through his body, relaxing all the tension in his muscles and promising sweet deep sleep. The mother stooped down low and stroked his cheeks, and her touch was so loving and gentle that Seeker closed his eyes and smiled.

"That's the way, my baby," whispered the mother. "No more fear, Mother's here."

Seeker heard his own voice in a sleepy murmur.

"Kiss me good night, Mother."

"Mother always kisses her babies good night."

He felt her sweet lips press softly against his brow, and the love flowed into his mind and heart, and he knew that he was safe forever and could let himself sail away into oblivion.

But somewhere deep inside him there sounded an echo of a voice from far away.

Refuse to play their game.

He struggled against the sweetness. He stirred beneath the tight, binding bedclothes. He forced his eyes to open.

"No, no, my baby," murmured the caressing voice. "My baby's a good baby and wants to go to sleep."

Seeker uttered a wordless sound. His mouth felt dry.

"Greedy baby! You want another kiss, don't you?"

The loving face descended. Seeker gathered spittle in his mouth. As she prepared to press the kiss on his brow, he spat.

For a fraction of a second, her expression changed. In place of the loving smile he saw a face twisted with hatred. Then the mother face returned.

"Oh, you bad baby!"

She stroked him. It was unbearably sweet. But he had seen her truth.

"Savanter!" he said.

This time the mask fell away altogether. He was staring at a woman in extreme old age, her skin blotched and gray, her teeth gone, her eyes cloudy. He streamed his power into her, hoping to flood her defenses. She staggered back, uttering a cry of fear, but he would not let her go. He knew this was his only chance to take control, and he held nothing back. He hurled his lir into her, and he felt her choke and gasp.

But she was strong. Stronger than he could ever have believed. Once the first shock was over, he could feel the elastic power with which she retreated before him, and he knew that at any moment now she would come stinging back.

Let it come. Not like a rock. Drink it in.

The half-remembered words echoed in his mind.

The savanter was back, smiling her thin dry lips.

"So I'm a savanter," she said in a crackly voice. "No good-night kiss for you."

She struck, fast and deadly, stabbing the blade of her will deep into his mind. Seeker knew as the blow came that it was more powerful than anything he could ever deliver in return. But he had no need to strike back.

He drank her in.

He heard her gasp. He felt her struggle. But he had her clasped to his very being. And as he gripped her, he sucked the force from her and felt himself swell with redoubled strength.

"How?" she stammered. "How?"

He drew a deep breath, directed his new lir to his arms, and with a single movement tore the bedclothes from his body. In that same moment, the savanter reeled back from him and covered her face with her withered hands.

She shook her head, shook all her body, as if to ward off the horror.

"It can't be," she said. "After all this time . . ."

Then she backed away into the mist. She moved with extraordinary speed. Before he could think to pursue her, she was gone.

Seeker jumped from the bed and ran after her, all down the long lines of empty waiting beds. Ahead he could hear the patter of her hurrying feet. He followed, into the ever-deepening mist.

⊰ 18 ⊱

Preparations for War

RADIANT LEADER AND AMROTH JAHAN, EACH ACCOM-
panied by a large retinue, arrived together to witness the
test. The Jahan was duly impressed by the massive structure that filled the imperial arsenal's yard, but his keenest
interest was in the little scientist.

"So you're the fellow who makes the bombs, are you?"

"I am, Excellency."

"Your own work, is it?"

"I'm proud to say, Excellency, that I am the only man
living who understands the complex process of making
charged water."

"Is that a fact? Then you must be some kind of genius."

Professor Ortus found this attention very agreeable.
Radiant Leader understood the Jahan's scheme and quietly
resolved to thwart it.

"Professor," he said, "would you be so kind as to walk over here with me and explain a point of detail? The scaffolding is still to be removed, surely?"

"Yes, Radiance. Any moment now."

When he had the scientist out of hearing of the Jahan, Similin whispered to him.

"You made a grave mistake in telling the Great Jahan that you alone can make the charged water."

"But it is true."

"The Jahan is a ruthless man. My informers tell me that as soon as Anacrea has been destroyed, he will close down your laboratory and have you killed."

"Killed! Me?"

"It will appear to be an accidental explosion."

"But why?"

"He fears the charged water. It's stronger even than his great army. With you dead, no more will be made."

The little scientist seemed to be badly shaken by this warning.

"So what should I do?"

"Go on as you are for now. You'll come to no harm. I too have plans."

"You'll protect me?"

"There will be an accident. But it's not you who will die."

Similin smiled at the scientist, then returned to the crowd of dignitaries. The scaffolding was now cleared, revealing a line of towers supporting a steeply sloping track.

"Let the test proceed!" he declared, with a sensation of satisfaction.

Workmen hauled on ropes by the tallest tower. The ropes turned a winch. The winch slowly raised a platform on which stood a wheeled truck.

"The truck contains sixteen glass bottles and a box of stone ballast," said Ortus. "The bottles are filled with water and sealed. For test purposes, this is plain water. If it were charged water, and all sixteen bottles were to be smashed at once, the explosion would destroy the city of Radiance."

"Remarkable!" exclaimed the Jahan. "This man truly is a genius."

Ortus bowed.

"And what is more," said Radiant Leader, "our genius is a patriot, who is proud to serve his homeland."

Ortus bowed again.

The truck reached the top of the ramp. Here it stuck fast. The watching leaders were not aware that anything had gone wrong. Ortus quietly instructed one of the workmen to climb the tower and release the obstruction. Meanwhile he drew the attention of the two leaders to a net stretched between two poles some way away from the great structure.

"According to my calculations," he said, "the distance from the launch ramp to the net is equivalent to the sea channel between the mainland and the island of Anacrea. The height of the ramp, the velocity of the truck, and the angle of uplift are all precisely gauged to project the truck over that distance and into the net. From the optimum position on the coast, this means the bomb will strike the side of the island just below the walls of the fortress."

"Astonishing!" said the Jahan. "I have such faith in your genius that I have no doubt at all that your calculations are correct."

Radiant Leader frowned.

The workman on the tower signalled that the truck was released. Professor Ortus turned not to Radiant Leader but to the Great Jahan.

"Shall I proceed, Excellency?"

"Yes, yes. Let's see it."

"When you're ready, Professor," said Radiant Leader between clenched teeth, "I will give the command."

"Oh, I'm ready," said Ortus. "If I wasn't ready, I wouldn't ask permission to proceed."

Radiant Leader bit back the sharp rejoinder that rose to his lips, and forced a smile.

"In that case, Professor—please proceed."

Ortus gave the signal, and the truck was set in motion. It rolled down the slope gathering speed, its wheels rattling against the boards, until it was hurtling so fast it seemed it must surely shake to pieces. But no, here it was swooping down to the bottom and riding up the other side and off the ramp, sailing out and up through open air, carried only by its own momentum.

All eyes watched intently as it rose to its highest point over the parade ground and then began to fall towards the far posts. It seemed for a while that it must fall short; but down it came at last and struck the net, buckling the poles with its descending weight, and so came crashing to the ground.

A cheer rose up from the onlookers.

"Perfectly calculated!" exclaimed the Jahan. "Sheer genius!"

"Highly satisfactory," murmured Ortus, blushing with pride.

"A word, if I may," said the Jahan.

Radiant Leader could do nothing. He watched, smiling, filled with rage, as the Jahan took the little scientist aside.

"This city is too small for a man of your stature," said the Jahan. "You should be acclaimed by the whole wide world."

"Your Excellency is too kind."

"Not kind, Professor. Ambitious." He lowered his voice. "Join me, and you'll have the world at your feet."

"And him?" Ortus cast a sly glance at Radiant Leader.

"I'll take care of him."

"An accident, perhaps?"

"A casualty of war," said the Jahan.

"Most regrettable." Ortus was positively smirking.

"But first," said the Jahan, "we deal with the Nomana."

The two leaders and their retinues moved on from the arsenal to the dockyard nearby. Here in long lakeside sheds men were at work constructing five floating bridges. Each bridge, once in place, would be wide enough for a company of mounted Orlans to cross.

The chief carpenter reported to Radiant Leader.

"One left to complete, Radiance."

"How long will that take?"

"By tomorrow noon."

Radiant Leader turned to Amroth Jahan.

"When will your men be ready?"

"When I tell them," replied the Jahan. "Now, if you want."

"The ramp has to be dismantled and towed to the coast. The bridges have to be dismantled and towed downriver. Both operations will take the best part of a day and a night."

He turned to the carpenter.

"Embark the completed bridges at first light tomorrow."

And to the Jahan, "March south in the morning. By the following morning, we will be ready to attack."

"By the following morning? What are we to do all day? When I give the order, ten thousand warriors will ride without ceasing. We'll be at the coast in hours."

"The ramp and the bridges will not be in place before tomorrow night," said Radiant Leader. "But you know best how to command your Orlans, Excellency. If you want them to ride without ceasing, let them do so."

The Jahan smiled thinly.

"And your all-powerful axers, Radiance? Will they be starting their march south soon?"

"The imperial army left at dawn."

This was true. What Similin did not say was that his axers were marching east, not south. Once the battle was over, and the Orlans and the Noble Warriors had done their worst to each other, Similin meant to have his entire army rested and unharmed and ready to impose his will.

In this way, with smiles of unity and promises of mutual support, the two commanders parted to prepare for a victory neither expected to share.

The Jahan summoned his company captains. These men, over two hundred of them, each had command of a band of Orlans and were encouraged by the Jahan to operate with a high degree of independence. There was no other command structure. In time of war, even the Jahan's sons were captains like the rest. The Great Jahan gave the order as to whom the army would attack and when; the captains decided for themselves how to fight. This made the Orlan army fast and flexible, responsive to all the changes that take place in a battle.

The captains were now gathered in the same open space that had held the jagga. Amroth Jahan, his two younger sons at his side, surveyed the alert weathered faces of his veterans with pride. Such men, he thought, had no equal on the face of the earth.

"My captains," he said. "We have feasted enough. Now we go to work."

A growl of satisfaction rose up from the gathering. These were hard men, accustomed to long days on horseback and short nights on hard ground. The luxury of Radiance had already begun to pall.

"We will ride south, to the coast. There where the river meets the sea stands the island home of the Nomana."

The captains nodded as they heard this. They had been expecting it. No one had dared to speak openly to the

Jahan of the humiliation he had suffered on the bridge, but all knew that the Nomana would be made to pay for it. They too wanted revenge. An insult to the Jahan was an insult to all Orlans.

"I promise you this—I, Amroth Jahan, who have led you to victory in every battle we have ever fought—by the end of the day the god of the Noble Warriors will be dead, and all the world will know that there is no power as great as the Orlan nation!"

The captains cheered and raised their fists in the victory salute. The Great Jahan raised his fist in response.

"Call out your companies!" he cried. "Ride south!"

As the gathering dispersed, he turned to his sons.

"What news of Sasha? Is the forest burning?"

The forest was not burning. Sasha Jahan and his ten companies had arrived at the forest's edge, and his men had set about building large fires of brushwood and fallen branches. They had built ten of them, one to each company, in a line all along the fringe of the Glimmen. But the rain of recent weeks had left the wood sodden and it proved slow to burn. When at last a sluggish white smoke began to seep from the pyres, an easterly wind carried it away from the forest and into the faces of the Orlans and their horses. Many of the horses bolted, to get out of the range of the smoke. Then rain began to fall, and several of the fires went out.

Sasha Jahan sat under the shelter of an open-fronted campaign tent, pulling at his thick bushy hair and brooding on the unfairness of life. His father had ordered him to woo the pale and beautiful girl who had dropped from the trees, and the girl had laughed at him. Then his father had ordered him to compete for the girl in the jagga, and he had humiliated him. Now his father had ordered him to burn the Glimmen, and the wood refused to burn, and the wind blew the wrong way. How could he return to his father and tell him he had failed? It was unthinkable. He could hear his father roaring at him, "What I have said I will do, I will do!"

So let *him* make a fire burn in the rain, thought Sasha bitterly. Let *him* tell the wind which way to blow.

One of his men rode up.

"Do I tell the men they can rest? This smoke's a real choker."

"Yes. Let them rest."

Sasha Jahan sat in his tent, listening to the rain falling on the taut canvas, and stared at the forest ahead. They were in there somewhere, he knew—the girl and her people, up in the trees like squirrels. He thought maybe he should send his men into the Glimmen to drive them out. But Orlans fought on horseback, not in the branches of trees. There was nothing for it but to wait for the wind to change.

Then as he gazed and brooded he became aware of movement among the trees. People were coming out of the forest.

His men came running to report.

"Enemy approaching, sir."

"Are they armed?"

"No, sir. Women, sir."

"Women?"

He emerged from his tent and mounted his Caspian. Accompanied by a dozen of his men, he rode forward to meet the party walking slowly out of the Glimmen.

He recognized the one in the lead: it was the girl called Echo Kittle. Behind her came seven or eight women, all slender and elegant but older than Echo. Beside her walked a Caspian.

He rode on until they were close, and then drew his men to a stop to let the women approach him at their own pace. Echo Kittle walked proudly, her head held high, but her face no longer wore the defiant look he had come to dread. Instead there was a deadness in her eyes.

She stopped before him. Her gaze took in the smoldering pyres.

"Your father has sent you to burn the Glimmen?"

Her voice was flat.

"Yes," said Sasha.

"The Glimmen is my home, and the home of my family, and the home of my people. I offer you my life for theirs."

"Your life?" For a moment Sasha Jahan didn't understand. "What am I to do with your life?"

"I will be your bride. As your father wishes."

"My bride?"

"I ask you not to burn the Glimmen," said Echo. "Take me instead."

Sasha's mind began to race. Could it be that his luck was changing? If he were to return with the girl, what would his father say? His father, who had himself been re-

jected. Sasha Jahan could still remember the thrill of astonishment he had felt as he had heard Echo's defiance of
his all-powerful father.

*You think you can have whatever you want, but you can't
have me!*

And this same proud girl was now offering herself to
him, to Sasha Jahan, eldest son of the Great Jahan, and
rightful inheritor of his prestige and power.

"Very well," he said. "You will return with me."

This caused a commotion among the women, which
he ignored. There was sobbing and weeping. But through
it all came Echo's flat voice.

"You'll put out the fires?"

Sasha Jahan gave the order.

"Put out the fires!"

"Then I'm ready."

Sasha Jahan studied her carefully.

"You'll obey me in all things, as a dutiful bride?"

Echo Kittle looked back, and there was no defiance in
her eyes. Nor was there any love.

"What I have said I will do," she replied, "I will do."

⊰ 19 ⊱

The Spiker Army

As they rode east, Morning Star and the Wildman passed a steady stream of travellers making their way more slowly in the same direction.

"Where are you going?" Morning Star called as they went by.

"Spikertown," came the reply.

They were fleeing the Orlan horde, seeking safety in the sheer numbers now assembling in Spikertown.

"We're all spikers now," said the Wildman.

On reaching the top of the last low hill before the descent to Spikertown, they dismounted to let Sky rest. They looked down on the bend in the Great River and saw a large crowd gathering in the water meadows. Faint but clear on the cold air, they heard the uproar of raised voices.

The Wildman scanned the distant crowd with close attention.

"It's a meet," he said. "The tribes have called a meet."

"What does that mean?" said Morning Star.

"It'll be on account of the invaders. They'll be choosing a leader." It was a good omen. He had arrived at the perfect time. "But they'll never agree."

Morning Star could see that the Wildman was energized by some new purpose.

"You should be their leader, Wildman."

"You think so?"

"You'd be a strong leader."

"Could be. We'll see."

When they remounted, he proposed that he take the lead position. She was happy to straddle Sky behind him. She wrapped her arms round him as they began their descent, and she pressed her cheek to his back. She was doing her best to conceal it, but his nearness intoxicated her. Every contact was precious to her. She asked for nothing but to be in his company and to see him happy.

I want him to be happy more than I want to be happy myself, she thought.

Such a surrender had never happened to her before. It frightened her and it excited her.

They rode down into the muddy shanty-lined alleys of Spikertown, then along the deserted main street towards the river. As they came closer they heard the roaring of angry voices in the crowd and the booming cries of the would-be leaders.

"I'm the father of all spikers! Follow me!"

"Not you, old man!"

"I'm as good a man as you any day, Branko!"

"Come and show me, graybeard!"

The roars grew louder and more violent.

"They'll be fighting any minute," said the Wildman. "That's all they ever do, fight each other."

Now the back of the crowd was in view before them. As the Wildman had predicted, a fight was about to begin. A big spiker with a full gray beard was advancing grimly towards a short stocky black-haired man, who stood with his arms wide, stamping his feet on the ground. The crowd had fallen back to open up a space for the combat. On one side ranged the supporters of Mully, the older man; on the other, the mountain men who followed Branko.

"Ya ha!" roared Mully, smacking his great hands against each other as he advanced.

"Ya ha!" responded Branko, pounding the earth.

"Go, Star," said the Wildman.

Morning Star slipped off the Caspian's back. The Wildman rode alone into the empty space.

"Heya, bravas!"

Astonished heads turned and gaped. Mully lowered his hands to stare. Branko swung round, and was fixed to the spot.

The Wildman spread his arms wide on either side and cried out his familiar call.

"Do you lo-o-ove me?"

Smiles broke out on all sides. Big Mully laughed out loud.

"You crazy Wildman!" he said. "Where'd you get that beast?"

The Wildman swung himself to the ground and tossed back his long golden hair.

"More where that one comes from," he said.

He stroked the Caspian's neck. She had been ridden hard and was now pulling in deep shivery breaths.

"I see you've all come out to welcome me home," he said, looking round. "I call that friendly behavior."

"We're not here for you," growled Branko. "We're here to pick a war leader."

"A war leader?" said the Wildman. He spread his arms wide once more and turned about and about, showing himself to the crowd. "Here I am!"

"Out of the way, boy!" Branko had no time for this gaudy youth and his antics. He swept the Wildman aside with one muscular arm. But instead of giving way, the Wildman took hold of his arm and turned the mountain man round to face him, then fixed him with his eyes.

"You love me, brava?"

He used no force. But to the surprise of the onlookers, Branko reached out his arms and hugged him.

"Sure I love you, Wildman."

The Wildman then turned to Mully.

"Branko votes for me," he said. "You vote for me too, old man?"

"I'm not dead yet, boy," replied Mully. "The day I vote for you is the day—"

The Wildman was staring at him. Mully faltered and fell silent.

"You love me too, brava?"

Mully sagged. His head bent in a bow of submission.

"I love you, Wildman."

"Then, heya!" The Wildman turned his laughing face on the assembled spikers. "Everyone loves me! Anyone here have a problem with that?"

He swept one hand through the air, and everyone who saw it felt the thrill of his power like a wind in their face.

"Wildman! Wildman! Wildman!" they cried.

Morning Star stood quietly by the Caspian's side and gloried in the change that had come over the Wildman. He was glowing with power: power shone from his beautiful face, power laughed in his smile and burned in his brilliant eyes. Here before a captivated crowd, he had become in public what he already was in her secret heart—someone whose every motion was perfect. He had shed all self-doubt. He was intoxicated by the love of so many people.

Now the whole crowd was calling his name, chanting his name, their eager faces laughing back at him.

"Wildman! Wildman! Wildman!"

He jumped up onto the hull of an overturned riverboat and spoke to them, finding the very words that were in their hearts, because in this moment, everything was easy and he could do no wrong.

"My friends! I'm a spiker like you. We're the people who don't belong. We have no country, no place of safety. We're called beggars and thieves. We're feared and despised. But we're everywhere! We're tramping down every road in every land. We're from every race and every tribe. We are everyone!"

Morning Star listened to the Wildman and she shared his pride, as she saw everyone in the great crowd sharing his pride.

So I'm a spiker now, she thought, and she smiled at the thought.

"Spikers have nothing," cried the Wildman, "but spikers are free! Will you fight for your freedom?"

"Yes!" answered the crowd, in one great shout.

"Will you fight together, bravas? All the tribes in one army?"

"Yes!"

"With me as your war leader?"

"Yes!"

"Then there's no warlord in the world can overcome us!"

The crowd cheered and cheered.

"Wildman! Wildman! Wildman!"

There came then a scuffling at the back and a shout of anger. The crowd parted to reveal a tall lean young man dressed in heavy furs but bareheaded and hairless. His skull was painted from his eyebrows to the nape of his neck with dark vertical stripes of yellow and black. Behind him came a large band of evil-looking men, all painted in the same fashion. The stranger strode forward with a spike in one hand, pointing with the forefinger of his other hand at the Wildman.

"I want you," he said.

"Tigers!" cried fearful voices in the crowd. "It's the Tigers!"

The stranger jabbed the air with his spike: the challenge to a fight. The Wildman jumped down from his boat and approached the stranger.

"I don't have a quarrel with you," he said.

The stranger's men gathered round him. The band known as the Tigers was big, more than a hundred men, all well armed with spikes and blades.

"Maybe I have a quarrel with you."

"Here I am."

The stranger moved closer to the Wildman. Morning Star, watching the Wildman's eyes, expected to see the stranger yield to the Wildman's will. Instead, the stranger spoke one word in the Wildman's ear.

"Chick," he said.

The Wildman started, as if he'd been stung, and staggered back, staring at the stranger. The stranger reached out one hand and rumpled the Wildman's hair, then broke into a laugh.

"You don't know me, do you?"

The Wildman stared some more and slowly a grin of recognition formed on his face.

"Snakey!"

They fell into each other's arms. The hard men of the Tiger band now all started grinning, too. The tension in the crowd relaxed.

"Snakey!" said the Wildman again. "Is it you, Snakey?"

"Nobody else," said the stranger.

"What have you done to yourself?"

"Grown up, Chick. Same as you."

And he rumpled the Wildman's hair once more.

They took themselves off arm in arm to the fat man's bar to celebrate their reunion, and a great crowd went with them. As soon as they were gone, the cheers faded, and the spirit of unity gave way to renewed bickering. Morning Star hung back with Sky, and saw all too clearly the waves of suspicion that rippled through the clusters of spikers. She saw it in their colors. Each group, their passions once more heightened by the sneers of rival groups, took on its own dominant color. It was a phenomenon she had never noticed before. There was the graybeard called Mully at the center of a large crowd of his own people, and all of them were wrapped in a shared aura that was dirty red in color. The color itself was no surprise: it showed the resentful anger of a group that felt itself threatened and underrespected. But never before had she seen a single dominant color form like a misty blanket over so many individuals.

Near Mully's band there was a crowd of mountain men, and they were wrapped in an aura that was orange in color. Where the two bands pushed up against each other the auras wavered but did not merge. It was the clearest evidence there could be that the spiker tribes were not united yet, but it was evidence that only Morning Star could see.

Sky pushed her nose against Morning Star's back, seeking her attention. She turned and stroked the Caspian's neck and spoke to her softly.

"You need water, don't you, Sky?"

The Caspian nodded her lovely head, and Morning Star rubbed her coat and saw her own colors slowly merge with Sky's colors, as they had done before. It struck her then that if she could share colors with a horse, she could do it with a person. She remembered how her combat teacher's colors had flowed out and wrapped round her, and how she had realized that one person's colors could change another's. An idea began to form in her mind.

She found him in the bar, drinking with the stripe-headed stranger. He called to her gladly as she pushed her way through the crowd.

"Heya, Star! This is Snakey. I told you about Snakey."

"I remember."

"Snakey looked after me when I was a kid."

"When you was a chick," said Snakey, and burst into laughter.

"That's what they called me," said the Wildman, blushing. "Chick."

"He was so small," said Snakey, "and he had this fuzzy golden hair."

He reached out his hand and ran his fingers through the Wildman's hair.

"And look at him now! He's the Wild Chick now."

He ducked as the Wildman took a swing at him.

"Watch yourself, Snakey. I'm the man."

"That's what I see. And to think you used to run round after me calling, 'Snakey! Don't leave me!'"

"Until you left me."

"I never left you."

The Wildman turned to Morning Star.

"Snakey got snatched by slavers. I thought he'd run out on me."

"I'd never do that, Chick."

"He was taken away in a cage to a faraway country to be sold for a slave. But they got more than they knew when they took Snakey. Soon as they let him out of the cage he slit their throats and off he ran. Nine years old."

"Eight, Chick. Eight."

Snakey stroked both hands over his smooth painted head and showed his uneven teeth.

"Those were hard days," said the Wildman.

"I don't see the days getting any softer," said Snakey.

"Wildman," said Morning Star. "There's something I want to show you."

On the Wildman's orders two large bands gathered in the main street of the town, one of northerners and the other of mountain men. The Wildman spoke to them, with Morning Star by his side.

"This is Morning Star," he said. "Whatever she tells you to do, you do. Just as if it was me telling you."

Morning Star then spoke to them.

"The warlord is on his way," she said, "and the spiker tribes have agreed to fight together under one leader. But you're not united. In your hearts each tribe is saying, When the battle comes, we'll fight better than the others. So you won't stand together as one great force. And that way, you'll lose the battle."

The men didn't like being told what to do by a girl.

They scowled and muttered to each other. Branko spoke out loud.

"Who's she to lecture us?"

"You listen," said the Wildman, "or you answer to me."

Morning Star continued.

"I have a way to bring you together."

"We've had truces," said Mully. "We know all about truces."

"This isn't a truce."

She looked from one group to the other. Their colors were clear and distinct, heightened by the challenge she laid before them.

"This is a bond."

She walked forward and placed herself between the two bands. Then turning first to the mountain men, she spoke to the one nearest to her.

"Don't move. I'm going to hold you."

She put her hands on his shoulders and looked up at the aura that reached over him and all his companions. She let his colors flow round her. As she did so, she felt herself fill up with all the fierce sensations that were surging within the mountain men. Then she turned to the second band and put her hands on the shoulders of one of Mully's tribe. There came a shuddering of emotions within her and of colors round her, and she saw the two competing colors swirl and stream in tangled threads of orange and red. She felt a giddy sickness as the two currents of anger seethed like waves within her. She closed her eyes and held her breath and tried to empty herself of all her own feelings, so that she became no more than a channel for the passions of the two bands. She felt them soak into each other and flow out from her again, and the nausea passed. She opened her eyes and could see it clearly: the two bands were merging into a single aura that embraced them all.

The Wildman saw nothing of the colors, but he did see the change in the men. At first there was little more to observe than a shifting about, as if they sought to find more comfortable positions. Then they met each other's eyes, warily, unsure what had happened. Then they grinned at each other and looked round more confidently. Finally there came a straightening of backs and a squaring of shoulders, and without realizing what they were doing, they formed themselves into a single battalion.

Morning Star stepped back, and turning to look at them, she felt an extraordinary burst of elation. One color was now uniting them all. She trembled with exhaustion. The effort had been far greater than she had foreseen, but it could be done. She knew now that she could add band after band, and each new group would share the dominant emotion of the main body. She was building the perfect instrument for war.

"They'll stand together now," she said to the Wildman.

"Heya! Will it work with more?"

"Many as you want."

"I want them all."

"Take them all," said Morning Star. "There's no limit."

"Every race and every tribe," said the Wildman, awed by the prospect before him. "Everyone. That's what I want. An army of everyone."

"I give it to you, Wildman," said Morning Star. Silently she added, Because I love you.

The Wildman spoke to the new spiker army, massed before him on the water meadows.

"Heya, bravas! Do you lo-o-ove me?"

Back came a pounding cheer.

"Wildman! Wildman! Wildman!"

"Are we afraid of the Orlans?"

"No!"

"Shall we drive the Orlans from our land?"

"Yes!"

"Will you follow me into battle?"

"Wildman! Wildman! Wildman!"

And to Anacrea? And into the heart of the Nom? And into the Garden itself? But these things he did not say aloud.

⚡ 20 ⚡

Savanters

SEEKER WALKED ON INTO THE CLOUD MORE SLOWLY now. He could no longer hear the sound of the fleeing savanter. He had no way of orienting himself. Then he became aware that the mist round him was in motion. Nearby it was too fine to see, but ahead, where it formed the ever-retreating wall that closed him in, it was slowly flowing. The flow was not uniform—it was a drifting eddying swirl, but it did have an overall direction. It was flowing towards him, from some unseen source. Insensibly Seeker was directing himself towards this source, as if following a river to its spring.

The ground was now descending. Little by little he sensed that the light was diminishing and that he was in the shadow of higher land to either side. Then the shadow deepened. In the gloom and the mist it was hard to make out his surroundings, but the sound of the air was changing.

I'm going underground, he thought.

If it was true, the entrance to this vault must have been very large. There was no doorway, no obvious change from outside to in. Only the shadowy mist all round and a soft echo of his own footfalls from above.

As he went on, he became sure that he was right.

The light was all behind him now. The farther he walked, the fainter it grew, that band of bright mist; until when he looked back he saw that it was indeed the mouth of a cave.

There came flickers of light ahead, and the scuffling sound of many slow-moving feet. Seeker shrank back. The flickers of light grew stronger and threw shadows— shadows of moving people. Then, round a bend in the cave wall, came a procession of men and women carrying lanterns, murmuring and sighing as they came.

They wore white robes. They staggered as they walked. Their eyes roamed about but saw nothing, and frequently, as if barely able to remain awake, their eyelids closed. Their cheeks were sunken. They breathed with difficulty. They were quite unaware that they were being watched.

As they went by, some of their murmuring voices could be heard.

"Live forever," they were saying. "Live forever . . ."

Seeker stared at them with horror and dread. These people were not old, or sick. They were empty. Their bodies still functioned, but the force that gave them life was gone.

The lir had been sucked out of them.

Even as he watched, one in the wretched shuffling line

stumbled and fell and did not move again. The others shambled on, unseeing and uncaring, their feet treading on the fallen man as they passed.

This was the work of the savanters. This was why he had been sent to kill them.

Seeker went on, deeper into the cave. Now the mist was streaming into his face as he walked. He was coming closer to its source.

Here and there lanterns lay on the ground, some still burning, offering the only illumination. Beside the lanterns lay more fallen bodies of men and women, all emptied, all dead. Seeker stopped by one of them, a youth not much older than he was himself. He reached down to close the dead boy's eyes. At his touch, the face disintegrated into a flurry of dust. Seeker started back, shocked. As the dust settled, he saw the side of the head: an ear, the neck, but nothing more.

The anger in him grew. Whoever did this, he thought, deserves to die.

He caught the shine of a new light ahead, a glow that was more than an abandoned lantern. The streaming mist made it impossible to know how large the cave was through which he was passing, but he now sensed that the space ahead was a great deal larger.

He walked towards the light. As he did so he saw that the mist was growing denser and that the mist at his feet was the densest of all. It was rolling towards him over the ground like cream, curling round his ankles and completely obscuring his feet as it flowed on down the long cave to the open air.

The source of light now revealed itself. It was a lamp, on a high lampstand, rising out of the mist. The lamp's brightly burning flame was shrouded by a handsome fringed lampshade made of patterned silk, amber on scarlet. The fringe was made of gold tassels. It was the sort of lamp you might expect to find in a rich lady's drawing room.

Seeker approached the lamp and so found himself in the presence of a small gathering of elderly people. They were watching him with intent and wary eyes.

There were four of them. They sat in a semicircle round the lamp, three in comfortably upholstered armchairs, one in a wheelchair, wrapped in a woolen blanket. Two were old men and two were old women. The one in the wheelchair had her head bent down to her chest and was asleep. Beside their chairs were low tables on which stood small bottles and half-filled glasses and vases of flowers, and books.

"A visitor!" said one of the old men, waving a crutch in the air.

"What does he say?" said the old woman in the armchair.

"He says we have a visitor, dear."

"No, I won't," snapped the old woman crossly. "Who am I to go visiting? Everyone I ever knew is dead. I won't be told to go visiting."

"No, dear. The visitor has come to us."

"Oh, leave the old goat alone," said the man with the crutch.

"I shall be very glad to receive the visitor," said the old

lady, "but my hair must be brushed first, and I like just the smallest touch of rouge."

"You haven't got any hair."

"A touch of rouge gives an air of animation and is not vulgar."

"Who did she say was vulgar?"

"No, no—"

"I'm not the one who does my doings in my chair."

"There he goes! On about doings again! And in front of a visitor, too."

Seeker stood gazing at this scene in utter confusion. The four before him, so extremely old, so helpless, so half out of their wits, could hardly be the enemy he sought. He could only think they were more of the savanters' victims. In which case, where were the savanters? He looked into the mist, expecting to find further passages, deeper caves. But all he could see within the reach of the lamp's light was the edge of a wide pool. At first it seemed the mist lay on the surface of the water. Then he saw that there was no water, only cloud. From this lake of creamy vapor flowed the mist that rolled over the ground and down the cave. This if anything was its source.

The old man pointed his crutch at Seeker and spoke.

"You! How old are you?"

"Sixteen," said Seeker.

"Sixteen! Very good! Well done!"

"What does he say?" chirped the old woman.

"He says he's sixteen, dear."

"Sixteen! That's a great big lie!"

"The visitor, dear."

"He always was a liar. But he doesn't fool me."

"Oh, suck an egg, you old goat."

Seeker felt it was time to intervene.

"I'm looking for the savanters," he said.

He caught a tiny movement from the old lady who was asleep in the wheelchair, or perhaps not asleep.

"Savanters?" The old man shook his head. "Never heard of them."

"Most likely dead," said the second old man. "Most people you want turn out to be dead."

"What is it he says?" said the old lady.

"He's looking for someone."

"Tell him to come nearer. I don't hear as well as I did."

Seeker was already moving forward. He went not to the old lady who had spoken, but to the one who was asleep in the wheelchair with her head on her chest. As he came close, she raised her head, turning it to the light.

It was the mother.

She screamed a high scream of fury.

"Don't let him touch me!"

At once a great change came over the old people. The senile gaping fell away, to be replaced by looks of keen and calculating intelligence. All four, old as they were in body, suddenly seemed powerful and alert.

"It's him!" screamed the mother. "He's come back!"

They all stared at Seeker in fear and hatred.

"Leave this to me."

It was the old man with the crutch who spoke, but his voice was now quite different. He spoke simply and clearly, in tones that sounded impossibly youthful coming from such a withered mouth.

He was obeyed at once. The mother sat back in her wheelchair and was silent. The old man turned to Seeker.

"Forgive our modest deception," he said. "We have learned to be wary of strangers. We are indeed savanters."

He bowed his head in a courteous greeting.

"Who are you?"

"My name is Seeker after Truth."

"You have been sent by the Nomana?"

"Yes."

"To kill us?"

"Yes."

"Here we are. You have the power. We are at your mercy."

Seeker hesitated. This was not the fearful encounter for which he had prepared himself.

"You know why, of course." The old man was watching him with a calm gaze. "You know why the Nomana fear us."

"You seek to destroy the Nom."

"That is so. But why is it so?"

"I don't need to know that."

"Our crime is that we have dared to seek truths beyond the limits set by the Nom. So you see, we too are seekers after truth. And for this reason alone, the Nomana fear us and send you to kill us."

"I have sworn to protect the Nom," said Seeker.

"To protect the Nom? Or the god who lives in the Garden?"

"The All and Only."

The ancient man held Seeker with his glittering eyes and his strangely young voice.

"Perhaps the All and Only is a prisoner," he said. "Have you ever thought of that?"

He smiled a bitter smile.

"We are the lords of wisdom," he went on. "We have devoted all the years of our long lives to overcoming the evils of existence. We have learned how to cure diseases. We have learned how to postpone death itself, perhaps forever. We have done all this so that we can ease the suffering of humankind. Is this not the true way to serve the All and Only?"

Seeker shook his head. He clung to what he knew. He had seen the husks of living men and women left to crumble in the cave.

"I've seen what you do to humankind."

"They feel no pain. They are sacrificed for the good of all. What you have seen distresses you. But every society makes sacrifices to ensure its own survival. In war many die in defense of their country. These few have given their lives in a far greater cause."

"They've given their lives for a lie. You tell them they'll live forever."

"Is that a lie? Look at us. We have overcome death. We have a kind of eternal life. But our cause is greater than that. What is eternal life without eternal youth?"

"Forever young," murmured the other savanters, like a prayer. "Forever young."

"We have not yet achieved our goal, but we're very close. We need a little more. Just a little more."

The old man watched Seeker intently throughout this exchange, to see if he showed any signs of opening his mind to what he was hearing.

"We are not deceiving you, Seeker after Truth. We deny nothing. We have no secrets. We are the enemies of the Nom."

"And I serve the Nom."

"What other truth have you ever known, in all your young life? But there are other truths. The Nom believes there must be limits set to how far humankind should go in the pursuit of wisdom. We believe there can be no limits. The Nom hopes to make the world just. We hope to make it wise. The Nom offers mysteries. We offer answers. If you think we should be killed for that, do it now."

He spread his thin old arms wide, as if to invite the killing blow. The others too spread their arms.

Seeker looked at them and neither spoke nor moved. He held tight to his loyalty to the Nom, but beyond that he felt his certainties beginning to crumble. He had set out on his pursuit of the savanters on the word of only one man, Narrow Path. Narrow Path had led him to expect great danger. If the savanters were to attack him, he would fight them as his declared enemies and kill them. But they did not attack him. How could he kill them in cold blood?

Now of all times he needed to hear the voice in his head. But nothing came. He recalled what the voice had said to him before.

Surely you know that where your way lies, the door is always open.

No doors here.

He recalled his night visit to the Garden. The figure of a man he had seen there had said to him, "Nothing is dependable. Nothing lasts." It had seemed like wisdom at the time, but it was of no use to him here.

He recalled Jango's words: "You must not defend. You must attack." But the savanters were not fighting him. They were reasoning with him.

He was on his own.

As he hesitated, the one who called herself the mother put her hands to the wheels of her wheelchair and set it in motion. She turned the chair about, moving slowly, and began to roll towards the cloud pool.

"Stop!" called Seeker.

She did not stop. The old man watched him, smiling his twisted smile, as if it amused him to witness his dilemma.

"Not so easy, is it?" he said. "You have to be so very sure, to kill. And you're not sure."

"No. I'm not sure."

"That's because you have an open and inquiring mind. It takes a closed mind to be sure. Intelligent people know there's always more to understand. And you are very intelligent."

The wheelchair creaked on its way. In a short time the mother would reach the edge of the cloud pool. Seeker knew the old man was trying to manipulate him. But he also knew that what he said was right.

Why have I been given this power? I'm no executioner.

The savanter's earlier words came back into his mind with sudden shocking force.

"Perhaps the All and Only is a prisoner."

Seeker could not doubt the reality and power of the god in the Garden, because time and again he had knelt before the silver screen and felt it for himself. But the brothers and sisters who guarded the Lost Child—could they be jailers? Why was the Garden not open, so that the Lost Child could come and go at will? Who was being protected, and to what end?

The All and Only was the ultimate source of the Nomana's power. No one gives up power voluntarily.

The old man seemed to read his mind.

"You have doubts," he said. "Only the intelligent have doubts."

The wheelchair reached the edge of the cloud pool.

He flatters me, thought Seeker.

Then suddenly he understood what was being done to him.

They've found ways to use the strength of others.

He had thought that meant his newfound power; but everyone has more than one source of strength. Seeker was clever and had always known it. The savanter was turning his own intelligence into the source of his weakness.

Fight them with craziness.

"My head is empty," he said. "I know nothing. I am a stupid."

Words from long ago. The old man frowned and blinked.

Seeker drew a long breath, gathering the lir in him to a sharp spike of concentrated power. The watching savanters realized what he was about to do. All three locked their eyes onto his and struck at him with all their force.

Seeker stood tall. He breathed more deeply still. He let their violence flow into him and fill him to the brim. He was at ease now. The attack had come. No doubts now.

The savanters saw with mounting horror that the force that should have obliterated Seeker was making him stronger with each passing second.

"Get back!" cried the old man. "Get away from him!"

They scrabbled for crutches and sticks. They heaved themselves out of their chairs. The old woman in the wheelchair rolled into the cloud pool.

Seeker released his breath and struck.

The force wave kicked over the armchairs and sent the tall lamp flying. It slammed the savanters to the ground and churned the cloud pool into a white storm. For a few moments nothing could be seen in the cave but the glow of the lamp on the ground, shining like a moon in the shroud of white mist.

Power without limits.

Seeker strode forward and righted the lamp. By its light he studied the bodies on the ground. They lay snapped like porcelain dolls, limbs twisted, eyes empty. Three savanters killed. Four to go. Seeker felt a burning in his chest and belly, and his whole body shivered with an entirely new sensation. It was more wonderful than anything he had ever known before. It was like being passionately hungry and eating your fill, both at the same time: desire and satisfaction blended together and gulped like wine.

I'm doing the job I was sent to do, he thought.

He strode on to the edge of the cloud pool into which the mother had vanished. He stepped into the thick swirling vapor. When he was immersed as far as his knees, he paused and looked back. Nothing had changed. The great cave was silent. So he walked on, deeper into the mist, and the surface of the cloud pool closed over his head.

THE FOURTH STAGE
IN THE TRAINING OF
THE NOMANA

BEING

*In which the novice achieves self-mastery
and becomes a Noble Warrior.*

⊰ 21 ⊱

First and Last

NARROW PATH KNELT BEFORE THE ELDER AND THE Community, with his head bowed. The Prior, standing by his side, slowly unwound the badan from his shoulders.

"By your own actions," he said, "you have cast yourself out of our Community. This is not our will. It is yours."

The Prior dropped the badan to the ground.

The Elder gave a sign.

"Let it be done."

Two brothers went to Narrow Path's side as he rose to his feet. They had no need to hold him, though they were there to restrain him should it prove necessary. He went without a murmur.

Outside the Chapter House, on the way to the wash-house, Miriander confronted him, unable to contain her anger.

"Why?" she asked him. "The boy was sent in our time of danger to save us. Don't you want the Nom to be saved?"

Narrow Path made her no reply and went on his way in silence.

In silence he was led into the washhouse and stripped to the waist. His thin arms were raised above his head and strapped to the high water pipes. In silence the brothers and sisters gathered round, and the taps were turned on, and the water streamed down over his bowed head and his naked upper body. He was so thin, there were hollows between his ribs where the water rippled as it fell.

Then the silence ended. The brothers and sisters began to make a buzzing sound. It began softly, on a low note, but little by little it rose in pitch and intensity until it filled the room.

The torment of the cleansing showed on the face of the dangling man, though he uttered not one cry. He twisted his head back and round, as if trying to escape the sound that drilled into his brain. His mouth and cheeks contorted, and his eyes rolled up in their sockets, and his bare feet kicked as if he was being hanged.

The relentless buzzing droned on, scraping and scouring into the deepest recesses of his mind, emptying him of all that had gone into the making of him, washing him out with the unceasing stream of water until at last there was nothing more to take, and the lines of pain that etched his face became smooth again, and the jerking twitches of his body ceased.

They untied him then and laid him down to rest. And when he was rested, they dressed him and escorted him to the outer gate of the Nom.

The Prior spoke the words of dismissal.

"All we have given you now returns to us. Take nothing with you as you go."

Narrow Path gazed back, his face empty of hope or fear.

"You are like a child born again. You are innocent again, and therefore forgiven. Go now, and may the One who understands all things have mercy on you."

Narrow Path set off, moving slowly across the Nom square. When he reached the top of the long steps down the hillside to the harbor, he turned back to look at his former brothers and sisters, and they waved him on. So he descended out of view.

At that moment, over the sea air there came a new sound—the call of a distant horn. Then another, followed by the rattle of drums. The eyes of the Nomana turned north, to the coast. There they saw a line of mounted warriors breasting the last hill before the shore. At first there were no more than thirty or forty, but as they advanced, the line spread and a second line came behind the first, and a third, until the riders reached from the riverbank to the distant fringe of trees. The lines kept coming, and became a swarm. The swarm became a multitude. Behind them, borne down the river by the fast-flowing current, sailed a long chain of heavily laden barges.

"So it begins," said the Elder.

Even as the Nomana watched, the whole strip of coast was turning black with mounted warriors, and the beat of their drums and the crying of their horns filled the air.

"How many more?" said Chance.

The same thought was in all their minds. The power of the Nomana was great, but it was soon exhausted. What if this invading army was so immense that it could soak up all the force they could throw at it, and remain undefeated?

"This was why the boy was sent to us," murmured Miriander. "But now he's gone."

The danger was suddenly all too close and all too real.

The Elder gave a quiet command.

"Let us open our minds and our hearts to the one Clear Light."

The members of the Community stood between the shimmering white pillars of the Cloister Court and gazed towards the Garden, and each submitted their will to the will of the All and Only. The Elder, too weak to stand, sat in his wheeled chair and fixed his old eyes on the green depths that could be glimpsed through the pierced silver screen. As he did so, those standing nearby saw tears form in his eyes. He was heard to murmur over and over:

"Not my will but yours . . . Not my will but yours . . ."

The Council of the Nomana regrouped in the echoing space of the Chapter House. Word came that the barges were being moored in the river mouth and that engineers had begun to build bridges across the channel. This news galvanized the members of the Council, and a buzz of urgent voices filled the octagonal space.

"They mean to enter the Nom itself!"

"The walls are thick. Let them try."

"One Noma can hold a bridge."

"But for how long?"

The Elder raised one hand for silence. As he spoke, the uncertainty slipped away from his voice. His words sounded frail but sure.

"We have only one choice. We will meet this enemy in battle. We will strike once. First and Last."

First and Last! The Nomana had no greater power than this mighty strike, which called upon the strength of all the Community, packed into one single devastating explosion. It was rarely used, and had always been overwhelming in its impact. But the First and Last could only be used once.

Narrow Path was rowed to the mainland and put ashore in some haste. The oarsman could see the mass of mounted warriors and had no wish to linger. Narrow Path saw the invaders too, but he was not afraid. He set off across the beach at a steady pace, looking round with puzzled eyes, wishing someone would tell him what he was to do.

When he came up with the riders, he walked through the middle of them, no more aware that they might be a danger to him than if they had been a flock of sheep.

"Hey, you! Where do you think you're going?"

"That's one of the hoodies!"

"Never! Where's his hood?"

A passing Orlan decided he had better take charge of the wanderer. Narrow Path made no objection.

"You come with me."

"Thank you," said Narrow Path.

The Orlan led him away to the band of trees and tethered him there like a calf. Narrow Path sat down on the ground and stared at the horses and rubbed at his temples with the knuckles of both hands.

Behind him, men with axes were at work felling trees. The rhythmic blows of iron on wood filled the air. Then there came new sounds: a fanfare of trumpets and the clang of steel on steel. Narrow Path watched as a chariot approached, bearing a figure on whom shone a dazzle of dancing light. A smile formed on Narrow Path's face for the first time since he had been cleansed. He thought this must be a god come to tell him where he was to go, and what it was he must do. He got onto his knees to show respect.

The men all round him were now beating their swords on their breastplates and cheering, so Narrow Path beat his chest with his hand, too.

The god's chariot stopped not so very far away, and the god pointed his whip across the water to the island.

"I am the Great Jahan!" he cried. "Let the Noble Warriors kneel in submission to me, or I'll hunt them down and kill them like rats!"

The Orlan warriors set up a chant. Narrow Path joined in, beating his skinny chest and crying out in his thin high voice, "Jahan! Jahan! Jahan!"

———

As the Orlan army massed on the coast, a second convoy of barges docked on the east bank a mile upriver. The cargo was off-loaded onto a line of waiting ox wagons under the watchful eye of Evor Ortus. As soon as each wagon received its burden, the ox team was driven off down the road to the coast. The transfer of timber sections from barges to wagons took many hours. By noon a line of ox wagons could be seen winding down the road south.

The last load to be carried off the barges was a wooden box the size of a blanket chest. Professor Ortus supervised the moving of this box himself, shouting to the men who carried it to take care as they lowered it onto a bed of straw in the waiting wagon. He then rode in this wagon himself, with one arm lying over the box, to make sure it remained in place on its journey down the rutted road.

"Steady! Steady!" he cried to the driver.

As they rode along he grinned at nothing and sang to himself.

> *"High, high, watch it fly*
> *Like an onion in the sky . . ."*

Soren Similin was waiting impatiently for Ortus at the construction site.

"They must work faster!" he said as soon as he saw him. "We have very little time. Why don't they work faster?"

"You don't want it to fall down, I suppose," said Ortus.

Similin was wearing a thick brown cloak and a fur hat with earflaps, partly to disguise himself and partly because his prominent ears felt the cold. He was in a state of extreme agitation. He paced up and down, bundled in his heavy cloak, and scowled at the workmen as they went about their task. Section by section, under the cover of a stand of tall trees, the ramp rose up. From the southern side of the trees, the island of Anacrea was in full view. Also in view, though partly blocked by the mass of the island, was the far bank of the river, where the Orlan warriors swarmed in their thousands.

When the upper part of the highest tower topped the trees, Similin's nervous tension reached a peak.

"They'll see it!" he exclaimed. "How can they not see it?"

"If they see it, they see it," said Ortus.

"They'll come and knock it down! They can, you know. They'll have it down."

"They've not troubled us yet," said the scientist. "And soon now it'll be too late."

"You're sure of your calculations? The bomb won't miss?"

"Oh, no. The bomb won't miss."

"And what then, Professor? What will he do then?" Similin looked across the river at the Orlan army. "Once Anacrea is destroyed, he won't need us any more."

Professor Ortus turned to Similin with a penetrating stare.

"What do you fear he will do?"

"Who knows?" said Similin. "But if it were to come to war between the empire and the Orlans, I fear the worst."

"You will protect us, Radiance. You are the beloved son of the Great Power above."

"Yes, well, I'll do what I can, of course."

He didn't sound at all convinced.

The little scientist laid one hand on Similin's arm.

"Who knows? Perhaps it will be my power that protects you."

"The charged water, you mean?"

"No. Me."

Similin almost laughed. How could this comical bald-headed midget protect him?

"Not as I am," added Ortus, "but as I will be."

"What are you talking about?"

The scientist lowered his voice, glancing round to make sure that none of the carpenters at work assembling the ramp could hear him.

"The charged water," he said, "can be absorbed into the human body. I believe it can make the human body invulnerable."

"Invulnerable!"

"I mean to test it on myself. So far I've only tested it on a small animal, but the effects were beyond all my expectations."

"What animal? What effects?"

"A mouse. A mouse in a stout well-made cage of timber frame and steel mesh. I infused the mouse with charged water. I turned away to seal the container. There was a crash. I turned back. The mouse was gone. The cage had been torn apart."

"Torn apart!"

"The radiant power stored in the charged water gives the body astonishing strength."

"Astonishing strength! But I don't remember any such result last year, when we tested it on the axer."

"That time, the charge was in the blood. This time, the charge will infuse the flesh."

"Can you be sure?"

"There is no certainty in this life, Radiance. But you will see. I mean to test it on myself."

Similin fell silent. He started to pace up and down once more, clasping and unclasping his hands behind his back. He looked up and saw the ramp assembly rising ever higher. He looked across the river and saw the thousands of Orlans massing there. He knew he had very little time. He came to a bold decision.

"Professor," he exclaimed. "I order you to do this test on me."

"On you!" The scientist goggled at him in disbelief.

"On me."

"But Radiance, it's never been tested on a man."

"I'll take that risk."

"I must test it on myself first. I have promised myself that honor."

"We don't have the time."

"But—but—but—I want it!"

Similin strode up to the little man and seized him by the shoulders and shook him.

"I am Radiant Leader!" he said. "I am the chosen son of the Great Power above! Your duty is to obey!"

Ortus trembled before him.

"Yes, Radiance. Yes, of course."

Similin released him.

"So let's get on with it. What do I have to do?"

"What courage!" murmured the little man, gazing on Similin and not moving. "What leadership!"

Similin clapped his hands sharply in the air before Ortus's face.

"Quickly! What do I do?"

"Do? Oh, that is simplicity itself. You drink."

"Drink? From a cup?"

"No, no. The charged water must not make contact with the air. You suck it through a thin tube. See—I have it here."

Ortus produced from his bag a metal cylinder from which protruded a rubber tube clamped with a metal clasp.

"Once in your body," he said, "the stored energy is absorbed into the tissues."

"And it will give me—what did you say?—astonishing strength."

"You will become invulnerable!"

"How long will it take?"

"With the mouse, the transformation took just a few seconds. Your mass is far greater, of course. I would anticipate many minutes. Perhaps as long as an hour. No longer."

"Then let's get on with it! We have no time to lose!"

The little scientist unwound the rubber tube and took hold of the clasp.

"Once you have the tube in your mouth," he said, "I will release the clasp. Suck the water up the tube and swallow it. Keep sucking and swallowing until it's all gone. Don't open your mouth. That is most important. Do not open your mouth."

"I understand."

Similin sat down and prepared himself. He was trembling, but he was determined.

"Soon now," he said to himself, "I will be—invulnerable!"

He took the tube in his mouth and began to suck. Evor Ortus watched with shining eyes.

Amroth Jahan, now mounted on Malook, rode slowly along the shore to the point where the bridges were being constructed. There were five of them, each one formed of eight barges, over which swarms of carpenters were fixing beams and cross-struts and surface planks. The beams were all in place. The planks were advancing, from the mainland side towards the island.

"How much longer?" said the Jahan.

"Soon now, Excellency! Very soon!"

The Jahan stared up at the high walls of the castle-monastery but could see no signs of life. One of his officers rode up with a request from the company captains. They wanted to know how much time remained before they were to go into action.

The Jahan looked across the river at the high ramp, now nearing completion. Then he looked back at the bridges, where teams of men were hauling the heavy planks forward and nailing them down so rapidly that it seemed as if they rolled a carpet before them.

"Tell the captains," he said, "to mount for battle."

This order was received with joy. Behind him, all across the great army, the Jahan heard the familiar sound of his

Orlan warriors mounting their horses and forming lines, company by company. But his gaze was still on Anacrea.

Now the last planks were fixed into place. The workmen ran back over the bridges, making them bounce on the water. The captains rode up to the Jahan to ask if they were to advance and take the island.

"Wait," said the Jahan. "Let them see the power at my command. I want the Nomana to beg me for mercy on their knees."

Even as he spoke, the great gate of the Nom began to open, and out came the Nomana. They came in silence, their badans over their heads, their eyes cast down. They descended the steep stone steps in a long file and wound their slow way to the island's shore.

The Jahan watched, also silent. His men watched, waiting for his command. The only sounds now were the crunch of hooves on pebbles and the restless movement of the Caspians and the ebb and flow of the sea.

When the first of the Nomana reached the bridges, they separated and spread out, so that shortly there were five lines crossing the five bridges. They advanced slowly and steadily, seemingly unaware of the presence of the great army drawn up before them. When they were halfway across the swaying bridges, the Jahan drew his group back, to place himself on a high ridge to one side of the line of the Orlans, on the upper shore. From here he could survey the battle to come. Before him, filling the great space between the river and the trees, his men were lined up company by company, ten ranks deep.

The Nomana now stepped off the bridges onto the

shingle and fanned out in a long line facing the mounted Orlans. Still the Jahan gave no signal for attack. He wanted them all before him, all at his mercy.

His eyes glanced over the river at the ramp. How soon before it was finished? It must be almost ready now. The builders of the ramp could see that the battle was about to begin. All he had to do was be patient.

Now all the Nomana were off the bridges and lined up on the shore. They formed a long shallow crescent. The Jahan guessed there were over a thousand of them.

He sent one of his captains to within hailing distance.

"Will you kneel to the Great Jahan?" he cried out. "Or will you fight?"

He received no answer.

The Jahan smiled a proud angry smile. He knew now they would fight.

There came a slow ripple all down the line of the Nomana. They were raising their heads, looking up. Hundreds of eyes, very still, very intent. In the center of the long crescent of hooded men sat one who was in a wheeled chair. He too raised his old head, then fixed his gaze on the Orlan army.

The Noble Warriors stood at the Tranquil Alert. They calmed their breathing and let the lir in them flow to a still, deep pool. They reached out to one another, feeding on one another's strength. Then they began to release their lir, letting it flow out of each one of them, to form a single massive charge of energy: the First and Last.

They waited for the Elder to give the command.

⊰ 22 ⊱

Lost in Whiteness

THE DENSE MIST Seeker WAS NOW BREATHING HAD NO smell and caused him no discomfort. If anything, he sensed a slight tang in his nostrils that was refreshing. The ground beneath his feet was sloping downwards. He only knew this because he could feel the soft pull of the slope. He could see nothing. All round him was whiteness. He could make out his own hand if he held it up before his face, but it was the hand of a ghost, veiled and insubstantial. He could hear the pad of his own feet on the earth, but even this sound was muffled and distant. He listened for other sounds, for the fleeing shuffle of the savanters, but he heard nothing.

There seemed to be no features in this lake of cloud, no buildings or trees or walls. He knew no way to orient himself and no reason to choose one direction over another; indeed, he was barely able to distinguish any direction from

another, when every way he turned presented the same vista
of milky whiteness.

It struck him then to wonder how he was seeing at all.
What was the source of light? As far as he knew, he was
still in the immense cloud-filled cave where he had met
the savanters. But the soft cool light that filtered evenly
through the mist on all sides had the look of daylight. He
had descended into the cloud pool; but somehow in going
down, he had found his way into open air.

Such puzzles troubled him little. He was no longer
concerned about finding his way. The killing of the savanters had changed him. He was filled with a new conviction that was more than the sensation of power. He felt
that everything he did was right.

"It doesn't matter which way I go," he told himself.
"My way is wherever I am. I'm not the seeker any more.
I'm the one who is sought."

This made his task simple. All he had to do was move
forward and be prepared to withstand attack. He no longer
had any doubts about the nature of the savanters. They
were a source of danger and evil to the Nom and to all
people. He was walking ever deeper into the cloud pool to
meet them. And he was the instrument of their destruction.

Now ahead in the whiteness, he began to make out
looming shapes. He walked on more slowly, his eyes
searching the cloud. The shapes were clearer when he
didn't look directly, when he glimpsed them from the sides
of his eyes. There were many of them, one beyond another: they seemed to be high frames, like scaffolds or gib-

bets. Suspended from each frame was a shadowy mass that was the shape of a human body.

His heart began to bump with fear. Was this some form of mass execution?

He came nearer. Now he could see the dark outline of the frames and the way they formed a curving line disappearing away from him. The frames were not vertical like scaffolds, but at a slant. The gray masses hanging from the frames were indeed human forms—there was no mistaking the outspread limbs. But where were the heads?

Seeker forced himself to keep moving, drawing closer to the leaning mist-shrouded scaffolds all the time, seeing more and more of the bodies that hung there, spread-eagled, headless.

Not headless. Upside down.

He could make out one of them now. A man in a white robe, strapped on his back to a steeply sloping frame, his legs spread out at the top, his head at the bottom. A band of folded cloth was tied over his eyes. His mouth sagged open. And from his lips oozed a thick creamy white syrup.

Seeker stopped and stared. The man seemed to be unharmed. But the sight of that white ooze trickling from his lips and over his cheeks to the ground was peculiarly horrifying. As the thick white substance dribbled down, it formed a puddle, and the puddle was steaming. White vapor rose from its surface and swirled up and away. Evidently on contact with the air, the dense ooze expanded and became a heavy gas.

Seeker looked beyond this nearest victim and saw through the mist all the other scaffolds curving away in a wide circle. Each one holding a victim, each one dribbling out this same ooze. No doubt deeper in the mist there were other similar circles. All that ooze forming puddles on the ground; all those puddles rising up as white gas. This, then, must be the source of the cloud.

Seeker had no way of knowing what the white substance was. Clearly it had no value to the savanters, because they allowed it to drain away and be wasted. It could only be the by-product of something they did want.

The initial shock now past, he moved closer still, and saw that a thin tube ran from the suspended body, over the ground, into the cloud. He tracked the tube to find the point at which it was fixed to the man's body. It ended in a long fine needle, and the needle was inserted into the base of his neck.

Seeker was so close now that he could see the slow rise and fall of the victim's chest. So he wasn't dead. He moved on, past other victims strapped in the same way to their high sloping frames, his eyes now on the slender tubes. Every frame had its tube, and the tubes converged on a central point. The arrangement was becoming clearer. A wide circle of victims, made up of a larger number than he had at first realized, were connected by tubes that snaked their way over the ground to the circle's center, which was lost in the mist. There, he presumed, he would find the remaining four savanters.

Seeker padded cautiously through the whiteness, following the tubes. They led him to a long low cylinder;

and beside the cylinder, a chair made of canvas and wood, like a garden recliner; and in the chair, an old man in a bathrobe, fast asleep. The cylinder that received the tubes from the victims was connected to the sleeping man by a single much thicker tube, which was fixed to the back of his neck. This tube was twitching as if it were alive. The old man's lips shuddered as he slept. A low humming sound came from the cylinder. At one end, there was a knurled wheel that looked as if it opened and closed an inner valve.

Seeker watched the sleeping man for a few moments, and the anger in him mounted. By what right did he feed on the life force of so many victims? Seeker knew he had not been sent here to save the victims from their own folly, but how could he leave them to die like this?

He stooped down and turned the wheel on the cylinder as far as it would go. The humming stopped.

Then, moving rapidly, he went back to the perimeter of the circle, to the first scaffold, and pulled the needle out of the victim's neck. He untied the straps, holding the man's limbs, and helped him to fall to his feet. He wiped the thick ooze from his face and pulled his white robes down over his shivering legs.

"There," he said. "You're free now. Leave this place."

The rescued victim stumbled and uttered a dismal groan. Seeker moved on to the next, and the next.

The one he had released first called after him through the mist.

"Please, sir, is this eternal life?"

"No," said Seeker. "You have to go home now."

"But we were promised eternal life."

"You were tricked. You nearly died."

They came limping after him, hands reached out to clutch him.

"You took us down too soon. We were on our way. Why did you bring us back?"

The scratchy querulous voices sounded all round him, tugging at him, as he hurried from frame to frame to set the victims free.

"We never asked you to do this. You should have left us alone. Where's Mother? I want to be put to bed. I want my good-night kiss."

They tried to take hold of him, but they were so weak that one impatient gesture was enough to send them tumbling to the ground.

"I've saved you from dying."

"No, no. We were the chosen ones. We'd been kissed good night. We were on our way to eternal life. You've woken us up. You've robbed us of eternal life. You've condemned us to death."

As this sank into their fuddled brains, they set up a thin melancholy wailing.

"We're going to die! You've killed us! Murderer!"

Seeker struggled to control his anger.

"Go home," he said. "Just go home."

"Murderer! Who are you? Why do you hate us? What have we ever done to you?"

It was hopeless. He had done what he could for them and must now leave them to go their own way. They began to drift off into the cloud, grumbling and lamenting as they went. He himself returned to the center of the circle.

He found the old man awake, sitting erect in the low chair, and peering at his reflection in a small hand mirror.

"I think there is a difference," he was murmuring to himself. "The sagging under the chin is reduced a little. And the skin round the eyes—yes, I feel a little plumpness returning there."

He became aware that Seeker was standing before him.

"Something has gone wrong," he said sharply. "The process has been interrupted."

"Yes," said Seeker. "That was me."

"It's very slow. Frustratingly slow. We need more. However—"

His eyes returned to the mirror, irresistibly drawn to the reflection of his own face.

"I do see a change in the right direction. And I do feel quite refreshed. But the wrinkles are by no means gone."

He fingered the skin round his mouth, alternately frowning into the mirror and smoothing out his features.

"I used to have a beautiful mouth," he said. "Everyone said so. An expressive mouth. Masculine, and yet also full. In a word, plump." He puckered his withered lips at the mirror. "It's the plumpness one misses."

He turned his attention back to Seeker.

"Did you say it was you who turned off the supply?"

"Yes."

"That was wrong of you. I wasn't finished. In fact, I'd only recently started, now that I remember. Why couldn't you have turned off Manny's supply?"

"Manny?"

"Manny. He's over there."

He gestured vaguely behind him.

"He'd very nearly finished. He was ready to go. Did Manny tell you to turn off my supply?"

"No."

The old man wrinkled his already wrinkly brows and glowered at Seeker, his anger slowly rising to the surface.

"Then you're a wicked interfering boy. You've done a very bad thing. I'm going to have to punish you."

He fixed his aged eyes on Seeker, and they burned with a sudden intense glow. Then, like the lash of a whip, came the bolt of deadly power. But Seeker was ready. He felt the savanter's strength flow into him. He gazed back unmoved. The savanter's eyes blazed again. Seeker breathed in slowly and saw the savanter blink in surprise.

"You wicked, wicked boy!" said the savanter in a peevish voice.

At that, Seeker unleashed a rolling wave of power of his own that smashed the savanter down into his reclining chair, crushing the chair beneath him, and sending both skidding backwards into the cloud. Enraged, he followed after him, ready to strike again, but there was no need. The savanter was spread out like a starfish, his head snapped back, dead.

Once again there came a rush of heat through Seeker's body that left his skin tingling. He wanted to shout, to let out a victor's cry, a killer's cry. Restless, excited, he began to dance from foot to foot. He was light as the curling mist, and also massive, immense, overpowering.

Show me who I must kill. I will crush them. One touch of one finger and their hearts will burst.

Four savanters dead. Three to go.

He set off into the dense white mist, striding fast, moving ever farther from the entrance to the cave. Somewhere ahead he thought he caught a glimpse of a figure, and he started to run. He ran easily, covering the ground swiftly, driven by his new strength. He saw the figure ahead once more, only now it seemed to have come to a stop and to be standing still. As he came up to it, he realized it was another of the slanting scaffolds, and on it was strapped another victim. To the left and to the right he could make out the ring of scaffolds vanishing into the mist. No time to release the victims. He ran on, into the center of the circle.

There was the chair. There was the savanter, asleep, like the last one. No foolish chatter this time. Kill and get it over with. Kill and grow stronger. Kill and enjoy.

He strode to the savanter's side. The sleeping figure was a woman. Her face was averted. But as he came up to her, she turned and looked at him with anguish in her tear-streaked face.

It was his mother.

"My son!" she cried out. "Help me!"

Not the false motherly face that had bent over him to give him a good-night kiss. His actual beloved one-and-only mother.

"Mama! Why are you here?"

"Take me away! Take me away!"

She reached up her arms, weeping. Seeker leaned low over her and let her clasp her arms round his neck, and he swung her up out of the chair. She felt so light. She clung so tight.

"I've got you, Mama. You're safe now."

She gripped her arms tighter still and pressed her face to his shoulder.

"You can let go now, Mama."

But instead she squeezed her arms round his neck ever more fiercely, so that it began to hurt him. He tried to pull her away, but in her terror, her grip had locked rigid. He started to choke.

"Mama!" he gasped. "You're throttling me!"

He pulled at her body and twisted every way he could, but her grip tightened further. This was more than terror. His own mother was strangling him. His own mother wanted him to die. If he was to save his life, he must fight back. He must strike at the head that pressed against him. The head that had looked at him with his mother's face.

He was choking. He couldn't breathe.

He reached for the woman's neck, gripped the back of her neck with the fingers of his right hand. He had the power. He could snap this neck if he chose. Snap his mother's neck.

He closed his eyes.

This is not my mother. I am not killing my mother. I am killing a savanter.

He gave a brutal twist of his right hand, jerking back the woman's head. He felt the snap of bone. The choking grip fell away. The woman slumped in his arms. Gasping for air, he stood holding her for a moment longer. Then he lowered her to the ground.

There before him was the bony wrinkled face of a very old woman. Her eyes were closed. She no longer looked like his mother. She was dead.

The fifth savanter.

Now, for the first time, he felt tired. This last killing had not brought in its wake the rush of joy. But it had made him stronger.

Let it be done. Let it be over with. Two more to go.

On into the cloud.

Now as he walked, the light became brighter and the cloud became whiter. It was not a pleasant sensation. His eyes were tired. He blinked to rest them from the intensifying glare. Then he closed them entirely, for seconds at a time, without slowing his steady onward tread. What did it matter, after all, if he walked without seeing his way? His way would find him. It made no difference where he went.

Then he thought he heard a sound behind him. He turned, opening his eyes. It was the cry of seagulls, far away, thin and high and already disappearing. But even as the sounds faded, his weary eyes were making out a form in the mist. He stopped and peered back, trying to distinguish the faint shape that seemed to hang in the surrounding whiteness. When he gazed directly at it, it melted away. When he looked aside, he thought he could detect it out of the corners of his eyes.

He moved towards the shape. It moved away. With that movement, he saw that it was the figure of a man.

He stepped back. The shape moved nearer.

"Who are you?" called Seeker into the mist. "Are you Manny?"

No answer. His own words sank like stones.

He raised one arm, meaning to beckon to his follower, and as he did so he caught an answering movement in the mist. It was almost too faint to detect, but it was enough for him to guess at what he was seeing. He raised both his arms. He saw his follower do the same.

My shadow.

He laughed. The light in the cloud pool was so dispersed that it had never occurred to him he could cast a shadow. But a moment's thought revealed that the light must come from the sun, far above, and so would come from one direction only. A shadow was inevitable. The mist was sufficiently dense to form a surface on which the shadow could be seen. There was no mystery here after all.

This unseen sun, he thought, could give him a direction. So long as he kept his shadow behind him, he would be walking towards the light. At least this way he could be sure he wasn't walking round in circles.

On he strode, and as he went, the light continued to grow imperceptibly brighter. From time to time he looked back at his shadow. As the light strengthened, the shadow took on more detail. It struck him then that there was something odd about his shadow, so he stopped once more to study it.

He stood still, his arms by his sides. There was his shadow, faint in the whiteness before him, as motionless as he was. Nothing odd in that.

Once more he heard the distant cry of seagulls. He

shuddered. It was cold in the cloud pool. He should keep moving.

But just as he turned away from his shadow, he caught a movement that should not have been possible. He turned back. The figure before him had raised its right hand, to reveal that it was holding the shadow of a long thin rod. The shadow's right arm rose slowly, and the rod swung round to come to rest in a horizontal line above its head.

This is not my shadow.

For the first time since entering the cloud pool he felt a chill of fear.

"Who are you?" he said.

The shadow stood before him like a warrior readying himself for the strike. Slowly Seeker raised his own arm, to match the shadow's stance, even though he had no weapon.

I've seen this before.

Then he remembered. He was sitting on the floor of the Night Court in the Nom, listening to his teacher Miriander speaking of the great warlord Noman. And Seeker was seeing the memory of Noman in the darkness above, his sword raised over his head in just this manner, going forward alone into the Garden.

"Noman?"

The shadow made no answer. But slowly, his arm came down once more. Seeker found himself lowering his own arm, as if he were the shadow's shadow. The fear had not left him. If anything, it had grown.

He moved a step back, and the shadow moved with him. He moved a step forward, and the shadow retreated. He walked away, and the shadow followed.

Seized by panic, he turned and ran. He ran through the cloud until he could run no more. He came to a stop at last, breathless and panting, and only then did he look back. There was his shadow, bent over just as he was, clasping his knees.

He straightened up, and his shadow did likewise. He waited, not moving. His shadow waited before him.

"Please," he said. "What do you want of me?"

The shadow then raised one hand and beckoned, motioning back the way he had come.

"You want me to go back?"

Seeker felt himself break into a sweat. He heard the crying of the seagulls, only this time the birds were far closer. He looked up, expecting to see their outspread wings passing overhead, but there was only the omnipresent whiteness. He felt his own heart beating, too loud, too fast. He was exhausted and frightened and lost.

"Please—"

A song came into his head from nowhere. It came complete with a jaunty little tune, as if he had known it all his life; but it was entirely new to him. He started to sing.

> *"Jango up, jango down*
> *Jango smile, jango frown*
> *Weep your tears, say your prayers*
> *No man hears, no man cares*
> *Seek a, seek a, seek a door*
> *Open wide for evermore."*

He sang it again, more loudly. Then he sang it a third time, shouting it out as loud as he could.

When he fell silent at last, he heard only silence all round him. The gulls were gone. And so was his shadow.

He shivered. Wind on his back.

He turned his face to the wind. It came from far away, but it tugged at him, calling him home. He heard laughter in the mist, thin and high and mocking and triumphant.

He started to run, running back the way he had come, running at a speed he had never known possible.

The Nom was in mortal danger.

❊ 23 ❊

The Battle for the Nom

THE ELDER LET OUT A SIGH. SLOWLY HE RAISED ONE hand above his hooded head. The Noble Warriors, standing four deep on either side, fixed their gaze on the army of the Orlans arrayed before them, and their power gathered in the air like a thundercloud. The Elder dropped his hand. The line of Noble Warriors rippled from end to end. The storm broke.

The shock-blast of pure force struck the mounted Orlans with devastating power, hurling rank upon rank back and across the open shore where the Jahan's army was drawn up. Men and horses screamed as they slammed into each other and still were driven on, tumbling, rolling, tossed and smashed into the hillside. The blast lifted earth and stones and trees in a hurricane of whirling destruction. For a while the full force of the strike was concealed by flying debris. Only when the air cleared again could those outside the region of the blast see the full damage.

An entire army had been swept away. The space between the river and the trees, where company on company had stood in serried ranks, was now empty and bare. Shouts and cheers rose up from the slopes of Anacrea, where the people of the island had come out to watch.

On the far side of the river Soren Similin felt the shock of the mighty blast, and heard the cheers from the island. There was a tingling all over the surface of his skin as his new power grew within him. He had dared to take a great risk. Soon would come his reward.

The Orlan army, perhaps even the Great Jahan himself, was destroyed. The Noble Warriors had served their purpose. Now it was their turn to die.

He looked up to see the progress of the bomb, which was even now being winched up the tower to the top of the giant ramp. To his surprise he saw Professor Ortus sitting on the truck, on top of the bomb, already almost halfway up the tower.

"Professor!" he shouted. "What are you doing?"

Ortus leaned over the creaking platform and called down. "I'm going with it."

As far as Similin could make out, he was grinning.

"Why?" he yelled.

The professor waved at him, as if he were on a fairground ride.

"I'm going to die!"

———

Sasha Jahan and his hundred Orlans rode back from the Glimmen in the best of spirits. None of his men had been harmed, and beside Sasha rode the prize even his father had been unable to win, the beautiful Echo. It was true that she rode in silence and never looked at him, but Sasha Jahan was untroubled. No doubt the girl hated him. Truth to tell, he didn't much like her. None of that mattered. What mattered was that by bringing back the runaway who had defied his father, and by showing that he, Sasha, had compelled her obedience, he would win his father's respect.

The Orlans were riding at a steady jog, their horses' hooves rattling over the stony track, so they didn't hear the runner until he came alongside them.

The runner was a young man, loping with long bounding strides that seemed to cost him no effort, but that carried him forward at a remarkable speed. He overtook horseman after horseman. Then he was loping past Sasha Jahan and Echo.

As soon as Echo saw him she was galvanized into action. "Kell! Go!"

She urged Kell into a gallop after the running figure.

"Stop her!" cried Sasha Jahan. "Stop her!"

His leading riders gave chase, whips out and cracking in the air. Echo forced Kell to his fastest speed, and so came up with the runner.

"Seeker!" she shouted. "Help me!"

The runner turned and saw her. He looked back and saw the pursuing Orlans. He made a rapid movement of one hand, without breaking stride, and the Caspians behind swung about in an abrupt turn, sending their riders tumbling. Others galloping up after them collided with the riderless horses, and they too were thrown to the ground in a tangle of confusion.

"Fools!" shrieked Sasha Jahan. "I'll have you all whipped!"

But it was too late. Echo was now far ahead, riding fast, with the runner pounding the track beside her. Shortly they were gone from sight.

The Noble Warriors stood motionless in their lines, their eyes on the ridge ahead. They could hear a sound that filled them with dread: the steady beat of horses' hooves.

Over the ridge rode a new line of mounted warriors. Just as before, the line grew and grew, and was followed by a second line, and a third, until as many Orlans were arrayed before them as there had been before.

The Nomana had delivered their greatest strike, the First and Last. They had swept away an entire army with one devastating blow. And now here facing them was a second army.

How many armies did the Great Jahan have? For how long, weakened as they now were, could the Noble Warriors withstand their assault?

The Orlan horsemen drew their short swords and leaned forward, ready to charge. A sharp cry came from their captains, a cry the impatient Caspians knew as well as their riders. The line broke into movement, jogging forward at a brisk trot. The trot opened into a canter, and then hit the full gallop of the charge.

The Elder sat still in his chair and watched them come. They were nearer this time before he raised his trembling hand. The Nomana reached deep into themselves, calling on all that was left of their fading strength.

The lead riders were a bare fifty paces off when the Elder dropped his hand. The Noble Warriors pumped out a single pulse of power, and the charging Orlans fell like skittles. This time there was no cheer from the slopes of the island. The people of Anacrea could see what the Nomana could not yet see. A third army of Orlans was riding up to the ridge.

The Elder saw that his brothers and sisters had no resistance left. He gave his order in a low weary voice.

"Evacuate the island."

The Nomana by his side heard this with shock.

"Abandon the Nom, Elder?"

"Evacuate the island. Get everyone off. At once."

The truck carrying Evor Ortus and his bomb was almost at the top of the tower.

"You're mad!" Similin shouted up to him. "Why do you want to die?"

"We all have to die," Ortus called back. "Even you."

"But your knowledge—it belongs to the world!"

"The world is full of fools," came the reply, "so I'm taking my knowledge with me." He was very high now, and his voice was faint. "The world is full of fools and villains. And some, like you, are fool and villain both."

"Then good riddance to you," cried Similin. "I don't need you any more."

"Not quite rid of me yet, my friend!" The scientist was leaning over the edge of the platform, three hundred feet up, his voice just audible. "I've left you something to remember me by."

"What?" shouted Similin.

"Whatever you do," came the reply, "don't—"

Similin could just hear him, but the shape of the words was blurred by the distance. It sounded like: enemy orb ladder.

"What did you say?" he yelled at the top of his voice.

But by now the truck had arrived at the top of the tower, and the scientist was out of sight. From there the descent would be rather more rapid. When it ended, there would be no more professor left to ask what he had meant.

Soren Similin didn't care. The tingling sensation was growing stronger all the time. Soon now he would be— what had Ortus said?—invulnerable.

The people of Anacrea came down the zigzag steps of the mountainside and across the bridges in response to the Elder's order. Old people and women and children, storekeepers and tradesmen, servants of the Nom and meeks, they all came. They had been on the western side of the island watching the battle, so the evacuation did not take long.

The line of Noble Warriors defending the bridges had not wavered, but as they prepared to face the third charge, there was no concealing their weakness. This next charge would break them. The seemingly limitless numbers of attackers had exhausted their powers.

The Elder called on his brothers on either side, lifting his arms.

"Help me up," he said. "This time I will fight."

"No, Elder," they urged him. "You're not strong enough."

"Help me, or I'll do it alone."

So they lifted the Elder out of his chair and stood him on his feet, to face the gathering enemy.

Amroth Jahan, mounted on Malook on the high ridge, looked down to the shore and saw the Elder rise, tottering, to his feet. He smiled a grim smile. This was the Nomana's last stand. He could see that across the river, the bomb had reached the top of the ramp. His horsemen would break through, the bomb would destroy the Nomana's god, and the power of the Noble Warriors would be broken forever.

He raised his whip hand to give the order for the last charge—and was startled to hear, from behind him, a wild whooping cry.

"Heya-a-aa, bravas!"

A wave of brilliant colors, a rage of howling voices, and the spiker army burst over the brow of the hill. They struck the Orlans from the rear, hurling their deadly spikes, closing in with flashing blades, yelling a wild war cry as they came. The Orlans, taken entirely by surprise, broke ranks and scattered, only to find yet more spikers cutting at their whip arms and dragging them from their horses.

In their lead was a golden-haired youth with a laughing face, who cried out as he slashed his way through the Orlan ranks.

"Chuck-chuck-chickens! Coming to kill you!"

The people of Anacrea saw the Orlans break formation, and they cheered. But already the Great Jahan was barking out orders, and more companies of his immense army were thundering into position. Now the spikers themselves were surrounded, and fighting on all sides.

Fighting, the Jahan noted with surprise, like an army. They worked in teams, covering each other's backs, delaying their strikes until the most effective moment, giving way before a charge, only to turn on the riders as they passed. Above it all sounded the cry of their leader, who seemed to be entirely without fear.

"Heya-aa, bravas! Do you lo-o-ove me?"

"That one!" ordered the Jahan. "The golden-haired one! Kill him!"

He never even noticed Morning Star standing on the brow of the hill, her eyes fixed on the battle below, a strange faraway expression on her face.

The Jahan had not forgotten the Nomana. In the midst of the battle, five new companies peeled off to face the insolent islanders he had sworn to destroy.

"Charge!" cried the Jahan. "Kill them all!"

Seeker and Echo reached the top of the hill just as the charge began. There below them the battle was raging, Orlans and spikers swarming round each other. Nearer to the shore, the weary line of the Nomana stood with bowed heads, awaiting the impact of the last charge. Seeker took in the danger at a glance, planted his feet wide apart on the tussocky grass, and summoned up all the immense power he now possessed.

Evor Ortus felt the truck roll from the platform onto the top of the ramp. The view was splendid. He was happier than he had ever been in his life. He was sitting on the wooden chest that contained the bottles of charged water, holding on to the straps that tied down the lid. He could see, far below, the gray of the winter grass and the brown of the shingle, the strip of gleaming water, the island with its castle-monastery, and the empty ocean beyond. It was all so petty, he thought, so unimportant. There was no greatness in this world. The gods men worshipped were all frauds, set up to give power to knaves like Similin. And the only god who might really exist was about to be wiped out. So what did that prove? That he, Evor Ortus, possessed the only true power in existence. And how did he use that power? To put it beyond the reach of all, forever. There was true greatness.

Now the truck was picking up speed. Before him the ever-steepening slope of the ramp dropped away to the ground, three hundred feet below. Now the rush was beginning. Down swooped the truck, wheels shrieking, and the speed-wind stung his eyes. Faster he went, and faster. Oh, it was thrilling! No stopping me now!

Seeker concentrated his power to a single point as sharp as a needle. Then he gave a crack of his entire body that made him ripple like a whip, and he drove all the amassed force deep into the ground. The earth shuddered beneath him. The wave of power rippled outwards. There came a great subterranean groan, and the land began to shake.

The bomb, with Ortus still holding on, hit the bottom of the curving ramp at top speed, swept up the shorter, rising track, and sailed off the end just as the earthquake struck. The land shook—the ramp collapsed—but the bomb was airborne. And as he sailed onward in his perfectly calculated arc over the water, Evor Ortus was singing.

> *"High, high, watch me fly*
> *Like an onion in the sky!"*

Seeker's earthquake stopped the battle dead. The heaving, bucking land threw the Orlan horsemen to the ground just as it felled the spikers and the Nomana and the frail Elder with them. They rocked like sailors in a storm, clinging to the surging land. But as the quake subsided, there came a second vibration.

It began as a shudder in the air. Then came a screaming wind. Then the island of Anacrea rose up and expanded in midair, a mountain of solid rock erupting into fragments and dust. The accompanying boom of sound filled the world, grand and deep and terrible. When at last the final echo had rolled away and the stunned onlookers dared to raise their heads, they saw in shock and disbelief that the entire island had vanished into a mile-high column of dust.

Seeker stood motionless on the brow of the hill above and knew that the worst had happened, and he had failed to avert it. The Nom had been destroyed.

His god was dead.

⚔ 24 ⚔

The Traitor

AMROTH JAHAN ROSE TO HIS FEET, BRUSHED THE DIRT from his breastplate, and looked round for his horse.

"Malook!" he thundered.

The Caspian struggled to his feet and came trotting out of the trees, his ears laid back in fear, yet obedient to his master's call. The Great Jahan mounted and rode out into the open ground where all could see and hear him. Malook had to pick his way through the bodies of the Orlans and their horses. The earthquake, and the explosion that had followed so closely behind, had left no one standing.

"On your feet!" roared the Jahan. "Form companies!"

The Jahan had been as astounded as anyone by the devastating end of the battle; but he had known it was coming, and he knew that it brought him victory. Now, as so often before, it fell to him to restore order and receive the allegiance of the vanquished.

Shocked, covered in debris and dust, the surviving Orlans rose and mounted once more. The spikers too staggered to their feet, unsure where to turn. The Wildman
was standing in silence, gazing in disbelief at the place
where Anacrea had been. Along the line of the shore, the
Nomana too looked on the seething shallows that had
once been their home and the home of their god.

The Jahan rode down the sloping shore, to the Elder
of the Nomana. The old man was lying on the ground.
The Nomana round him were tending to him where he
lay, and they were weeping. One of them looked up as the
Jahan approached, and spoke with quiet bitterness.

"You have murdered all the good in the world today."

"You opposed me," the Jahan replied. "Those that op-
pose me I destroy. I am the Great Jahan."

He swung his horse about and saw with satisfaction
that his orders were being obeyed and his army was re-
forming. There was still the matter of the spikers, but they
showed no will to continue the fight. They could be dealt
with later.

The Great Jahan smiled to himself as he surveyed the
devastation of the battleground. He sniffed the dust in
the air. He heard the groans of the wounded. This was the
moment he loved best of all—the moment when silence
fell over the field of battle, and the blood sang in his ears,
and he knew he had won.

His two sons, Alva and Sabin, were weaving their way
towards him through the men and horses. The Jahan looked
on them with an affection born of his victorious mood.
They weren't bad boys. Maybe he should give them a little

more responsibility, a little more power. He thought then of Sasha, his eldest, whom he had sent to burn the Glimmen. By now the forest would be ablaze, and that ungrateful girl would be wishing she'd never spat in the face of the Great Jahan.

"Alva!" he cried. "Sabin! Here's a job for you both. These so-called Noble Warriors seem to have run out of tricks. Line them up in an orderly way. I want to see them kneel before me."

"Yes, Father."

"And all the rest of the riffraff too, while you're about it. Tell them the Great Jahan is merciful. But they must kneel."

"Yes, Father."

At this moment, to his great surprise, he saw riding towards him the pale and beautiful girl he had honored with an offer of marriage. He could still hear, ringing in his ears, her contemptuous words: "You think you can have whatever you want. But you can't have me." Well, it seemed she had changed her mind. It seemed she had decided he wasn't so very old after all. This too was one of the sweet fruits of victory.

There were others accompanying her, walking by her horse's side, but he paid no attention to them. His eyes were on Echo. He would require her to kneel to him once more, he decided, and to kiss his hand. Then he would forgive her. He might even tell her one day how much he had admired her spirit of defiance. But only when she was suitably submissive.

She had an odd look on her face for one coming back

to ask forgiveness. She kept glancing to one side, at the youth who walked on her right. This youth had a soft, almost childish face framed in the gray hood of the Nomana. So he was a young Noble Warrior, come home to find he had no home any more. The Jahan smiled and looked to see how he was taking his loss.

The youth was looking at him. His eyes were not childish. Not soft. The Jahan felt a cold shiver go through him.

He was gazing into a bottomless pit of rage.

"Off your horse," said the youth.

"Nobody gives me orders—"

Oof! A crippling blow caught the Jahan square in the chest, throwing him from his horse to the ground.

"Make him kneel!" said Echo. "Make him kiss my hand!"

The Jahan started to crawl to his feet, when he found himself struck again, and again, until he was lying below Echo's horse.

"Kneel," said the youth. His voice was the most terrifying sound the Jahan had ever heard: ice-cold, stripped of all human feeling.

His sons came riding to his help.

"Boys—"

The young Noma lifted one hand and held out two fingers together, and Alva and Sabin crashed screaming to the ground. The same two fingers then turned on their father.

"Kneel," he said, "or I crush the life from your body."

Amroth Jahan was in too much shock to respond. He didn't understand what was happening. He was the victor.

He was the leader of a mighty army. Why did his men not seize this youth and punish him for his insolence?

"He doesn't kneel," said Echo. "Crush him!"

The Jahan felt an irresistible weight bear down on him, a weight that filled the sky. He knew he could do nothing against such power.

"Please!" he cried. "Please!"

His army, looking on in stupefaction, saw their feared and mighty leader lying on the ground, untouched by anyone, pleading for his life. They saw him struggle, gasping, to his knees and crawl to the girl on the horse.

"I'm kneeling," he said. "I'm kneeling."

"Now kiss my hand."

She reached down her hand. He took it and kissed it.

Echo looked up at Seeker, her eyes bright and hard.

"Now kill him," she said.

"No!"

The cry came from Morning Star.

"No more!"

"Why not?" said Seeker savagely. "You think I do this for her? I do it for all of us! This warlord has killed our god. He must die! Every man who fought with him must die. I mean to kill, and go on killing, until I've rid the world of the last warlord, and no one will ever dare to make war again!"

"Then," said Morning Star, "you will be the last warlord."

"Don't tell me what to do!"

"I'm not telling you what to do. I'm telling you what you are."

"I am what I have been made!"

Seeker stabbed one finger towards the river mouth, where once the island had stood.

"Look what they've done! The Nom is gone! The Garden gone! The Lost Child gone! We swore to protect all of it, and we failed! Everything I loved, everything I believed in, everything that made sense of my life—gone! So what am I now? Tell me that! What's left of me now?"

He was almost sobbing in his rage and his grief.

"You're not to blame, Seeker," said Morning Star.

"Of course I'm to blame! I'm the one with the power! I was too late!"

He swung away from them all and strode into the trees, choking with tears.

Amroth Jahan clambered slowly to his feet.

"Any trouble from you, old man," said Echo sharply, "and I'll call him back."

The Jahan shook his head.

"No trouble."

Amroth Jahan indeed felt like an old man. His body ached all over; but worse by far, his proud spirit was broken. He stood before his men, and he no longer commanded them. His sons watched him with pity. The Jahan had no experience of such a condition. He didn't know how to behave, or even how to feel. He was bewildered.

Echo gazed down at him and saw that there was no fight left in him, and she found she didn't feel as satisfied as she had expected. The fingers of her right hand were pulling and stroking her left little finger.

"You should give your sons more respect," she said.

"Yes," said the Jahan dully.

"You should go home to your wives."

He looked up and met her beautiful eyes. He had heard the change in her voice. She pitied him, too.

"I have been shamed," he said quietly. "I can never go home."

Soren Similin was giddy with triumph. He had seen the downfall of the Jahan's army, and the awesome destruction of Anacrea. His finest moment was come. He regretted that Evor Ortus had chosen to take his own life, because his respect for him had never been higher. Every part of his construction had worked. Every calculation had been accurate. The man had been insane, but he had been a genius.

All the more reason to trust in the power he had given him before his death. Similin could feel it burning within him but he wasn't yet sure what form it would take. The little scientist had spoken of astonishing strength. He had said it would make him invulnerable. Then he had said, in his final madness, "I've left you something to remember me by. Whatever you do, don't—enemy orb ladder."

Surely this was important. Everything else Ortus had done had come to pass precisely as he had predicted. This too would therefore come to pass. He, Similin, must take care not to—enemy orb ladder. Of course, that was nonsense. Ortus must have said something else, which sounded like that. But what?

He became aware at this point of some movement among the Orlans on the far side of the river. As far as he could tell from this distance, all was not going according to plan. Suddenly it struck him that there was some urgency to his affairs. He must confirm his new power beyond doubt. He must cross the river.

He hurried towards the riverbank. There he found a row of fishermen's huts and, drawn up on the shingle before them, a row of fishing boats. There were no people in sight.

He picked out the smallest of the boats and dragged it over the pebbles to the water's edge. He was no sailor, but he reckoned he was capable of paddling the craft the short distance across the river to the far bank. He was just in the process of heaving the boat into the water when its owner emerged from his hut.

"What do you think you're doing?"

The fisherman was a big, powerfully built fellow, with a shock of dark hair and a face the color of seasoned timber. Here, thought Similin, was his chance to test his new power.

"Taking your boat," he replied calmly.

The fisherman did a little dance of fury.

"First you shake my house until everything in it's smashed! Then you take the island! Now you take my boat!"

"My need is greater than yours," said Similin.

"I'll give you need!"

The fisherman bore down on Similin, clenching his fists. Similin turned to face him, entirely unafraid, feeling the tingling of his power all down his arms. The fisherman came up close and drew back one stout arm to strike.

"Stop there!" commanded Similin, raising one hand.

The fisherman's fist hit him full and hard in the face, knocking him into the shallow water. Half stunned, he floundered about, gasping and gulping in river weed. The fisherman took hold of his boat and dragged it back up the bank.

"You want more," he called back to Similin, "there's more where that came from."

Similin rose unsteadily to his feet. Blood was streaming from his nose. His injured face hurt all over. But worst of all, his whole body was shaking with fear. He did not want any more from the fisherman.

What had gone wrong? Where was his power? Had the mad professor lied to him? It made no sense. How could it benefit Ortus to put him through a charade of sucking water that he supposed was charged, when it was only plain water after all? And anyway, he had felt the tingling in his body. The water was charged, he was sure of it.

I've left you something to remember me by.

Similin now recalled the look on Ortus's face as he had called out these words: it had been a smile of hatred. He'd thought nothing of it at the time, aware of how easily the little scientist took offence. Now it struck him that in some as yet unknown way, this must be Evor Ortus's revenge.

Whatever you do, don't—enemy orb ladder.

The fisherman came stomping back towards him, his fist once again clenched and threatening.

"You going or staying?"

The fist was there to help him make up his mind.

"Going," said Similin.

"What you've had so far," said the fisherman, "that was just a starter."

"Just a starter. Right."

"You touch my boat again, I'll rip off your head and piss in your neck."

"Right. Well. I'll be going, then."

He made his way back up the riverbank, to the fields. Here the timbers that had made the great ramp lay smashed and scattered. Similin walked slowly, in a state of confusion. The fisherman had humiliated him, but that he could deal with later. Right now he needed to find out what Ortus had done to him.

Over on the far side of the river, the Orlan army seemed to be dispersing. The Nomana were still there, now clustered into a great gathering, no doubt trying to decide where to go and what to do now that their home and their god were destroyed. The column of dust thrown up by the bomb was breaking up and being carried away by the freshening wind. There was a smell of rain in the air.

Similin thought of the fisherman's threat and shuddered. Piss in your neck. Where does an ignorant brute like that get such a potent image? Presumably from his ignorant and brutal life. No doubt he's proud of his pissing power. A man that size must have a bladder as big as an ox.

Similin came to a stop.

Bladder.

"Whatever you do, don't—enemy orb ladder."

Yes, that was what he had said. Only, of course, it

wasn't quite that. It was something far more ordinary. And far more terrifying.

Whatever you do, don't—empty your bladder.

"The Elder is dying."

Seeker heard Morning Star, in shock. Then he turned from the trees and ran back to the shore. He pushed through the Nomana who were gathered close round the Elder, laying their hands on him, already beginning the quiet chant with which a Noble Warrior is sung to his rest.

"Not yet!" he cried. "Don't leave me yet!"

He knelt by the Elder's side, begging him to speak before he died.

"Make me understand! How could our god have allowed this to happen? Why was I not with you? Why was I given so much power for nothing?"

"Let him be," said Miriander. "Can't you see how weak he is?"

"He has to tell me," insisted Seeker. "He's the only one who understands. He can't go without telling me."

But the Elder said nothing. His breathing was faint now.

"Don't die!" cried Seeker in anguish. "I need you!"

Miriander looked up and caught Morning Star's eyes. She signalled to her to help. Morning Star knelt down by Seeker's side and put one arm round him.

"Let him go in peace," she said.

Seeker grasped hold of her hand, as if she could give him the answers he so desperately needed.

"He knew the Orlans were never the true danger," he said. "Why did he abandon the Nom?"

"He did the best he could."

"The Nomana don't make war! Why was the Nom abandoned?"

Suddenly remembering, he leaped to his feet.

"There was a traitor in the Nom!" He turned on Miriander, his eyes burning. "You! Was it you? Are you the traitor?"

"No, Seeker," said Miriander.

"You, then? Is it you? Or you?"

He turned from Noma to Noma, his fierce gaze hunting for an enemy to fight. They all shrank back, shaking their heads.

"Where's Narrow Path? He's the one who told me. He must be the traitor!"

Morning Star was watching the dying Elder. She saw something there that none of the others could see.

"Seeker," she said quietly.

"We've lost everything because of one man!" cried Seeker. "Our god is dead because of one traitor in the Community!"

"I know who the traitor is."

"I'll tear him to shreds!"

"He's lying before you."

Seeker looked down in consternation.

"The Elder?"

Morning Star nodded.

"It can't be!"

He dropped once more to his knees beside the dying man. As he did so, the Elder's eyes flickered and opened. Seeker beseeched him.

"Help me, Elder. Tell me who has betrayed the Nom."

The Elder's lips moved. Seeker put his ear close, to catch the faint words.

"Forgive me . . ." he heard. "You'll understand . . . One day . . ."

Seeker felt a great heaviness tighten about his throat. The old man's eyes closed once more. The breaths that had expelled those last few words were his last.

Seeker rose to his feet, his face drained of all expression.

"What did he say?" asked Miriander.

"Nothing," said Seeker. "He said nothing."

Soren Similin knelt down by the riverside, and cupping water into his hands, he drank as much as he was able. The water escaped through his fingers and soaked his garments, but still he drank on. Then when he could drink no more, he rose to his feet and set off walking as fast as he could. He wanted to avoid standing still. He knew that as soon as he relaxed his muscles he would want to pee. And he must not pee yet.

It had never been an issue in all his life before. He could go for long hours without peeing at all, when his mind was engaged on some pressing matter. But now, when he understood with hideous clarity that he must not empty his bladder, all he could think of was how desperately he wanted to do just that.

He cursed himself again, as he had been cursing himself ever since he had worked out the monstrous details of Ortus's revenge. Why had he not anticipated this? He had known full well that the charged water exploded when exposed to the air. Why had he not stopped to think that what goes in must sooner or later come out?

His only defense against the coming catastrophe was to dilute the charged water within him with plain water. He had drunk all he could. Now he could only hope that the river water would make its way through his system before the need to pee became irresistible.

As he walked he cried out to the savanter who had controlled him for so long.

"Mistress! Help me!"

But there came no answering voice in his head.

Next he appealed to the Radiant Power, the sun god in whose name he had ruled, knowing full well that there was no such god: but desperation makes believers of all men in the end.

"Great Power! Help me!"

As if to spite him, a dark cloud swept by overhead, casting him into ever deeper shadow on this dull winter day.

So then he called to the first gods he had ever known, the father and mother who had raised him in a humble town in the north, the father and mother he had never thought to see again, because they were the little people he had outgrown.

"Mama! Papa! Help me!"

When there was no one left to turn to, and his bladder was at the point of bursting, he stopped calling for help and threw all his hope into his luck.

"I can't die," he told himself. "I'm too special. I'm too clever. I'm too superior. Death is for the little people."

Encouraged by this thought, he determined to risk what

anyway he was powerless to stop. Out of pure force of habit, he sought out a clump of bushes. He unlaced his breeches behind the bush and prepared for sweet release.

The explosion startled the rooks out of the high elms but otherwise went unnoticed on that day of explosions. It was the last and the smallest. But it was big enough.

⚔ 25 ⚔

Parting

A COLD RAIN WAS FALLING AS THEY BURIED THE ELDER.
The Community's cemetery was gone, along with the entire Nom, so the old man's body was laid to rest in the fishermen's graveyard on the hillside between the woods and the sea. He was lowered into the grave, without coffin or shroud, because the Nomana had lost everything. But they sang for him, as they had always sung for every brother and sister at the time of their passing.

> *"Light of our days and peace of our nights*
> *Our Reason and our Goal*
> *We wake in your shadow*
> *We walk in your footsteps*
> *We sleep in your arms . . ."*

Seeker stood in the rain with the rest, but he did not sing. His heart was heavy with bitter thoughts. He saw

Miriander watching him with her grave beautiful eyes, and he knew what she was thinking, and he looked away. He no longer wanted the burden of her expectation. His power was hateful to him. What point was there in being able to dominate all others if the All and Only had ceased to be? The Clear Light had been snuffed out. There was no reason and no goal.

The sweet voices sang on as the rain fell.

"Lead us to the Garden
To rest in the Garden
To live in the Garden
With you . . ."

It made him angry. They knew as well as he did that the Garden was gone. Why sing on as if nothing had changed?

The brothers and sisters covered the old man's body with earth, each throwing a handful into the grave to the accompaniment of some private words of farewell. Some shed tears. Seeker looked on dry-eyed, tormented by his bitter thoughts.

"This man betrayed you all," he cried, but only in his mind. "It's because of him that our god is dead."

He knew it must be so. Morning Star had seen the color of betrayal. The Elder himself had said, "Forgive me." He had also said, "You'll understand one day."

Seeker did not understand and felt that he would never understand. How could the Elder have sought the end of all he had lived for? What possible purpose could he have had in leading the Nomana out to a futile battle against such a great army? The Noble Warriors did not fight wars. The youngest novice knew that. There was no meaning to it but for a bad meaning, a poisoned meaning. The Elder had become their enemy.

One day perhaps he would understand. But he knew he would never forgive.

After the burial, the brothers and sisters, and the people of Anacrea, and the spikers who had stayed on to help, set about building themselves some shelters for the coming night. Working with borrowed tools, they cut up the timber felled by the Orlans and made small frame houses in the old way. They were glad to be busy, not wanting to look back or forward.

The men cut the main posts and struts. The women wove pliant branches between the struts. And the old people and the children scraped up mud to pack between the woven branches. The steadily falling rain slicked the mud to a gleaming sheen.

Seeker joined the children in gathering handfuls of mud. It was the humblest of the tasks. He wanted it to be known that, for all his powers, he was no better than the rest of them. After a while Echo joined him and worked alongside him without speaking. Her beautiful pale hair was dark with rain and clung close to her head, making her seem even more slender and lovely. From time to time she looked at Seeker, and he knew that she wanted him to speak to her, but he said nothing.

The Wildman had got himself an axe and was splitting logs for the great fire, alongside Snakey. Morning Star was one of the party building the fire. She went back and forth from the Wildman to the fire stack, carrying the split logs in the rain. All this Seeker saw.

When the fire was built, a hollow was dug into one side and filled with wood chips. Here, where the rain didn't reach, a spark was kindled. It smoldered on the damp fuel and issued a plume of white smoke.

Seeker said to himself, "If the fire catches, we will survive. If the fire goes out, we will die." No more than a foolish superstition, but he wasn't the only one to cling to small signs on that terrible day. Like him, everyone was as busy as they could be, in order not to have to speak the words that hung above them like smoke, like a sentence of death: it's over.

He went to the stream that bubbled out of the wood, and plunged his mud-caked hands into the water. By the time he returned, there was a flicker of flame in the heart of the smoking pile. Then came a crackling sound, and all at once the fire burst into life. Now the fire would be stronger than the rain and would last through the night. As if in acknowledgment of its defeat, the rain began to pass, as twilight set in.

The people huddled round the great fire, to dry their drenched clothing. As the heat grew, they backed away, forming an ever-widening ring. Other fires were built from this, the master fire, and so the people of Anacrea and the Community of the Nom, hardly realizing they were doing so, arranged themselves in neighborly clusters that echoed the courtyards and streets of the lost island. The spikers gathered round their own fires, just as they had always lived apart from the settled townships.

Seeker sat alone, within reach of the great fire's warmth but outside the circle. At such a time it would be customary for a pot of soup to be heated at the fire, and baskets of oatcakes to be passed from hand to hand, perhaps with a jar of brandy to moisten the lips; but there was no soup, no oatcakes, no brandy. All would go to sleep hungry tonight.

Echo watched Seeker and saw his unhappiness and wondered at it. She had witnessed his extraordinary power in action. She could still feel the way the ground had kicked beneath her, she could still hear Kell's terrified braying call as he fell, she could still see the sight that had met her eyes moments later—a battlefield stilled by one blow from one man. And that man barely more than a boy. Such a one could command all the world. Why then was he alone and sad? His island home was gone, but all its people were safe. And as for his god—Echo had never had a god of her own, and she found it hard to imagine what it was. Maybe Seeker's god was dead, but his power remained, and surely that was what mattered.

That gave her an idea.

"Do you mind if I sit with you?"

"I'm not good company," Seeker replied.

"I don't mind."

Echo settled herself down cross-legged by his side, facing the fire.

"I have to thank you. When you made the Jahan kiss my hand, that was the best moment of my life."

Seeker looked at the distant fire and said nothing.

"If you'd killed him," Echo went on, "that would have been even better. I don't know why you didn't. He lost. He should die."

Seeker shook his head.

"He's not my true enemy. My true enemy hasn't lost."

"What true enemy?"

"There's someone."

He fell silent, not wanting to explain.

"Then kill him, whoever he is. No one has as much power as you. You can do whatever you want."

"There's nothing I want any more," said Seeker.

"What! That's impossible!"

Echo herself wanted so much, so intensely, that she could only think Seeker spoke this way out of weariness.

"You think there must always be more to want, do you?" he said.

"Yes. Of course."

"What do you want?"

She was about to say she wanted to be home again, when she realized there was something she wanted much more.

"I want to do something," she said. "I don't know what. Something good and strong. Then I'll be good and strong, too."

"Aren't you good? Aren't you strong?"

"No. All I care about is myself."

Seeker looked at her in an odd half-attentive way, but he said nothing.

"If I had your power," she said, "I'd do such things!"

"And then what?"

"Then what? Then nothing. Then, we just live."

Seeker shook his head.

"That's why there has to be a god," he said. "Just living isn't enough."

"There is a god," said Echo. "You just aren't looking in the right place."

"Where am I to look?"

She pointed one slender finger straight at him.

"At yourself."

This was her idea. Seeker had the power to move the world. Why should he not be a god?

"Me?"

"Only a god could do what you have done."

He laughed softly, with an edge of bitterness.

"Me? I'm no god!"

"How do you know?"

"Because I've seen the true god. I've seen the All and Only."

"You could still be a god."

"No. Believe me, I'm no god. I'm just—"

He hesitated, unsure how to describe what he now felt himself to be.

"I'm just somebody with something given him to do."

Echo reached out and touched his arm, to make him look at her.

"Let me go with you," she said, "wherever you're going."

"No," said Seeker. "I have to go alone."

"Why?"

"Because I won't come back."

Echo looked into his eyes for a long moment, and she knew then there was nothing more she could say. She rose to her feet.

"If you ever pass through the Glimmen," she said, "look up into the trees above you. Call my name."

All this time, Morning Star had been sitting with the main band of spikers, beside the Wildman and Snakey. The spikers were in high spirits despite the lack of food and drink. Never before had so many spikers come together as a unified force and fought as an army and been victorious.

"We're the top dogs now," Snakey was saying, spreading his hands in the orange glow of the fire. "The ones whose homes get burned, the ones who tramp the road and beg for food, the thieves, the bandits, the cutthroats. You got yourself a wolf pack for an army, Chick."

But alone among the spikers, the Wildman was not rejoicing. In the heat of the battle, he had burned with the bright light of ecstasy. Was he not a warlord, at the head of his own mighty army? Then the world shook. Then the world changed. Anacrea was no more. The Nom was no more. The Garden was no more. How now was he to find his peace?

The great warlord Noman had conquered the known world, but he had not stopped there. Caring nothing for danger to himself, smashing every rule and every prohibition, asserting his will as his right, he had burst his way into the unknown. There the Wildman longed to follow.

That dream was now ended.

He looked up and saw Morning Star watching him.

"Heya, Star."

"Very quiet, Wildman."

"You too."

"Me too."

"Bad work today."

He gestured at the night sea, towards the place where the island of Anacrea had been.

"I still can't believe it," said Morning Star.

She looked out into the emptiness of the night, and she too grieved. For so long her young dreams had flowed towards the secret green light of the Garden. Now she too must find new dreams.

"What will you do now?" she asked the Wildman.

"Who knows?"

"You got yourself an army."

"Thanks to you."

"Can I come with you, wherever you're going?"

"Sure you can," he said. "We're friends."

Friends.

"As to where I'm going," he said, "I guess it's Spiker-town for now."

"Spikertown's as good as anywhere."

And anywhere's good for me, she wanted to say, if you're there.

Wildman rose to his feet.

"Get some sleep," he told her. "Been a long day."

He walked away into the trees.

Morning Star turned and looked into the darkness behind her and saw that Echo Kittle was no longer talking to Seeker. He sat alone, his arms wrapped round his knees, gazing into the night. She caught the faint shimmer of his colors and knew that he was unhappy.

She went to him and sat down by his side. She took his hand and held it in hers, to show she shared his grief at all they had lost. There was no need for words.

The fires blazed on into the night, and one by one the drowsy children were carried away to sleep in the huts, and one by one the others followed. Then, as the stars began to show in the breaks in the clouds above, Morning Star fell asleep, her head on Seeker's lap, there in the open air. Seeker watched her as she slept, and saw the dying firelight flicker on her cheek, and allowed himself, just once, to stroke her hair.

Shortly before dawn a little group of people came to Seeker and sat before him: Chance and Miriander and his brother, Blaze, and other members of the Council of the Nomana.

"You know what we come to ask," said Chance.

Seeker knew.

"No one has ever had so much power. You must be our leader now."

"I don't want the power," said Seeker. "If I could let it go, I would."

"It's been given to you for a reason," said Miriander.

"I was given the power to save the Lost Child," said Seeker. "What use is my power now?"

Others joined them, black silhouettes gathering round, rimmed by the faint glow creeping into the dawn sky. Seeker's father and mother came forward for the first time since the battle and knelt before him. They looked at him with frightened eyes.

"My sweet boy," said his mother, her voice trembling. "We're all so afraid. Only you can help us now."

"We didn't know," said his father. "But we know now."

Seeker reached out to his mother, and he kissed her and embraced her. He kissed his father too, and saw in his father's eyes an uncertainty that had never been there before. How could it be otherwise? He had lost his entire world: his social position, his daily routine, his purpose in life, all turned to dust along with the honors board on which his name had been painted in gold letters.

"I told you, my boy," said his father, coughing a little as he spoke. "Do you remember? I said you weren't the same as the others. I said you were superior to them. You see, I was right."

"Yes, Father. You were right."

The crowd round them was growing all the time.

"Little brother," said Blaze, "everyone's waiting for you to speak."

"What am I to say?"

"Tell them you'll protect them from danger. They're frightened. Tell them we can rebuild what we've lost. Tell them there's a future."

"I see no future."

"Then pretend."

Seeker looked at all the faces turned towards him, and he saw there the fear and the longing. He couldn't tell them what Blaze asked of him.

Miriander watched him and understood.

"You've been given power without limits," she said. "There must be a reason."

"I was given the power to kill the savanters."

"And have you done so?"

"There're two still alive. But what does it matter now? The All and Only is gone."

"You do have a future, Seeker. But you don't know it yet."

"When will I know it?"

"You must wait. You're not lost. You're just young."

"Young?"

This simple word struck deep. It expressed exactly what Seeker was feeling: that he was still a novice, still a disciple. He wanted a teacher. He wanted a father so that he could still be a child for a little longer.

"But you will grow older," said Miriander. "And day by day, year by year, you'll come to know more and more. Then one day you'll look back and find that you had a future all the time, because now it's become your past."

Her words gave Seeker some comfort.

"So it doesn't matter that I feel this way?"

"Live your life simply and in the truth."

There were the faces all round, waiting for him to tell

them what to do. Seeker drew a deep breath, and addressed them.

"Give me a little time on my own," he said. "Let the sun rise. Then I'll speak."

He went alone to the stream to wash away the dust of the night and to drink. He felt hungry.

He crossed the encampment and crunched over the shingle to the shore. Here an early fisherman was up and rigging his boat for the day's work. Seeker came to a stop by the sea's edge and looked out at the dark horizon.

"Clear day dawning," said the fisherman.

"Yes," said Seeker.

"Maybe the world's coming to an end. But it's not ended yet, and there's still fish in the sea."

He took hold of his boat and began to haul it into the water.

"You want a hand?" said Seeker.

"That would be kind."

So Seeker helped him, and between them they got the fishing boat into the shallows. The fisherman then opened a tin box and took out a breakfast of nut bread and smoked fish, which he shared with Seeker.

"Not enough for everyone," he said, "but enough for two."

Every mouthful Seeker ate was delicious.

Light began to spread across the eastern sky.

"Time to get wind in my sail," said the fisherman.

He gave Seeker a friendly wave, pushed off from the

shelving beach, and slipped out to sea in the freshening breeze.

Seeker remained on the beach, watching the approach of dawn, thinking of nothing. The clouds of the previous night had dispersed, leaving only a low bank on the southern horizon, which now began to glow rose pink with the light of the not-yet-risen sun. It reminded him of the day he had stood by the Elder's side on the high overlook of Anacrea, and the Elder had said, "Have you ever wondered what lies beyond the horizon?"

Other lands.

And does the Clear Light shine beyond the horizon?

As this memory passed through his mind, the sun rose, and its light streamed across the water like an answer to his question. How could the Clear Light not still shine?

It wasn't an answer. It was the return of hope. Dawn makes the unknown future endurable.

He turned about and climbed back up the slope to the encampment, his shadow long and clear before him. The first person he met was the school meek, Gift. The old man was peering at him with anxious eyes.

"You will speak to them, won't you?" he said. "They don't know where they're to go."

"Yes," said Seeker. "I'll speak."

"The words will come," said Gift.

This was what Seeker too had come to believe. He had no god and no guidance, only the sense that this was not an ending but a beginning. So he decided to enter each new moment without foreknowledge and find what was to be found there.

The fires had been rekindled by now, and most of the people were up. As they saw him approaching, they began to gather, in the hope that he had a message for them. The Nomana gathered, and beyond them the people of Anacrea, and beyond them the spikers. Already they looked on him as living proof that their god was not dead.

"My friends, my teachers, my elders," he said, his eyes travelling over the grave faces of the Nomana. "My brothers and sisters. Each of us has made the same vow, to possess nothing and to build no lasting home. If what we held to be true was true before, it's true still. Our mission remains unchanged. We use our powers to bring justice to the oppressed and freedom to the enslaved. We are still Noble Warriors. And the little that we can do, we must do, so that others will know good men too can be strong."

This had been spoken by Noman long ago, as they all knew. So it turned out not to be so hard to find the words to say after all.

"I go on my way alone, leaderless, without certainty. So must you. One day we'll hear the call of the Nomana again. We'll come together again then, stronger than we were before."

How do I know that? he thought as he spoke. Our home is destroyed, our god is dead.

"For now we hope without hope and keep faith without faith. We'll travel light, don't you think? We'll go far. We'll blow away on the wind. And when we float to Earth again, what will be left of our Community? Memory— and love."

He found he was smiling as he finished, for all the gravity of his words. His brother, Blaze, came forward and embraced him.

"I'll be waiting, little brother. Call me, and I'll come."

Together they sought out their father and mother, to make their farewells.

"Are we to go on the road, too?" said their mother.

"No," said Seeker. "You're needed here. Look." He pointed to the makeshift huts. "Already a new town is being born. Think how much there is to be done."

"But the Nom is gone. What are we to do here without the Nom?"

"People must still eat, Mama, and be clothed. Roofs must be raised, and streets paved, and cattle reared, and fences built. You'll want a meetinghouse and a town council, and you may be a councilor. And you'll want a school, Father. The children must have a school. New walls, new honors boards."

"Ah, now, as to the honors boards," said his father, "I've been thinking of a different approach. It strikes me that our boards were too small. What we need is names all over the walls. The name of every child who passes through the school."

"And will all the names be in gold?"

"Oh, I think so, yes. You see, one can never quite tell how any of them are going to turn out. So it seems wisest to honor them all."

Seeker then embraced his father and kissed his mother and left them with his brother, Blaze. He passed from friend to friend, making his farewells. He bowed before his teachers Miriander and Chance. And so he came to the group of spiker chiefs, where the Wildman stood waiting for him.

"You a bandit again, Wildman?"

"Bandit and spiker and Noma, too," he replied, showing his badan. He had it tied round his waist like a sash. "Don't know what I am. Don't know what you are, either."

"I'm your friend."

"Heya, Seeker! To the end of the world!"

Seeker glanced across at Morning Star.

"She going with you?"

"Seems so."

"You watch over her."

"She'll watch over me, more like."

And so, last of all, Seeker made his farewells to Morning Star.

"I'll not forget you, Star."

"You'd better not."

"I hope you find what you want."

"Where I'm going," she said, "I don't think I'll find anything I want. But I'll go, anyway."

"None of us get to choose our own way."

"So who's doing the choosing?" she said.

"I don't know."

"If you ever find out, you come and tell me. I've got a whole lot of complaints about how my life has been run so far."

"I wouldn't want you any other way. Well, apart from one or two minor changes."

He knew she could read his colors, so she didn't pretend not to understand.

"You're the best friend I have in all the world, Seeker," she said. "And you always will be."

She held up her palm, and his hand met hers, and they interclasped their fingers.

"Don't say good-bye," he said.

With that, he left her and strode away briskly up the slope. At the top of the hill he turned back, knowing they were all watching him, and raised his hands high above his head in the Nomana salute. Then he passed on out of sight.

⊰ 26 ⊱

Through the Door

ON THE ROAD WEST, SEEKER PASSED MANY BANDS OF Orlans, no longer in their companies or under the command of the Jahan's captains. The humiliation of their leader had shattered the cohesion of the horde, and it had disintegrated into hundreds of smaller bands of stragglers and marauders. Many were heading back to the land of their origin. Some reckoned to stay and take advantage of the collapse of the empire of Radiance. All knew only one way to survive: by pillage and plunder.

None of those Seeker passed on the road gave him a second glance. Word had spread rapidly that the god of the Nomana had been killed, and in that land of many gods, it was taken for granted that those who lost their god also lost their power. Seeker did not wish to disabuse them. He had no desire to attract attention.

He walked on steadily down the road, his badan drawn tight round his head against the cold, until the white sun began to decline in the sky. He needed to rest and to eat. So seeing a roadhouse ahead, he decided to allow himself a short break.

A number of Caspians were grazing untethered by the roadside. An Orlan band must be in possession of the house. He thought of moving on to somewhere less troublesome, but he was tired and hungry. With luck, they would ignore him.

He opened the door and found a drunken party was in full swing within. Orlans crowded the benches, but not only Orlans—there were spikers at the tables too, and on the tables. Those on the benches were beating the boards with their fists and singing, and those on the tables were dancing and singing. Empty brandy bottles rolled about on the floor. Plates of rice and beans, half eaten, lay here and there on the tables, where they were stamped on by the dancing boots. A bright fire roared in the hearth.

No one heard Seeker come in, and no one asked him his business as he settled himself down in a corner by the window. He took up one of the plates of rice and beans and quietly set about finishing off what had been left. As he ate, he watched the drunken dancers.

The dancing was not quite as wild as at first he had supposed. There was a sort of order to it. The dancers formed two rough rings. The outer ring was made up of the true drunkards, still with bottles in their hands, who flailed their limbs about without any reference to the rhythmic beats of the song. The inner ring were attempting the steps of the dance, a staggering affair that lurched from right foot to left foot and back again, in time to the table-banging of their companions.

> *"No home but the road for me!*
> *No roof but the sky for me!*
> *No law but the knife for me!*
> *So what's to do but drink!"*

Then they held their bottles high and gave a cheer and drank. A gap opened up briefly in the rings of dancers, and Seeker saw a swarthy Orlan, with a bottle in one hand, singing at the top of his voice. He still wore his bright armor and had his whip and his sword in his belt. His face was red as a tomato, and he was beaming with pleasure as he joined in the song.

It was Amroth Jahan.

Seeker looked on in amazement. What had happened to the proud warlord? Anger was to be expected, and despair, and shame. But dancing and laughter?

Then he saw through the jumping figures that the Jahan was not alone in the center of the circle. He was dancing close to a woman. The woman had her back to Seeker, but he knew he had seen that rich mass of black hair and that voluptuous figure before. When she turned in her stamping dance and he saw her face, he remembered her name. It was the Wildman's friend Caressa.

The dance came to an end shortly, terminated only by the emptying of the brandy bottles. Amroth Jahan, profoundly drunk, had to be helped off the table to the floor.

There he slumped to a sitting position, his back against the wall, grinning and calling out.

"Here, beauty! Want you, beauty! Kissy kissy!"

Caressa dropped down by his side and he took her in his arms.

"Say it again!" he cried, holding her tight. "Say it again!"

"Youngster!" she said, laughing. "Stripling! Colt!"

"Where's the old man?"

"I see no old man. I see a young fellow. Big and strong and young!"

"Oh, you beauty! Kiss me again!"

Seeker looked on in sadness. He felt no joy in the Great Jahan's downfall, and no desire to inflict any further punishment. What was done was done. It was enough that the once all-powerful warlord who had set out to conquer the world was reduced to groveling for the flattery of bandits.

He finished eating, then rose, meaning to leave as quietly as he had come. But at this point, one of the bandit gang spotted him.

"Heya!" he cried. "A hoodie!"

Others turned at the cry and, seeing Seeker, began to jeer.

"Hoodie, hoodie, lost your god!"

"Boom-bang! Bye-bye god!"

Seeker realized with a sinking heart that they supposed his powers had died with the destruction of Anacrea. He bowed his head, not wanting to provoke a conflict, and made for the door.

"Not so fast, little hoodie!"

They gathered round him, prodding at him.

"Not so noble any more, eh?"

Caressa now came to see what her gang had found. She recognized him from their brief encounter in Spikertown.

"That's one of the kiddies went off with the Wild-man," she exclaimed. "So you're a hoodie now?"

Shab, who was right behind her, gave a mocking laugh.

"A saddy, more like."

"Hey, sad boy," said Caressa, coming up close to Seeker. "Think you're better than everyone else, do you?"

"No," said Seeker. "I've no quarrel with you."

"How about I've a quarrel with you, boy?"

Amroth Jahan now came lumbering through the crowd. When he saw Seeker, he burst into laughter.

"Why, that's the one! That's him! He was there in the battle!"

"You and your battle!" said Caressa. "If I'd been there, you'd be telling a different story."

"He's the one that made me kneel!" cried the Jahan.

He dropped to his knees and shuffled forward.

"Look, I'm kneeling again! I'm kissing your hand!" He tried to take hold of Seeker's hand. "Don't care any more. You want me to kiss your feet, too?"

"Get up, you fool," said Caressa, laughing and pulling him to his feet. "He's just a sad boy."

The Jahan wrapped his arms round her and grinned at Seeker.

"See, sad boy? I've got a beautiful woman in my arms and I'm young again. So I don't care if the whole world kisses your hand. I've got a woman who kisses more than hands."

He fell to smothering Caressa's lips and cheeks and neck with wild drunken kisses.

"Get off me," said Caressa, still laughing. "You'll get all the kissing you want. Right now I mean to teach this sad boy how to dance."

"Heya!" cried the bandits. "Dance lessons!"

"Make a ring for our guest, boys! Shab, see to the fire."

The bandits pushed back the tables and formed a ring round Seeker, their blades now drawn to make it plain that he was not at liberty to go. The Jahan shook his head vigorously from side to side and tried to stop them, but he kept bursting into laughter and forgetting what he meant to say, so he gave up and sat down on a bench to watch.

"You'd better let me go," said Seeker quietly.

But Shab was scattering hot coals from the fire over the open space of the floor, and the bandit ring was tightening. The points of their blades poked at Seeker, nudging him onto the coals.

"See, boy," said Caressa, "I don't like you hoodies. You took my Wildman and stole his soul and made him into a sad boy. So now I'm going to make you dance."

Seeker looked at her and said nothing. For all her taunts, he felt no anger. They didn't understand. That was no crime. He didn't understand himself. So it seemed to him the simplest way to silence her was to do as she asked.

With his mind he reached down into the soles of his bare feet and prepared them, making them strong. He gathered the lir in the tips of his fingers and the palms of his hands. Then he stepped onto the hot coals and felt no pain. He stooped and picked up the hot coals in his hands and was not burned.

He held out the hissing coals to Caressa. She started back from him, her eyes now wide with fear. Seeker saw the meaning of that look. He had become a strange and monstrous creature.

"Let's go, boys!"

The bandits and the Orlans melted away, taking the Jahan with them. Seeker put the coals back in the fire. They had not so much as singed his skin.

By the time he was out on the road again, they were gone. He had put them to flight. Once again he was the victor. But there was no glory in it. He had not sought these powers, and he didn't know how to use them. He had broken the army that had attacked the Nom, but the Nom had been destroyed, anyway. Now all authority was overthrown. The land was in the grip of anarchy. It was one thing to win a battle, but who was then to rule?

Seeker made his way down the road, following the line of the old ruined wall. It seemed to him he had been given an immense responsibility, but he felt helpless in the face of it. Was he supposed to be the bringer of order? Was he supposed to set himself up as king?

The spikers were right. He was just a sad boy.

So why had he been given so much power?

I didn't ask for it. I'm no one special. All I ever wanted was to be a Noble Warrior. All I ever wanted was to live in the Garden.

The Garden was gone. Once more, desolation gripped his heart. Why the voices? Why raise his hopes, only to leave him with nothing?

Who is doing this to me?

The questions echoed through his mind, one after another, circling and calling like seagulls. There were no answers, only more questions.

Where am I to go? What am I?

Who am I?

He felt a lurching shock within himself. It was as if with this last simple question he had stumbled on some hard obstacle that blocked his way. The question turned out not to feel so simple after all. And yet surely he knew the answer. He knew his own name, and his parents' names. He could describe himself. So why did it feel all of a sudden as if he did not know who he was?

He remembered the shadow in the cloud. It had been his shadow, but it had not been him.

Nervously he looked now for his shadow. There it was, faint in the cold gray winter light, and unremarkable.

I am Seeker after Truth. I was born on Anacrea. My father is the schoolteacher. I have been trained as a Noble Warrior.

But that was all only a small part. There was so much more. Most of him was hidden from himself.

I am more than I know.

Seeker had no idea where this strange notion had come from, but now that it entered his mind it would not leave. It frightened him to think he could be someone or something other, but it also came as a relief. Ever since he had first heard the voice in the Nom, he had felt as if he was living inside a maze. Somewhere was the right way to go, the way that would let him out of the maze, but he never knew which turning to take. Now it seemed to him obvious that he did not know and could never know. If the self that was trying so hard to make sense of everything was not his real self—or was only a small part of a much bigger self—then of course he wouldn't know. His little finger didn't know why he was walking down the road. All it could do was come along with the rest of him. His present notion of himself was perhaps like that: too small to comprehend the greater purpose of which he was a part.

Who am I?

More than I know.

Keep walking.

He began to sing the song that had come to him in the cloud.

> *"Jango up, jango down*
> *Jango smile, jango frown*
> *Weep your tears, say your prayers*
> *No man hears, no man cares*
> *Seek a, seek a, seek a door—"*

And there was the strange old man, seated on his sitting-stick, between the road and the old wall ahead. And right by the place where he was sitting there was a door in the wall.

Jango raised one hand in greeting.

"Here at last! Young Hero! Or maybe you've got yourself a new name by now, eh? New names for new times."

"Did you know I was coming?"

"Why else am I here? The faithful keeper of the key to the door. Not that I have a key. But then, nor does the door have a lock."

He studied Seeker with his little brown eyes.

"You're getting the hang of doors by now, I should say."

"I don't think I'm getting the hang of anything."

"But there's no getting anywhere without doors. And surely you know," he added with a mischievous smile, "that where your way lies, the door is always open."

Seeker stared at him.

"How do you know that?"

"The same way you know it."

"You hear voices, too?"

"All the time."

"Where do they come from? Do you know?"

"Yes, I know. And so do you. But you've forgotten."

"Then, tell me! Make me remember!"

Jango smiled and shook his head.

"Please!" said Seeker. To his shame he felt tears rising to his eyes. It was all so difficult. He had lost so much. The sadness could not be kept inside any more.

"Dear boy!" exclaimed Jango, much moved. "My dear boy! This won't do."

He produced a faded scrap of handkerchief and dabbed at Seeker's cheeks.

"What has happened to distress you so?"

It seemed the old man knew nothing of recent events. Seeker told him how Anacrea had been destroyed and, with it, the Nom and the Lost Child he had sworn to protect. Jango listened and clicked his tongue in dismay.

"And you believed you were meant to prevent this?"

"Why else have I been given the power?"

"To kill the savanters. I thought that was quite clear."

"I have killed the savanters."

"All of them?"

"All but two."

At this, Jango looked very grave.

"That is unfortunate. Do you know where to find them?"

"In the cloud."

"The cloud has gone."

"Gone?" Seeker was dismayed. Where was he to find the savanters now?

"You will have to go another way, I think."

"But I don't know any other way."

Jango pointed at the old wooden door in the wall behind him.

"This way, perhaps. If it is a way."

He rapped on the door with his knuckles.

"To be exact, I suppose it's a door. And yet when you start to think about it, you discover that there is nothing exact about doors. I mean, what is the essence of a door? A plank of wood isn't a door. Nor is a hole in a wall. Nor is a plank of wood fixed into a hole in a wall. It must open. One must, you see, be able to go through."

Seeker felt confused and disappointed. Why was the old man rambling on in this way?

"Yes," he said. "Obviously."

"Obviously? It took me years to understand that. So you believe you can identify the essence of a door?"

"No, no." Seeker shook his head. "I don't really know what you're talking about."

"Yes, you do." Jango gave him a reproachful look, as if he were a student who had forgotten a recent lesson. "It's the threshold, of course. The threshold is the essence of a door. The threshold lies between here and there." He pointed with one finger. "You cross from here, over the threshold, to there."

"Yes. I can see that."

"Excellent. That's cleared that up, then. Where were we? Oh, yes. The last two savanters. You must find them, you know. It is your mission."

"It was. But now the Nom is gone. The Garden is gone. The All and Only is gone."

"Your Nom is gone," said Jango. "What makes you think it's the only one?"

"There's more than one Nom?"

"Of course. It would be a poor sort of a god that could be sent packing so easily."

As he spoke, there came a soft creaking sound from behind him. The door in the wall had opened a few inches.

"Well, well!" murmured Jango, and he smiled his sweet smile. "The door seems to have been left open."

Seeker paid full attention to the door for the first time. It was made of wood and had once been painted white, but the paint had long since peeled away. All that was left of the pigment was a thin line in the cracks between the boards. The door had a curving top that fit into a stone arch built in the wall. The threshold too was stone, worn by the tread of many feet over many years into a smooth hollow.

Through the gap now opened up between frame and door, Seeker expected to see a plain white room, a table, a blue flower. Instead he saw the branches of trees. He began to feel a very strange feeling.

"Am I to go through?"

"If you want to," said Jango.

So Seeker pushed the door open wider and stepped across the threshold.

He found himself in a large wood of tall leafless trees. A path ran in a straight line between the trees towards a dense stand of evergreens ahead. Seeker followed the path, feeling with every step a mounting excitement that he could not explain.

Where the evergreens began, the path passed through a gap in the thicket of yew and holly that was just wide enough for a man. Seeker went through the gap. Beyond, the evergreens fell back to create a circular clearing that was walled and roofed with dark foliage. Very little light penetrated the canopy, but where it did, it fell in narrow beams that laid stripes and speckles on the woodland floor.

Seeker stood still, in silence, hardly daring to breathe. Could it really be so?

He turned to look back. There at the end of the path between the trees, he could see the wall and the open door and the old man standing silhouetted in the doorway.

He looked round him, his heart beating fast. He had been in a space much like this before. It had been called the Night Court.

He looked back once more. Jango raised his stick and held it horizontal over his head, echoing the stance of Noman long ago.

"Go on, Seeker," he said, his voice sounding close though he was far away. "Your life is an experiment in search of the truth."

Seeker pressed on. Beyond the dark vaulted clearing was a grove of aspens. Their smooth silver trunks stretched out before him in the winter light, like pillars of alabaster. He had come into the Cloister Court. There was no path now. Every way between the trees was the right way.

Now he knew what he would find. He felt it before he saw it, in the awakening joy of his heart. A glimpse of brightness between pale trees. A dazzle of green. He trod quietly forward, and little by little he made out a high tangle of bramble and vine, a natural screen that rose up beyond the aspens, guarding and concealing the space within. Between the knotted tendrils there were little gaps and crannies, like the pierced stars and diamonds in the silver screen, and through these apertures he could make out green grass and the bright ripple of water and the scarlet and gold of flowers.

He closed his eyes. Even without seeing it, he knew it. The sensation of sweet tranquillity was so powerful that he could feel it in every part of his body, in the unknotting of his muscles, in the softening of his skin.

He had come back to the Garden. The Wise Father was watching over him still.

He opened his eyes and saw through the web of brambles that there was a person in the garden; just as he had seen before. The light was behind him, as it had been before, and was bright, so that he could make out no details of the person's face. The figure was seated and did not move.

The light was growing brighter. Seeker wanted more than anything to see that face, but he felt his eyes burning, and could look no more.

He dropped to his knees and prayed.

"Wise Father, forgive me for doubting you. Now I know that you are Here and Now, Always and Everywhere. My All, my Only. My one true god."

A soft voice then spoke to him out of the Garden.

"Save me."

William Nicholson is the author of the heralded *Seeker,* the first book in the Noble Warriors sequence, as well as the acclaimed Wind on Fire trilogy and the screenplays for *Gladiator* and *Shadowlands,* both of which were nominated for Academy Awards. He lives with his wife and their three children in Sussex, England.

www.williamnicholson.co.uk